Shrader Marks
and
Keelhouse

Revised Edition

Also by Rob Smith:

Poetry:
Eyes on Mars: A Poetic Memoir
The Immigrant's House
Mzungu, Hello: a Poetic Journal (color chapbook)
256 Zones of Gray

Novels:
Children of Light
McGowan's Journey, which includes complete editions of:
    McGowan's Call
    McGowan's Retreat
    McGowan's Return
    McGowan's Pass
Sand Dollar Island

Literary criticism and commentary:
Cultural Perspectives on the Bible: A Beginner's Guide
Hogwarts, Narnia, and Middle Earth: Places Upon a Time

Tween's literature:
The Spell of Twelve

Shrader Marks
and
Keelhouse

Revised Edition

Rob Smith

Drinian Press/
Huron, Ohio

Cover design, photos, and illustrations by Drinian Press LLC

Drinian Press LLC
PO Box 63
Huron, Ohio 44839

www.DrinianPress.com.

Library of Congress Control Number: 2025936103

ISBN-13: 978-1-941929-19-3

Printed in the United States of America

Contents

Saint Lawrence Seaway

(Lake Ontario to the Gulf of St. Lawrence)

1) Lake Ontario
2) Sodus Bay
3) Oswego, NY
4) Cape Vincent, NY
5) Massena, NY
6) Cornwall, ON
7) Montreal, QC
8) Quebec City, QC
9) Ile d' Anticosti
10) Gulf of St. Lawrence

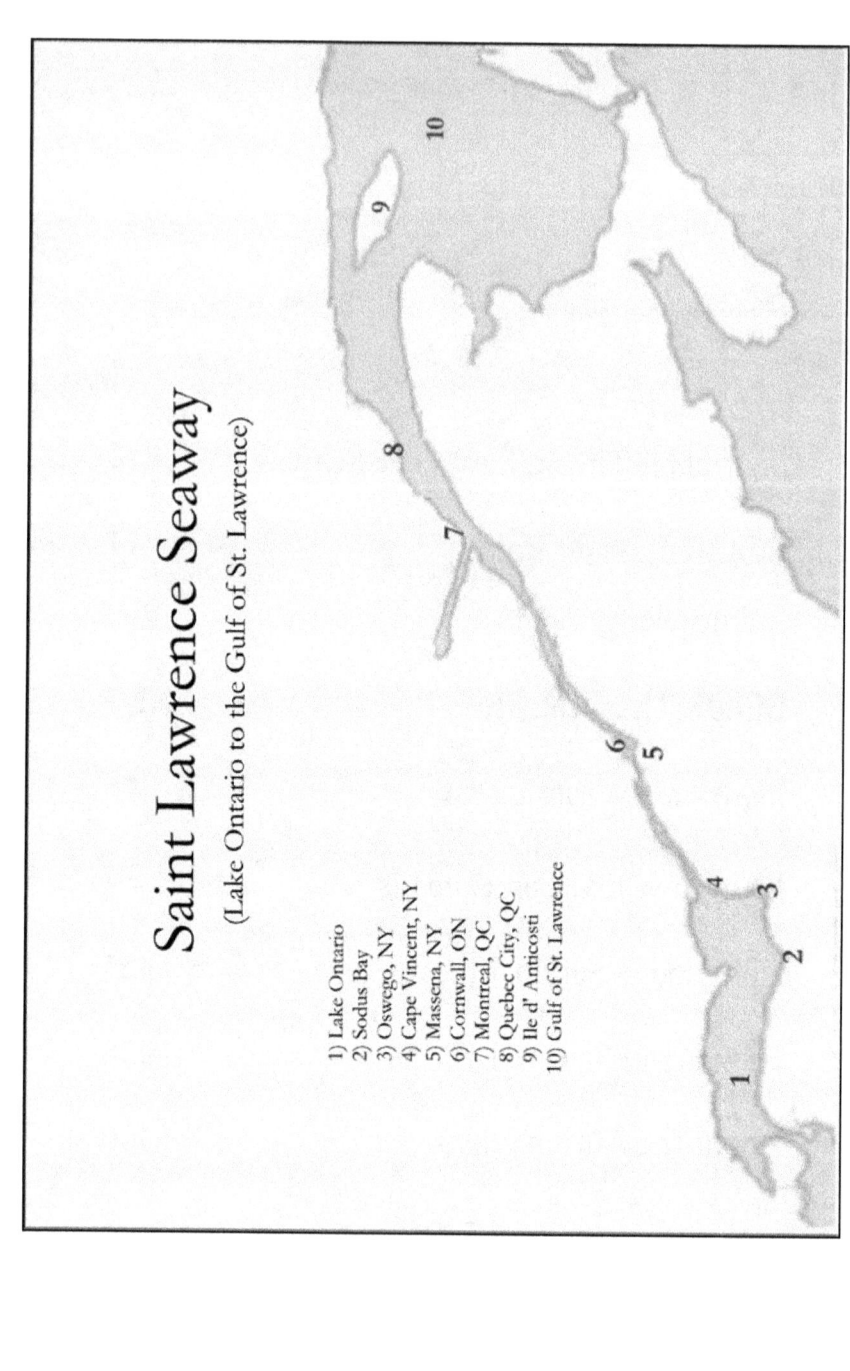

BOOK I

NIGHT VOICES
(The story of Shrader Marks)

To Court and Libby

Those who went down to sea in ships,
doing business on the great waters,
they saw the deeds of Yahweh,
and his wondrous works in the deep.

Tehillim 107

NIGHT VOICES

1

"Shrader!" a woman's voice carried over the water. He swung around on his jet ski, salt spray cutting across his face as he sped forward. Ahead of him was a small flotilla of sailboats. There was something unusual about their deck layouts, but Shrader was more alert to the cry that had drawn his attention. Then he saw her. She was out on the bowsprit of the starboard most boat. Someone was moving toward her. It was a man, and there was a glint of steel in his hand.

"Shrader!" she repeated. He did his best to focus, but couldn't make out either person as he gunned the jet ski toward the boats. Power surged beneath him, but there was no sound from the engine. He raced forward, and then he woke up.

Shrader Marks was in his hotel room in Orlando. It took a minute for his heart to stop pounding. This was the third time that sleep had carried him through this sequence of events. He was a man who seldom dreamed, or, at least, never remembered dreaming. He turned on the light and retrieved his watch from the bedside table. It was 3:45 a.m. Next to the watch was the envelope that contained the access card for his room. It was labeled *Mark Shrader*, a testimony to an error that plagued his whole life. People seemed to have an aversion to hearing his name in the proper order, but his current and growing aversion was sleeping. He found himself fearing sleep or rather the prospect of dreaming the reoccurring nightmare. It was so vivid in his memory, and so troubling, and that bothered him most. He could not understand the intensity that the dream worked in his gut. He loved the water. He loved sailing. Why was he seeing these images? Why were they so disturbing? And who were the people?

Shrader sat up in bed and reached for the book on the night stand. It was Rupert Hartley's treatise on the Neolithic stone circles of Great Britain. As usual, he could not open the book without seeing the glances of his more literary friends who shunned his taste in reading. "What normal person reads a textbook for fun?" was what they'd ask. For that he had no good answer except that Stone Age culture was his passion, and non-fiction in that realm seemed more creative than science fiction.

Tonight, reading didn't divert him from the memory of the dream. His mind kept turning back to relive the images. He closed his eyes remembering the line of sailboats. He recognized their basic profiles. They looked like the common boats of the Great Lakes. There were the contemporary lines of the Tartans and the classic lines of the Island Packets. If there was anything over forty-five feet in length, it could not have been too much larger. Most of them seemed in the thirty-two to forty foot range.

The woman on the bowsprit must have been on one of the Island Packets. Who was she? Shrader tried to make her features look familiar. She might have been Cathy. He never could remember her last name. At the marina, people mostly knew each other by first names. It could have been her, but she and her husband, Phil, didn't sail a Packet. She didn't look the same. *Maybe it was the parka?* thought Shrader. It was the first time that the thought had come to his consciousness. The people on the boats were dressed for winter. He shrugged off the image and exchanged his book for the TV remote. He had already spent too much time on a wild dream.

He wandered through all the late-night channels, forwarding through one old movie after another until he found a news channel. He normally avoided the repetitive sound-bites that passed for news, but tonight he was looking for distraction and not current events.

The newscaster reported on a gathering of geologists in Geneva, Switzerland. They were discussing the ramifications of meteor strikes in relation to plate tectonics. The debate was considerably heated. Some suggested that volcanic eruptions could be triggered that would pour enough ash into the upper atmosphere to create a short-term ice age. Shrader's mind began to link the TV images with his book on the Neolithic period. He thought of the early maritime culture on the shores of Labrador. As he listened, his mind was drifting back to a time he'd only imagined, a time when Stone Age peoples lived on the edge of retreating glaciers. They traversed the North Atlantic in dugout canoes following the migratory path of the Great Auks moving toward their nesting grounds. It was an old image in Shrader's mind. One that, for a reason he couldn't explain, was comforting to a man who felt a kinship with the creatures of the sea. He fell back asleep.

"Shrader!" cried the same insistent voice from his dream. Behind closed eyelids Shrader fought back his terror. This time he would face his nightmare. He swung his jet ski around and raced toward the flotilla. They were familiar boats. All of them bore the NY numbers of their New York registry. But why were they here in salt water? He scanned the decks and saw why the cabin trunks looked different. The ports were all covered with plywood. The people on deck were focused toward the woman who was calling to him. It was Cathy. Through the haze he could make out other winter-garbed shapes, but no faces. They wore surgical masks. Before he could wonder, Shrader was choking. It was not haze that obstructed his vision. It was snowing ash. He could taste the sulfur in it.

"Shrader, we need you now!" An entire chorus of frantic voices called his name.

He tried to gun the engine of his jet ski, but the hand grips vaporized. Quickly he tightened his knees for balance. Instead of an engine's vibration against his thighs, he felt a heartbeat. Whatever he was riding, it was alive. The throb of that heartbeat echoed in his head until it pounded his brain into consciousness. He was back in his hotel, and it was the sound of his own racing heart that flooded the room.

2

A shiny oak table dominated the room. Around it were dignitaries huddled in animated pairs as a frustrated moderator tried to keep the discussion focused on the new information. Malcolm MacBrin was losing control and he knew it. The point-counterpoint of the debate was aggravated by dozens of side conversations and translators reverting to their native tongue mid-sentence.

"Please," he said in a moment of desperation. "We all agree that the issues are absolutely critical, and we don't have a lot of time." The tone of his voice drew all eyes back to the head of the table. He continued, "The talks in Geneva can't hold the attention of the press for very long. Eventually people will realize that they're looking at the window-dressing. Those of us here at Camp David must come up with a recommendation for the United Nations." A fresh wave of murmuring erupted. MacBrin raised his voice, speaking over the rumble. "I remind you that the potential for a meteor strike is now highly probable. The trajectory can now be projected from earth's observatories. That means that the initial images from the Hubble telescope have now been verified by the Mount Wilson Observatory. Somebody last night referred to it as 'double Hubble' and, in spite of the play on words, the results will not be pretty. The planet is going to be hit!" Everyone understood the reference to Edwin Powell Hubble whose name was born by the telescope and whose life's work defined Mount Wilson. "Within the next few days we expect to hear a lot from amateur astronomers who will have a pretty clear idea of what's going on."

"Can we project an impact point?" asked the Russian delegate through his interpreter.

MacBrin nodded. "There's a 95% chance that it will strike in the southern hemisphere, and a 65% possibility that it will be close to Antarctica, if not a direct hit."

"In Wilkes Land or on the Peninsula?" asked the Australian representative.

"I wish I could tell you, Andrew," offered a sympathetic MacBrin. "It would be a roll of the dice to say which side of the continent will feel the impact. I'm sure the Argentines would prefer Wilkes Land, and your side of the Continent." There was some tense laughter scattered throughout the hall. "It's good that we can still laugh," assured MacBrin. "I just wish we had more options."

Abraham Gatu from the African Council of Nations spoke the question that was on many minds: "What about the use of missiles, conventional or even nuclear, to redirect the meteor path? Gatu's impeccable English sounded more British than MacBrin's Ulster lilt.

"The use of the nuclear warheads was dismissed out of hand," answered MacBrin. "We aren't positive what effects a strike would have, but we can be fairly sure of what a shower of radioactive debris would mean at that magnitude. Lesley John from the Centers for Disease Control can speak to this."

A confident woman in a navy suit spoke from across the table. "In the first few years we'd see cancer rates increase between twenty and forty percent," she said. "Those numbers might be worth the risk, but with the plutonium being shuttled by the jet stream..." Her voice trailed off. "Well," she continued, "we wouldn't expect any significant human survival rates beyond twenty years." With that, the room went silent.

"That still leaves the option of a conventional warhead," said MacBrin. "But the news on that account is not hopeful either. Major General Copleston from the Joint Chiefs has studied that option." A large man in a dark suit rose to his feet. His clothing did not show any rank or insignia, but the crease in his trousers and the shine of ebony shoes whispered his identity.

"MacBrin is right." offered the General with the voice of command. "We know that though we can hit or divert the meteor cloud, we cannot predict the path of any diversion. We've had to ask ourselves whether a strategic action on our part will make things better or worse. The conclusion is that we just don't know. But face it, if we have to take a hit, we couldn't choose a better spot than Antarctica."

"Spoken like a true resident of the Northern Hemisphere," said Andrew Harris of Australia. There were a lot of nods of agreement from other delegates. The General flushed red, but continued without a change in inflection or tone.

"North Pole or South wouldn't matter," he said. "Let's suppose we can shatter the largest of the meteors, or even divert them two or three degrees. What then? We may actually worsen the situation for everyone. Let's talk cases here. We break a meteor up and scatter the pieces. Half of them miss the earth altogether, but one, maybe a tenth the size of the original, hits Sydney. Or worse, we know that this meteor cloud is passing so close that we'll take a few hits. But, we are on the edge of that cloud, and suppose most of the cloud passes by. That would mean that most of the mass of the material is going to go into the sun. Sending a missile into that cloud may actually increase the number of particles that come under the influence of earth's gravity. We could look like what we saw on Jupiter in 1994 when the comet hit." Again, the room went silent.

"That brings up a question that has been on my mind during this whole presentation," said Carlos Menendez. "I don't understand why you are calling this a meteor strike. I think we are dealing with an asteroid, probably the core of a comet that has lost its plasma."

MacBrin shifted uneasily at the suggestion. "I am familiar with the data that has been received by the radio telescope at Arecibo," he answered. "Yes, I agree, we are probably looking at the core of what was once a comet. As such, we know its mass is only a fraction of that of an active comet."

"A fraction?" interrupted Menendez. "Try thirty percent, hardly a minor consideration."

"But it's not that simple," argued MacBrin who was beginning to lose his temper. "It's unlikely that we are looking at a solid mass. You know as well as I do that the readings are more apt to be a cloud of associated materials. Granted, some may be pretty hefty, but I have to believe that most are more like sands that will burn up in the outer atmosphere. We'll probably have a spectacular sky show."

Menendez did not look satisfied by the answer, but he wasn't given another opportunity to protest.

"We need a plan," said MacBrin at last. "We have to walk out of this room humming the same tune. We're into 'double Hubble'," he said to soften the tension. "Amateur astronomers are beginning to report anomalies. We have to take a stance, and quickly. That's if we don't want widespread panic and speculation. Are we together on this?" The silence which followed was eerie. If it did not constitute assent, it at least ratified the implacable truth. None of them had much choice.

3

"Cathy? Cathy Pearson?" asked Shrader. He was standing in a corner near his boarding gate at the Atlanta airport, hoping for a bit of privacy as he spoke into his cell phone.

"Shrader, is that you?" came the reply. "This is very strange, but I knew that you'd call today."

"How could you know that?" questioned Shrader. "I didn't even know that myself."

"It's about the dream, isn't it?" said Cathy.

Shrader came up short. It didn't make any sense that she would know about his dreams. Confusion swirled in his mind and found no place to rest.

"Shrader, are you still there?" came Cathy's voice as a call back to reality.

"Have we been sharing the same dream?" he said at last.

"I don't know," answered Cathy. "But I've had the oddest dream. It happens over and over again, and you are there. I tried to talk to Phil about it, but he just blows it off like it's silly. It doesn't feel silly."

"No," responded Shrader, "Silly is not the word I'd use. It's a nightmare. I always wake up in a panic. It makes me afraid to go to sleep. It's just too real. Was someone coming after you? Who was it?" He asked as much to test her knowledge of the dream as to identify Cathy's assailant.

"I don't have any idea who he was," said Cathy, without missing a beat. "I just knew that I had to get you to help me. I didn't expect such a dramatic arrival, however. Neither did the fleet captains. You really took all of us by surprise."

A flood of questions flowed through Shrader's mind and found their way to his voice. "Where were we? Did you know that the water was salty? Why were we out there in the snow?"

"Whoa," she said. "It's a puzzle to me. I just know that we were running from something, and I needed to call you. Where are you now?"

"I'm waiting for a connecting flight. I'm on a layover in the Atlanta airport," answered Shrader. "I'm supposed to be at a graduate supervisor's conference at the Peabody in Orlando, but this dream..." his voice trailed off.

"I know what you mean," responded Cathy. "Yesterday I left for the office, and ended up at the mall looking for parkas. I bought three of them. It was the most bizarre thing that's ever happened to me. My brain kept saying that the whole thing was stupid, but I just handed over the credit card anyway. I just don't understand it."

"I'm sure that my wife thinks I'm crazy. I called Lynn last night to say that I was flying home early, but I really called to get your phone number from the marina directory. It's a dream, but it feels like it's more than that, too."

"If you want my opinion," added Cathy, "we're on the edge of something that's about to happen."

"I should be back in Syracuse by early evening," remarked Shrader. "I'll phone you then. Do you suppose anyone else is having this same dream? I don't understand it."

"Phil is miffed that you've appeared in my dream, so I haven't been able to talk to him about it. I don't think it's going to be something that we'll understand. This will sound psycho, but I think we're being given some kind of warning. It's about something that we have to do. I thought that I was going crazy, but the fact that it's happening to both of us..."

"I don't know, Cathy. I'm not too sure I know what is real right now. Maybe I'm dreaming this call."

"No, this isn't part of the dream," she answered. "Whatever is happening, it's real and it's making us do things that don't make any sense."

"Like my leaving the conference early and your buying parkas?" asked Shrader.

"Exactly," said Cathy. "People will think we are crazy, and maybe they'll be right, but at least I don't feel so quite alone since you've called."

"I'll call when I get home," assured Shrader. "Cathy," he continued hesitatingly, "you said that in your dream everyone was surprised by my dramatic appearance. Why was that? I was just riding a jet ski."

The line went silent for a moment. "Shrader, you were riding on the back of a killer whale."

4

Shrader was usually willing to strike up a conversation with fellow travelers, but today he wasn't in the mood to chat with the sales rep in the aisle seat next to him. Instead, he looked out the window at the mountainous billows of the clouds below. In his lap was a well-read issue of *Sail* magazine with a cover story on the latest GPS navigating systems. He and Lynn were considering adding one to their thirty-foot sloop. Most people at the marina were already on their second or third generation GPS system with color readouts and various electronic interfaces. Shrader had never even owned a handheld unit. For him, dependency on technology seemed antithetical to the art of sailing. Those who touted the advantages of hi-tech readouts could not convince him that a computer chip connected to an LED screen would improve his sense of direction. A magnetic compass and what others described as an uncanny sense of the weather served him quite well. Now, even as he looked out over the clouds, he could sense the plane's direction of flight. With no features of earth below to guide him, he knew that they were flying east. The jet rolled slightly as the pilot changed headings. *We must be heading almost true north*, thought Shrader through the haze of fatigue. He slid down the protective shade over the port, and slumped down in his seat. His exhaustion overcame his fear of reliving the recurring nightmare. He fell asleep. This time his sleep brought a new dream.

The night air was chill, and the stars silhouetted the horizon. He was on the water. Beneath him was the familiar decking of fiberglass non-skid. Around him were the sounds of rushing water. He was on a boat under sail at night. He had the feeling that there were others there too, but the boat was dark. It was running fast without lights.

He looked to the stars for guidance and cursed his lack of knowledge of celestial navigation. He strained to calm himself. He tried to match his heartbeat to the rhythm of the waves striking the bow of the boat.

Suddenly, he was not alone in his thoughts. Someone else was there. He heard the other voice speak with a most inhuman quality, "Follow the path of the *Inuksuk*."

It was an Inuktitut word that Shrader understood. In his dream he looked toward the darkened horizon. He did not know what he was looking for except shapes against the night sky. He had seen *Inuksuk*, standing stones, along the coasts of Labrador and the Canadian Maritimes. He strained to see shapes against the brilliantly speckled sky. Broad on the port bow, he saw what he was looking for. Dark shapes blacked out the stars like spiked pinnacles reaching up out of the water. Experience told him that they were probably twelve miles away, somewhere near the outer edge of the horizon, but their scale could have been misleading.

"It's just off the port bow," he heard himself shout. He felt the boat respond to the helm, and turn more to windward. The breeze picked up, and he heard the winches grinding as the sails were sheeted in.

"I think you've been reading too much of that sailing magazine," said the friendly face of the man in the aisle seat.

Shrader blushed. "I guess I must have been having a dream," he confessed. "It only proves that my wife is right in saying that I talk in my sleep. Sorry."

"No problem," said his companion. "I take it that you have a sailboat. Where do you sail?"

"Lake Ontario," answered Shrader.

"Where?" asked the man. "We have a runabout for water skiing with the kids. We went up to Ontario once, but mostly we use it on Seneca Lake."

"We sail out of Sodus Bay," offered Shrader. The man looked blank. "It's about midway between Rochester and Oswego," he added.

"I like it," the man said. The comment took Shrader by surprise.

"Like what?"

"Being on the water. Oh, I'm not a sailor like you, but there's that time in the evening when the sun is just going down, and the water is shimmering."

Shrader laughed, "You have the makings of a sailor, or a poet. Sometimes I think they are the same. But you're exactly right."

"Someday I'm going to have to give it a try. Do you think if I drove over to Sodus Bay during the summer, I'd find someone to take me out for a quick lesson?"

"Probably," said Marks. "Just don't wear one of those goofy captain's hats; it's not politically correct. In general sailors are a friendly group and like showing off their boats."

"How about you?"

"Are you in sales?" Marks said with a wink.

"Is it that obvious?"

"The fact is I don't think I'll be there this summer. I'm thinking about sailing out the Seaway." Shrader looked at the man. Genuine disappointment flashed through his eyes. "I'll tell you what," he added. "Give me your card and I'll talk to the marina owner. Sometimes they have get-togethers at the dock. He could put you on the mailing list, and if you showed up, there'd be someone who'd take you out. I'll tell him that you might be interested in buying a boat."

"Now who sounds like a salesman?" said the man reaching back to fish a wallet from his pants' pocket. He opened the bill section and retrieved a slightly bent ivory card. "C.J. Conway," he said as he handed the card to Marks.

"Shrader Marks," came the reply. "You go by 'C.J.'?"

"Never could stand 'Chuckie', and 'Charles' meant I was in big trouble."

"I understand completely. I've lived with 'Shrader' all my life. It's bad when you have to explain your name."

"Would you rather explain your next cruise?"

"I'd love to, but it's still a little unclear."

Time passed quickly as the two men chatted. When the plane docked at the boarding gate, C.J. jumped up to retrieve his bag from the overhead compartment. Shrader had checked his luggage and showed no interest in fighting the other passengers to the forward hatch, only to stand and wait at the baggage carousel.

A sudden change in cabin pressure announced the opening of the hatch. C.J. leaned back in Shrader's direction. "Good luck," he said. "I hope your trip comes together the way you want. Sounds like the adventure of a lifetime. You won't forget about our deal, will you?"

"I won't," said Shrader, placing his hand over his breast pocket where he had stowed C.J.'s business card. The line of passengers started to move forward, and then he was gone.

5

Malcolm MacBrin was still bleary-eyed from his transatlantic flight. He quickly finished another cup of coffee before entering the seminar hall. He felt like the pea in the shell game of a magician's trick. He had to act as though he had been in Switzerland, when, in fact, he had been in another hemisphere. The Camp David meeting had achieved its purpose, but the duty of making the first public announcement fell to him. To keep the charade intact, the podium for the communiqué was located in

Geneva, Switzerland. At first, members of the press corps were surprised that an unknown delegate from Ulster would deliver the prepared statement, but then a rumor was circulated that it was a symbolic gesture meant to give status to a country emerging from its own violent past. In other words, it was "politics as usual". In the end, Malcolm MacBrin was not challenged in what appeared to be a sudden shift in conference leadership.

"Ladies and Gentlemen," began MacBrin. "This conference, which began three days ago, was meant to bring together the greatest minds to discuss an issue that has more than academic interest. The effect of meteor strikes on our planet is a difficult subject, and the theorists cannot entirely agree. On the other hand, the earth stands in the path of a great many meteors. The public, in general, is not aware of the fact that as many as two hundred million visible meteors occur in the earth's atmosphere every day. Most are so small that they burn up before ever hitting the earth's surface. Those that have hit the earth are relatively small and, while the effect of a particular episode seems negligible, it is estimated that the aggregate effect is that the weight of the earth is increased by 910 metric tons daily."

MacBrin's comments left the audience unmoved. Simple facts would not merit primetime coverage. He paused to prepare his hearers for the real story.

"We now have enough evidence to announce," he continued, "that we are entering a new period in earth's history." Some of the more alert observers sat up to listen. "It is apparent that the planet is about to be bombarded with meteoroids of more significant mass."

Suddenly the room was a hubbub of shouting reporters calling out questions. "Please," said MacBrin, raising his hands, "I'm not accustomed to news conferences, so let me finish my prepared statement, and then you can ask questions." As quickly as the chaos broke out, order was restored.

"Thank you," said a patient MacBrin, returning to his text. "It is apparent that the planet is about to be bombarded with meteorites of significant mass. Those of you with scientific backgrounds will know that the definition of *significant mass* in the case of meteoroids is not really very large at all when compared to the mass of the planet. Just a little history lesson, the Tunguska meteorite that hit Siberia in 1908 was estimated to weigh a few hundred tons, but it scorched a twenty mile area." He paused to study the expressions on the faces in front of him, but they offered no help.

"From the geological record," he continued, "we know that there is a 640-kilometer wide depression on the eastern shore of the Hudson Bay in Canada that was caused by a meteorite. So we have some idea of the kind of damage that might be expected." Again, tension rose in the room, and it felt like a second flurry of questions would erupt. MacBrin hurried on.

"One of our foremost concerns relates to the extent of damage that we can anticipate. The answer is that we can't say for certain. The meteor cloud that we are currently tracking is not so well-defined that we can predict the sizes of the meteors and how many will succeed in hitting the ground as meteorites. In fact, there is almost universal agreement that most, and let me reiterate *most* of the particles contained in the cloud will be influenced by the larger gravitational pull of the sun. They will not hit the earth at all." Two correspondents in the second row jumped to their feet, but Malcolm ignored them.

"The hopeful news," offered MacBrin using the lilt of his accent, "the hopeful news in all of this is that we are confident as to where the strike will occur. The anticipated *ground zero* is the continent of Antarctica." He stopped to let his statement take root before continuing. "Before we announced this press conference, we notified the twelve nations that have been heavily involved in Antarctic research and exploration. Even as I speak, evacuation protocols are being implemented. I also add that provisions have been taken into account to remove human-related risks. That means all the nuclear fuel used to generate electricity at McMurdo Naval Air Station will be removed when the personnel depart. We have also issued warnings and procedures for the coastal regions of the southern hemisphere. Here, I can show you."

He turned to a large scale Mercator map that formed the backdrop for his presentation. "We have identified several zones where we anticipate some level of danger. The first zone is Antarctica proper and its coastal area. This area, as I have said, is subject to immediate evacuation. The second danger area is coastal regions up to the fortieth parallel. These areas include the south island of New Zealand, Tasmania, the southern portions of Chile and Argentina, and of course, the island chains such as the Malvinas/Falkland group. This is a huge area, and our concern is with regard to tidal surges. We just don't know what will happen. There is even a remote possibility that ocean levels may rise on a planetary scale, so all coastal regions should keep alert." He waved his hand over the continental land masses indicated on the map.

"Before I answer questions, let me say that we are predicting a worst-case scenario. Ocean levels rising, for example, would be the result of the ice cap melting appreciably. Most of the world's fresh water is held in Antarctic ice, so if there is any significant melting due to impact, we could see a notable rise in water levels, especially at high tide. Now, I will open the floor for a few questions."

"What do you mean by 'a notable rise'?" shouted a member of the press, picking up on MacBrin's final comment.

"It's a matter of scale," answered the Irishman with a hint of a smile. "Most people have no idea of the size of Antarctica. Maybe it's the fault of the tourist industry." A ripple of laugher drifted through the audience. "There is enough ice to raise the average ocean depth more than 150 feet, but that would be assuming a 100% meltdown. Geological evidence tells us that 65 million years ago a collision with the earth left a crater just north of the Yucatan peninsula that has a 180-kilometer diameter. That is one of the largest impact craters ever identified, but in terms of a comparable effect in Antarctica, well, it could not produce a total meltdown. The distance between the Palmer Peninsula and Wilhelm II Coast is about 5,230 kilometers, almost thirty times the diameter of the Chicxulub crater. Next question."

A flurry of hands begged for recognition, but a shouting voice took precedence. "So you're saying that the planet can absorb the impact?"

"That's our best educated guess," answered MacBrin. "But let's handle these questions in an orderly fashion," he chided as he pointed to a heavyset reporter from Reuters.

"Yes," said the man in a calm tone that MacBrin had expected. "For decades, space theorists have been saying that a collision with an asteroid is inevitable. Some popularists have even advocated that this is the premier reason for space exploration; and certainly for the development of missiles to divert extraterrestrial objects. But what can be done to avoid the impact altogether?"

"The issue has been discussed thoroughly, and all plans to redirect or break up the approaching meteor cloud have been abandoned. The missiles that we possess are from a twentieth century arsenal and were designed to hit targets on earth. They can achieve earth orbit altitudes, but were not functionally designed to hit more distant targets on the other side of the solar system. If we waited until the meteor cloud came closer, we would run the risk of diverting particles toward the earth rather than away. This could render a more adverse affect on populated areas. Next question!"

A woman reporter was invited to speak. "You keep describing this as a 'meteor cloud'. One of my colleagues just used the word 'asteroid'. Can you be more specific?"

MacBrin cleared his throat. This was the critical question, and he had already predetermined that it would the last he would attempt to answer. "What we believe we have discovered is the remnants, the rocky core, of a comet. It is a short-period comet that has lost its plasma, and therefore did not show the characteristic tail as it approached. The ice and frozen gases, that made it a comet, are gone. What are left are the solid parts drifting in close orbit. I remind you that the cores of comets are not solid like a stone in a snowball. While there may be large chunks of rocky material, most of the bulk is probably fine particles that will flare-out and give a spectacular light show. They will burn up before getting near the land surface. We suspect, however, that the core will also have larger particles that will survive atmospheric burn-up and strike the earth. We also know that some of these larger masses will glance off the atmosphere and be drawn into the sun. That is why we have called this conference. Something is going to happen, and we need to warn the planet so that we can brace for a worst-case scenario. Thank you for your attention, and your help. We do not want to cause panic, but we should be alert. We will be keeping you informed as more data becomes available."

The press corps jumped as they realized that MacBrin was cutting them off. Before they could stop him, he had left the podium and was out of the room.

In the back hallway, MacBrin took a deep breath. He had intended to hide his fears and apprehensions beneath some techno-jargon, and he had.

6

The drive from Syracuse to Sodus Bay was usually pleasant for Shrader, who enjoyed the rolling hills of the Erie-Ontario lowlands. Today, however, it seemed like his car was crawling along. He had not even given a glance at the small marinas that lined Onondaga Lake as he skirted its shores and drove northwest toward the south shore of Lake Ontario. Had he allowed himself to think about it, with his federal tax return lying unfinished on the dining room table, this trip in early April would seem foolish. This was a trip that had eclipsed all else, and his wife, Lynn, was clearly worried.

"You are not usually an impulsive person," she noted. "Why are you doing this?" It was a question for which Shrader had no clear answer. Nevertheless, he felt driven to complete this journey. His one thread of hope was Cathy. If he were going crazy, he would be dreaming his nightmare alone, but she was experiencing similar visions. *Similar was not the word for it, more like identical*, he thought. As a teacher of anthropology he had done a lot of reading on primitive cultures and shaman religion. He had given lectures on the role of dreams in the spirit communication of primitive peoples, but nothing had prepared him for his own dreams.

His grip on the steering wheel relaxed as he approached the turn-off at Route 14. He would see the Bay soon. It was always a little odd approaching the marina in early spring. The parking lot was full of sailboats on cradles and jackstands. They looked like many beached whales; their massive bulk revealed in a way that belied their sleek appearances on the water.

Shrader pulled off to the side of the road next to the sign of the Sodus Point Marina. He turned the key and the car was overwhelmed with silence. For a moment he sat, staring blankly ahead at the road that led to the abandoned lighthouse. It stood as a sentinel for a small town that slept in the winter, but sprang to life when the Ontario boaters returned in the spring and summer. Shrader could not tell how long he sat there, but he was awakened from his trance by a sudden sharp knocking on his passenger side window. It was Cathy. He reached across the car and unlocked the door. She pulled it open and a draft of chill air invaded his senses.

"It's cold out there," said Cathy as she slid into the passenger's side.

"The water temperature can't be much above fifty degrees," answered Shrader. "The air over the water will be cold for at least another month."

Cathy nodded her agreement. "They have started launchings, however," she said. "I'd say that they have about ten boats in the water. Mostly sloops, a few cutters," she added, referring to the long-keeled Island Packets.

"Last ones out, first ones in," commented Shrader. "I wish I had insisted that they not pull *Strider* until November. She's probably wedged in behind a dozen others."

"Right next to *Affinity*," said Cathy. She had gone to work for Affinity Technology Services when things got rough financially for the family. Her husband, Phil, was a private consultant, and the nature of his business sometimes led to a problem with cash flow. When Cathy took the position with ATS, Phil renamed their boat saying that it only seemed fitting since ATS was now paying his *entertainment* expenses.

"Which boats are in?" asked Shrader.

"I made a list of the more seaworthy ones," she said reaching into her jacket pocket.

"We *are* on the same wavelength, aren't we?" remarked Shrader. "I figure we have to go with boats that are in the water or that can be launched within the week."

"This is happening way too fast," said Cathy. "But, we don't have a lot of options, do we? Right now, in the water, we've got: *Fairwinds, Rol's Royce, Major Blunder, Well-heeled, Dream Dancer, Wave Chaser*, and one I've never seen, *Mutiny*- but it's spelled M-e-w-t-i-n-y."

"Cute! Do you figure they have a cat onboard?" asked Shrader.

"Probably," agreed Cathy. "Do you suppose the litter box helps mask the odor of the head compartment?" The two laughed. The requirement of holding tanks on the Great Lakes made for some interesting cabin smells in the hotter months. "I talked to Gary at the marina office about getting *Affinity* and *Strider* on a priority launch list. As usual, he won't make guarantees, but I think it's only a matter of moving two or three boats."

"We may need to light a fire under a few people before this is over," commented Shrader. "We have to get to *Manitoanna* as soon as possible."

Cathy's blank expression told him that she didn't follow. "Where?" she asked.

"What did I say?" he asked. "I was thinking of the Thousand Islands at the entrance to the Seaway."

"That I would have understood, but you said some name that started with an M."

"I don't know what I said," confessed Shrader. "But I know we have to get positioned to enter the Seaway. Have you and Phil ever locked through the Saint Lawrence?"

"No, but it's always been one of those adventures in the backs of our minds, or at least in my mind. Philip's not what I would call the adventurous sort. When I'd describe the trip, he'd always pass it off as a huge endeavor. But to sail to Montréal and even the Canadian Maritimes, well, that would be something. I remember figuring that, to do it right, it would take a couple of weeks at least."

"A dreamer with courage," said Shrader almost to himself. "You'll need both."

"What do you know that you're not telling me, Shrader?"

"Let's go look at the boats, and I'll tell you," he said. "Then you can tell me if I'm going crazy." He pulled the door handle. A rush of air reminded them both of the realities of springtime on Lake Ontario. Once outside, the two zipped their windbreakers and pulled the drawstrings to seal the nylon hoods over their heads.

"Okay, what do you know, Shrader?" Cathy repeated.

"I don't know anything, really," he answered. "It started with the dreams, and then all this news coverage about meteorites. I can't help but think that the two go together."

"I feel the same way," confessed Cathy. "The scientists are acting confident enough. CNN even announced that they are going to cover it like a news event with camera teams and everything."

"I know it's all supposed to be benign, but..." Shrader's voice trailed off.

"But, what?" asked Cathy.

"But a comet strike has been blamed for the eradication of most dinosaur species. The dust from the impact got trapped in the jet stream, blocked the sun's rays, and sent the world into a mini-ice age. The combination of diminished food supplies and colder climate led to a mass extinction. Okay, that's an oversimplification, but it just doesn't square with the *worst-case* scenarios that they're talking about on TV. I have the feeling that we are being given Civil Defense drills like the school children of the 50's who were told to get under their desks in the case of nuclear attack."

"We're being lied to, then?"

"Maybe not 'lied to', but we're not being told everything," answered Shrader. "I don't know if you even know what I do for a living, but I teach anthropology at Syracuse," he continued.

"I didn't know that," said Cathy.

"One thing that keeps haunting me about that stupid dream is the question why the boats are in salt water. But the answer is so clear. In an ice-age world, the ocean is the place where the food is kept."

"What?" asked a confused Cathy. The two had managed the twisted maze created by the beached sailboats and were standing beneath the faded blue of *Affinity's* bottom paint. The wind had either diminished or the hulls blocked it out, but the air was still. Shrader ran the palm of his hand along the boat's underwater surface feeling for blisters and imperfections hidden beneath the chalky anti-fouling paint.

"Did you ever take anthropology in college?" he asked.

"Are you kidding?" answered Cathy. "I was a business major. No offense!" The two laughed.

"Okay, then," responded Shrader. "It's time for my revenge, the dreaded 'pop quiz'. Where is the birthplace of civilization?"

"This isn't a trick question, is it?" asked Cathy.

"Not for me," said a grinning Shrader.

"Then I will say *Mesopotamia*?"

"A popular answer," remarked Shrader, "one based on the Judeo-Christian legacy of the Western world. But what if I told you that there were people living in established settlements on the Gulf of St. Lawrence and crossing the North Atlantic in boats 3500 years before Abraham? When he left his family and kindred and set out on his pilgrimage of faith, there were already families along the Atlantic coast that had been there for millennia."

"Thirty-five hundred years?" repeated Cathy.

"You got it! They lived on the edge of retreating glaciers, and they lived off the sea."

"How did they survive?" asked Cathy.

"Apparently, very well," remarked Shrader. "They had a network for trading stone tools that stretched across the Atlantic and as far south as what's now New Jersey. Who knows what else they traded? Only the stone tools survived to the present. What's this? Here's a problem."

Cathy looked to see where Shrader had knelt to inspect the rudder. "What is it?" she asked. He pointed to a hairline vertical crack on the front edge of the rudder blade.

"It looks like some water got into the rudder and split the housing when it froze this winter," he answered.

"Is it difficult to fix?"

"No. Well, not in temperatures above sixty degrees. It'll have to be epoxied, or else you'd be risking rudder failure at sea. Our problem is raising the outdoor temperature by twenty degrees. That shouldn't be a problem, but then there are some who are beginning to conclude that I'm a madman. Do you trust me?"

"Yes," said Cathy, "and what does it say about me if I think a madman is the sanest one around? Right now, we have to get two boats ready to be launched. You take care of the outdoor temperature; I'll try to get some batteries out of winter storage."

"Okay," said Shrader. "Let's hope we have enough time."

7

Muoshti looked over the ridge at the vast herd of caribou. His heart always leapt at the sight. The antlered beasts were so strange to him, and unlike his cousins of the sea. By now, the hunt was well under way, and clansmen were moving among the herd draped in the skins of cows. Soon they would attempt to isolate a part of the herd, and attack before the bulls could ring their defense or stampede the throng.

Muoshti had not joined the hunt. His reluctance was not due to his age. At fourteen his manhood could not be doubted. His refusal to hunt the caribou was credited to the list of strangeness that was being whispered around the settlement. Only *Whaleman* seemed to approve. Muoshti clutched the orca effigy which hung around his neck. The coolness of the stone spoke to him of the waters, and the voice of the waves soothed his mind.

In the hunt he could see his brother, Vuhar. He was the stalker who knew the ways of the beasts of the tundra. He hunted them and even revered them, but the spirit of the caribou was not within him to understand their wisdom. Muoshti wondered if the great beasts could speak as clearly as the orcas, if only the humans could learn to listen. *Whaleman* had told him that such was possible. Muoshti suspected that *Whaleman* spoke to the animals of the sea long before he himself had discerned the voice of the whales. Many of the villagers distrusted the *Whaleman* and his eccentric ways, but they needed him. When the fishing fleet lost their way, *Whaleman* would call out to the spirits of the sea. The fishers feared him for that. They hated him also for the fact that he would not let them harvest the great killer whales when there were no cod or swordfish to be found in the deep sea waters.

It had taken Muoshti all his courage to confront *Whaleman* the first time. He had been taught to shun the strange ways of the shuffling old man. But when he was eight years old, curiosity overcame his fear. One morning the eastern sky awoke with a telltale red that made the fishers fear. Muoshti saw *Whaleman* move away from the village and make his way down to the cove where the huge dugouts had been beached. He followed at a safe distance as the old man crossed the beach to a spit of rock that extended out into deeper water. There the shaman squatted cross-legged and began to whistle as he opened a skin sack and carefully set its contents on the rock in front of him. As Muoshti listened, the whistling evolved to a rhythmic chant as *Whaleman* arranged and rearranged pieces of bone and carved images. When the arrangement met with his satisfaction, he sprinkled them with red ochre. At first the blood-red powder was scattered low over the fetishes and the rock table, but as the chanting rose, so too did the hand that sprinkled the dust until it caught the breeze and drifted onto the waters. *Whaleman* watched as each passing of his arm sowed the redness to the winds.

Muoshti stood in silence, unsure whether *Whaleman* was aware of his presence. The shaman seemed lost in a trance until he broke it by beating a boudran that he had withdrawn from his sack. The sound was sharp and clear in the morning air. Muoshti thought that it might have been the heartbeat of the earth, but he was wrong. It was the pounding of the seas, and soon the waters were teeming with motion, swirling black and white. The orcas had come to *Whaleman* who rose to his feet and held outstretched arms to the eastern sky. Out of the sea a great orca rose opposite him, its white underbelly appeared as a shadow of light reflecting the *Whaleman's* straight form. He did not seem old in that moment. Nor was he crippled by the partial paralysis that deformed his gait. He spoke words that called forth fear in the watching boy.

"Muoshti, come out on the rock," he said. "Step out here so that you may meet your brother."

"My brother is Vuhar," he said finding his voice.

"Your brother is the orca, and the sea is your mother. I know you well, Muoshti," said the shaman. "Come out on the rock."

Muoshti felt compelled to obey. A tentative step was followed by another until he stood with the *Whaleman*. The killer whales made the waters churn beneath the rock. Muoshti heard a voice from somewhere. Perhaps it was inside his own mind. "Who is the little one?" it asked.

"He is our brother, Muoshti," said the *Whaleman*. "He hears your voices, but does not yet know how to call out to you."

A voice like the voice of the sea answered, "Bring him to us, Caller Brother." Muoshti recognized the name that had been given to the *Whaleman*.

"Do not fear your brothers, Muoshti," said the shaman. With that he took hold of the boy and threw him into the deeps. The water was cold and cut him to the bone. But Muoshti was not alone. His sodden clothes felt heavy against his skin, but he was buoyed up by an orca that swam beneath him.

"Hello, Little Brother," came the voice.

"Hello, My Brother," said Muoshti taking a mouthful of water. "I am Muoshti."

"You are *Whaleman*," came the reply. Muoshti knew that it was true.

8

When Cathy reappeared, she was pushing one of the dockside carts. Shrader had fabricated a polyethylene tent around the rudder of *Affinity*. He was pressing down the duct tape that attached the upper edges to the smooth sides of the fiberglass boat.

"So that's how you control the temperature," she commented, understanding what he was trying to do.

"I may be going insane," said Shrader, smiling, "but it's a pragmatic insanity. Looks like you're carting quite a load. Do you need help?" he asked referring, to the four marine batteries that tested the weight capacity of the sagging bicycle-wheeled cart.

"Yes," said Cathy. "I had to wear Gary down to get these out of storage, and it took all I had to get them into the cart."

"Well, I'll help you get them up into the boats. Do you have a space heater or a hair dryer in the boat?" asked Shrader. "I'm going to try to keep the air around the rudder warm enough to allow the epoxy to set-up."

"I'm sure we do," answered Cathy. "You help me get these batteries into the boats, and I'll get the heater."

In the water, *Strider*'s keel extended five and a half feet below the surface. The depth of the keel meant that on her cradle, the boat's rail was somewhere near eleven feet above the asphalt surface. *Affinity*'s keel drew only four feet, so her deck was slightly lower. Nevertheless, carrying four forty-pound batteries up a rickety ladder proved more of an ordeal than Shrader expected. By the time the last one was lowered into the cabin of *Affinity*, his arm muscles were beginning to spasm. "It's been a long winter," he said as he massaged his biceps. Cathy had pulled aside the cushions on the rear quarter berth to expose the battery cases. Shrader eased the heavy battery into one of the cases, and then positioned the second one next to it.

"Thanks," said Cathy. "I can handle the power connections." She paused for a moment before asking again, "Shrader, what do you think is happening?"

"Besides my going crazy and the two of us dreaming the same dream?"

"Yeah, besides that."

"I wish I knew," confessed Shrader. "I've given lectures on the relationship between dreams and future-telling in primitive cultures, but this isn't the way it's supposed to be. I have a feeling more than a plan. Something is going to happen, and our future is tied with being out on the water. I've always prided myself on being a realist, keeping emotion from tainting reason, but this really scares me. When I found out that you had the same dream, I knew that I was experiencing more than the breakdown of my brain chemistry. How about you? Have your dreams told you anything new?"

"I'm afraid that I've stopped dreaming," offered Cathy cautiously.

"What?"

"Ever since you called from the Atlanta airport," she said. "The dream hasn't come back. In fact, I don't have any dreams that I remember."

"Then I'm dreaming this stuff alone," said Shrader anxiously. "Maybe I am crazy."

"No," interrupted Cathy, "I didn't want to tell you because I was afraid that you'd think I made it all up. It's not like that at all. After you called, it was like a weight had been lifted. I didn't have to dream it anymore. It cleared my thinking, and I knew that we were still in touch with whatever it is that's trying to warn us. When we talked later, I began to feel guilty about sleeping so well, but then I told myself that *you* are the link. I just have to trust your dreams, and help figure out what to do."

"Then I should be asking you what all this means," said Shrader. "My senses feel stretched to where I can't trust myself. Hell, Lynn doesn't even trust me. She thinks I'm absolutely bonkers–Says I blew my best chance for tenure when I left the conference in Orlando. When I told her that I was driving up here to meet you, she just said she wasn't going to lie for me when the university called."

"I'm sorry, Shrader," consoled Cathy. "I know that the dreams are real. I also believe that they're a warning. Someday, Lynn will realize that."

"I hope so. What did Phil think?"

"He wanted to know who was going to drive the boys to soccer practice. Does that tell you where he is in this marriage?" she added.

"Okay," said Shrader. "Now it's my turn to say that I'm sorry. But I guess that's not why we're here. Apparently, I'm the one suffering from sleep deprivation, and you're the one thinking clearly. What do you think is happening?"

Cathy paused before speaking. "I'm almost afraid to say what I've been thinking, because it's too strange."

"We've been dreaming each other's nightmares," interrupted Shrader. "What could be stranger than that?"

"I guess you're right. It can't get much stranger. Okay, here's what I think: the dream is a warning. The fact that we both experienced it means that it's not a chemical imbalance in the brain. Unless, of course, we both have the same malady, but that's not very likely. Some force has planted this image in our minds, and has brought us together. After all this, we start hearing reports about the meteor strike in Antarctica, and I think that we are being warned about something that is going to wack-out the world or at least a big part of it. Whatever we have to do, it has to be done in the next two or three days. I think you were right when you said that we have to get our people together and get out to the Thousand Islands in order to be ready to head out the Saint Lawrence."

"I said that?" commented Shrader.

"Yes, you did. Don't you remember when we were sitting up in the car? You said we had to get to *Manitoanna*."

"Where's that?" he asked.

"That was the name you used in the car. I asked you what it meant and you said that you were thinking of the Thousand Islands. Well, while I was waiting for Gary to locate the batteries, I browsed one of the new books in the ship's store. There was a new Great Lakes cruising guide, and *Manitoanna* was the Native American word for "Garden of the Great Spirit," their name for the Thousand Islands."

"I am an anthropologist," said Shrader. "But I don't remember knowing that as a name for the islands. What is happening to me, Cathy?"

"I don't know," she said sympathetically. "But I know that you aren't crazy." She placed her hand on his arm. There was strain on his face. She could not explain her own sense of energy. "Come on," she said. "We have boats to outfit before the party."

"The party?" asked Shrader as he snapped back to reality.

"Yes," she said. "Three days from now, we are going to have an on-the-water meteor party. You'd better be thinking of who you want to invite because they're going to be shanghaied for a voyage to *Manitoanna*."

"Aye-aye, Captain," snapped Shrader with a smile and a salute. He felt relieved to hear a plan that was not of his own making. He was not ready to trust himself.

9

When Muoshti emerged from the water, he was a different person. He had crossed the boundary that humans had imposed upon themselves. It was not something that he could easily tell the others who lived in his area of the stone longhouse. He did risk telling Vuhar. His brother sat in the corner of the chamber flaking a piece of chert, shaping a tool to scrape the hide of a caribou.

"Vuhar," said Muoshti.

"Yes, Brother," he answered.

"Vuhar, I have ridden with the orcas."

"I saw you," he answered, without looking up. "You were with the *Whaleman*. Did he teach you?"

"No," confessed Muoshti. "The orcas called to me. I heard their voice." He stared at his eight year old twin, who did not look up from his work. In the dim light, Muoshti saw tear streaks on his brother's brown skin.

"Then you have been chosen," commented Vuhar. "I will miss you, My Brother."

Muoshti knew that Vuhar's few words represented a truth that he had not considered. The gift of hearing the voice of the whale set him on the fringe of the community. Though his insight would be integral to the Council of the Elders, never would he be welcomed again into the circle of an easy kinship. That very evening Muoshti folded his few possessions into a skin blanket and went to the hovel that was the home of the *Whaleman*. For a long time, he stood quietly in front of the stone lintel that marked the entrance to the private world of the shaman. The biting wind of the Labrador coast seemed far away from him, though it nearly froze his body through. At last, he stepped across the threshold and through the layered portiere. The inner sanctum was warm, and dimly lit with an oil lamp. The *Whaleman* was seated in front of a flat horizontal rock that he was using as a polishing stone. In his hand was a piece of black soapstone.

When Muoshti had left his home, his brother Vuhar had been making a sharp cutting edge. Here, in his isolation, the shaman was smoothing an object of beauty. He looked up at Muoshti and gave him a broad, yellow-toothed smile. It was an expression never before seen on the face of the old man, who quietly turned back to his work. Muoshti looked again at the object of the shaman's attention. It may have been a fishing plummet. Whatever its form, it had cost the *Whaleman* the skin of his fingertips which were bleeding as a result of inadvertent contact with the polishing stone. A few more strokes against the stone and a second smile crossed the shaman's face. He examined his treasure in cupped hands, shielding it from Muoshti's view.

Content with the results, he rose to his feet, but his legs betrayed him and he fell hard against the packed dirt floor. Muoshti jumped to his aid, but the old man gestured him off as if this were a normal occurrence. When he got up the second time, his legs held, and four shaky steps brought him to the place where the eight year old was standing.

"Hold out your hand, Orca's Brother," said the *Whaleman*. Spoken words were foreign in that place of solitude, but Muoshti did as he was told and extended his hand. The shaman placed the soapstone object on his palm. It was still warm from the friction of the polishing stone. It was an effigy, a black orca. The old man gazed with uncertainty into the face of the boy. Muoshti smiled as he fingered the smooth stone and recognized the killer whale image as a mark of his gift. His smile jumped onto the face of the *Whaleman*. Then both erupted into laughter. It was the sound of pure human joy, a sound not heard at that edge of the village for ages. But it was not heard in the longhouse that night, for the sound of it was swept away by the howling of the North Atlantic.

10

The temperature fell to thirty-eight degrees in the Sodus Bay area. Cathy and Shrader slept in sleeping bags in *Strider's* main cabin. Neither slept very well. Cathy was awakened several times by Shrader's fitfulness. While she regretted his discomfort, she used her sleeplessness to good advantage by going over her plan in her mind. She had already contacted the owners of the launched boats to try and sell them on the idea an Antarctic Comet party. To her surprise, the idea was greeted with enthusiasm. Out of the seven boats, only two failed to get positive results. The owner of *Mewtiny* actually hung up on her when she called, and she had been unable to get hold of the owners of *Well-Heeled*, the Bedfords, who were on a business trip in Nairobi, Kenya.

Weather forecasts for unseasonably warm conditions helped her lure the boaters who were already getting anxious about the sailing season after a winter of inactivity. Nobody seemed too concerned that actual news coverage of the Antarctic events would be limited to network coverage on the nine inch screen of *Affinity's* TV. Access to cable television would be nonexistent onboard the boats since the marina did not provide hookups.

It was about five a.m. when Cathy spoke into the darkness. "Shrader, are you awake?"

"Yes," came the reply.

"I have been thinking about *Mewtiny* and *Well-Heeled*," she said. "I guess there are a few things that really scare me. Okay, there are a lot of things that scare me, but at some point, are we going to need those boats? I mean, with or without the owners?"

"If you mean we're going to become pirates," answered Shrader. "I think we already are. I've come up with a list of things we need to get. It's mind boggling. If we're right, we have to sail off with provisions to last for years. We'll need food, at least enough to last until we can harvest our own from the sea. To do that, we'll need to latch onto some good way to catch fish, but

I'm not so sure we want sport fishing gear. We need to be efficient."

"I hadn't really thought about that," confided Cathy.

"The only sane thing I know about this insane plan is that the sea will be the only reliable source of food if a planetary disaster hits. On top of that, we'll also have to worry about hygiene, changes in diet, and weather exposure. In the dream the people were wearing winter clothes. It's spring now, but wherever we are going, it's going to be cold."

The two allowed silence to surround them as they lay in settee berths on opposite sides of the cabin. At last, Cathy spoke. "Shrader, I'm scared."

"I know. So am I," he answered. "But I would be more frightened if you weren't. Do you have a direct discharge fitting on your head? Can you flush the toilet into the lake?"

"What?" Cathy roared. "I tell you that I'm on the edge and you ask about the toilet."

"I guess I'm just one of those sensitive males," added Shrader, "or still full of that practical insanity from this afternoon when I epoxied your keel."

"And filled my boat with toxic fumes," said Cathy.

"It was the only way that I could get you to sleep with me," said Shrader.

"You are the sly one, then."

"Or afraid of the dark," he said. Again silence took over the two.

"No," said Cathy, after a pause.

"No, what?" said a confused Shrader.

"No, *Affinity* does not have a direct discharge. They are illegal. Our sewage goes into a holding tank and we have to go to the pump-out stations."

"How would Phil like it if I cut a hole in the bottom of the boat and make it possible to flush your toilet directly into the lake?"

"He'd calm down a week or two after he killed you," she said.

"Then, what do you say we not tell him right off?" suggested Shrader. "We aren't going to be able to find any pump-out stations where we are going, and holding tanks take up room where we could store provisions."

"But direct discharge into the Great Lakes is illegal," she continued to protest.

"See, we're already pirates," observed Shrader.

11

The caribou seemed jittery as Muoshti watched from the ridge. Vuhar and the others were moving toward an isolated group on the fringe of the herd. Muoshti could feel the wind in his face, and he knew that the hunters were downwind of the animals. It could not be their scent that was betraying them, but he could sense something. Then he saw them. Upwind from the herd, there were gray shapes slinking close to the ground. *Tundra wolves*, thought Muoshti. *But why were they upwind?*

He wanted to warn the hunters, but his signal would stampede the herd and endanger his brothers. He could do nothing but watch the drama unfold. Vuhar was in position, not twenty yards from an antlered bull. He set a spear into the hooked end of his *atlatl* to fling it with great force. Suddenly, as if on command, the wolves howled and sprung to full charge toward the very animal that Vuhar was stalking. The large animal leapt for fright. Muoshti saw the spear fly. Blood spurted from the neck of the hulking animal, but the wounded beast lowered its head and lunged forward catching a surprised Vuhar and dragging him thirty yards before falling dead upon him.

Chaos broke loose as the commotion telegraphed panic through the entire herd. The hunting party broke for high ground as the thunder of the earth sounded across the plain. Muoshti lost all sense and broke toward the carcass. A clansman passed nearby shouting warning, but he veered away when he realized that it was one of the *Whalemen*.

Instinctively, Muoshti cried out to the orcas, but this was not the place of their power. In any case, there was little that could be done. Vuhar's crushed body seemed little as it laid there next to the bull. He had been gored badly in the abdomen. It would have been a slow agonizing death had the beast not fallen and crushed the life out of him. Muoshti's hand went to the effigy around his neck. It was cool to the touch. He listened to his own racing heart, and then he let his heart rate slow to the memory of the pounding surf. "I will miss you, My Brother," he said to the lifeless body. It was then that he realized that he was not alone.

At first, he thought the hunters had returned. He sensed their presence. When he turned, however, he faced a hunter of another sort. It was the dominant wolf. Behind him, crouching close to the ground, were his minions.

The wolf spoke to him. "Why are you here, *Whaleman?*" he said.

"Because this one is my brother," answered Muoshti.

"Your brother knew how to hunt," said the wolf. "I am sorry that we had to betray him."

"Why did you approach from upwind?" cried Muoshti.

"Because my brothers are hungry," explained the wolf. "We have followed this herd for four days and they have given us nothing. We would have starved until we saw that your brother would shoot for us."

"You stampeded them on purpose!" he shouted, fighting back the tears.

"It is our way to hunt. It is our way to eat. Your brother knew that. We needed the flight of his spear; he gave us that gift."

"Then give me a gift," said Muoshti. "Let me take my brother's body while you eat his prey. The hunters will return soon to get the caribou. If you are still here, they may have darts for you."

"That is their way," said the wolf. Soon, the other wolves came and began to tear at the soft underbelly of the dead animal. Muoshti slid Vuhar's body free and lifted him up to his shoulder. He did not look back at the pack as they went to work.

"Tell my friend Creonduk that I will pick his bones if he is tired of them," called the wolf to Muoshti. The *Whaleman* did not answer. The weight of his brother was heavy on his shoulder and heavier on his heart.

12

Shrader had only a vague idea, actually more of a feeling, of what would soon be happening. On the Monday that he and Cathy had met at the marina, he had commented on getting a flotilla to the Thousand Islands. As his thoughts distilled, the enormity of the task began to catch up with him. Cape Vincent and the entrance to the Saint Lawrence River were sixty-nine miles across the lake. The Iroquois Lock, the first lock on the outward trek, lay seventy-three miles down river from Cape Vincent. At an average speed of six knots, it would take a boat eleven hours to cross to Cape Vincent. It would be tricky, if not impossible, to navigate the Thousand Islands area at night. So an overnight harbor would have to be found. Without exceptionally good luck, at the end of two days, they would still be on the Ontario side of the Iroquois Lock.

"It won't work," said Shrader to himself as he lay in the darkness of his berth in the main cabin of *Strider*. He was surprised to hear an answer. He had forgotten that Cathy was in the berth opposite him.

"What won't work?" she asked.

"Not enough time," said Shrader. "Under best-case conditions, sailing nearly at hull speed, it'll take twenty-four hours to reach the Iroquois Lock. We don't even have twelve hours of daylight this time of year. If we leave early on Saturday, the best we can hope for is to reach the Iroquois late on Sunday, and we'd have to wait to lock through on Monday. It's too late."

"So, we sail at night," said Cathy matter-of-factly.

"I don't think we can navigate the river at night," answered Shrader. "There may be ice and snags this time of year."

"No," replied Cathy. "We sail the first leg, the Ontario leg, at night and reach the Saint Lawrence at dawn."

Of course, thought Shrader. "It's perfect," he said aloud. "We arrive at Cape Vincent by dawn and have all day Saturday to make our way to the Iroquois. We can spend the night and lock through on Sunday. It'll work!"

"Just seems logical," she answered. "The lake is ice-free, and barring bad weather there won't be any shore hazards to contend with." Shrader laid back with his mind at ease. The voyage would begin in darkness. Somehow, it seemed fitting. He drifted off into sleep. Mercifully, he did not dream his nightmare. He had a new dream. He was whitewater rafting in a kayak. There was one thing that did not make sense, however. His kayak had a wheel instead of a paddle.

13

Muoshti carried the body of Vuhar to the ridge overlooking the bay on the outskirts of the village. Carefully, he set his brother on the ground and aligned his body face up, his head directed toward the sea and his face to the open sky. He arranged Vuhar's arms so that they crossed over his chest. For a long time, he stood looking down at his twin. Tears ran down his cheeks as he began to chant. From the sea came the answer of the great orcas as they churned the waters and spouted wisps of spray from their blow holes.

Muoshti sang to his brother, Vuhar, and to his other brothers, the whales:

> Brothers, come to me in the spirit of the morning.
> Brothers, come to me over the paths of the sea,
> for Vuhar has passed beyond sight,
> but not beyond my longing to speak to him.
> He is my brother, guide him beyond my seeing
> to the place of my longing.

Just then, the *Whaleman* cleared the ridge. He crawled on his arms dragging his useless legs. The sight was so familiar to Muoshti that he took no notice.

"The Hunter has been betrayed," said the shaman.

"The tundra wolves were hungry and Vuhar's spear fed them," answered Muoshti.

"They are an ancient race," said *Whaleman*. "They have survived many things, and they feed their pups with their cunning."

"They gave me a message for one I do not know," replied Muoshti. "They told me to tell Creonduk that they would pick his bones if he was tired of them."

The *Whaleman's* visage changed as though he were staring beyond time. "Yes, they would remember Creonduk. They honor him with their offer, for they are hunters and would have the old hunter run with them. It would be a fine thing," he answered. "Tell me of Vuhar," he asked changing his gaze to the present. "How did he die? How did he live? How is it that he is so truly your brother?"

Muoshti recalled the hunt and the stampede that resulted when the wolves purposely moved upwind of the herd. It was easy to explain Vuhar's death, more difficult to tell how he was a brother. "We were sons of the same mother," he began. "We were twins, two alike."

"But what made him your brother?" asked *Whaleman*.

Muoshti paused to consider the question. There are bonds deeper than kinship. For as different as he was from the great orcas, he knew them to be his brothers. At last he spoke:

"Vuhar was my brother when we pulled a seal through the breathing hole in the ice. He was my brother when I shared the food that Grandfather gave me in his last winter, in the time for the children to die. Vuhar was my brother when the sky turned green and dropped its curtain of light in the north; and before the long darkness when our parents ceased walking the paths of earth." When Muoshti stopped talking, the hillside seemed eerie in its silence.

"Now I know how he is your brother," answered the *Whaleman*. "And I know why you are shaman." The old man reached into the leather satchel that he had dragged with him and retrieved the familiar pouch of red ochre. He sprinkled Vuhar's lifeless form. "We must kindle fires to mark his place," he said.

Muoshti took his meaning and began to gather bits of moss and dried dung from the caribou trail. He placed the fuel in small piles directly north and south of the body of his brother.

"Bring coals from his own hearth," said *Whaleman.* "Bring them together with fire from your home." Muoshti nodded, rose to his feet, and headed back toward the settlement.

Eyes watched him as he walked past the entrances to the stone longhouse. The hunters, returning with the carcass of the wolf-gutted caribou, saw him also. Muoshti bent low as he entered Vuhar's chamber, the place that had once been his home. He scanned the dimly lit space until he located a small piece of leather. He laid it on the earthen floor in front of the fire. With a piece of kindling he scraped at the floor to loosen the packed dirt. He coated the hide with the soil to serve as a barrier. Then he nudged charcoal from the fire to the perimeter of the edge of the skin flicking the hot coals onto the prepared surface. He wrapped the bundle and left the chamber. He turned toward the edge of the village and went to the hovel where he and *Whaleman* quartered. He entered and collected hot coals from his fire. When he emerged, he saw that a crowd was gathering outside the longhouse. Clansmen were pointing to the ridge where he had carried Vuhar's body. Muoshti turned back toward the ridge. The throng began to follow at a distance. Muoshti rejoined *Whaleman* on the hillside. He sat on the ground and opened the folded skin. The smoldering contents brought a familiar smell to the overlook.

While he had been gathering the coals, *Whaleman* had managed to erect several small slabs of stone around Vuhar's body. Muoshti saw his purpose and without instruction began to help him complete the cyst. Once the body was entirely encircled with stones, the shaman spoke.

"We must turn him over to face the earth, his new home," he said.

"May he find new family there who will recognize him as a brother," added Muoshti.

"They will know him," consoled *Whaleman.* "He looks like his twin, Muoshti, who has many brothers."

45

"Then I will give him my token," offered Muoshti as he slipped the rawhide thong that held the whale effigy over his head. "This one is a brother of a *Whaleman*. The spirit that meets him will know that." He slipped the effigy over his dead brother's head and rolled the body facedown as the shaman had instructed him. He then tended the fires. Deftly, he shifted the burning coals to the two ritual fire sites. He used his fingers to transfer the embers. Then kneeling to the earth, he blew into the live coals and ignited the fuel. For a brief time the flames leapt up and then withered to smoke. Back along the ridge stood the men, women, and children of the clan. They heard the two *Whalemen* sing to the universe:

> Greet our Brother, Mother who bore us.
> Greet our Brother, Earth that sustains us.
> He was a hunter with the spirit of the Wolf.
> His darts sped true, and he honored his prey.
> Send us another like him, a man of the hunt,
> a man of the Wolf, a man like Vuhar.
> He is our Brother still, O Earth, that holds him.

When the chanting had finished, the clan began to move in toward the site. Already they were collecting rocks and boulders to raise a cairn over the sanctified body.

"We must leave now," said the shaman. "Others will now bring their tears. Help me stand, Muoshti. I want to go down to the water walking as a man." The request was an unusual one. As weak as he had become, the *Whaleman* had never asked to be lifted. Muoshti helped him to his feet, and bore most of his weight as the two slowly descended the ridge to the shore. Once on the sandy beach the shaman seemed more determined than ever. "Let's walk out to meet our Brothers," he said referring to the orcas which had gathered in response to their chanting.

"You walk as a young man, Old Friend," said the killer whale. As the water deepened, the shaman became more buoyant and less heavy on Muoshti's shoulders.

"I wondered if you would remember me in my youth, Keeper," said the shaman.

"I remember," said the Whale. "As you have remembered my name, so I recall yours, Creonduk. But why do we name ourselves again?"

"The Wolf has spoken my name to ask if I am yet weary of these bones."

"Are you?" asked the orca.

"Yes," came the reply. "The hunter offered to take me with him."

"But the tundra is not your home, is it?" questioned the Whale.

"No, Brother," said the shaman. "My bones are too heavy to walk the earth. My Keeper travels the paths of the sea. In the water I am light and I am young again."

Muoshti was having trouble grasping the conversation. "You are Creonduk?" he said at last.

"Yes," said the old man. "And you are the *Whaleman*." He slipped his own well-worn effigy off over his head and slid it over Muoshti's.

"Long after my people had forgotten the name of Creonduk, the Wolf remembered. Hearing it again makes me young. One day, I will come to you *Whaleman* to speak the name that all others have forgotten. On that day, we will be young together, and we will swim with our Brothers."

Muoshti felt the water swirl around him as Creonduk rose out of the water. Keeper had lifted him and he was seated with his back to the great dorsal fin. The two sped off into the deeps.

"When you have forgotten your own name, I will speak it," called Creonduk. "And we will laugh together, my Friend."

That was the last time that Muoshti saw the *Whaleman*. The water was very cold.

14

Shrader Marks was impatient as he waited for the elevator door to open. When it did, it revealed a part of his private world as an instructor of anthropology. Before him was the subterranean world of the junior faculty whose offices were off the archive storage area of the natural science building. He was not sure why he had made this last pilgrimage. He had told his wife, Lynn, that he was driving over to his office at the university, and she seemed relieved at the behavior that approached normal. But Shrader was feeling anything but normal.

In his own mind, he was saying good-bye to all that was familiar, to the school, the profession, and unless he could persuade Lynn, to a childless marriage of fourteen years. He walked quietly between the gray stacks of drawers neatly labeled and full of the relics of past civilizations. His small office was at the end of the asphalt-tiled aisle. That was where he was headed when, to his own surprise, he stopped and pulled open one of the wide, shallow drawers that lined the corridor. He knew what was inside. It was the one object that captured his mind and imagination from the time he unearthed it near Red Bay on the coast of Labrador. Simple and elegant in form, there was no mistaking the stone effigy's likeness to a killer whale. He reached in to touch the smooth, cold flint.

Shrader did not particularly believe in magic, but this piece of black chert made him feel a kinship that spanned seven-and-a-half millennia. He remembered his excitement when he first uncovered the red ochre, a telltale sign that this was a burial site. Lower in the cyst was found the skeletal remains of a young boy, still wearing the whale effigy.

"Why don't you just take it?" came a voice from down the aisle. It was John Romig, a geologist who had been with Shrader on the summer expedition in Red Bay.

"What, and risk losing all this?" answered Shrader with a smile.

"In a few days, I don't think it will matter," commented Romig. Shrader looked hard at the man who was about his own age and height, and usually lighthearted.

"What are you talking about, John?" asked a guarded Shrader.

"Oh, I've just been on the Internet for four hours and consensus of opinion is that we might well be on the edge of oblivion."

"Now, that's a cheery thought," observed Shrader with growing interest. "Is it the meteor strike? I've heard that it is supposed to be fairly benign."

"That's what T-Rex said just before Mother Earth installed the Chicxulub crater sixty-five million years ago," John scoffed. The two had had similar discussions before, and Shrader knew that John was referring to an impact crater off the north coast of the Yucatan peninsula that is credited with the mass extinction of the dinosaurs.

"Okay, John, spill it!" invited Shrader.

"It's all lies. That's all," said Romig. "They aren't taking the geology into account at all. They are saying that we're going to get hit by a burning fireball, but it's okay because it'll land in an icy area. They act like we're talking about defrosting the freezer." Romig was getting more agitated as he spoke.

"You'd think they'd never heard of continental plates," he continued. "Well, two days ago the powers-that-be broke rank. Carlos Menendez put out the word on the Internet. This whole press release is nothing more than the scientific community crossing its collective fingers. This so called meteor is turning out to be more like a dead Apollo or even an asteroid. It could be a mile in diameter, and solid."

"Whew," whispered Shrader who was beginning to understand John Romig's sense of upheaval. "CNN is planning to cover the event like it's going to be nothing more than a spectacular meteor shower."

"I know," agreed Romig. "The reporters don't know it, but they've been assigned a suicide mission. Then again, maybe we all have."

"Now you're exaggerating. It can't be that bad." Shrader found himself arguing against his own intuitions. What Romig was saying was bringing a scientific basis to his nightmares, and he still hoped that they were unfounded.

"No," said John. "I'm not exaggerating. Antarctica is not a floating ice cube; it's a continent. It sits on its own tectonic plate at the junction of most of the major continental plates. What we have is the possibility for any number of chain reactions beginning with volcanic actions on the Antarctic plate to

SHRADER MARKS & KEELHOUSE

underwater earthquakes and the resulting tsunamis. Imagine the ocean levels at one hundred and fifty feet above normal and a fifty to a one hundred foot tsunami on top of that. What if it triggers seismic or volcanic activity all the way up the Pacific rim?"

"It will," said Shrader in a low voice. "I tasted the sulfur in the air."

"What?!" asked Romig. It was his turn to be taken by surprise.

"John, if I tell you something, you've got to promise you won't think I've gone completely bonkers. Well, at least keep an open mind. Okay?"

"Okay," said Romig hesitatingly. "But I can't imagine anything..."

"Trust me," interrupted Shrader. "This is weird. You know I was supposed to go to the supervision conference in Orlando?"

"Yes," answered John. "I was surprised when you were back so soon."

"So was everyone else. In fact, I walked out on the seminar. I started having dreams. When I'd wake up and think about the dreams, they seemed strange, but not scary. Yet, I'd be terrified while I was dreaming them. I was with a group of Lake Ontario boats, but we were in salt water. It must have been cold because all the people were dressed for winter. The air, I remember, tasted like sulfur."

"So after what I said, you think it was a premonition?" asked John Romig.

"No, there's more," corrected Marks. "I dreamed the same thing three or four times, and started to recognize people. One of them was a woman who sails out of the same marina. I don't know her very well, but in the dream she was in trouble and called my name."

"Is she a *major babe*?" asked Romig with a wink. Shrader's glance told him that this was no time to joke.

"Anyway," Shrader continued. "When I called this person on the phone, she had had exactly the same dream, viewed from her perspective on the boat." Shrader thought of telling him Cathy's comment about his riding a killer whale, but thought better of it.

Romig's silence told Marks that his words were not being dismissed as trivial. "How do you understand it?" was his answer.

"I don't," said Shrader. "At first I tried to think of it in psychological terms. I even reread Carl Jung, but it doesn't feel like a normal dream if there is any such thing as that. When I found that Cathy was having the same dream, I figured that it wasn't coming out of my subconscious."

"Then where from?" asked Romig. "Genetic memory?"

"I thought about that, too," answered Shrader. "But it doesn't seem to fit the definition, unless genetic memory is more than behavior patterns from the past. Maybe it also includes a way of dreaming that foreshadows the future. Listen to me. I sound like the kind of person that they lock away for hallucinations."

Romig studied him for a moment. He turned his gaze away and looked into the open specimen drawer. The black whale effigy sat in a neat row along with other stone artifacts. He reached to touch the polished image. It was cool to his touch. "Where were you in your dream?" he asked.

Shrader was surprised by the question. "What?"

"Instead of asking yourself what the dream means or what the dream is, ask yourself where you were," explained John.

"I was in the water," began Shrader. "It was salt water."

"You already told me that. What else did you see?" urged Romig.

Shrader Marks closed his eyes. In his conscious mind he drifted back to the world of his sleep. He saw the sailboats moving along together, crawling along the coast. It was then that he noticed a rocky shoreline. The boats were approaching the shelter of a bay. On the barren ridge above the beach were markers, standing stones. One stood erect, a second at an angle that formed a right triangle. "*Inuksuk,*" said Shrader.

"Standing stones?" inquired Romig. "Where are you?"

"Labrador." he said without hesitation. The answer surprised them both, but brought a look of satisfaction to Shrader's face. "Labrador," he said again.

"Couldn't you dream of some place warmer?" asked John.

"But no place safer," commented Shrader.

"Wait a minute, Marks," protested Romig. "I've been to Labrador, remember? There's nothing there. It's cold, barren, and hostile. How can you say *safer*?"

Shrader could feel the tension level dropping as the tone of John's voice began to take on a playful banter. "There's plenty of open water, fish, and caribou. More importantly, there are no dangerous humans like academic deans and tenure committees."

"Can I sign up for the trip then?" said Romig with a chuckle. When the laughter died, he asked again with a quiet seriousness which could not be ignored. "You do have a plan, don't you?"

"Cathy and I have nine boats, either in the water or they will be within twenty-four hours. All we have to do now is convince people to trust in the nightmares of an anthropology instructor whose own wife thinks he's nuts."

"Lynn doesn't buy any of this?" asked Romig. Shrader shook his head. "I know that when we were on the Red Bay expedition, you two were having problems. Things haven't gotten better?"

"No," confessed Shrader. "She's tired of the itinerant life of an instructor. She likes it here at Syracuse and has basically said that she isn't moving. So, if I'm not granted a tenured professorship at the end of my six years, I'm going to have to decide on my wife or my profession."

"I'm sorry," consoled John. "We both know that there won't be any openings here for a while unless some wealthy alumnus endows a chair."

"Not likely," said Shrader.

"Not likely," repeated Romig. "But I think that's a moot point right now. I wasn't being facetious when I asked about signing on. I've known you long enough to know you're not a flake, and I know what the geologists are saying. The Internet is rife with survival plans. Some are talking of escaping to the mountains, others to the tropics, but no one has offered Labrador as a haven."

"Pretty crazy, huh?" added Shrader.

"Yep," agreed Romig. "It's right off the wall until you give it some thought. We know humans can survive there in an ice age. The sea will provide a food larder, and human populations are not dense enough to cause upheaval over the scarcity of resources."

"We're announcing a meteor-party at the marina for Friday evening, and a first-sail-of-the-season shakedown on Saturday." said Shrader. "It was Cathy's idea. We need to get people together on the boats and try to convince them to follow us out the Saint Lawrence. Pretty feeble, isn't it?"

"Maybe you need a geologist to talk hard facts. Shrader, I'm volunteering," pleaded Romig. "Look, it only makes sense. If a dead comet is going to hit, I'd like to have some a better plan than the current *nothing*! If the doomsday scenario turns out to be way overblown, I'd be glad to say 'OOPS' and settle for an April sail on Lake Ontario. The price isn't too high if we are wrong, but it's incalculable if we are right and do but sit and wait."

"There's room on my boat for a geologist and his family," said Shrader. "Especially one that *almost* has me convinced that I am not absolutely crazy."

"You are not crazy," said John. "I don't know how you are receiving your premonitions, but they seem to square with a growing number of scientists who are not convinced that the rock that's going to hit the earth on Sunday is going to disintegrate into a cloud of sand and gravel when it hits the outer atmosphere."

"Sunday?" questioned Shrader.

"Yes, that's pretty certain, now," answered Romig. "The thing is being tracked, and it evidently appears to be a solid mass and not a dehydrated mud ball that will eventually fall apart."

"I told Cathy that we had to be through the Iroquois Lock by Sunday. How did I know that?"

"Maybe you've got ESP or some divine revelation, but who cares? The point is that you are right on the money," said the geologist.

"Thank you, John," said Shrader.

"What the hell for?" asked Romig.

"For listening, for not laughing, for believing in me when I'm finding it difficult to believe in myself. That's all," added Shrader. John Romig just shrugged his shoulders. "Would you be willing to do me one other favor?" asked Marks.

"Sure, if there's time," offered Romig.

"Talk to Lynn. I hope there's time."

15

"They're for our Girl Scout summer camp archery program," said Cathy to a dubious clerk in the sports department.

"These are not the sort of arrows that kids should be using," he protested for the third time. "You need the ones with blunter tips for target shooting. These are razor sharp and meant for bow hunters, not target practice."

"Look," said Cathy in her best see-here-you-male-chauvinist-pig voice. "This is not a recreational program. We are teaching young women to be safety-conscious bow hunters."

"Okay, okay," he said. "I'll see if we have any unopened cases in stock. But I can special order some and have them for pick-up by Tuesday."

"No, I'll take what you have in stock. The program leaders gave me a list of things to purchase for the first overnight camp this weekend. I just shouldn't have put it off for so long." The clerk seemed satisfied with Cathy's answer and disappeared through a swinging door marked *Employees Only*. She was not fully prepared for all the storytelling that had to accompany the purchase of sporting goods. She already had four cases of arrows under blankets in the back of her minivan, and six compound bows. Her shopping list read like something out of some maniacal survivalist community. It didn't surprise her that a woman buying arrows by the case, twenty-four at a time, needed an accompanying explanation. She wondered whether Shrader would have had the same problem. The two had talked about food gathering strategies, and had settled on bow hunting.

"I know that firearms seem like the logical choice," said Shrader. "But that technology will be obsolete when the last bullet is fired." Cathy was quick to realize that he was correct. "Besides," he added. "There is a waiting period on the sale of guns, and we can't wait. Even if we could manufacture our own gunpowder and reload shells, we do not have the time for the bureaucratic process."

"Phil has a couple of shotguns and a rifle," offered Cathy.

"That would be some insurance," commented Shrader.

"What do you mean by that?"

"Only that it will take some time before any of us are proficient with primitive hunting tools," he answered. "Having firearms will provide a margin of safety for novice hunters."

The sight of the sales clerk dragging two cartons of arrows brought Cathy back to reality. "These are the last two in stock," said the clerk.

"I really appreciate your effort," answered Cathy trying to make up for her earlier harsh tone.

"No problem," said the young man. "Like I said, in a week we should have a new shipment."

"I'll remember that," she said. "I think these will do for now. You've been a lifesaver." The two lifted the oversized boxes to her waiting shopping cart.

"You'll need to take these to the customer service counter for check-out if you want to use your tax-exempt number," he added.

"What?" asked Cathy.

"The Girl Scouts," he said. "Doesn't your council have a tax-exempt number to save the sales tax? Those check-outs are only done at the customer service station."

"Oh, sure," Cathy stuttered. "I'd almost forgotten that. Thanks." She made her way to the front of the store and wheeled her cart along the first aisle until she found an open register. She ran her MasterCard through the card reader as the cashier totaled the sale. As she slipped the plastic back in her wallet, she thought about what she had just done. *I am a pirate,"* she thought. *I just signed for an expense that I won't be around to pay.*

16

Shrader was encouraged by John Romig's reaction and his willingness to join the conspiracy. In the meantime, he was shopping for the birth of a new community. His first stop was the local pharmacy where he cleared a shelf of multi-vitamins and a sizable amount of antiseptic ointments. He chose the longest expiration dates and poured over label warnings on bulk laxatives and anti-diarrheal medications. He could not begin to guess the physical reactions of people to the radical change in diet that would have to take place. Fuel for cooking would not last indefinitely, and heart-smart, low-fat diets would be replaced by high-fat diets to generate the calories to survive cold temperatures.

He checked his list again. It was an odd assortment of items: can openers, cases of canned meats, beans, and spaghetti, butcher knives, axes, tree saws, bailing twine, and fiberglass epoxy resin and roving material.

"I can't forget the permanent markers," he thought. Every can would have to be labeled as to contents. In the marine environment the paper labels would soon peel away from dampness. He grabbed the markers as he went past the school supplies on the way to the register.

I wish I had some access to antibiotics, he reflected. In wilderness survival, infection always posed a serious threat. A broken leg could be set and splinted. Even if it didn't heal perfectly, it would heal provided that infection could be avoided. As an anthropologist, he knew the diseases that plagued primitive societies, particularly in colder climates like Labrador. Shrader's mind turned to the remembrance of a long evening discussing the subject with John Romig.

In Red Bay, so close to the Arctic Circle, the evening twilight lingers far after the cities of the lower forty-eight states have turned to darkness. Scurvy and rickets seemed likely candidates for the mass of the population, but Romig had alertly noted other possibilities.

"Being so far north, I'd guess more incidences of multiple sclerosis," he said. "I've heard of studies pointing to higher rates of MS among people who live their first fifteen years in colder zones."

"For a geologist, you seem to be up-to-date on medical research," observed Shrader.

"Well, I pick up information here and there and try to apply it," answered Romig. "For instance, here's a bit of trivia. Antibiotics require a doctor's prescription, but did you know that you can buy them over the counter if you know where to look?"

"Does the FDA know about this? And will I be frisked in the parking lot outside the drug store?" said Shrader with a laugh and a wink.

"Yes," confessed Romig. "The FDA knows, and no, you won't get followed home to see if you actually own tropical fish."

"What?" exclaimed Marks.

"Hey, this is a first," said Romig. "I actually surprised you. You can buy sulfa and tetracycline in the fish departments of pet stores. They aren't great antibiotics, and outdated tetracycline is even dangerous, but it might be better than nothing."

The memory of that conversation came back as Shrader added *fish supplies* to his growing shopping list. *It's scary,* he thought. *In two days I am going to have to tell practical, sane people to place their lives in jeopardy because I had a weird dream.*

17

"What are you doing?" asked Cathy as she climbed over the gunwale and boarded *Strider*.

"I'm doing a little research for a project that I have in mind," answered Shrader. "I'm learning how to launch boats using the old crane," he said as he cast his gaze over the port side of the boat. Cathy followed the direction of his glance. From their perch on the beached boat she could clearly see the marina work crews as they slowly prepared *Affinity* for launching.

"I take it that you didn't get anywhere with Gary?" she inquired.

"No," said Shrader. "He seems more responsive to you than to me. I don't know whether it's your sex appeal or the fact that your boat is worth five times the cost of *Strider*, and he knows that an anthropology instructor will never be buying a new one."

"I vote to believe it's my sex appeal," said Cathy.

"Probably right," quipped Marks. "Anyway, he says that he's not going to get to *Strider* until Monday. *Affinity* is the last on this week's schedule."

"Did you explain to him about the party on Friday?" asked Pearson.

"Yes, and I think it only managed to piss him off. Apparently, we're not the only ones who are planning a comet party. He's going to one on Friday, too. He's declared the entire day a holiday and doesn't intend to set foot in the marina. The way he sees it, it'll reduce employee hours for the pay period and put money back in his pocket. These are his words, 'Your fuckin' boat is going to stay on its cradle until Monday.'"

"Is that right?" asked Cathy.

"No," said Shrader. "I think my *fuckin' boat* will be in the water tonight. But I'll need an accomplice."

"I think you already have one," added Cathy.

"Good," observed Shrader with a smile. "I've been watching how they are handling your boat. The first trick is to get *Strider* into position under the crane. They used the tractor and the low flatbed trailer. The problem will be backing that thing up while sliding the trailer under the boat. With my luck I'll flip *Strider* onto her side and the whole line of boats will fall like dominoes."

"My guess is that you'll do just fine," consoled Cathy. "I suppose that it'll be my job to direct traffic?"

"You got it," said Shrader. "Oh, and maybe one other thing."

"What would that be?" asked Cathy cautiously. "Do you want me to shoot Gary with a poison arrow or anything?"

"That would be a pleasant thought," he said. "But what I need isn't quite that illegal, no homicide involved."

"Hey, I was joking," she added. "But I have the feeling that you aren't. What do you have in mind?"

"Keys," answered Marks. "I'll need to know where I can get keys for the tractor and how they power-up the crane. Gary is watching me like a hawk, and I'm sure that he'll never let me get near the maintenance shed."

The two sat in silence for a moment as they focused on the launching of *Affinity*. It was a common procedure at the marina, but the prospect of having to launch a four-and-a-half ton boat like *Strider* gave the study greater intensity. Once it was moved into position under the crane, a worker climbed up onto the deck to handle the lifting straps that were passed under the belly of the boat fore and aft of the mast step. The ends of the straps were attached to a heavy steel frame suspended from the crane. Gary stood with his back to Cathy and Shrader. They could see that he was operating a handheld control box. With what looked like a computer joystick, he raised the crane slowly until all the slack was out of the four-inch wide straps. The electric motor whirred easily, then droned lower as it began to take the full weight of the boat. Gary called to the deck hand who scurried down the ladder that had been propped against the hull. Once the worker was clear of the boat, Gary engaged the complaining motor. The tires on the flatbed trailer returned to a rounder shape, and the wooden cradle creaked as the weight of the craft was lifted free. Shrader could see daylight between the fiberglass and the padded supports of the welded steel cradle.

Gary set the control box on the ground and climbed onto the rusty-colored tractor. He gunned the idling engine and a puff of putrid black diesel smoke belched into the air. He let out the clutch and the tractor pulled away. Slowly, the cradle slipped out beneath the slightly swaying boat. Once clear, Gary killed the tractor's engine and returned to the crane's control box.

Affinity dangled like a ponderous eight-ton pendulum. The deck hand slid a timber beneath the long keel, and Gary lowered the crane slowly until the weight of the craft was brought to rest on the six-by-six block of wood. With practiced skill, the waterline was masked in preparation for a spray coat of anti-fouling paint on the boat's bottom. Shrader watched through binoculars as the painters donned masks and fired up the compressor for the spray gun. He did not focus, however, on the activity of the workers, but on the control box that Gary had set on a piling alongside of the hoist. It was in the middle of what appeared to be a power cord.

"It looks like it's just a heavy electrical cord with a toggle switch to control the current," said Shrader out loud.

"What?" asked Cathy who was watching the paint crew spray the underside of her boat.

"The hoist is powered by that special extension cord," he answered. "See, one end runs into the shed." He pointed to the heavy orange cord that went through the door to the blue maintenance building. "The other end," he continued, "seems to plug into a junction box on the side of the derrick." Cathy followed his gaze and located the metal housing that concealed the end of the cord.

"We can probably jury-rig a cord so that by reversing poles we can change the direction of the motor," he added.

"Why not just use the control box?" offered Cathy.

"It'll be locked away tighter than a drum when Gary leaves for the weekend," observed Shrader.

"Why don't you leave that to me?" said Cathy with a wink. "You won't believe how devious I've become since meeting you."

"You're enjoying this, aren't you?" Shrader looked at Cathy's smiling face. "I have a pretty accomplice," he heard himself saying. No sooner had the words escaped his lips than he realized that he had not meant to say them. Cathy was indeed an attractive woman, and their work together had drawn them close in a short amount of time. He didn't want to confuse their relationship with romantic notions and had pushed all such thoughts from his mind.

Cathy took the comment very well. Her smile broadened. "That's nice to hear," she said. "But I think your judgment is clouded by exhaustion. When is the last time you slept?"

Shrader looked away. "I slept some last night," he said.

"Well, you should sleep some right now," she interrupted. "Tonight, you will be launching a boat, and you'll need to be alert. I'll find a way to get into the shed so that we will have access to the control panel."

Shrader trusted her implicitly. Her words washed over him with a wave of relief, and an unexpected tiredness flooded his senses. "Maybe I should take a nap," he said rising to his feet. Cathy was over the lifelines before his foot hit the companionway step. By the time he was standing on the cabin sole, she was walking across the parking lot through the thinning maze of keels. He threw himself down on the quarter berth and was quickly asleep. Cathy approached the work crew as they were wet sanding a spot on the underwater surface of *Affinity*. Drop cloths were spread out beneath the hull to catch any runoff of the toxic paint. "The EPA would be proud," said Cathy.

"They sure have changed the way we do business," offered Gary who was watching the crew members who had donned protective clothing, masks, and gloves.

"Are you going to be here this weekend?" asked Cathy.

"No," said Gary. "Why is everyone so interested in my weekend plans?" He gestured toward the cradle where *Strider* was perched.

"I'm not sure what you mean," said Cathy coyly. "I was just asking to see if anyone would be around tomorrow in case Phil wants to borrow a swaging tool. He'll be up here for the weekend and was thinking about reworking the lifelines."

"Oh," murmured Gary in a surprised tone. "Why don't I just loan it to you today and you could see that it gets back to me by Monday?" he said apologetically.

"That would be great," said Cathy. "Phil will really appreciate that. He gets these projects in mind and gets very frustrated when he can't get them done."

"Remind me to get it for you when your boat is off the crane," added Gary.

"I hate to bother you when you're so busy," she mewed, "How about if I just get it from the shed? I think I know where it is."

"Okay, if you don't mind the mess. This time of year everything gets kinda junky." Before Gary could finish his thought, Cathy was walking toward the blue maintenance shed. She knew that Gary was watching her movements so she purposely let her hips roll. It was a distraction that worked effectively. He could not see her smiling as she walked. Her eyes were trained on the object of her mission, an orange power cord that disappeared through the open door of the shed.

She looked over the threshold of the dimly lit interior. The power cord snaked into the room and disappeared over the lip of

61

a galvanized steel drum. She walked over and looked down into the can. A few coils of cord were at the bottom of the drum, and the bitter end was plugged into a greasy wall outlet located just above the open container.

"That answers one question," said Cathy to herself. "This is where they lock up the power cord." She looked around the room. Along the back wall was a cluttered workbench. She approached it carefully as she stepped around the hodgepodge of cans and drums and boat parts. Her eyes came to rest on the Nicropress swaging tool. She picked up the familiar tool that looked like a large set of bolt cutters. She wouldn't have much time before Gary would become suspicious. Above the bench was a row of nails with keys dangling down. Deftly she poked and prodded the odd assortment of metallic shapes. A single blue key caught her attention. It looked pristine with the word *Ford* molded on its face. She smiled as she lifted it off its hook. She clutched it tightly in her fist then retraced her steps to the door. Her pulse raced with an adrenalin-rush that followed with the discovery of a tractor key that would not be missed on a Thursday night by workers anxious to get home for their comet-extended weekend. But her luck carried her even further when her eyes were drawn to the glint of shiny steel in the archway of the door. It was a new padlock dangling on the hasp of the door. Suspended at the bottom of the lock was a wire ring with a hanging key.

"What's this?" she said lifting the lock in her hand. It was a new lock complete with the two keys that came packaged with it. She slid the keys from the padlock and retreated into the shadows of the building's interior. Quickly she split the ring and slid a key off the flimsy loop. She slipped a key in her pocket, and returned the second one to the padlock on the door. When she emerged into the sunlight, she blinked from the brightness. Gary took a step toward her. She lifted the swaging tool as if in a victory salute, and he settled back with a smile. "Thanks," she called back. "I'll lock it in my car until you're done with *Affinity*." She could hear the sound of her own heart thumping in her ears.

18

Sleep came easily to Shrader who was approaching his physical limit. Unfortunately, his dreams remained his bed-companions. Familiar images came back to him now as he slept in the bowels of *Strider*. He was in the water riding at the surface of the water's level. The salty spray stung his lips, and Cathy was calling his name from the deck of *Affinity*. The scene switched. Now he was in a kayak, whitewater rafting through a high-sided canyon. He felt the boat under him sliding toward the sheer rock wall as the turbulence rolled beneath the thin skin of the hull. He paddled hard against the sideways pressure trying to move the slippery boat to port and into the center of the channel. As the wall loomed closer, he could see that they were fabricated from scraped and scarred concrete. He was going to sheer it when suddenly the boat hit the crest of a leading wave and surfed through the front edge of the spray. The churning water sent the light boat spinning, and he found himself facing back on the course he had just traveled. Still, he paddled to face into the next wave as the kayak continued to race stern first.

Looking back through the surging waters, he saw another boat coming through the slot. "Keep left! Steer to port!" he found himself shouting, but the warning was too late and the sound of grating fiberglass echoed through the canyon. With the noise came a crash of something out of the sky, and Shrader awoke.

He was in the main cabin of *Strider*. He looked up at the white vinyl of the cabin liner and could see through the smoked glass hatch cover. It was still daylight.

"Was it a new dream?" said a voice that he recognized as Cathy's.

"No, not new. Just more intense," he said. "They are all more intense these days. The problem is that I don't know what I'm seeing. It's just pictures that flash into my mind."

"Would you sleep easier with these in your pocket?" she asked. Cathy pressed two keys into his hand.

"What's this?"

"It's your ticket to an early launch," she added. "They'll give you access to the control box for the crane and to the tractor." Marks opened his hand and saw the keys.

"You are amazing!" he said.

"Sure," said Cathy with a smile. "But why don't you try to sleep a little longer? I'll sit with you a while." Shrader didn't argue. He closed his eyes.

Cathy reached out to take his hand. She folded his fingers over the warming metal treasures, but she did not withdraw her touch. He fell asleep with her beside him. It was his first untroubled sleep in months. When he opened his eyes, it was dark inside *Strider's* main cabin. The only light was from the sodium vapor security lights that illuminated the marina.

"What time is it?" asked Shrader.

"Nine-thirty," said Cathy from close by.

"How could I sleep so long?" complained Shrader. "I should be working!"

"No," said Cathy. "You needed to sleep, and you couldn't have done anything anyway. Gary only left ten minutes ago. He was working in the shed. I would have woke you up you as soon as I was sure that he wasn't going to come back after something."

"I've been complaining about that guy all week," remarked Shrader. "The truth is that he's a hard worker."

"Fortunately, he didn't miss the second key when he closed the padlock," said Cathy. "I watched him close up, and he just pocketed the key without hesitation."

"Then he's gone for the weekend?" asked Shrader.

"Seems that way," she answered. "And now it's time for this conspiracy to go public."

"You're right about that," he said as he pulled himself up out of the berth. Cathy went to the icebox in the galley and retrieved a plastic milk carton. She poured a glass of milk and set out a sandwich with it in front of Shrader.

"I hope you like peanut butter? It's all I could find in your cupboard. Then again, you bought it."

"Guess I'm not much of a cook, that's all," he answered. "But as a matter of fact, I like peanut butter, and I have a feeling that it'll be a long time before it becomes a staple part of our diets again." He lit into the sandwich with a ferocity that even surprised himself. Obviously, he was hungry. He washed the meal down with the milk and reached for his jacket. "It's going to be cold out there. I'll bet it'll be a real blow before the night is over."

"It's cold, but it'll help us burn off some of this winter fat." The two zipped their outer garments and climbed up out of the main hatch. The night air was brisk. Cathy was first over the gunwale and down the boarding ladder. Shrader raised his head and looked into the night sky. The stars were spread out like campfires across a great valley. His mind was flooded with images that he could not understand. Strangely, fear was not in him. He felt a kinship with the night, with the stars, and with the water. Below, he could see Cathy walking across the marina yard toward the maintenance shed.

"Here I am," he found himself saying to no one. His voice sounded small. "Here I am," he repeated.

19

"I know what's trending on the 'net," said an exasperated MacBrin. He'd done well to keep his temper in check, but was approaching his limit. "Look," he continued. "What we said was true when we first announced it! There *was* a possibility that the object we were tracking was basically granular. If that had been true, it would have been less destructive than we now suspect. On the other hand, we gave all the warnings that needed to be given in a timely way. There's not a whole lot that can be done in the face of a worst-case scenario."

"So you finally admit that this is a *worst-case!*" shouted Carlos Menendez.

"Okay, I'll admit it," said MacBrin. "But what the hell good does it do if you say, 'I told you so', and what difference would it have made two weeks ago if we'd made it public knowledge?"

"What difference?" came an incredulous voice. It was Major General Copleston who had held his tongue throughout the debate. "We could have used missiles after all. That might have saved a lot of lives."

"Look, General, I understand your frustration. But believe me, if your solution was practical, we would have suggested it. It's just that the whole problem is out of proportion with anything we might have thought at first."

"What do you mean by that?" asked an unidentified voice from the corner of the room.

"What he means," began Carlos Menendez, "is that we are not facing a meteor cluster at all. It has been confirmed as a solid mass. This thing is probably an asteroid with a diameter of five or six kilometers. We are no longer worrying about a polar meltdown. The interest now is in the area of plate tectonics. The big question is how the impact will affect the continental plates. My guess is that we will see major plate shifts and fissure eruptions along the Antarctic plate and even up into the Pacific Rim."

"But that's all speculation," interrupted MacBrin. "And I think you've provided quite enough fuel for that fire on the Internet."

"I only told the truth while you were stonewalling," shouted Menendez. "People have a right to know."

"Even when they have no means of escape?" countered MacBrin.

The room grew suddenly silent while the last words took effect. MacBrin realized that he had to offer some explanation. "Carlos is right," he confessed, "but there is not much that can be done at this point. Frankly, there was never much that could be done." His voice trailed off.

General Copleston picked up on his awkward silence. "You mean that we waited too long to get the warning out?"

"No," answered Malcolm. "Warnings are provided to give people time to prepare or a chance to escape. There will be no escape from this one!"

20

The night air bit into Shrader's face as he directed his flashlight toward the controls on the hydraulic trailer attached to the old Ford tractor. He had to teach himself how to operate the lift system before he attempted to add the nine thousand pounds of *Strider* to the lifting bed. It was a simple collection of levers all drawing power from a single twelve-volt battery. Cathy came to watch his progress.

"It's not unlike a hospital bed," he said at last. "Watch this." He pulled on one of the levers and the back of the bed started to lift. He activated a second and the front of the bed rose to an equal level.

"Great," observed Cathy, "are you ready to try it on the real thing or do you want them to find us frozen here in the morning?"

"Okay," agreed Shrader, "it's now, or never." He shut down the power on the trailer and mounted the tractor. With a turn of a key and the press of the starter button, the engine coughed and complained before settling down to an idle.

"So far so good," encouraged Cathy, over the sound of the motor and the flapping clang of the exhaust baffle. Shrader nodded and pushed the gear shift forward and let out the clutch. The rig lurched with a start that would have toppled both boat and cradle. He looked back at Cathy and saw the same fear in her eyes.

"Can't lose nerve now," he said to himself.

Without thinking, he offered a prayer to the darkness of the night, and was surprised to hear an answer: "We called you out, and we will not abandon you now."

Shrader shook off the feeling. "This isn't a time to go schizoid, Marks," he said aloud. He depressed the clutch and the brake to bring the tractor to a halt. He then tried more delicately to set the vehicle in motion. After four or five practices, he was getting the feel of the clutch action. Cathy's expression seemed to relax as well. By now, he was approaching the spot where *Strider* sat on her cradle.

He swung the tractor in a wide arc, grateful that the marina crew had launched the larger boats that had blocked *Strider's* path to the launching crane. He pulled forward to straighten the trailer, then, looked back over his shoulder in time to see Cathy checking the alignment with the timbers of *Strider's* massive cradle.

"That's good," she called out. Her voice sounded weak in the growing wind. A sense of urgency sharpened Shrader's focus as he wrestled the gearshift into reverse and began to back up. The end of the trailer's flat bed slipped under the forward edge of the cradle. "Stop," cried Cathy as the trailer made contact with the cement blocks that held the frame of the cradle off the ground. Shrader slammed on the brakes, shifted to neutral, and engaged the parking brake.

"Wait a minute!" exclaimed Cathy. Headlights flashed at the marina entrance. The two stepped back in the shadows. A car pulled in between two darkened boats in the upper lot and the driver doused the lights.

"Great," said Shrader. "We have company. Maybe we've been spotted."

"Security's never been an issue here, at least I never heard of cops patrolling or anything like that," said Pearson. "Makes me think that, whoever they are, they're the ones afraid of getting busted." Shrader looked confused. "Kids—"she continued, "it's a school night and they told their parents that they had to go to the library, so on the way home they swing by here for some privacy."

"Aren't you the romantic one?" observed Shrader.

"No, I'm the mother of a teenager," she said with a smile.

Shrader stepped out from the shadows into the glow of the security lights. "Stay here," he whispered as he walked up the steep drive toward the upper parking level. At the brow of the hill, he turned back to Cathy. "I'll bet the battery terminals just need tightening, Gary," he shouted at the top of his lungs so *whoever* could hear. "I have a better flashlight in my car."

His heart pounded as he approached the parked car. He slapped the hull of a nearby boat. He let the sound carry on the wind as he recognized the name on the transom, *Murphy's Law*. He pulled at one of the lines that held the winter tarp over the deck. Then, as if to the boat, he spoke in a clear voice, "Living up to your name again, Murphy. Well, I'll be right back to add a line to your cover as soon as I deliver this flashlight." He walked beyond the parked car and out of sight of any occupants. He pulled his flashlight from his parka and switched it on. He ran the beam along the gunwale of *Murphy's Law*, letting it inadvertently strike the four-door sedan parked alongside. No heads were visible. Thoughts of club-wielding vandals loose in the boat yard welled up in his mind and tensed his nerves. He took ten steps out of sight of the car and crouched down alongside of a fifty-five gallon steel drum.

He did not have to wait long for an answer. In a moment the sound of a car ignition dispelled fears of intruders. The shadow of a car pulled out into the open drive, and crept forward to the main entrance. At the street the headlights boomed like a streak of lightening which was followed by the squeal of tires.

Shrader had a satisfied look on his face when he returned to Cathy. "It was as you expected," he said. "I just hope they don't run into Gary on the way home and ask him how he could be in two places at once."

Cathy was busy sliding a plank under the front of the frame of *Strider's* cradle. "Here, let me help you with that," said Shrader, stepping over the low frame of the flatbed trailer. They slid the heavy plank along its track on the inside edge of the trailer until it was aligned with the front timbers of the cradle. Shrader went to the hydraulic controls at the front end of the rig and pushed a lever that set off the whir of a motor that fed the hydraulic lifting device. The sound slowed as the rising plank met the weight of the boat. The cradle creaked, then lifted off the cement blocks.

"It's clear!" shouted Cathy as she began to slide away the cement blocks that had supported the weight of the boat. Shrader ran to the opposite side and pulled away the companion block. *Strider* was now supported on the ground by two blocks on the aft end of the cradle, and by a free sliding plank on the flatbed.

"My fingers are getting numb," observed Cathy. The wind was now blowing at about twenty knots out of the northwest.

"Just hold on," said Shrader. "When we get the whole thing on the trailer, we can go aboard *Affinity* and warm up." He knew that the trickiest part was yet to come. "Stand clear while I back up the rig," he ordered. "If I get this twisted, the whole thing will come down around us."

Cathy nodded her understanding but made no move toward safety. "You'll need me to signal when you are at the back edge of the cradle," she added.

Of course she was right, and Shrader knew it. They were in the middle of a balancing act. They had nine thousand pounds of fiberglass hanging on the back end of a trailer no more than eight inches off the ground. A miscalculation would roll the boat and set off a chain reaction of toppling boats. Shrader mounted the tractor and placed it in reverse. Slowly he eased off the clutch to keep it from lurching. In spite of his precautions, a shudder jolted the cradle, but *Strider* held firm. The rig began to move slipping beneath the cradle as the timber bearing the weight of the boat slid forward on its track.

"That's good!" shouted Cathy. Shrader hit the brake and brought the rig to a halt. The steel frame of the trailer now rested against the aft blocks that held the boat cradle off the ground. Cathy struggled to pull free the six-by-six blocks that they needed to shim the cradle against the frame of the trailer. They would not budge until Shrader kicked them hard with his heel. They had frozen against the bed of the trailer, but broke free with the solid impact of his boot. Once the blocks were set in place, Cathy and Shrader took positions on opposite sides of the trailer.

"Okay," explained Marks. "We need to pull back on the levers in unison so that we can raise the boat evenly." He was referring to the control handles at the back of the trailer bed. Each one operated an independent hydraulic lift that would elevate one side of the bulky boat and cradle. "Let's take it slow," urged Marks. The two pulled on the switches simultaneously.

There was a quick high-powered whir until the shimming blocks made contact with the timbers of the boat's cradle. The motors then strained to lift the weight.

Shrader's side lifted first. One inch, two inches, the clearance gap began to widen when Cathy cried out. "Stop! It's not lifting." The shim block fell off the trailer bed and the cradle began to creak and twist. "Bring your side back down," she ordered. Shrader reversed the control lever, but it was no good. The control was dead. Instinctively, he put his hand against the belly of the boat as if he could steady the massive weight of the craft. What he felt instead ran through his freezing flesh like a brand of hot steel. The boat was swaying. He recognized the sensation. *Strider* was beginning to heel, to roll with the wind.

"It's going over," he called out. Cathy ran out from under the boat. Shrader called to her, "Help me shore it up!" he said, diving beneath the frame to retrieve the fallen six-by-six, but she was gone and his only answer was a gust of wind in his face.

The wedge had fallen forward to the hard pavement. Shrader reached through the cross-members of the cradle to try to lift it back in place, but it eluded his grasp. Quickly he dropped to the ground and slid under the frame. The tips of his fingers gripped the block, and he inched it back toward himself. The cradle over him was rocking against his shoulder blade reminding him that he would be crushed instantly if the twisting timber frame came apart from the stress.

Suddenly, there were lights shining in his eyes. A car was careening down from the upper lot and heading toward *Strider*. It slowed as it came through the maze of dry-docked boats, and stopped just inches from the tractor. Shrader heard the spring latch of the hood being released. By the muted light of the interior dome, he could see Cathy opening the van door. She leaped out, carrying something in her right arm. Without regard for Shrader, she lifted the hood and attached the jumper cables to the battery terminals of her idling engine. By now, Shrader had shimmied his way out from under the trailer dragging the support behind him. He slid it back on the trailer frame almost catching his hand beneath the madly rocking cradle. By the light of the headlamps, Cathy found the positive terminal on the trailer's battery pack and clamped on the red-handled lead from her cable. The ground she clamped to the trailer frame.

"Try the control lever now," she called as she retreated to her car and raced the engine. Shrader understood, and reached for the handle on the low side of the trailer frame. The bed began to lift, catching the base of the cradle and firming it up.

Shrader felt his heart slow to a sprint. "That was quick thinking," he said at last. "I thought you had run to escape a crash."

"I figured that the cold weather had done in the battery," answered Cathy.

"You're a lot quicker than I am. When am I going to stop being surprised by your competence?" asked Shrader rhetorically.

"Just admit it," said Cathy with a smile. "You're a male chauvinist pig at heart."

"And I have no doubts that you will cure me," answered Marks. "Thank you."

"For calling you a pig?"

"No," said Shrader, "for saving *Strider*, and me."

"I can't take the chance of losing you now, Shrader," she said. "We're in too deep." The two worked for the next half hour in near silence. Cathy opened the maintenance shed and retrieved the control cord for the hoist, and the two rehearsed raising and lowering the steel I-beam structure that would carry *Strider's* weight.

The wind was biting. "We can't stay out here much longer," warned Cathy. Her voice was beginning to fade after all the shouting over the howling of the wind. She also realized that Shrader, disregarding the numbness of his extremities, was working deep in himself. His right hand was cut and crusted over with blood. "This is crazy," she chided. "We are going to take a break. Let's board *Affinity* and I'll take care of that."

He did not argue. His energy was sapped. Cathy looked around the yard. *Strider* was safe on the trailer and the hoist was lowered out of the wind. "Everything will hold for an hour," she said taking Shrader by the hand and leading him away toward the quayside berth where her boat had been temporarily docked.

Shrader nearly stumbled over the lifelines as he stepped up to board the forty-foot sloop. Cathy had rigged the dodger that sheltered the companionway from the wind. She slid back the hatch cover and lifted clear the lap boards that sealed the entrance. A draft of warm air washed over them. She gestured toward the main saloon below, and Shrader retreated to the warm glow of the cabin. Cathy replaced the lap boards, and glided the overhead cover back to its closed position.

The two stood in the warm silence for a moment before Shrader spoke. "Do I still have feet?" he asked. They burst out in laughter.

"Yes, you have feet," said Cathy. "You almost lost your boat, however."

"Not even close," bantered Shrader in his best macho voice. "I was in control the whole time. I was just testing your reaction time."

"Now you sound like Phil," she said. "Only I know you're joking."

"And he wouldn't be?"

"No, he wouldn't be," she said with sadness. "In his eyes I can't get much of anything right."

"That's sure not my impression. You have been right all along. Including getting out of the wind, I think that I have frostbite," he said rubbing his palms together. Cathy stepped toward him and placed her hands around his. Her touch was warm. Their eyes met with a startling awareness that neither had expected. They both turned aside. Cathy opened a galley cabinet and retrieved an electric kettle which she filled from a gallon jug on the counter. Shrader thought she was blushing. His own face felt flushed, but he attributed it to the warm cabin air and the senses returning to his cheeks.

"There's something we'll all miss," he said pointing to the kettle.

"What's that?"

"Power," was his immediate answer, "Being able to heat things or cool things quickly. Running our engines to keep batteries charged for lights."

"I've thought about that, too," answered Cathy. "The people who go with us will probably think that life at sea will be like what they've been used to on summer cruises."

"Then the fuel will run out," agreed Shrader. "*Strider* will be the first, then the diesels."

"What do you mean?" she asked.

"Gasoline," was the answer. "*Strider* has an old Atomic IV gasoline engine. It guzzles the fuel ten times faster than your diesel. If we have to motor to the Thousand Islands and can't refuel, I'll probably only have enough left to lock through the Seaway and nothing for the thousand miles beyond Montréal."

"Pardon my larceny, but why don't you hijack one of the newer boats?"

"We'll need them all." Shrader went silent. Cathy knew his moods well enough to tell that something was amiss.

"What have you seen?" she asked.

Marks did not look at her directly. "We're going to lose some boats."

"What?"

"We're going to lose some boats," he repeated with more confidence. "At least one–and I think I'll even know it as it's happening, but right now it's only a mental image." Cathy nodded in understanding as the kettle began to whistle.

It was an hour before the two were willing to brave the cold and the actual launching of *Strider*. Before they left the cabin, Cathy and Shrader reviewed the steps of the process: Shrader would climb up on *Strider's* deck and Cathy would pass the lifting strap under the hull and up to deck level. Marks would then attach the free end to the I-beam frame that hung from the crane. Cathy would raise the boat clear of the cradle, and Shrader would tow the cradle away with the tractor.

"I'm afraid that if the squall hasn't let up, *Strider* may rattle around like a five-ton wind chime," confessed Shrader. His fears were without merit, however, and when they emerged from the cabin to face the night, the air was still, and the stars were shining with the crispness that only the winter sky could divulge.

"It's spectacular," said Cathy.

"The clear sky will make it colder, but it really helps that the wind has died," he responded. The launch itself proceeded exactly as planned. "I think we're more efficient than Gary's crew," said Marks when the hull was safely afloat.

"Of course," agreed Cathy. "But we're not being paid by the hour either." Their laughter emptied the tension of the night into a universe that scattered it into nothingness.

Shrader had already pulled the tractor and cradle out of sight by the time Cathy had secured the spring lines that snugged *Strider* against the dock. When he returned, she handed him the end of the yellow power cord that she had pulled from the lazarette. Shrader walked it aft and plugged it into the shore outlet near the base of the crane. In a moment he was back on board checking the battery charger and electrical systems.

"I'd say we put in a pretty good night's work," encouraged Cathy, looking at her watch. "And it's only 2:30, time to crash."

"Just one more thing," said Shrader. "I won't sleep until I know that the engine is going to turn over." He turned the battery selector switch to the *All* setting and went up into the cockpit. He turned on the blower to exhaust any fumes in the engine compartment. The whir of the small fan motor gave him some assurance. He pulled out the manual choke. "Cross your fingers," he said as he threw the toggle that brought the starter motor on line, and depressed the ignition button. It cranked slowly, coughed and sputtered before blasting out the antifreeze in a surge of white smoke. It caught, and Shrader smiled as he pushed the hand throttle forward and revved the engine.

"When they run, it's a miracle," he said.

"The real miracle will be if you slow down and get some rest," she added. "*Strider* is in the water and barring any overnight surprises, we will be half way to the Thousand Islands at this time tomorrow."

"And sailing into a nightmare," continued Shrader.

21

The *Whaleman* stood on the brow of the hill where he had stood many times waiting for the return of the caribou.

"Tell me what you see," he said to the young boy at his side.

"I see many children laughing with shining faces and full stomachs," was his reply.

"You see much then," said the *Whaleman*. "The herd gives our children life. Now, look to the water and tell me what is there." The boy turned to the vista of the great gulf. The ball of the sun sent warming rays of scattered light across the surface of the gently rolling surf.

"I see the home of our brothers, and I hear them singing to the morning sun and to their friend. It is a name that I have never heard before, *Whaleman*," he said.

"What name is it that they call?" asked the shaman, "for my ears have grown nearly as weak as my eyes."

"They call to one named *Muoshti*," said the boy. "It's a name I don't know."

"And one that I have not heard for many ages of my people," said the *Whaleman*. "Please, young one, go to our brothers and tell them that their song has been heard, that it is the *Whaleman* who greets them. Tell them that."

"But I cannot leave you here alone," protested the boy.

"I will not be alone, and it is time for you to go to them by yourself."

"But they will want to see the *Whaleman*."

"Don't be afraid. Seeing you, they shall see the *Whaleman*. They will sing a new song, and your heart will rejoice."

"But how will you see the hunt without my eyes?" the boy's voice pleaded.

"You speak too much and obey too little. My eyes still see many things and my ears hear voices you have not yet understood. You must go speak to the Keeper." His voice softened, "You have outgrown your teacher. I have gotten smaller and you, bigger. One day you will be small again, and we will talk." The discussion was over. The shaman turned his back to the sea and faced the great blur of vision that was the herd of caribou. As he watched through eyes grown dim with age, he began to see other scenes. Below him was his brother Vuhar and to his ears came the strains of a young boy singing. It was his own voice:

> Brothers, come to me in the spirit of the morning.
> Brothers, come to me over the paths of the sea,
> for Vuhar has passed beyond sight,
> but not beyond my longing to speak to him.
> He is my brother, guide him beyond my seeing
> to the place of my longing.

"I am not beyond sight," came another voice. Muoshti turned to see Vuhar standing on the ridge of the next hillock. The distance between them collapsed on itself as they spoke.

"Vuhar?" questioned Muoshti.

"Did you not suspect that I would be here at the hunt, my Brother?" said Vuhar with a boyish smile.

"But I can see you with clear eyes," said the shaman.

"The circle of our lives has drawn close again," offered Vuhar. Muoshti puzzled for a moment then stretched his gaze to touch the endless horizon. He felt like he was at the point where earth and sky touched.

"Muoshti, does your name sound new to you?" said another voice. "Or are you still the *Whaleman*?"

"There is another *Whaleman* now," he said, turning to the voice. Before him stood a familiar form, one who stood straight and firm of limb. "Creonduk," he cried with joy.

"Did I not tell you that we would laugh together, my friend?"

Muoshti threw his arms around the ageless man. "Yes, you did. You said you would speak my name when I had forgotten it, and your call has given me life again."

"I am glad to see you," said Creonduk. "I have been walking without you for too long."

"Where have you journeyed?" asked Muoshti.

"I have been wandering in a day beyond the cycle of years. In that day the sun still shines and the circles of many lives become one."

"Can I walk with you again?" asked Muoshti.

"That is why I have come to you," said Creonduk. "It is why this door has been opened for you."

"I see no door," offered Muoshti.

"That is because you are standing in it," explained the shaman. "Take a step, and you will pass through it."

Muoshti slid his foot forward and stepped out of the world.

22

Shrader stepped to the electrical panel beneath the companionway step and switched on the nav-station circuit. He then turned to the VHF radio mounted on the port side of *Strider's* main cabin. He pressed the "WX" symbol on the keypad to tune in the National Weather Service broadcast:

> ...the National Weather Service broadcast for waters within five nautical miles of the south shore of Lake Ontario. Today: unseasonably warm with temperatures in the low to mid sixties and winds from the southwest at ten to twenty knots, decreasing to ten to fifteen knots by evening. Tonight: continuing unseasonably warm with lows in the mid to upper forties and southwest winds fifteen knots.

"What do you think?" said Cathy who called down from the cockpit.

"I think we're damn lucky," answered Marks. "The ice is off the bay, the temperatures are mild, and the wind will be at our backs. What more could we ask for?"

"How about a receptive audience at around 2:00?"

"That I will leave up to your powers of persuasion,. Until then, do you have a guess as to who is actually going to show?"

"Believe it or not, the numbers are increasing," said Pearson. "I phoned Phil, and he said that the Barkers have changed their minds and will be here in force with their three kids. Bill and Connie Morgan on *Wave Chaser* will be here, too. So that's seven that we didn't know about yesterday."

"I guess the nice weather is giving everyone sailing fever," commented Shrader.

"Maybe," said Cathy. "But it may be hysteria. At least that's Phil's conclusion."

"Why's that?"

"The news is making everyone a little jumpy. Phil says that the planet is going crazy. Every religious group is predicting the end of the world. Half the population is making peace with God and the other half is trying to corner the market on unrestrained debauchery. The survivalists are buying out the groceries and the fatalists have decided to pray or party 'til the end of time."

"Where does that put us?" asked Shrader. "We've been stashing food for a week and sending out invitations to a comet party."

"Strange as it sounds, Shrader Marks, they might nominate you for a *sanest-person-on-the-planet* award."

"That's scary. But then again, we might have a chance at spreading our particular brand of insanity this afternoon."

"The media has done us a favor by getting everyone on edge. I figure that people tend to grab at hope, and that's what you'll be offering," consoled Cathy.

"I'm glad you have confidence. I've been running on adrenaline too long. My biggest fear is that someone didn't top off their fuel tanks before winter storage and we won't be able to cart enough fuel down here to get the engines running in time."

"I think you fear too many things." Said Cathy. "There's a time when you just have to let go and deal with life as it comes. This will never turn out to be a situation that you can control, and it's going to get worse before it gets better."

"That's for sure," agreed Shrader.

"But whatever happens, it won't be your fault," she continued. "You are giving these people a choice that they otherwise will not have. They may try to blame you, but it's their choice."

"Thanks," he said. He looked at Cathy and really saw her for the first time. Her blond hair was pulled back and held in place by a baseball cap. The expression on her face was serious, and her gray eyes seemed to take in everything. Shrader laughed. His display of pure delight confused Cathy. "You are a wonder," he said. To his own surprise he kissed her on the cheek which brought a rosiness to her winter-pale skin.

"What was that for?" she asked.

"For whatever you like," he offered, "for friendship, for believing in me when I don't believe in myself, for courage, or how about for grand larceny?"

"That I understand," she said as she joined him in his laughter. The rest of the morning was spent with the two running in separate directions. Cathy gathered up as many jerry-jugs as she could find on the decks and in the lazarettes of the dry-docked boats. Loading them in her minivan, she made a foray into town to buy diesel fuel. It was not the simple task that she had imagined. Sodus Bay was a sleepy town except in the height of the vacation season. Even so, the streets were unusually quiet. It felt more like a morning after a major snow storm when no one could emerge from house or garage, but there was no snow. Nevertheless, the shops remained closed, and one by one she passed gasoline filling stations closed and locked.

Finally, on the edge of town she came to an open gas station with a black pickup truck parked out front. She pulled in front of the pump marked *diesel* and began to fill the empty fuel containers.

"You almost didn't make it," said a voice over her left shoulder. Cathy turned to see a middle-aged man in blue coveralls approach her. His sleeves were rolled back to reveal a tattoo of an eagle and the cuff of his greasy thermal underwear.

Cathy turned with a start. "What do you mean?" she asked.

"Just that I was about to close," said the man. The name *Bert* was embroidered in script over the left pocket of his coverall.

"Haven't you heard that it's supposed to be the end of the world?" He stepped closer to her. Cathy could not say why, but she felt uneasy.

"Does that mean you won't take a credit card?" she said, forcing a smile.

"The diesel will be on me," he said. Even at a distance, he smelled of beer. "Consider it a little gift, but then you might say you *owe me.*"

"How about if I just pay in cash?" said Cathy who had finished filling a five gallon can. She fumbled with the cap while keeping an eye on the attendant. "Would you do me a favor?" she asked.

"Anything you want, Pretty Lady," said the man licking his lips in a gesture that he meant to be seductive.

"Would you put this jug in the back of my van?" She tugged at the heavy container.

"No problem," he countered, grabbing the handle of the jug with one hand and slipping his free hand up under the loose waistband of her windbreaker. His movement was so fast that it caught Cathy unaware. "What do you say that we climb in your van, too?" he said as he roughly squeezed her left breast. "You pump the diesel, then, I'll pump you." As if she were nothing, he lifted her off the ground in the crook of one arm. In that instant, she realized that she would not be able to match his strength. Her mind raced.

"I'll bet you are quite the man in bed, too." She felt his arm relax beneath her ribcage as he set her down. "Just give a girl a second to catch her breath," she added pulling an empty container from the van. She placed it strategically between herself and the man. In one deft motion, Bert swung the full fuel can over the bumper and into the back of the van. He turned back to face her.

Cathy noticed a look of indecision on his face. He was not accustomed to playing the rapist, and under ordinary circumstances, would not have dared such a brutish advance. "You seem so anxious." She wanted to get him talking.

"They say the world is coming to an end today," was his answer. Cathy heard a final rush of air from the canister and the nozzle clicked off. She replaced the lid. Bert whisked it away and put a third empty in its place.

Cathy thought to herself, *This man doesn't know whether he should be a rapist or a boy scout.*

"They're probably wrong about that," she offered, trying to soften her tone.

"I don't think so. They say the earth is going to crash into another planet, and *boom!* We're all out of business."

"Shouldn't you be with your family or somebody? Your mother?" She saw him move a step closer. The indecision had gone from his eyes.

"I think that I'd like to go out with a bang," he said glaring at her, "and you're pretty. I'll bet you're a real screamer, too!" Cathy braced herself. As he stepped close, she raised the fuel nozzle out of the mouth of the jug. A thick stream of diesel spewed out. She directed it up his left leg before letting it click off.

"I'm sorry," she said. "You'd better wash that off."

"Why?" he said, moving even closer. "Are you hot enough to start a fire?" He swung his arm to grab at the nozzle. Cathy squeezed the lever and doused him from the waist down.

"You're asking for it, Bitch," he sneered. "I'm going to..." But he did not get the words out of his mouth before Cathy had redirected the hose to his face. He coughed and sputtered as the smelly fuel oil gushed from his mouth. His hands clutched his face as the fluid washed into his eyes.

Three quick strides and Cathy took hold of the door handle on the driver's side of the van. She pulled it open and swung herself into position. She hit the electric door lock switch and breathed a sigh of relief at the familiar click of the locks being driven home. Outside the van, the attendant railed against her, and he began beating on the sides of the van with his closed fists.

"The keys!" Cathy exclaimed. They had slipped from the pocket of her nylon windbreaker. She looked out her side window. She could see them lying on the ground near the feet of her assailant. She turned away her gaze in fear that he would discover her situation. But with the soaking he had taken, she doubted whether he could see anything very distinctly.

"You are going to pay for this," he shouted as his fists struck the glass. She felt the vibrations of the blow like she was inside a drum. Suddenly, he turned and ran into the station. It was the only cue Cathy needed. She unlocked the door, pushed it open and dove for the key ring. She had no time to waste, and made it back into the cab as the wild man reappeared carrying a short-shafted sledge hammer. She fumbled the key, but managed to engage it and the still-warm engine burst to life. She jerked the gear shift that spun her tires on the wet pavement. The rush of blood in her ears was broken by a hollow thud that did not penetrate her conscious thought. She raced over unfamiliar roads before calming down enough to turn back toward Bay Road and the marina. Her first thought was that she had to find Shrader. Her second was to wonder why her front seat was covered with rock salt.

She made the marina entrance, stopped, and took a deep breath. It was cold in the car and her breath was steamy. "I can't let Shrader see me this way," she said aloud as if taking inventory. Another deep breath, and she took her foot off the brake and began a slow descent to the lower parking level. Ahead of her, Shrader was standing dockside speaking with another man. She pulled the van into an empty space and opened the door. To her surprise, Shrader was rushing toward her.

"Are you okay?" he asked. "What happened?" She wanted to burst into an explanation, but she had promised herself that she would remain composed.

"I'm all right," she said.

"All right?" questioned Shrader. "You're covered with blood!" Cathy looked down and realized that he was right. Her jacket was spattered with it. Shrader took her by the hand and led her to where *Strider* was docked. She remembered very little of what happened during that time period. When she came to herself, Shrader was washing caked blood from her scalp and dabbing hydrogen peroxide on a one-inch gash on the back of her head.

"You're still in shock," she heard him saying. The hatch opened and a tall slender, dark-haired man stepped down into the main cabin. "This is John Romig," said Shrader, looking up from his work. "John, this is Cathy Pearson. The one I told you about."

"You must have had quite a run-in with someone," said Romig to Cathy. "A sledge hammer shattered your van's side window, and very nearly took your head off from the look of things. Your front seat is full of glass pellets from where the window blew out."

"Phil told me that things were going crazy, but I never...," her voice trailed off.

"He's right," offered Romig. "The news of the meteor strike is making people do strange things; obviously some are giving license to their more violent fantasies, and the thing hasn't even hit yet! I can't imagine what will be unleashed when things really start happening."

"I only got ten gallons," said Cathy.

"What?" asked Shrader.

"I only could get ten gallons of diesel before the guy came after me."

"Don't worry about it," consoled Shrader. "We'll make do even if we have to siphon off the tanks of the boats on the cradles. This is the deal: none of us leaves the marina except by boat this evening. It's just too risky, and it will get worse when the strike takes place." He threw a last tissue into the plastic-lined wastebasket where it joined half-a-dozen others that were caked with blood. "There," he said. "You may be pretty sore for the next few days, but it's a clean cut and it ought to heal all right." Shrader turned to Romig. "How are Laura and the boys taking all this?"

"Laura doesn't know what to think. Mostly she's scared, but we've been married long enough that she's willing to risk it. Cameron and Ben just think it's a big adventure."

"Laura is John's wife," said Shrader to Cathy. "She and their sons are settling in on *Mewtiny*."

"Are you a sailor, John?" asked Cathy.

"No, not at all, but Marks thinks I can learn on the job," he chided, looking sideways at Shrader. "I think Laura's more scared of that than anything else. She can handle the idea of a meteor strike. It's navigating Lake Ontario with me at the controls that really has her worried."

"At the helm," corrected Shrader. "You'll be at the helm or you'll take the wheel. The first lesson has begun. It's called *learning the proper terminology.*"

"See how pathetic I am?" said Romig to Cathy with a smile and a shrug.

"For the first few days at least you won't have to know much about sailing," reassured Shrader. "Tonight you'll motor along with us, and that will just be a matter of maintaining a compass course. Once we get to the Thousand Islands we'll begin the sailing lessons." Turning to Cathy, he added, "Give John the extra fuel. He'll be motoring more than the rest of us. Tonight's forecast sounds like we'll be able to sail."

Cathy nodded with understanding. "Let's get the diesel," she said to Romig. "Then I'd like to meet Laura and the boys. I might be able to answer questions that will make them more comfortable on *Mewtiny*. I have two sons and a daughter myself. Besides, I need to get a better idea of *Mewtiny's* hardware. I have the sneaky feeling that I'll be your sail instructor."

"She's been having a lot of sneaky feelings lately," said Shrader. "But she's got good judgment and you could do a lot worse for an instructor."

As if on cue, Cathy and John moved to the companionway, climbed the four steps, and stepped out into the cockpit. Shrader, who had joked a moment earlier, felt a wave of anxiety come over him.

"Will you be okay?" said Cathy, who had turned and looked back down into the cabin.

"Are you a mind-reader, too?" responded Shrader.

"Not at all, I just know you."

"Now there's a scary thought," said Shrader sidestepping the issue. "I'll be fine."

"At some point you will have to trust somebody, Shrader. Just so you know, I'm here, and your dreams don't scare me." Cathy turned to leave.

"Cathy," called Marks.

"What?"

"Thanks," he said.

"For what?"

"For being my friend, for not letting me hide any more. I do want to talk, but I don't have the words yet." His confession surprised himself. Cathy's response was an understanding smile.

"The words will come when you need them," she said as she disappeared from his view. John Romig was waiting on the dock for her. Shrader, alone in *Strider's* cabin, went into himself searching for words. In his mind, he saw a boy of eight asleep on a bed in a familiar room. It was his room. The boy stirred in his sleep as if running away. He began to call out, "No, no!" and struggled against the bed clothes until he had kicked them clear of his skinny body. Tears streaked the boy's face and he choked while trying to catch his breath. His blue eyes opened suddenly as his breathing became a steady pant. He sat up and looked steadily into Shrader's eyes. "Why did she have to die?" he asked.

Shrader studied the boy's face, and he knew himself. "I don't know," he said. "I just don't know."

Alone in the belly of the boat he had remembered the question of his childhood, a question he had spent his adult life ignoring.

"Do you remember her?" asked the boy. Shrader paused trying to recall images of his mother.

"No," he said at last, "not at all."

"Do you remember me?" Shrader looked into the eyes of his boy-self and saw all the sadness that comes from unanswered longing.

"Yes," he said. "I remember you, and I remember the nights that I called out to the darkness and there was no answer. I remember falling into *the nothing*, the place where words do not fit, and passing through to the other side where life returns."

"Shrader," asked the boy. "Are we shaman?"

It was a question that he had never considered. It brought him back to the reality of time and space. It brought him back to the settee berth in the main cabin of his sailboat. "Is that what's happening to me?" he said aloud. "Am I shaman?" The word was one that dotted the pages of his anthropology library and filtered through the reams of papers that he had written over the years. Always the shaman was a shadowy figure living on the boundary between the visible and invisible world. But in his mind, the shaman belonged in primitive societies, not in the information age. Without thinking, his hand came up to clutch the orca effigy around his neck, the same one that he had taken from the specimen drawer at the university. "I don't know," he said aloud to no one.

23

Cathy Pearson and John Romig crossed the parking lot toward her minivan. She lifted the rear hatch and John took hold of one of the five gallon jerry-jugs of diesel fuel.

"I can't believe that I didn't feel that," said Cathy, pointing to the shattered side glass behind the driver's seat.

"You were pretty shocky when you pulled in here," remarked Romig. "But Shrader and I figured that something pretty traumatic had happened."

"It's still a blur, and I'm not ready to talk about it. There's too much to do."

"You and Shrader are a lot alike," observed Romig. "When you drove up in your van, I was telling him about Lynn. He's not ready to talk about that, either."

"What about her?" asked Pearson.

"She's not coming here today."

"Not coming?" said Cathy. "Poor Shrader; he loves her."

"Yes," John agreed. "But in her mind he has stepped beyond the limits of reason. Actually, I think it's been building for years."

"You mean they've had a lot of problems?"

"Not really," answered Romig. "It's more situational. As an instructor, you get bounced around from university to university. Academia has a way of using people and then throwing them away. They let you believe that if you work hard you'll be given tenure, but the fact is that it's cheaper to hire PhD instructors and let them go every four or five years, rather than offer tenure and a living wage. I think his wife just got tired of it and blamed him. She'd pretty well decided that she'd made her last move."

"Have you told Shrader?"

"I started to. I had just told him and he didn't react much. I thought he hadn't heard. Then you pulled in and we could see that you were in trouble."

"I guess my timing isn't so great," stated Cathy.

"No, it's not that," answered Romig. "I don't think he can deal with it. He's known it for a long time. The last time we talked at the university he as much as told me that Lynn wouldn't be here. I think he's been alone in this for a long time, but hasn't admitted it to himself. Except for you," his voice trailed off.

"Yes," she answered, "except for me. The odd thing is that we didn't really even know each other until two weeks ago. Now it seems like we've known each other for ages."

The two had been walking slowly across the marina. John shifted the five gallon can from side to side periodically in a fruitless effort to find a comfortable way to carry the bulky container. At last they approached the berth where *Mewtiny* was docked. They stopped and looked at the craft. She was a cutter-rigged Bayside 38.

"You'll be sailing a pretty boat, Captain," said Cathy as she looked at the traditional lines of the boat and its surplus of decorative teak.

"There's only one flaw," answered Romig. "I don't have a clue as to what it takes to sail a boat of any size and this one seems as long as a football field."

Cathy studied the boat for a moment before speaking. "You have a few things in your favor," she said at last. "First, the boat is facing out toward the bay, and no one is tied off in front of you. You'll just have to cast off the lines, throw the engine into forward, and wait until the helm responds. Second, I think I'll loan you my daughter Brittany. She's only fourteen, but knows a lot about sailing and boat handling. That is, if you don't mind taking orders from a teenager?"

It was Romig's turn to ponder the situation. "You'd trust your daughter with me?" he asked.

"No," she answered. "I trust my daughter, and you'll need someone with some experience out there. Besides, Shrader says it'll be an easy night. The winds will be moderate, and you'll be motoring. Brittany has been racing dinghies since she was eight and has a good weather sense."

"But this thing is no dinghy," offered Romig.

Cathy smiled. "Relax, John. A boat like this is very forgiving. You make a wrong move, and she might roll and scare you, but she'll not go over. Dinghies tell you that you made an error by giving you a bath. Brittany will keep this boat afloat."

"Can I ask another dumb thing?" John whispered. "What did you mean when you said that to get out of this space I'd just have to throw the engine into gear and 'wait until the helm responds'?"

"I sometimes forget how many little things there are to learn about sailboats," said Cathy. She chose her words carefully. "It's just that there is no steering unless there's water moving under the boat. Let me explain it better. In a powerboat, you turn the wheel and the propeller shifts one way or another and directs the engine thrust to push the boat forward." Cathy gestured with both hands as she attempted to explain the physics of engine propulsion. "A sailboat steers with a rudder, a sort of blade that sticks down in the water and bends the flow under the boat. It only works when water is actually moving around it. The propeller from the engine is stationary. It doesn't move side to side. It just churns up the water and pushes it back against the rudder. When it gets enough force going, you can steer the boat. Until then, there is always a moment when the wind or the current is going to have more control over the boat than the operator."

"There's a pleasant thought," broke in Romig.

"It's just something you have to get used to. You just can't start and stop. You have to stay alert to the other forces on the boat and anticipate. Always try to keep some forward momentum, otherwise you'll be adrift."

"And that's not good, right?"

"Most of the time, it's an embarrassment," said Cathy. "In light winds you bring the boat around and the wind dies on you and you just sit there. You can spin the wheel, but you'll just sit until you start the engine or push out a sail to catch some new wind. In a storm, however, well, that's another story. You can hit a wave wrong and it stops all your forward progress. You're dead in the water with no steering and you know that the next wave is going to hit you and roll you sideways, and they'll be another after that and so on until you regain some sort of forward momentum."

"And if you don't, you sink!"

Cathy laughed. "John, are you always such a pessimist? No, you don't sink! At that point, anything that isn't stowed properly below gets loose and starts crashing about, the crew gets seasick, and the people out in the cockpit get drenched. But the boat won't sink. Boats sink when water gets into the hull through an opening. So you close the hatches, tie down everything below deck, tie the crew to the boat, and pray that you don't run out of water."

"Run out of water?"

"You know, hit the shore or something solid," said Cathy with a wink. As she spoke, a short-haired woman stuck her head out of *Mewtiny's* companionway.

"John," said the woman who was about Cathy's age. "It's got a bank of two batteries for cabin power and a third to turn over the engine."

"That's Laura," said Romig to Cathy. "Her dad had a service station when she was growing up, and she worked her way through college as his chief mechanic. Laura," he said turning toward his wife. "This is Cathy Pearson, Shrader's friend."

"Hi Cathy," said Laura, stepping up out of the cabin. She was tall and wiry, reminding Cathy of a long distance runner.

"John tells me that you're a mechanic," began Cathy, "do you think you can keep this thing running?"

"It looks pretty clean," offered Laura. "I drained off some diesel, and it looks pretty good. No evidence of gelling."

"What did I tell you?" said John with a note of pride in his voice.

"How about if I come aboard and give you a few hints about stowing gear and safety equipment?" suggested Cathy. "And then Laura can give me a lesson on starting diesels in cold weather."

"Sounds like a good deal," said John. The two stepped over the double life lines that ran fore and aft along *Mewtiny's* hull.

24

August William Gundersen had spent his adult life working for the Saint Lawrence Seaway Development Corporation. Like his own name, the name of his employer was a mouthful. Fortunately for Gus Gundersen, very few of his friends knew what the initials, A.W., in his name stood for, and even fewer remembered the years in high school when he had been victimized by the nickname *Root Beer*. If they did, they would not have mentioned it in front of him now. He had earned the privilege of their respect. If the Development Corporation brought in college-educated managers to oversee the Seaway locks on the U.S. side of the Saint Lawrence, it did not take them long to realize that the Eisenhower and Snell Locks were the personal domain of Gus Gundersen.

It was not that Gundersen threatened, bullied, or cajoled, just the opposite. He understood the river. From the beginning, he knew that the technology and massive bulk of the lock system was nothing compared to the power of the water that fell drop by drop from the clouds and subsequently flowed into the Great Lakes watershed. As a result, it was Gundersen who would be called in the middle of the night when there was an equipment malfunction or consulted when water levels seemed abnormally high or low. Lock operators on both sides of the border knew his name even if the joint project administrators did not.

He had spent all his working years on the Seaway, and owed his life to it as well. Five years ago when his wife of thirty-eight years died suddenly, he could not bring himself to face anyone. Two weeks later, Ray Anderson, an operator on the Snell, called him at 2:30 a.m. with a problem. Whether by force of habit or determination of will, Gus donned his khaki coveralls and drove his four-wheel drive from his bungalow in Massena Center to the Eisenhower Lock. When he arrived, he found that there was no real problem at the work site, just a friend and a few quiet hours. He would always remember that night. The stars were crisp and the full moon caught the ripples off the still waters of Lake Saint Lawrence. His mind went back to his childhood in the early fifties and fishing with his father along the river. As a boy, he had stood watching the workers pour the concrete for the massive locks. Years later, he had seen the first passenger ship lock through the newly completed Seaway. The actual date was etched in his memory, thanks to a gift given to him by his father. The treasure of his childhood now occupied a place of honor over his desk. It was an imprinted business envelope, matted and framed. On the left side of the white envelope was the silhouette of a lighthouse and the words *S.S. South American: First Passenger Ship Through the New St. Lawrence Seaway.* It was postmarked from Massena, New York and dated Sept 6, 8 p.m., 1958. Gus Gundersen and the Seaway had grown up together, and now in his late sixties he thought of it as the most enduring relationship of his life.

The parking area at the end of the private access road was emptier than usual. In the summer, vacationers would fill the upper lot in order to watch the ships locking through the waterway. But in the winter, the skeleton maintenance staff would only fill the lower spaces near the walkways that led to the control station. Gus turned off the ignition and climbed out of the cab of his Jeep Cherokee. The air was unusually warm for April, but then the ice had been off the river for some time. It was one of those atypical years when the Great Lakes region would experience a long spring. More common was a short spring when the frozen waters kept the breezes cool. When the ice disappeared, temperatures would leap to summertime levels. Already some commercial shipping had resumed along the seaway, and Gundersen wondered why the start of a new season did not expand the population of employees' cars.

Must be all the hoopla about the damned comet, he said to himself. He did recognize Betty Montgomery's green Toyota and knew that at least one of his operators had shown up that morning. Once inside, he took off his brown leather flight jacket and entered the control room where he could see Betty glancing at the surveillance monitors of the various locks. "Looks like we have a lot of no-shows, Betty," he said.

The middle-aged woman turned to look at him, and then turned back to the controls. "Hi, Gus," she said. "We're checking the seals on the downstream gates. But, you're right. No one has shown up for the shift change."

"Why wasn't I notified?" asked Gundersen.

"Nobody was notified," said Montgomery sharply. "I mean, no one called in sick or anything; they just aren't showing up! I've been on for twelve hours already, and so has everyone else. We're about dead on our feet."

"Okay," said Gus. "I'll get on the horn and start raising hell."

"It won't work," warned Betty. "They aren't answering their phones. At least that's what Tim Hartwell said. He normally stops to pick up Zack Schuster and when Zack came out to say that he wasn't coming in, Tim told him to expect a call from you."

"Tim got that right," interrupted Gundersen.

"Wait," continued Montgomery. "Schuster said he wasn't worried about a phone ringing, since machines can do the answering and, besides, you'd not be able to fire the whole shift."

"Why, that little bastard," sneered Gundersen. "I'll go out and bring them all in by the scruff of the neck if I have to."

"I don't think you have time," warned Betty. "This came over the fax about half an hour ago." She handed Gus a curling piece of paper. Gundersen read the first few lines and sat down in an empty chair.

"What the hell does this mean?" he said. "I've never seen anything like this before."

"I know," consoled Betty, "it sure scared the shit out of me. Why else do you think we started all this testing so shorthanded?"

"According to this," continued Gundersen as though he hadn't heard anything Betty had said, "according to this, we are going to have more traffic than we can handle moving up river into Ontario."

"That's the way I read it, too," agreed Montgomery.

"What the hell can they be thinking will happen that would make them try to move boats a thousand miles inland? And in the next twenty-four hours! I can't imagine that there's that much shipping in the pipeline. The ice hasn't been off the river that long."

"According to that," said Betty pointing to the fax in Gus' hand, "there's been a fleet headed our way for three weeks."

"Nothing too big, I hope," observed Gus. "Leave it to the planners to forget that we have some size limitations, no big container ships or aircraft carriers. Oh well, by the time they reach the Snell, the Canadians will have weeded out anything that we can't handle. Any ships too large for the Saint Lambert Lock will have to stay in Montréal."

"That could make quite a logjam," noted Betty, "but what about vessels coming down river from Lake Ontario?"

"There aren't going to be any," announced Gundersen. "As of today, the Seaway is a one-way street. We'll bring in everything we can from the Gulf of Saint Lawrence, but nobody gets out. How are the tests going anyway?" They both turned to look at the control board and the overhead monitors.

"Looks good," said Montgomery. "No ice damage or malfunctions that I can see."

"Good," said Gus. "Get on the phone and call the bums. Leave messages on the damn machines if you have to. Tell them that it's a national emergency, and we need to get a lot of tonnage out of the reach of a rising ocean. Tell them it might be the best thing they'll ever do."

"They're scared, Gus. That's the simple truth. I'm not sure this will make them any more anxious to leave their families when the world around them is going crazy."

"Hell, we're all scared," countered Gundersen. "Some of them will see the sense in that and do the right thing. Tell them to bring their families if they'd like. I'll call the Development Corporation and see if they can't take over a school for a shelter. We'll need a round-the-clock crew and it would be good to have a place close by where they could eat and sleep. Their families could stay there, close by. And I'll call Ray Anderson; he'll help out."

"But he's been retired for three years," protested Betty.

"I know," answered Gus. "But he called me out once during a crisis. I think I owe him the same favor, now." Betty didn't understand Gundersen's remark, but let it pass. Gus was already at the phone ringing the private numbers of the supervisors of the Saint Lawrence Seaway Development Corporation.

25

"So you are proposing that we *go out* the Seaway at the very moment that all the scientists in the world are predicting a major rise in ocean levels?" It was the third time that Phil Pearson had challenged Shrader's presentation. And the third time that John Romig stepped in with a calm, logical response.

"It really isn't as crazy an idea as you are trying to make it sound," said Romig. "I've spent a lot of time in Canada with Shrader, and the sea will supply our survival needs for quite a long spell. The Gulf of Saint Lawrence is relatively sheltered. We won't be subject to the storms of the open ocean. We'll have access to land and to waters rich with cod and other fish."

"But it would be safer to stay right here," interrupted Pearson. "Even if the oceans were to rise to the level of Lake Ontario, which I seriously doubt, we are still above that here, and we have the resources of civilization." Romig rolled his eyes, and looked to Shrader.

"Don't be a fool, Phil," said Shrader whose voice sounded as hard as ice. "There will be no civilization on the planet, at least not one that you'd be able to trust. Even if the authorities can hold order for a time, it will have to be by force. People will be fighting for food, and desperation will quickly strip away law and order."

"And no one ever said that the oceans would rise to Ontario's level." John Romig was back to his argument in an attempt to divert Shrader's impatience from fueling the fire of Phil Pearson's red-faced rage. "We're 245 feet above sea level. The seas could rise—maybe as much as 160 feet, but that's it. We won't have to worry about floods here. But the state of Florida will be gone. The coastal lowlands of every continent will become ocean floor. New York City will be nothing more than rocks jutting out of the water. What do you think will happen to all the people? And it will be worldwide! Do you think Homeland Security will handle it better than *Katrina*? Those who can escape will create a refugee explosion unequaled in time. Those who do not escape will be a source of disease and contamination."

"I figure it this way." The voice that spoke was calm and sure. It was Cathy. She looked around the small gathering of captains. "We don't have to try and guess the fate of the planet. Face it; the best scientific minds on the planet are having problems doing that. What *we* have to do is fairly risk-free. It is unseasonably warm. While it's still on the chilly side, a lot of you are champing at the bit to get in the first sail of the year. The way that I see it is that there's no reason to panic. We travel together on a night sail. Tomorrow we'll probably motor-sail through the Thousand Islands and try to get through the Iroquois Lock before evening. If the wind stays light, we might be able to raft up in Lake Saint Lawrence. That's when we'll have to make the final decision. If the planet is going to fall apart, we'll know by then. If this whole comet-thing fizzles, well, we can start back on Monday and we'll tell of our adventure at a cruising comet party."

"Cathy is right," said Roland Koenig, the skipper of *Rol's Royce*. "Since I retired, Marty and I have done a lot of early season sailing. Wear a wool sweater and carry a thermos of coffee and it's great!"

"But you don't have kids to worry about," voiced Tish Barker of *Fairwinds*. "Jim and I have three. "If it's too cold to be out on deck, you can bet that we'll have a cabin full of motion sickness to deal with."

"Has anyone heard the latest forecast?" asked Cathy.

"Winds light and variable today, increasing to ten to fifteen knots tonight, waves less than two feet, building to three by morning." Cathy turned to face Bert Jenkins, who repeated the weather report with an accuracy that fit his years of military service.

"Thank you, Major," said Cathy.

Jenkins smiled sheepishly. "I can do better than that, Commodore," he said to Cathy. "I have an SSB on *Major Blunder* and can get the actual printouts of the weather charts from the

National Weather Service." Cathy could see confusion on the faces of some of the people.

"Does everyone here know everyone else?" she said as a follow-up to Jenkins' statement. "Our high-tech expert is Major Bert Jenkins," she added. "Maybe we all ought to introduce ourselves and our boats. I'm Cathy Pearson and this is my husband, Phil. We sail on this boat, the *Affinity*, and we have three kids, Brittany, fourteen, Justin, twelve, and Christopher, ten." Her husband nodded grudgingly, and she turned to her right where John Romig stood.

"I'm John Romig, and this is my wife, Laura. We have two sons, Cameron who is eight and Ben who is six. We're new to this marina. We sail on *Mewtiny*." Romig glanced at Shrader who gave him a reassuring wink.

One after another the crews introduced themselves. There were the Koenigs, Jim and Tish Barker aboard *Fairwinds*, Vince and Rhonda Ragni who owned *Dream Dancer*, Bill and Connie Morgan on *Wave Chaser*, and Bert and Tiffany Jenkins on *Major Blunder*. Tiffany seemed very quiet and reserved, never making eye contact during the introductions. Cathy guessed from her Asian features that she was still unaccustomed to American straightforwardness.

Mentally, Cathy made a quick headcount. She tallied seven children besides her own, which brought the total number to ten. There were fifteen adults on eight boats. That was counting Shrader who was alone on *Strider* and the Romigs who were hijacking *Mewtiny*.

"I've been retired from the Air Force for five years now," said Major Bert Jenkins. "But there are certain things you never forget when you are flying a mission. One of them is *chain of command*. I called Cathy *Commodore* a little while ago because I think she's got the right perspective on this whole thing. I don't know whether Shrader or Phil is right, but we don't have much to lose by sailing out as a fleet. Worst-case scenario is that the comet does everything Romig says. It is Romig, isn't it?" he said, turning to John. "If that happens we'd at least be at the staging area and in a position to decide if the mission is a *go*. If we sit here, we're betting that nothing will happen. If you lose that bet, you lose it all. On the other hand, if we get out as far as Lake Saint Lawrence and find that it's a false alarm, we come back and change the name of *Strider* to *The Sky Is Falling*."

Everyone laughed except Marks and Romig. "I'll pay for the new graphics when we get back," gloated Phil Pearson.

"Well, Commodore?" continued Jenkins. "When do you finish the briefing, and when do we sail?"

Cathy turned to Shrader who quickly looked away.

"It's a stupid idea," began Phil Pearson, "but I'll work out the compass course and get back...."

Cathy cut him off mid-sentence. "There will be a Captains' meeting at 9:30 this evening in the main cabin of *Affinity*. Each boat that plans to go has to send a representative. We'll be sailing at 10:00." She racked her brain to remember all the details that she and Shrader had discussed. "It's about seventy-five miles to Clayton and we want to time our arrival so that we can reach the islands in daylight. That means that for the trip across the lake, we'll try to average between six and seven knots. I don't think that should be a problem, except some of the long waterline boats may have to hold back. We need to stay in the open water of the lake while it's too dark to navigate by line of sight. Any questions?"

The group was silent until Jenkins spoke. "No questions, Commodore," he said. "The lady knows her stuff," he said with a wink as he looked around the circle of attentive faces. Most of the expressions were pensive and impenetrable. Two were not. Phil was red-faced and stern. Shrader had a broad smile, like a proud parent whose daughter had just scored the winning points in a grudge match. Cathy closed her eyes and took a deep breath. It was over, or rather, it was beginning.

26

"How do you think the meeting went?" asked Romig as he and Shrader stood at the end of the dock. Shrader did not answer. He gazed rather blankly at the bay. John tried to follow his line of sight. In the gray water, Newark and Eagle Islands stood as bleak reminders of the passing winter. But he understood that Shrader was not looking at anything that stood in time. "How do you think the meeting went?" he repeated.

"Sorry," said Shrader, shaking himself back to reality. "On the whole, I'd say it went well. You kept countering Pearson, and Cathy was great!"

"That Phil Pearson was mad," observed Romig.

"Phil Pearson's a fool. I don't know how Cathy ever got mixed up with him!"

"I suspect that there was a lot more going on with him than contention with the plan." Romig studied Shrader's body language.

"He's just used to being in control, that's all," stated Marks. "He's up against something he can't understand and so he's trying to play games."

"For a Ph.D. you're a friggin' idiot," replied John. "Pearson's reaction has nothing to do with the comet. It's about you and Cathy."

"You've got to be joking. That's way out of line, John," protested Shrader. "A week ago I barely knew her. I had to call Lynn to even find out her last name."

"But things have changed a lot in one week, and Phil can see it."

"What have we done to set him off? We have done nothing, except to try and get ready to save a piece of his world. We've come too far to let him get in the way of that!"

"That's what he's afraid of," commented Romig. The two men stood silent for a long moment. The sun was behind them now, and threw a glint across the waters. A gull cried overhead. John turned toward the direction of the bird's call.

"Did you hear what he said?" asked Shrader.

"Who?" answered a startled Romig.

"John, I think I am crazy. Lynn is right to stay away. I could swear that the gull just said 'It has started'. But you didn't hear it, right?"

"I heard the thing screech, which is what you probably heard, too."

"No, I heard words," said Shrader. "There have been a few times this week when I've heard voices. I thought it was sleep depravation or something, but that was too real. You didn't hear anything out of the ordinary?"

"Sorry, Shrader, I didn't. But that doesn't mean ..."

"That I'm a basket-case," said Marks, finishing the sentence. "Lynn was right not to trust me."

"She's not coming today. I really tried to convince her."

"I know, John. I guess I've known for a long time that she'd never agree to be here. I just thought that if somebody else asked. Did she say anything?"

"Nothing much," said Romig shrugging his shoulders and looking away.

"In other words, nothing you want to tell me," answered Shrader.

"I guess," came the reply. "Nothing that would serve any purpose at this point." The sound of running feet came on the breeze. The two men turned to see a girl running toward them. "It's Brittany," said Romig. "She's been helping us aboard *Mewtiny*."

"Dr. Marks," she called.

"Yes, Brittany," responded Shrader. "Are you okay?" The young woman's expression told him that something troubling had happened. "Did something happen to your mother?"

"No," said the girl. "She wanted me to tell you that the TV reports have started to come in. It's really big, an asteroid or something like that."

Romig looked at Shrader in disbelief. "You knew," he said.

"Tell your mother we'll be right there," called Marks. The girl turned to reverse her path. "Brittany, don't be afraid," added Shrader. The teen hurried off, leaving the two alone again.

"You do love her," stated John Romig.

"Of course," replied Marks, "we've been married a long time."

"Not Lynn," corrected Romig, "Cathy."

Shrader started to protest, and then stopped himself. "I don't know," he said at last. "I don't know."

27

"Okay," said Cathy, "the reports of the strike in Antarctica have us all shaken. If there's anyone here who wants to turn back, this is the time. If not, we should start making our way out of the bay and into the lake. We'll be moving northeast on a heading of 30º magnetic north which puts us on a direct course for Cape Vincent and the entrance to the Seaway. Three-fourths of the way across, we'll approach Galloo Island. Keep a wide passage to avoid the shoal. It's marked with a flashing light, but then again, it's early in the season and the winters have a way of rearranging the marks and putting them out of commission."

"Where are Shrader and the guy from *Mewtiny*?" asked Bill Morgan from *Wave Chaser*. "Have they bailed out on us?"

"No," said Cathy quickly. "John Romig was having some trouble with his boat and Shrader is helping him out. They're already up-to-speed with the plans and will be joining us. From what I can see, no one has bailed out."

"I thought about it after our meeting this afternoon, but the comet strike brought me back." It was *Dream Dancer's* owner, Vince Ragni, who spoke up. "CNN has suspended coverage and the Air Force is enforcing a gigantic *no-fly* zone south of the fortieth parallel. Shrader might be off his rocker, but so far, he seems to have it right. I'm staying with the game plan, at least for now."

"Good," said Cathy confidently. "The thing we have to watch out for is that what's happening with the asteroid doesn't make us so jumpy that we make mistakes. The plan is to get eight boats safely into Lake Saint Lawrence by tomorrow afternoon or early evening. Let me run down my checklist to make sure that I don't leave anything out." She unfolded a piece of lined yellow paper from a legal pad and began to read. The representatives from five other boats began to copy down her main points. Phil, her husband, sat in the corner of the settee berth with an open chart on his lap.

"A few safety rules first. You all know this stuff, but bear with me. After dark, it's always good to wear your life jacket with a flashlight or a whistle. Besides, this time of year a PFD will help keep you warm. Use a harness and a tether if you have one. We aren't expecting high winds or waves, but things happen and it's better not to go overboard." Phil let out a heavy sigh as a protest to what he considered his wife's trivial comments.

"It looks like we'll be able to sail tonight. The winds will be off the port quarter so we'll be on a broad reach most of the way. Since we're going about the same direction of the wind, it will reduce wind chill. But bundle up with layers of clothing. My goodness," she added, "I'm starting to sound like somebody's mother." The cabin broke out in mild laughter which affected everyone except Phil.

"Try to maintain a speed between six and seven knots. This will get us through the open waters during the darkness and ready to approach the islands at daybreak. This isn't a race. If your boat wants to jump ahead, reduce sail, or take the sails down and use the engine. Same thing if you can't maintain at least six knots. Turn on your engine and motor-sail. Phil and I will lead out on *Affinity*. Shrader will be last on *Strider*. If you have adequate battery power, you can monitor channel 68 on your radio. That's going to be our working frequency. If you don't want to keep the VHF on the whole time, we will be voice-checking each other on the hour and on the half-hour.

"I know you all have enough people on board to share the responsibility for the helm. I'd suggest two three-hour watches followed by two two-hour turns. Those of you who have autopilots, don't get lazy and leave the thing unattended or fall asleep on it. This time of the year there'll be no commercial traffic on the lake, but remember, there will be eight of us on the same course and we don't want to be running into each other. I think that's it, unless you have questions," she concluded.

"What if we get separated?" asked Jim Barker from *Fairwinds*.

"Good question," Cathy assured. "If you lose your radio and can't make visual contact, head for the Cape Vincent Village Dock. It's on your charts and should be easy enough to find. We won't be able to wait there all day, however. So, if you have a problem, get on the horn right away. Shrader's boat has an old Atomic IV and has enough power to tow a tank. If there's trouble on the lake tonight, we can help each other. But, if we don't find out until tomorrow that you're stranded out there, we can't come back and get you."

"All the good battlefield officers are tough," said Bert Jenkins leaning over to Marty Koenig who was representing *Rol's Royce*. Her husband, Roland, was busy changing a fuel filter on their diesel.

"Any more questions?" The group went silent. "Good," continued Cathy, "*Affinity* will be leaving as soon as you all clear out. We'll keep a 30º heading and you just follow out as you're able. The first radio check will be in forty-five minutes," she said after looking at her watch. "That will be 10:30."

"In other words, 'get out and get going'," said Bill Morgan.

"Good briefing, Commodore," offered Bert Jenkins. The hatch cover over the companionway slid open, and cold air rushed into the stale cabin. One by one, the people stepped up the ladder and out into the cockpit.

"Thanks, Cathy," said Marty Koenig. "Do you want me to cover the hatch?"

"That's okay, Marty. Phil and I have to come out to disconnect shore power and cast off. I can't be late after sounding so tough." The two exchanged smiles before Marty disappeared into the night.

As she looked out of the hatch, Phil came up behind her and put his hands on her hips. "Did I do okay?" she asked.

"Sure did, Commodore," he said with mock sweetness. He pushed her roughly aside. "You may have them fooled," he added, "but we both know who's in charge on my boat, right?"

Cathy did not answer, and Phil did not wait to hear it in any case. In a few steps he was unplugging the shore power. The cabin went dark. "Switch on the battery power, Commodore," came a voice colder than the wind.

28

"Don't worry, you'll be fine," consoled Shrader. From the look on Romig's face, he wasn't so sure that John believed him. He passed the last dock line to Laura who stood on *Mewtiny's* bow. "Laura, get him to relax, would you?" he said reassuringly. The diesel was cooperating with a nice steady sputter as the hull started to gain forward momentum. Brittany stood at the helm. She appeared to be the only one who had no concern. *You are your mother's daughter!* Shrader thought to himself. To her, he asked, "Are you going to motor or sail?"

Brittany gave him a long look. "Are you kidding?" she asked.

"Yes, I'm kidding, Brittany. Have a good sail."

"Thanks, Dr. Marks," she said in answer to his smile. The boat slid by quickly and they were out of earshot. Shrader watched as she followed a steady course parallel to the peninsula that jutted out into the bay. She would have to round the point and then come back to enter the narrow channel that linked Sodus Bay to the waters of Ontario. He looked at his watch. It was already 10:20.

"I'd better get a move on it," he said aloud. "I'll be the only one not underway at the first radio call." He climbed over the rail and stepped down into the cockpit of his boat. The large stainless steel wheel was mounted on a white binnacle post. The post was capped with a floating compass. The engine controls were mounted on the right hand side. He made sure the gearshift was in neutral. He pulled out the piston choke, and started the blower motor to exhaust the gasoline fumes. After a few minutes, he threw the kill switch and depressed the starter button. The motor cranked, then caught. He pushed the throttle forward and the engine surged. Beneath the boat came the gurgling sound of water shooting out the exhaust pipe. So far, everything was operating correctly. He jumped ashore and released the spring line that held the boat tight against the dock. *Strider* began to drift out until it reached the limits of the bow and stern lines, and Shrader realized that the wind was going to make the boat drift quickly. All that held the boat were two half-inch lines. He loosened the stern line, and then the bow line before climbing back aboard. He went forward and pulled in the bow line. The boat started to swing out, pivoting on the stern. Quickly, he ran back and released the stern. Now the boat was drifting freely. If he did not move quickly, he would find himself up against the docks on the opposite side of the channel. He pushed the gearshift forward; he felt the transmission engage. The boat continued to drift sideways. He gunned the throttle and the propeller grabbed at the water. The boat began to move forward, and Shrader turned the wheel. *Strider* responded by heading up into the center of the channel, along the same course that *Mewtiny* had followed.

Shrader sat behind the wheel, and leaned his hand over the transom so that he could read his watch in the illumination of the stern light. It was 10:28. In his rush to get out on the lake, he had not remembered to turn on his VHF radio. *Damn!* he thought. It was going to be a trick to keep *Strider* under control and get the radio online for the first check-in. The fact was that the boat was neither rigged for single-handed sailing, nor did it have an auto-pilot which would permit him to leave the helm for extended periods of time.

Shrader rounded the point of the peninsula and brought the boat to a more northerly course which placed him in the channel to leave the bay. *Strider* slid through the dark water as he steered through the narrow neck that connected Sodus Bay to the vast waters of Lake Ontario. On his right he passed the four-second flashing green light that marked the channel entrance. The familiar sights looked very different after the fall of darkness, and Shrader said his quiet farewell to Sodus Bay with a backward glance. Ahead of him was the open water of Lake Ontario and seven ghostly boats. Their billowing sails reflected the masthead running lights like Japanese lanterns floating on the water. The closest of the boats was *Mewtiny*. She was running on her mainsail. *Good for you, Brittany,* thought Marks. The Romigs were getting their first lesson. Shrader looked at his watch. It was 10:40. He decided to make radio contact before getting under sail. He turned *Strider* due north on a different course than the rest of the fleet. He throttled back the engine to a crawl, and locked the wheel into place. The precautions would hold the boat on a straight course for a few minutes and well out of the path of the others. Quickly he went below and turned the VHF to channel 68.

"*Affinity, Affinity, Affinity* this is *Strider*," he said into the handheld microphone. He waited for a response.

"*Strider*, this is *Affinity*. You okay, Shrader?" It was Cathy's voice.

"I'm fine. I just don't have long to talk. Has everyone checked in?"

"They're all under sail, and have their watches organized. You're the only one that I'm worried about," said Cathy.

"Me? Why?" asked Shrader.

"Because you're trying to do this alone. Tomorrow we have to put someone else with you aboard *Strider*. You're going to be dead after sailing all night single-handed."

"Let's see how John and Laura do with Brittany aboard," agreed Marks reluctantly. "Maybe John can come with me when we motor down the river."

"I'm going to hold you to that," said Cathy.

"Okay, but for now, I'm fine. Just don't worry if I don't answer your hail too quickly, but I'll be able to hear you. I can turn up the volume on the radio, but I can't leave the helm if there's any wave action or we're in close quarters."

"Understood," agreed Cathy. "Get back to *Strider*. You're already falling behind. *Affinity*, signing off."

Shrader grabbed the harness that he had left in the galley sink and climbed back out into the cockpit. A quick look around and he understood Cathy's concern. The other boats were now far to starboard as *Strider* had begun to travel in a wide arc toward the northwest. He unlocked the wheel, and turned it clockwise to correct the course. The wind was now blowing at about fifteen knots out of the southwest. It was a bit of luck for Shrader who would have had a tough time raising the mainsail alone. With the wind at his back he would not need the main at all. He would be able to make good time with just his headsail, a roller furling 155 genoa. Setting that sail was an easy task. He simply uncleated the furling line and pulled on the starboard jib sheet. The massive front sail rolled out smoothly like a window shade gone mad. It flew out ahead of the boat until he winched it into the shape of an enormous vertical airfoil. *Strider* showed her appreciation by leaping ahead, picking up speed as she slid into the night.

Shrader assumed the helm, reaching down to throw the switch to kill the engine. The mechanical throb of the motor was replaced by the sounds of the water and the bow of the boat pushing ahead into the waves.

"Shrader, where do you get off messing with my boat?" The voice of Phil Pearson came unannounced over the radio. "What the hell did you do to my holding tank?"

Shrader laughed out loud at the controlled anger in Pearson's voice. *He's got to be busting a gut holding back the four-letter words,* thought Marks. VHF signals are monitored, and Pearson was not about to announce to the Coast Guard that he was dumping sewage into Lake Ontario. Shrader laughed again as the radio went silent. After putting on his harness and snapping on a tether that would attach him to the boat, he settled in for a long night.

His senses began to sharpen, and he felt himself a small island of light in a dark sea. Ahead of him a quarter of a mile was *Mewtiny*, and beyond her was another in a long string that headed off into the darkness that opened up before them and wrapped around them as they passed. The eight boats were spread out over four miles, and Shrader felt a curious sense of peace come over him as the journey began. Beneath his harness, beneath his windbreaker and two wool sweaters, he felt the killer whale effigy that he wore around his neck. Suddenly, he knew that he was not alone.

"Who are you?" he called out to no one.

"Who are you?" came the unexpected reply. The peace of a moment earlier was shattered as his heart raced. He felt the same sense of confusion as he did in the instant when he heard words in the call of a gull. The voice came to him again, "Who are you, *Whaleman?*" Shrader's hand went to the whale effigy that hung around his neck.

29

"It's amazing! Just amazing," said Gus Gundersen as he hung up the phone.

"What's amazing?" asked Betty Montgomery.

"The way people respond to some words on a curly sheet of fax paper."

"Well, the fact that it comes from the Office of the President and specifically requires all federal, state, and local authorities to offer their full cooperation doesn't hurt," she added.

"And I thought it was my personal charm!" laughed Gus.

"Maybe more than you think," said Betty. "People around here trust your word. If I read anyone that fax over the phone, they'd want some proof that it was legit. You read it, and no questions asked."

"Well, I don't know about that," said a blushing Gundersen. "How are you doing on calling in the troops?" he added, changing the subject.

"I've been talking to several machines, but my guess is that they'll be here. They really aren't bad. Their hearts are in the right place."

"I know," agreed Gus. "I hired most of them, and I don't blame them for wanting to keep their families close by. I expect that some of them will take up my offer to bring them up to the vocational school for safekeeping."

"You're right about that. You were also right about calling Ray Anderson out of retirement. He jumped at the chance to help, and is going to manage the setup at the tech school and get it operating as a shelter. He also said that he'd round up some of the teaching staff to operate the shop equipment they have up there. He said that in three hours he'd have a maintenance facility that could rewind, rebuild, or fabricate anything that breaks down anywhere on the Seaway."

"He'll do it, too," said Gundersen. "That's something that I'd never thought about."

"What do you mean?"

"Just that we're geared up to keep locks operating, and not to give road service to a bunch of boats that don't know the waters. But, with the amount of traffic coming up the river, we'll have to keep a whole fleet moving along. It's obvious that we're supposed to get as many boats as we can into Ontario. My guess is that a lot of these crews have never traveled the Seaway, and we'll be improvising like crazy to get the majority of them through."

"Maybe not," added Betty. "If the Seaway Authority doesn't get onboard with the program, not many of those ships will reach the Snell."

"This will be the test of U.S.-Canadian cooperation. Four Canadian locks before you get to ours," observed Gus. "I can't imagine that the Montréal fleet hasn't been given the same orders as ours. Not to mention all the Canadian registry ships that will come in from the Maritimes."

"And I don't think that they're all going to be polite and say 'After you' when it comes time to enter the locks."

"Worse that that," continued Gundersen, "if Ottawa and Washington have to agree on a procedure for protocol, we'll be waiting until doomsday for the first ship."

"Do you suppose there's a Canadian version of Gus Gundersen?" quipped Montgomery.

"I've been told that I'm one of a kind," said Gus. "Usually, I'm told that just after the person has read off my pedigree. Still, what could it hurt if I just ran up the president's phone bill by calling a few of the lockmasters? By the time the pols figure it out, we'll have the job half done."

"Only half?" said Betty with a smile.

30

Whatever pyrotechnics may have been exploding in the atmosphere over Antarctica, the skies over Lake Ontario didn't whisper a hint of the secret. The black night was etched with crystal stars from the far horizon to the dome overhead. Shrader had just returned to the helm after his tenth trip below deck to check with the fleet. It was now 3:00 a.m., and the twenty-eight miles that *Strider* had traveled did more to invigorate him than to tire him. Earlier, the lights of Oswego, New York had been clearly visible off his starboard quarter, but now even their aura had disappeared, and Shrader was surrounded by water and sky. If he had wanted, he could have seen his closer partners in the flotilla, but they had become points of light no brighter than the stars and seemed to crawl along at the same slow pace as the rotation of the night sky.

After months of wishing for sleep, Shrader welcomed the alertness of his senses. He locked the wheel and stepped below. This time, it was not to call on the VHF radio, but to turn off his navigation lights. He rationalized the action with the belief that he was saving battery power. In point of fact, however, he wanted to rid his eyes of the night blindness that came from his running lights and reflections off the huge genoa sail. He poured a mug of coffee from his steel thermos. The steaming liquid was sweeter than he liked, but the sugar was a gift to his metabolism against the chill of the air. At the wheel he began to hum a tune which had unconsciously come to mind. It cycled through his brain a few times before he remembered it as a round. It was the Tallis' Canon, and snatches of words came to him like a lullaby from childhood. "Keep me, O keep me, King of Kings, beneath thine own almighty wings."

Now where did that come from? he asked himself.

You mean you don't remember? said a voice from within. He stretched his mind, but came up empty.

"I don't remember," he said at last.

It was when we had fallen into the place beyond words, and knew that no one would reach us unless the sky had hands.

"I do remember that place," said Shrader. He realized that he was talking to himself or at least to a part of himself that was more present to his own past than he allowed himself to be.

That was when we became shaman.

"Why do you keep saying that? I am not a shaman."

You're not? What are you then?

"I am a lot of things, but not that! I'm an academician. I'm an anthropologist. I'm a lousy husband."

And your dreams invade your waking life, you wear a stone orca around your neck, and you sing to the night!

"But what does that have to do with anything?" His question trailed off and was lost in the rhythmic sounds of the water against the hull. Throughout his career, he had studied primitive cultures with what he considered scientific detachment. He could recite the functions of a shaman/priest. He knew hundreds of Native American stories and the visions of trance dancers, but that learning was safe. It was always outside of himself in the form of answers on an essay test or the subject of a thesis. Now he was becoming aware of his own dreams, and safe detachment was not an option.

"But what if I don't want to be a damn shaman? What if it's not something that I would chose? Who in their right mind would choose such a thing?" he asked himself.

It isn't something that anyone would choose, is it? It's just something that happens to you. Do you think any of the ancients put up a sign outside their hovel announcing office hours and fee schedules?

"I know that! But they also knew or sensed what needed to happen and people took their word."

Shrader, look over the water! How many boats do you see? His eyes scanned the horizon ahead of him. Among the stars, he could see the glowing sails of *Mewtiny* and *Dream Dancer*. Beyond those were five others, and beyond the five, the universe stood out like the masthead lights of a billion sailing ships.

"That's an illusion," he called out. "They're following Cathy. She's the one they trust."

And she's following you. It's a very large circle. She leads the fleet. Her boat is in the front, but she follows your vision. Can you see that?

"Yes, I can see more than I want to admit. What I see makes me a stranger to myself, like I am on the edge of the world looking in."

That is because you are at the center of the circle. At the center, motion and stillness come together and are one. You are at the axis which never moves. They are in time, but stillness is eternity.

"Who are you?" asked Shrader. "I thought I was talking to myself, but I do not recognize your voice."

"You stand at the center, but you are not the center. When you stand at the axis of time, you are not alone."

"Who are you?" repeated Marks.

Who are you, Whaleman?

31

The voyage aboard *Affinity* began in relative silence, but not in peace. Phil Pearson was clearly building up a head of steam, and Cathy was just staying clear in the event of the explosion that was bound to come. Once out of the bay, Cathy went up on deck to remove the cover from the mainsail, a job that was routinely handled by her daughter.

"Where the hell is Brittany?" remarked Phil.

"She's helping the Romigs aboard *Mewtiny*. They are new to that boat and have never night-sailed. Shrader and I thought that an extra hand might help a lot."

"What about our boat? Did you give any thought to that?" snapped Pearson.

"We can sail this thing by ourselves without any problem. Besides, we've got the boys if we get in a pinch."

"Then let them get the sails ready. Justin, Christopher," he said to his sons, "get up on deck and get the sails ready." Turning back to Cathy, he said, "you get down here in the cockpit and get ready to hoist the main."

Cathy thought it better not to protest. She knew she could not win an argument when Phil was in one of his moods. At least, he would never acknowledge her reasoning and would make her pay dearly for the right to an opinion. Some battles were not worth it. This was one of them. She looked at Chris and Justin. They exchanged knowing glances as the twelve-year-old and the ten-year-old scrambled up on deck to prepare the mainsail.

"Don't be stupid like your mother," said Phil to the boys. "Get your life jackets on. We don't sail at night without PFD's." The boys slipped their bulky orange life vests on over their heavy parkas. A plastic whistle dangled from the foam-filled pouches on the front of the vest. "Remember the rules," continued Phil. "If you go overboard, blow the whistles. We might not be able to see you, so we'll have to find you by sound." To Cathy he said, "You'd be a better example to them if you had on a PFD." She stared at him behind the wheel. He wasn't wearing one. "You got some kind of problem?" he asked.

"No," said Cathy as she rose to her feet, stepped over the companionway, and down into the cabin. Once below, she walked forward to the hanging locker where the safety equipment was stowed. She opened the cabinet door and stooped down to rummage through the closet's contents. The open door shielded her from the view of cockpit. She felt tears rushing down her cheeks. *It doesn't matter,* she said to herself. *He can't hurt me anymore.* She knew that was a lie.

Cathy pulled off her gloves and wiped her cheeks with her hands. The base of the cabinet was stacked with a half-dozen of the clumsy, orange utility lifejackets, but she was looking for something else. At the bottom of the locker she found them, a pair of safety harnesses. They would be more comfortable than the PFD's, and it gave her some small satisfaction not to do exactly what her husband had ordered. She stood, and slipped her arms through the webbed straps of the harness. She clipped a six-foot tether to the stainless steel buckle in the center of her chest. Scooping up the second harness and tether, she returned to the cockpit where Phil was turning the boat to face the wind.

"I thought you might want one of these, too," she said, tossing the harness onto the cockpit seat next to where he was standing. Cathy clipped the snap-hook at the end of her safety tether to the recessed cleat in the cockpit coaming.

"Not now," said Phil. "I need you to hoist the main." Cathy knew the procedure. She put three turns of the main halyard around the winch and looked up to the top of the mast to get a view of the lighted wind vane. As the boat circled into the wind, the indicator pointed straight ahead.

"Boys, you'd better come down here," she said softly, "just in case the boom starts swinging. Sit down and just scootch along on your bottoms. That'll be safer," she added. Chris and Justin slid along the cabin trunk and down into the cockpit. Cathy loosened the mainsheet and began pulling in the halyard. Briskly, the mainsail rose up the mast. The aluminum boom along the sail's lower edge began to swing as the sail fluttered in the wind. The sound of the flapping Dacron was deafening. With the sail at its highest point, Cathy cleated the halyard, and Phil turned the boat to starboard, and out of the wind. The fluttering stopped as wind filled the sail. The boom swung out over the starboard side of the boat. Cathy allowed it to swing widely as the boat came around to a run. She secured the main sheet, and the strength of the wind seemed to die as the boat picked up speed. In point of fact, the wind maintained a steady pace, but the wind relative to the boat lessened as *Affinity* moved along in the same direction.

"At least we won't have to deal with much of a wind chill," she observed.

"Ready on the jib?" said Philip. Cathy looked at him for a moment. She knew he was giving her the command to unfurl the front sail.

"Do you think we need to fly the jib?" she asked. "We'll be fairly close to a run all night. With the wind behind us like that, the main sail will just blanket the wind and the jib will be useless. Besides, we've got enough wind to make six knots easily."

"It's not the crew's place to question orders," commented Pearson. "Ready on the jib?"

Cathy uncleated the furling line and wrapped the starboard jib sheet around the winch. "Ready," she said.

"Hoist the jib," commanded Pearson. Cathy pulled the sheet, and the head sail began to roll out. Suddenly, halfway out, the sail shuddered and stuck.

"Damn! Can't you do anything right?" he said. Cathy ignored his comment as she tried to determine the problem. In an instant she saw that the furling line had kinked up in the turning block, preventing the sail from opening fully. She grabbed the bitter end of the line and yanked. The tight bend in the rope snapped clear and the line ran out. With it, the jib opened and billowed free. Quickly, she sheeted in the sail.

"You're going to have to do better than that, Commodore," he remarked. The jib began to luff. The main sail was blocking the wind from reaching it. "There must have been a wind shift," observed Philip. He steered the boat to port to catch a little wind.

Glancing at the compass, Cathy recognized the course heading. If they maintained their current heading, *Affinity* would be heading for Prince Edward Bay, thirty-five miles to the west of the rendezvous point.

"That wind shift is going to cause us trouble," said an unflinching Philip. "Better prepare to furl the jib."

"Isn't that what I said in the first place?" she muttered under her breath. "You're going to have to do better than that, Captain." The words had no sooner come out of her mouth than she wished she'd bit her tongue. Her husband glared at her with fire in his eyes.

"Is *this* what comes of letting you hang around with Marks?" he said.

"Shrader has nothing to do with it. You can be a jerk without his help."

"And you can be put in your place very easily."

Cathy looked around and caught the wide-eyed stares of Justin and Chris who hovered in the corner of the cockpit. She had always tried to shield the children from the disputes and temper tantrums that characterized her marriage with Philip. She always suspected that they sensed them. "Hey, boys," she said, trying to steady her voice. "The water is pretty smooth tonight. It won't be bad to go down below and take a nap. In fact, I'm going to go to bed pretty soon, too. We're going to be sailing all night, and I need to rest while your Dad sails. In the middle of the night, I'll take a turn while he sleeps."

"Can I get up when you do, Mom?" asked Justin.

"We'll see," said Cathy smiling warmly at her ten-year-old. "Right now, you both need to brush your teeth and get out your sleeping bags." The two scrambled below and Cathy watched them go straight to their tasks of recovering their dark green mummy-bags from the stowage locker in front of the main cabin bulkhead. "They are such good kids," she observed.

"If you'll take the wheel, I'll pull in the jib," said Philip whose tone had softened.

"I can do it," offered Cathy.

"No," he said. "I also want to go below to use the head before you and the guys settle in for a few hours."

Cathy took hold of the wheel and slid around behind it as Phil moved forward to take position for pulling in the jib.

"Bring us around to the correct heading," ordered Philip. "That should take the wind out of the sail." Cathy slowly turned the wheel clockwise, then straightened it out when the compass started to respond. Her husband released the jib sheet, and the sail hung loosely from the wire forestay. He braced himself in the cockpit and began to pull hard on the furling line. The front edge of the sail began to rotate causing the sail to wind in on itself. When completely furled, Phil cleated and coiled the long line. "I'll be right back," he said as he stood and prepared to go below. "Did you check the holding tank before we started?" He did not wait for an answer before stepping down into the cabin. Cathy could see him lifting the cushions over the settee berth where the holding tank had been housed. She braced herself as he looked beneath. Instead of a waste holding tank, he found rows of neatly labeled canned goods.

"What the hell!" he cried out. "Cathy, there's no holding tank! Explain! And it better be good!"

"Shrader set up a direct discharge so that we could reclaim the storage space."

"That bastard! He never quits, does he? When we get back on Monday, he'll pay to make this right!" He stepped back up into the cockpit and grabbed the handheld VHF radio that was clipped in front of the wheel on the binnacle.

"What are you doing?" asked Cathy grabbing at the transmitter.

"I am going to give your boyfriend a piece of my mind," he said.

"Don't be stupid. You've got at least seven boats, and who knows who else, monitoring that frequency. Control your temper. Shrader was only trying to maximize our supplies."

"I'll maximize his ass," he quipped hotly, as he depressed the transmission button on the handheld. "Shrader, where do you get off messing with my boat?"

32

"Are you feeling any better?" asked Marty Koenig.

"Yes," said Roland. "The nitro seems to be working."

"This whole thing is just too much stress for you," observed his wife. "I still think that we should call Cathy and tell her that we're going to have to turn back."

"No, let's wait until morning. If the trip goes well, then we'll stick with it."

"But give me this, at least," pleaded Marty. "Let me take a three hour watch to your two hours. You've got to take care of yourself."

"Okay, I'll give you that," said Roland with a smile. "And thanks." The boat became as silent as the night that wrapped around them.

"Rollie, what are we going to do?" she asked, breaking the stillness.

"We're going to have a beautiful night sail, motor up the river, and lock through the Iroquois and into Lake St. Lawrence."

"You know that's not what I meant!"

"I know," said Roland. "I just don't have a good answer. If this asteroid situation fizzles, we'll sail back and, when the angina gets severe enough, I'll have a bypass. We both know that more angioplasty is out of the question."

"And if the dire predictions are true?"

"What a way to go!"

"Rollie, be serious. You're hiding behind a flip answer."

"Maybe there are no better answers on this one, Marty," he said in a muted voice. "As wild as this plan is, I prefer it to sitting at home. This morning when Marks and Romig were talking, my mind was going a mile a minute. Can you imagine what will really happen if the ocean levels rise like they predict?"

"No, but I'd guess you have an answer." She smiled and settled back to hear what she knew would be a full-blown presentation by a former VP for market research. Her body language was not wasted on her husband.

"Okay," he said. "I'm shifting into corporate mode. They can retire me early, but they can't put my brain out to pasture! Anyway, I remembered a project that we worked on some time ago. We were asked to develop a strategy for reaching new markets in emerging countries where there would be a real distrust of multi-nationals and U.S.-based corporations. There were no real innovations in the plan except the naming of the regional units. We recommended subsidiaries that had the word *Coastal* in their name. The idea was blasted, but there's real merit." Marty smiled as she watched her husband of forty years grow more animated in his speech.

"Just think," he continued. "The word has an equivalent in every language. If base offices are first established in coastal cities, the word in the title has a distinctly local sound to it. Branch offices in the interior of the country would not seem like a foreign intrusion by the population. Like I said, it was a good strategy, but some lackluster from headquarters made a big joke about the people in Denver thinking that the Californians were invading their ski slopes. The idea got lost in the laughter, even though we pointed out that more than sixty percent of the world's population lived within thirty-seven miles of a coast."

"More than sixty percent?" repeated Marty.

"Now do you see why think we shouldn't discount Shrader's wacky dreams?" said Roland. "If things go as badly as they're predicting, I would guess that bypass surgery for an over-the-hill executive would be considered a luxury. So the way that I look at it is that it's better to be doing something other than sitting at home and letting it take both of us a little at a time."

The two sat silently staring into the dark night. The sounds of the water were accompanied by small clicks and whirs from the autopilot as it sensed changes in the boat's heading and rotated the wheel to correct the course.

"Ahoy, on *Rol's Royce!*" came a voice over the water. Rollie and Marty turned in the direction of the cry and saw the ghostly shape of *Dream Dancer* moving up behind them on the starboard quarter. Standing in the cockpit was a large silhouette which was unmistakably that of Vince Ragni. The two waved back.

"He looks like he's having fun," observed Marty.

"That's Vince," agreed her husband.

"I guess we haven't been keeping a very close watch if he could overtake us without our noticing," she said. "One of us should be trying to sleep anyway. How about if you go below and sleep for a few hours?"

"Give me the difficult job, why don't you!" said Rollie with a wink. "I know I have some chest pain, but there's another part of me that feels like the youngest child at Passover."

"And what do you think will be the prize for finding the afikomen, little boy?" said Marty playfully.

"Guess I'm willing to be surprised," he answered. "But, if the world is going to end, I'd just as soon be with you here on the boat as in a cardiac care unit somewhere."

"What about Jeffrey and Carol?" she asked after a pensive moment.

"They've been on my mind all day," came the answer. "This has turned out to be a very different day than when we had breakfast at home. We were going to work on *Royce*, attend a party, and drive back home. Now, we're on the way out the Saint Lawrence. Jeff's going to think we've lost it completely. He needs to be told."

"He needs to be invited. Rollie, if this is true..." her voice trailed off.

"I know," he answered. "It's like running out of a house that's on fire. What do you try and save?"

"The children come first."

"I agree," said Roland. "I think we need to make a phone call." He flipped open his cell phone, but the signal was only one bar and that was shaky. "We're going to have to do this the old fashioned way," he said. He tuned his VHS radio to channel 25, depressed the switch on the handheld mike, and spoke slowly. "Marine operator, this is *Rol's Royce*, whiskey-bravo-echo, seven-five-two-five." The two waited in silence for a long minute before repeating the hail. This time it was answered.

"This is Rochester marine operator, KLU788, go ahead *Rol's Royce.*"

Roland again spoke into the microphone, "This is *Rol's Royce* calling 555-7654 in Watertown, New York. Over."

"Thank you, *Rol's Royce*," answered the operator. "How should this call be billed? Over."

"Make it a collect call to anyone at that number. My name is Roland Koenig. Over." The line went dead. "I guess that I could have used my credit card this time," he said over his shoulder to Marty. "What would it matter if someone eavesdropping on this frequency got hold of it?" Again, the night grew quiet as they waited. Finally, the marine operator's voice returned.

"*Rol's Royce*, this is Rochester marine operator. Your party is now on line."

"Dad?" came the confused sound of Jeffrey Koenig. "Dad, are you on the boat?"

Roland pushed the button on the microphone. "Yes, Jeff. Remember, I can't talk and receive at the same time, so give me a chance to answer between sentences. Over."

Jeff understood the request. "Where are you? What is going on? Over," he said.

"It's a long story. First, tell me what is happening with the comet. Over."

"There's no news. Evidently, tsunamis have been detected in both hemispheres, but earlier coverage shut down quickly after the thing hit. Over."

"Okay," said Rollie. "We're in a small group of boats on Lake Ontario. We have a plan for riding out this asteroid strike. Over."

"The predictions are pretty gruesome, Dad. Over."

"Then maybe you won't think that your mother and I are completely bonkers. How are Carol and the children? Over."

"They're scared. Hell, we're all scared. Over."

"Do this for me. Get your warmest clothes and meet us at Cape Vincent. We will be at the village dock just after sunrise. Over."

"What's going on, Dad? Over."

"Can't explain now. Just meet us in the morning. What do you have to lose? Over."

"I'll try," said Jeff. "Over."

Roland waited for a moment to swallow the lump that had formed in his throat. "Your mother and I love you all. This is *Rol's Royce*, whiskey-bravo-echo, seven-five-two-five. Out." He returned the microphone to its bracket. He looked at his wife. "The house is on fire," he said.

33

The size and shape of a wave are dependent on several factors. The speed and duration of the wind as well as the depth of the water play determining roles. Great Lakes' sailors see the results very easily. The waves on Lake Erie tend to be steep due to an average depth of only sixty-two feet. Ontario's waters are ten times deeper at their deepest point, and the waves spread out in longer patterns. Longer still are the wave troughs of the great oceans of the world.

Five hundred miles off the coast of Brazil the *Empress of Saxony* held her position in about sixty-five hundred feet of water. The captain, wary of sketchy marine reports, had elected to hold the tanker in position over the Brazil Basin rather than to head into the port city of Salvador. It was a strange day. The southern skies were dark with a heaviness that he couldn't explain, and the seas were flat.

"Maintain the current heading," he said as he stepped out of the pilot house and into the fresh air. From the railing he looked out over the water. "Damn," he thought. "There are no fucking waves here at all!" From the south he saw the crest of a small wave approaching with what seemed like lightning speed. It washed harmlessly against the stern of the *Empress*, and moved on in a single line that stretched beyond the twelve miles that his eyes could see from his vantage point. The seas again were flat, but the captain waited and watched until he could make out a second wave crest moving parallel to the first.

121

"Oh my God!" he said aloud. At last he understood what was happening. The seas were not calm. The wave crests were so far apart that the troughs were several miles wide. Here in the open sea, the waves tended to flatten out. In shallower waters, they would pile up to a great height. He burst back into the pilot house. "Get on the radio. Start broadcasting a warning to the coastal areas. It's a tsunami!"

34

Gus Gundersen stood on the parapet of the Eisenhower lock and gazed at the hint of dawn emerging on the eastern horizon. Wearing shirt sleeves against the breeze, he marveled at an April morning more like late spring than the usual lingering winter. "Well, what do you think, Ray?" he asked.

"It's the calm before the storm," answered Anderson as he looked over the railing and into the empty flight lock below. "In a normal winter we couldn't do this. Here it is, mid-April and who would have believed that we've been ice-free since February?"

"Somebody's watching out for us," agreed Gundersen. "But I've got to admit that I'd feel a lot better if we had some tonnage to boost up into Ontario."

"It's on the way," offered Ray. "The Canadians have started to work around the clock and they've got all four of the eastern locks in full operation. I don't know what you said to them, but they've even turned the whole damn system into a one-way street."

"It's really amazing what can be done *without* an act of Congress! And, for the most part I didn't have to yell," added Gus. "Of course, a couple hundred ships coming up the river and knocking at the gates of the Saint Lambert might have helped."

"I'll bet."

"There's also plenty of water in the system to run the locks one direction," continued Gundersen. "I don't care what the new superintendent of the Iroquois thinks."

"Is he still holding out?" asked Ray.

"Spineless mealyworm!" muttered Gundersen. "Ontario is three feet over chart levels and he's worried that opening the seaway to such heavy one-way traffic will take too much water. Says he won't agree to anything except normal traffic until he hears differently from Ottawa."

"Do you want me to try to convince him?"

"I don't think that it will be necessary. When we open the Eisenhower and begin pouring boats into Lake Saint Lawrence, I'm sure he'll get the message and speed up his operations. Besides, you're too important here."

"Hardly that," protested Anderson. "There's more help at the tech school than anyone would need. Guess there's nothing like a crisis to make good people pull together."

"Did you ever think it would end like this?" asked Gus.

"End? Do you really think that this is the end?"

"Who knows? Some people believe it is. I want to know how you thought it would happen."

"Well," answered Ray. "Never gave it much thought. It's like there's supposed to be a natural order to things. I never thought about the world ending. I figured that I'd be the one to end, and, well, the story would go on without my being a part of it."

The two companions stood quietly. Gus looked out toward the horizon. "When I was a boy growing up on the river, I thought that I'd understand everything when I got as old as my father. It seemed to me that he could fix anything. When he died, I knew that wasn't true. Did you know that I watched them build this lock?"

"You told me a few times," said Anderson with a smile.

"I guess I have, old friend," answered Gus. "But I didn't tell you about what I swore on my sacred oath. I've never told anyone that. Well, I told one person, but she's not here anymore." Ray turned to look squarely at his friend, but Gundersen continued to stare off at some unseen distance.

"This sounds serious. Are you sure you can trust me with this?" asked Anderson.

"It's a stupid thing," said Gus. "I was just a kid, twelve years old or something like that. Anyway, they had just poured the last footing for the Eisenhower. There were already rumors that the lock would be named for Ike, even though he was still president. I thought that was great. He was my hero. He was everybody's hero. My Dad fought in the European theater during the war, and all I heard about were Bradley and Ike. Anyway, I sneaked through the barricades and got down to the work site. It was the scariest thing that I'd ever done. They were working twenty-four hours a day and doing a continuous pour, so there were men everywhere. But I made it down and put my hand against some pilaster that's now underground and swore an oath of allegiance to the General Eisenhower."

"Even then you were pretty gutsy," commented Ray.

"Guts had nothing to do with it," retorted Gundersen. "It was one of those solemn oaths that we took when we were young and naïve. I thought that it was my duty to my country to move these great ships. Or maybe it was that I thought this lock was about the greatest thing I'd ever seen, and I'd be somebody if I could learn how it worked."

The two looked out at the lock with its massive concrete walls and huge water gates. "Do you know what the dumbest thing is?" continued Gundersen.

"No. What?"

"The longer I worked here, the more I realized how puny this lock really is. I mean, we can lift tankers ninety feet and dump them into Lake Saint Lawrence. Hell, we move nearly sixty million metric tons of cargo up and down the river each year, but it's nothing. We are entirely at the mercy of the water flowing downstream. The river just keeps flowing down through the locks just like she would if the locks weren't even here. When they built the big hydroelectric plant at Cornwall, everyone said that we had effectively harnessed the flow and power of the river. That's a real crock! The river just lets us cooperate around the edges. She's got all the power she ever had, and *the General* may have slowed her down, but if we opened all the water gates, you'd see that she's still there in full force."

"Well, I'd say that you kept your promise to the Eisenhower, Gus," remarked Anderson.

"I guess I did, even if it was a kinda childish loyalty," answered Gundersen. "I've also learned that I don't always see things right."

"What do you mean?"

"Just that it's easy to get distracted from what is important. I looked at all the concrete and the water gates and the monitors in the control room, and I nearly forgot that it was the river flowing quietly under and over and around every obstacle in the way that makes it all happen."

"Never thought of that," said Ray.

"When my wife died, it was the same. I thought that it would have been better if I'd crawled into the casket with her and just died, too."

"I remember," said Anderson. "You were in pretty rough shape."

"Then I got a call from a friend, from you. And I came here to the Eisenhower, driving up 131 along the river. It looked a lot like I remembered it as a kid, even before the locks were built. Some things don't change, even when something gets put in the way. I know that my love for Cassie didn't change, not even after she died. It was strange, but I felt close to her again that night. I've always wondered what would have happened if I hadn't been called out to work."

"Gus, you've become quite a philosopher in your old age."

"No," replied Gus. "It just takes me a long time to thank a friend."

35

Shrader sipped the last of his coffee from the stainless thermos that he had filled the night before. The sky around him was growing brighter. Already he could see the diminishing shadow of Galloo Island off his stern. He heard his VHF squawk, and Cathy spoke out clearly with no trace of fatigue.

"*Dream Dancer, Dream Dancer, Dream Dancer,* this is *Affinity.*" Shrader looked at his watch. It was 7:30.

"Everything is good here, *Affinity,*" came a halfhearted reply from a woman. Shrader guessed it was Rhonda Ragni.

"I wonder if she ever had second thoughts about marrying Vince because of the way her married name sounds," he said to himself. *Still, she's hanging in there.*

"I make our position to be just off Cape Vincent." It was Cathy's voice. "We are ready to pass through the channel by Wolfe Island. I don't think that we were passed in the night. Sodus fleet, please report."

One by one, the boats checked in and reported their relative positions. Last of all, Shrader locked his wheel and rushed to the cabin to call. He hailed *Affinity*. Cathy answered and her voice softened. "How are you doing, Shrader?" she asked.

"I'm tired like all the rest," he answered. "But not nearly as cold as I thought I'd be by now. We're lucky; the temperature has gotten warmer, if anything."

"I've got a report on that." An unidentified voice broke into their conversation.

"Who's there?" asked Cathy.

"This is Bert Jenkins on *Major Blunder*. I've been monitoring the single-side band radio and some military frequencies. It appears that the asteroid strike has triggered some volcanic activity along the Antarctic plate and up into the Pacific Rim."

"Thank you, Major," said Cathy. "Are there any more details, and can you continue monitoring?"

"There's a problem with that," answered Jenkins. "First reports were fast and furious. They talked about significant geothermal energy being released with planetary effects, but I haven't heard anything for the last half hour."

"Maybe there's just nothing new to report," offered Marks.

"No," Jenkins responded quickly. "The coded frequencies are buzzing. We just aren't able to eavesdrop."

"What does that mean?" asked Cathy.

"Just that things are being said that we're not supposed to hear," replied Bert. "My guess is that it's not good news, and the belief is that it would cause a general panic."

"Can you keep monitoring?" asked Pearson.

"I'll listen, but I don't think it will do much good," he answered.

"We need to have a powwow as soon as we make the Cape Vincent docks," announced Cathy. "How long before you can get there, Shrader?"

"I'd guess I'm about an hour-and-a-half behind you," answered Marks. "We need Romig there, too. Are you monitoring this, John?"

"I'm here, Shrader."

"Well, what do you make of it?"

"If we're being affected in the northern hemisphere, even a few degrees, the energy release must be massive. I can understand why the powers-that-be are worried about panic."

"What else can you tell us?" asked Cathy.

"Let me think about it, okay? This probably isn't the best forum. A little too public for speculation."

"Okay," agreed Cathy. "We will meet at the rendezvous point as soon as *Strider* can make port. This is *Affinity* standing by on channel 68."

Shrader returned the microphone to its bracket and paused to consider the conversation that had just passed. Suddenly, the sound of flapping sails pulled him back to reality. There was no one at the helm of his boat, and *Strider* had wandered off course. He scrambled up the companionway stairs and jumped to the wheel. A glance at the jib told him what had happened and the compass confirmed it. *Strider* had traveled in a great, counterclockwise arc and was trying to sail directly into the wind, an impossibility that set the Dacron sails fluttering uselessly. Quickly, he unlocked the wheel and turned the wheel to starboard, but the boat did not respond.

"Damn," said Shrader out loud. "What a time to go into irons." He knew that he could wait and hope that drifting in the wind would deliver enough forward momentum to give him back his steering, but he was growing impatient. He reached down to engage the engine's choke mechanism. He threw the contact switches and engaged the starter. The engine cranked, but it didn't catch. He worked the throttle and tried again. It was no good; the engine would not start.

"Shit!" Mentally, he took stock of the situation. Providing the wind held, there would be no problem sailing up the channel between Cape Vincent and Wolfe Island. Once around the point of the cape, he might have trouble making headway in the sheltered waters and docking under sail. With the wheel hard to starboard, the hull was beginning to turn and wind pushed out the foresail. Shrader watched his knotmeter as *Strider* picked up speed. The digital readout flashed the increasing forward motion. When it reached 5.5 knots, Shrader locked the wheel and went back to the radio.

"*Affinity, Affinity, Affinity*, this is *Strider*."

"Go ahead, *Strider*," said a man's voice. It was Phil Pearson.

"I've got a problem here, Phil," said Shrader in the most natural voice he could muster. "My engine won't start. I'll be coming into the docks under sail. Could you have someone stand by if I need a tow?"

"I always knew you were sailing a piece of junk," responded Philip. The message trailed off to garble.

"Are you okay?" it was Cathy.

"Yes, I'm fine. I got stuck in irons when we were on the radio earlier, and I tried to start the engine to catch back up. I can keep up with the fleet as long as the wind holds. It's docking that will be tricky."

"Any chance that you can get the engine going?" asked Cathy.

"Not without someone at the helm," said Marks. "The best bet is to work on it when we get to the docks."

"Who's near you?" asked Cathy.

"We can see *Strider*," offered another voice. It was Marty Koenig on *Rol's Royce*.

"Any ideas, Marty?" queried Pearson.

"Roland says we can drop off speed until we're close enough for me to board *Strider*. I could at least keep her on course while Shrader works on the engine."

"The water is pretty cold right now," warned Shrader. "I think it's too dangerous."

"That's why I volunteered," answered Marty. "My heart is better than Roland's. Besides, I've got a wet suit. We'll approach you under power so we'll be able to match your speed. Shouldn't be too big a risk at all."

"Sounds like you've thought it through, Marty," answered Cathy. "Shrader, prepare to be boarded."

"But...," protested Marks.

"You are the one who's in a hurry," chided Pearson. "We can't hang around Cape Vincent all day while you try to fix your engine. Do what you can while you're underway."

"We're closest to you, Shrader, and you're starting to wander again. Better get back to the wheel." When Marks emerged from his cabin, he knew that Marty was right. *Strider* had begun to swing around. This time he caught her in time to maintain her forward progress and correct the course. About a quarter of a mile off his port bow, he could see a boat turning into the wind to furl its jib.

So that's where you are, he said to himself. It was *Rol's Royce* taking down her sails and coming about to meet him. What had appeared as a miniature ship now grew as it approached. Marty was standing out on deck; her arm was looped around one of the shrouds leading up to the masthead. She called to him, but the words whistled off in the wind. Shrader shrugged his shoulders so that she would know that he hadn't heard.

The two boats were on a collision course, and Roland's hand was steady on the helm. When they were close enough for the sound to carry, Marty told Shrader her strategy.

"We'll come up behind you," she said. "You just maintain your heading and I'll board you on your port side."

Shrader nodded his understanding, and watched as Roland skillfully swung *Rol's Royce* to the right and rounded up behind his own boat. Marks glanced at the compass and the speed. He was making 6.2 knots in three-foot seas. Slowly the bow of the Koenigs' boat crept up on his position. He glanced to the left and saw the curling waters of the bow wave of the approaching boat.

Roland kept about eight feet between the boats until the beam of *Rol's Royce* was even with *Strider's* cockpit. Shrader was about to shout out a warning to Marty, who seemed poised to jump, when suddenly Roland rolled his boat to the left. The widest part of the boat seemed to lurch within a foot of *Strider's* lifelines, and then it headed off away toward open waters. Marty was standing in the cockpit with him. Marks' reaction bought a wide grin to her face.

"That was smooth," he said at last.

"Did you think that I was too old for this?" she asked.

"No, I didn't mean..." said Shrader, trying to recover.

"It's okay. I'm just teasing. The fact is Roland used to be a great racer, and I just think that he proved to himself that he can still handle a boat in close quarters. What's your guess about the engine?" she said, changing the subject.

"Well, I changed the points and plugs, so barring anything just plain breaking loose, my guess is that it's the spark coil. And I don't have a spare." He showed Marty the starter button and went below.

Shrader braced himself against the rolling action of the boat. He dreaded what would have to come next. Working on engines while at the dock was always a challenge. They were tucked away in the most inaccessible recesses of the boat. Under sail, the boat's motion was bound to catch him off balance. "I'll be a mass of bruises before this is over," he complained to Marty.

"Aren't you glad that I came over to help you?" she offered. He unlatched the catches that held the companionway ladder in place, and then lifted the backing panel out of place to open the access to a dimly lit cavern that extended back under the boat's cockpit. Lurking within was the golden brown cast-iron hulk of an old gasoline engine.

Shrader scrounged around for a small flashlight. He turned on the light and surveyed the wiring. Everything looked like it was in place. He reached over the engine block to feel for the distributor cap. It seemed solidly in position. "Crank the engine," he called to Marty. The starter engaged, but not a cough or sputter emerged from the motor itself.

Shrader signaled for Marty to lay off the starter. He pulled the cap off the closest spark plug, retrieved some insulated pliers from his tool kit, and held the tip of the plug wire next to the engine block.

"Try it again, Marty." The starter cranked, but no spark appeared. "Forget it," he called back. "Not much I can do down here." He replaced the plug wire and set the companionway steps back in place, sealing the engine compartment.

"Is it what you expected?" asked Koenig.

"Yes. It's the spark coil, and I don't have a replacement on board."

"Can you get hold of one in Cape Vincent?"

"That's the stupid thing. On a normal day, any auto parts store could supply one, but who knows what we're going to find when we get there? This old boat has a Delco ignition. I could have taken the coil out of my car and it would have worked. I can't make it up the Seaway to the Iroquois Lock without an engine. So, for the sake of a twenty dollar part I may have to leave *Strider* behind."

"There's got to be another way. Roland says there's always Plan-B."

"We could loot an auto parts store or pry open the hood of a parked car. We just don't want to get caught in the act. One thing for sure, we'll have a lot to do before we can leave *Strider* behind."

"And why is that?"

"This boat is one huge storage locker. Cathy and I have stowed away enough food and supplies to keep the fleet alive for six months, maybe a year."

"Food? What else?" asked Marty.

"A little bit of everything. Arrows, fishing tackle, tools, canned goods, even medicine. We haven't really told everything to the other captains. Cathy and I have been planning this since before the asteroid strike was announced."

"Before? How did you know?"

"It's a long story and when I say it out loud, it sounds even crazier. We just knew that something catastrophic was taking place. When the announcement came, we thought maybe we'd been given a chance. For some unknown reason, we were."

Marty looked over across the water where Roland was motoring alongside in *Rol's Royce*. "Do you have any nitroglycerin among your medical supplies?"

"What?" asked Shrader.

"Over there," said Marty, gesturing toward her husband. "Look at him. Roland thinks that we've been given a chance, too. He has heart disease, but he thinks that we should be here, and doesn't he look grand?" A tear ran down her cheek. "In my eyes, he looks like the young man I married. He's strong and handsome and dying!"

"I'm sorry," offered Shrader.

"Don't be. He's not," she replied. "I think that he believes in you, Shrader, even though you don't yet believe in yourself."

"What?"

"He's a marvelous man," she said. "You hear women complain about their husbands, but mine is my best friend. I can't say that I always understand him, but his instincts are pretty good. He thinks that it's better to be here with you than in a cardiac unit somewhere else. He's a man with a nose for life, and he's casting his lot with you and Cathy."

"But I didn't ask him for anything," protested Marks.

"Of course you didn't," said Koenig. "You can't ask a person to trust you. They either will or they won't. He trusts you, and you're stuck with it."

"And the man he trusts is going to limp into harbor on a piece of junk, as Phil Pearson thinks of it."

"Maybe not," said Marty.

"What do you mean?" asked Shrader. "Do you have a spark coil?"

"Maybe," she said cryptically. "Do you have room for a few passengers?"

"I guess so. If you ask Cathy, she'd say I shouldn't be out here alone anyway. I could take on passengers. What do you have in mind?"

"Roland and I made a ship-to-shore call last night. We hope that our son and his wife and children will be meeting us at Cape Vincent this morning. I'll trade you a couple of berths on *Strider* for the spark coil out of their car."

"You trust me that much?"

"Yes, Shrader, we're betting our lives on it."

36

Shrader reported his findings to Cathy on board *Affinity*. She, in turn, sent word to the other boats that they were to dock along the breakwater at the town docks. "If there's a problem," she warned, "the Anchor Marina is just down river beyond the state fishery. They probably won't have their docks set up this early in the season, but the waters are sheltered there and we can improvise something. *Strider* has had some engine problems, and will be approaching under sail. So, leave an open approach to the dock, use a lot of fenders, and stand by to help him in."

Cathy dispatched Bert Jenkins on *Major Blunder* to scout out the Anchor Marina. "Bert," she added. "We're going to have to get Shrader's engine running, but it'll have to be done quickly. If we can't, we'll have to transfer all his stores to the other boats, but I'm afraid that time will be working against us. It's nearly 8:00 and the sun will set tonight about 6:30 so we have maybe ten-and-a-half hours to get to the Iroquois if we expect to lock through today. That's seventy-five miles, and at flat-out speeds, it'll take every minute to get there."

"Sounds like it's pointless to put in at Cape Vincent," answered Jenkins, "at least, for the majority of the boats."

"Agreed," said Cathy. "By the time everyone's docked, we'll have lost a couple of hours. Here's what we'll do. A few of the longer boats can stop to help Shrader. They have faster hull speeds and will be able to catch up. You'll take the others on ahead."

"Sounds like I just volunteered to lead the advance party, Admiral," said Bert.

"If you please, Major Jenkins," said Cathy, with a hint of softness creeping back in her voice.

"Not a problem," he answered. "I think it's a reasonable solution. What sort of window do you think we're looking at in terms of getting *Strider* up and running?"

"I'll give him half an hour. But if we let everyone land, it'll just create confusion and take too much time."

"You're probably right. What would it take to convince him to skip the repairs and just transfer over to another craft?"

"At this point, I don't think that would be possible, and it won't be necessary if he has the correct diagnosis of the problem. Besides, Marty and Roland are sending in the cavalry to the rescue."

"What?" asked a confused Jenkins.

"We're all hoping that the spark coil out of their son's car will solve the problem. He's to meet them at the village docks."

"Understood," responded Bert. "Tell me who's going to be in your squadron. I'll round up the rest and begin heading down river."

"Phil and I will be here on *Affinity*. *Rol's Royce* is already involved, so I think just one more. What about the Barkers on *Fairwinds*?"

"Sounds good," agreed Jenkins. "Do you have a rendezvous point in mind?"

"Look at your Seaway charts," said Cathy. "On the south side of Galop Island, there's a place called Red Mills. It's on the U.S. side of the river just opposite Cardinal."

"Okay, I've found it," said Jenkins.

"The lock is only five miles beyond that point," continued Cathy. "According to my directory, it's only open seasonally so there may not even be a place to dock, but it looks like there's an inlet just to the east."

"I see it," answered Bert. "That's where we'll head. But I'm not moving on through the lock without you."

"I don't think you'll have to worry about that. *Fairwinds* and *Affinity* are the longest boats in the fleet and we should be able to average a knot-and-a-half faster than most of your boats. I'll probably catch you at about eight hours into the voyage."

"You have everything figured out, don't you?" said Jenkins with admiration in his voice.

Philip was at the helm of *Affinity* as Cathy spoke through the cockpit radio. He laughed at Jenkins' remark. "Wait until they start calling you *Admiral Screw-up*, and I have to bail your ass out of trouble."

Cathy winced, and was glad that she had not yet depressed the transmission button on the VHF. "Thank you, Major," she said, controlling the hurt in her voice. "It'll take a team effort from all of us. My worry right now is getting Shrader to the rendezvous point. *Strider* is a thirty-footer and probably the poorest performer under power. If she can average better than six knots, I'd be surprised."

There was a pause while Major Jenkins did a quick calculation. "He doesn't have enough time to make the Iroquois before dark then. Can you convince him to just leave the boat at Cape Vincent and forget the repairs?"

"Are you listening, Shrader?" said Cathy in the next exchange. "I wish that I could, Bert, but he won't be budged by my logic. He says that *Strider* will be there on time, and who am I to say? He senses a lot of truth that I don't."

"I won't pretend to understand that last comment, Admiral," offered Bert. "But as far as I'm concerned, you're in charge, and I will meet you at Red Mills, if you don't catch up to us sooner. This is *Major Blunder* continuing to monitor channel 68, out."

"Thank you, Major. This is *Affinity* monitoring channel 68, out."

"At least I'll have the satisfaction of leaving your boyfriend behind," mocked Phil. "Maybe someone will be willing to pick up his pieces on the way back tomorrow; then again, maybe not. By the time we're on our way back from this wild goose chase, your names will be mud. Maybe I'll give you to him as a present, a loser for a loser."

Cathy felt the pain that she had swallowed for years gathering in the pit of her stomach. She gave him the most disdaining look that she could, then quickly turned away and headed below into the cabin. She didn't want him to see her cry. "I have to check on the boys," she said.

The teak interior of *Affinity* was still in twilight. Chris and Justin were asleep in their settee berths. Lee cloths were stretched the length of the bunks to keep them from rolling out with the boat's movement. Cathy smiled as she watched them breathe slowly and deeply. She wanted to reach out to them, but feared that they'd awaken at her touch. Walking aft, she entered the rear cabin and crawled under the thick comforter of its double berth. She shivered at the coldness of the blankets, but as her body warmed the insulated fabric, her mind wandered off into an unexpected sleep.

37

"Shrader, you have to be careful. Philip is looking for a fight. Don't give him any opportunity."

"I won't," whispered Marks as he pressed himself closer to Cathy. Their naked bodies intertwined warmly beneath the coverlet, defying the chill in the air that showed their breath whitely. He kissed her gently on the cheek, and she turned to meet his mouth. His hands explored the smoothness of her flesh, and hers, the contour of his chest.

"Shrader, we're rounding the point." The voice was that of Marty Koenig. "I think that you ought to be at the helm if we're docking under sail," she said. "You know how she handles."

"Sure," answered a dazed Marks. It was a new dream, troubling in its own way, but one from which he did not wish to awaken. He looked at the cluttered cabin of his boat. His tool box lay open in front of the gaping cavern of the engine compartment. The dead spark coil rolled in the sink with the movement of the boat. Shrader threw off the blanket that he had pulled around himself. In an instant, he lost the envelope of warmth that had made him forget the reality of waking life. He had removed the companionway ladder to gain access to the engine; now he had to use his upper body strength to pull himself up to the cockpit. He stepped from the rear quarter berth to the rim of the galley sink, then out into the morning air. He scanned ahead of the boat.

"We're further in than I thought," he observed as he scrambled to take the wheel.

"You must have been sound asleep," remarked Marty. "I called you several times."

"Yeah," agreed Marks. "I didn't realize how tired I was. What are we looking at?" Neither one of them had ever docked at Cape Vincent, but they had copies of the marine charts that identified the buildings along the shore.

"On the left is the break wall. There," she said pointing, "it's flashing red." Shrader's eyes followed the direction that she indicated. "Over there," her arm flailed 180 degrees, "is the restaurant that's shown on the chart, and when we round it, we should be able to see the ramp and the village docks beyond."

They followed the path of *Rol's Royce* which was now ahead of them. Roland had already furled the jib and was under diesel power. They watched as the other boat took a broad swing to starboard and disappeared behind the shore structures. They held their course. Slowly the view opened as they passed the obstructions to their sightlines. Masts came into view, three of them. At the dock, *Affinity* and *Fairwinds* were secured. Their crews were on the walkway signaling to Roland to stay out and away from the dock.

"They're having *Rol's Royce* hang back in case we need a quick tow to keep us off the shore," said Shrader. "It looks like we will need all the fenders on the starboard side, Marty." Without further instruction, she went up on deck and moved all the inflated, white bumpers to the right side of the boat to cushion the fiberglass hull from impact with the dock.

Shrader uncleated the jib sheet and held the line tightly in his hand. The plan was simple. He would sail toward the dock until he judged that he had enough forward thrust to drift into place. Then he would let go of the jib sheet allowing the sail to fly free like a flag. With the wind out of the sail, the boat would begin to slow against the friction of the water. The danger was to misjudge the boat's momentum. Too little and the boat would stop dead in the water, too far away from the dock to toss a line. In that case, the sail would have to be sheeted in to circle around, or *Rol's Royce* would have to have a towline ready. If the boat drifted into the dock with too much force, it would be up to the shore crew to fend off a nine thousand pound impact. Shrader had confidence in his knowledge of *Strider's* handling characteristics. He held the line that controlled the jib. His speed was a steady five knots. Patiently he watched and waited as the boat moved ahead, closer and closer to the dock. *Fairwinds* was the closest of the boats. Suddenly, a picture loomed in his mind. It was a boat careening through a concrete canyon. He heard the rending of fiberglass. It was *Fairwinds*.

"Shrader, pay attention!" called Marty. Quickly he released the jib sheet, but he was closer to the dock than he would have chosen. Shrader watched the speed fall off, four knots, three, two-and-a-half. Experience told him that a collision at even one knot could tear a significant gash in the hull. A gust of wind brushed his cheek.

"Somebody is watching out for us," he said aloud. The strong gust started to push the boat sideways. He turned into the wind to counter the effects. Hands grabbed at the lifelines, but the boat was at a dead stop when Marty handed the bow line to Cathy.

"You made that look easy," said a tall man in his mid-thirties. Shrader looked at the stranger for a moment. He was a younger, thinner Roland Koenig.

"Jeffrey," called Marty. She was on the dock before Shrader could hand the stern line to a very quiet Philip Pearson. It was a silent moment that Marks was not willing to break. His eyes went back to the family reunion and two small children waving to a grandfather who was circling in *Rol's Royce*.

"Okay, everyone," called Cathy. "How about we help Roland get over here to hug his grandchildren?" A sudden outbreak of sanity sent the people scurrying to dock another boat. Cathy stepped aside as they took to the task. She boarded *Strider* and stepped toward Shrader.

"Had any interesting dreams lately?" she asked. Marks blushed at her question. "I know," she continued. "I think we're having the same dreams again." Shrader started to protest, but it was no good. "You'll need this," she said, offering him a black spark coil. "It's off Jeff Koenig's car. They seem as nice as his parents."

"Thanks," said Shrader, who was glad to have the subject changed. "It won't be long before we'll know if this will work."

"I want to move some of the stores off your boat. We'll pass them up the front hatch so that we won't be in your way."

"Cathy," he said in a serious tone that stopped her short. "Don't put anything on *Fairwinds*."

"Why not?" she asked.

"They aren't going to make it," was all he would say. "At least the boat won't make it," he added after a pause. Cathy nodded. She didn't understand Shrader, but she trusted him. By now, *Rol's Royce* was securely at the dock. When Roland killed the engine, the only noise left was the sound of *Strider*'s jib flapping uselessly in the wind.

"Better furl your genoa before you get some wind damage, Mister," said Cathy with a smile.

"Aye, aye," snapped Shrader.

Cathy quickly stepped over the rail and on to the dock. She turned back suddenly. "You know, it was good advice. You need to steer clear of Philip."

38

"Try it now," called Shrader from down in the cabin. Cathy pushed the starter button and the engine erupted in a full roar. Everyone on the docks burst into cheers.

"Less than twenty minutes, too," observed Cathy looking at her watch.

"I still have to straighten up a few things down here," answered Marks. "Cut the engine, would you? I don't want the boat full of fumes."

"Still, I'm worried about your making it to the Iroquois before dark." Cathy was pleading her case in a losing battle, and she knew it.

"Stop worrying," remarked Shrader. "Maybe I'm starting to trust these intuitions, but I know that I'll be there on time. I just don't have any logical argument to explain how. Speaking of wasting time," he mused, "didn't you want to transfer some of the stores to the other boats?"

"Changed my mind! It's a woman's prerogative." She smiled broadly as Shrader met her gaze.

"It's good to hear you joking again," he said. "It's been a long night, and the burden seems to have shifted your way."

"It's been fine," she said, shrugging off his comment. "I don't think we could have hoped for anything better. Still, I wish we could have had our little meeting here this morning. I'd like to know what John Romig makes of this weather. Look at them."

Shrader took a tentative step up the companionway ladder which he had just set into place. It held, so he stepped up high enough to peer over the cockpit coaming. He looked over at the Barkers aboard *Fairwinds*. "What about them?" he asked.

"They're wearing light jackets. Unzipped, at that." Ashley Barker who was twelve was trying to corral her seven-year-old brother, Aaron, who was trying to escape from nine-year-old Kelly. "This is not April weather."

"Maybe we shouldn't complain about the gifts we're given," observed Shrader. "There have been warm spells before. And you still haven't told me why you changed your mind about transferring some of the supplies to other boats."

"Not much point in it, is there? You told me that *Fairwinds* isn't safe. That leaves my boat, which already has the other half of the supplies, and *Rol's Royce*, which is taking on at least three passengers and their gear. I figure we might just as well go on and save the time."

"I tell you, time isn't a problem. At least it doesn't feel like there's anything to worry about in that department. I want to scout around here before we shove off."

"Shrader, what if you're wrong?"

"It wouldn't be the first time, but I'm not wrong about this. Just give me thirty minutes."

"No more," relented Cathy.

"Better yet, get the other boats on the way. I'll catch up to you at Red Mills, that's where you told Jenkins that we'd meet."

"But I want someone with you during this leg of the trip. Jeff Koenig has agreed to help you with the steering today."

"He needs to be with his family, and I need to be alone."

"You've been awake all night, and you have a full day ahead. You have to take Jeff with you." Without realizing it, their voices had raised enough to draw the stares of the Barker children on *Fairwinds*. Jim and Tish Barker even turned to look, perhaps more at the sudden silence of their kids, rather than directly hearing Shrader and Cathy.

"Come down here," ordered Shrader indicating the interior of *Strider's* cabin. The two stepped below. "Listen," he said with an intensity that showed the depths of his conviction, rather than a trace of anger. "There are some things that I can't explain. Two weeks ago I thought I was crazy. Yesterday, a bird told me that the asteroid had struck the planet. Today, everyone is worried about the time, but I say it's not a problem. I think that you are the most marvelous person that I have ever met. In twenty-four hours you have won the trust of this whole fleet. This is my promise to you, Cathy Pearson. I will never say 'yes' to you when I know that the answer is 'no', and I will never let you move ahead if the way feels unsafe. I will be the one who will cause you all the trouble, because I will never follow you blindly." Cathy began to speak. "No, let me finish," he said. "I will, however, be the best friend that you could ever have, and I will love you." His last words surprised even Shrader. Cathy searched his face, and knew that he spoke the truth. She clutched at him, and he put his arms around her.

"Thank you, Shrader. I'm so scared. I'm afraid that I'll do something stupid and really things up. I didn't choose to be in charge."

"None of us chose this," agreed Shrader. "But we're here. Before it's all over, we will both need a friend."

The kiss that followed seemed natural, and did not spring from a conscious decision. The fact that it lingered stunned their senses. They began to weep with release and lift with joy at a passion that had lain dormant for so long.

"I'm glad that I am dreaming with you again," said Cathy as she pressed close to him. "When I woke up, I didn't feel so alone."

"It did seem real," said Shrader, "and very nice."

"Okay," said Cathy, composing herself. "My friend is not going to agree with me. Just what does the *Whaleman* propose?"

"Why did you just call me that?"

"Call you what? *Whaleman*? I don't know. Maybe it's the effigy, or remembering the dreams. Does it matter?"

"No, I guess not. It's just that, last night, in the dark, something or someone else called me that, and it's a bit troubling."

"I'm sorry, then," apologized Cathy.

"No, it's okay. It isn't what you said, it's the fact that it may be true. I am the *Whaleman*, I just hadn't named myself yet." His hand touched the orca effigy that had worked its way out from under his collar. "What were we talking about?" he asked.

"I asked you what you had in mind for today."

"Oh yes," said Shrader, remembering. "I need to be alone, and I need some time on shore. Jeff Koenig might not appreciate what I'm going to do to his car. Besides, with half the fleet thinking I won't be able to catch up with the rest of you, it'll just make his family worry all day. Take the others and get going. I will be at Red Mills in plenty of time."

"You *Whalemen* are all alike," bantered Cathy as she mounted the companionway steps.

"Aye, aye, Admiral" was Shrader's reply.

Once outside in the air, Cathy turned around and leaned back into the cabin. "I love you, Shrader Marks. Just be damned sure you get to Red Mills before dark!" The exchange of smiles was remembered by both of them for a long time afterwards. "We're shoving off right away," called Cathy to the others. "Jeff, I think you ought to stay on *Rol's Royce* until your family gets settled in. Shrader is sure that he'll be able to join us at Red Mills before dark." No one offered a note of protest.

"They do trust her," thought Shrader. Only Philip seemed skeptical. He looked sideways at Shrader, then set his attention on loosening dock lines.

39

For the next half hour, Cathy and Shrader were busy with the other boats. First, they helped load the remaining gear that had been brought along by the Koenig's son and family. One piece of luggage was unmistakably a rifle in a long, black canvas bag.

"Stow that well out of sight," warned Marks. "We are going to be playing fast and loose with the Canadian border, and customs officials get nervous about firearms." Jeff Koenig took the hint, and hid the awkward package under the v-berth in the most forward part of *Rol's Royce.*

"Where's Philip?" asked Shrader as he and Cathy tossed the bow and stern lines onto the deck of *Fairwinds.*

"He said he was going to stretch his legs before heading back out on the water," answered Cathy. Shrader placed his booted foot against the rub-rail of *Fairwinds* to hold the boat off from the dock while Jim Barker pulled away from the jetty, stern first. Once clear, Barker put the engine into forward gear. The reverse-drift of the boat slowed. He pushed the throttle, and *Fairwinds* eased forward, turning on a dime and heading out to the wide channel of the Saint Lawrence River. The only boat left besides *Strider* was *Affinity.*

"I take it that you'll be motoring all day?" asked Shrader.

"I think so," said Cathy. "I expect that a few of the captains will raise sail now and again, but to make consistent time, river sailing isn't the best."

"Well, I've got the gasoline engine problem," remarked Shrader. "Those of you with diesels are carrying enough fuel to make it to the ocean. I'll be running on empty in two days."

"You're not going to try to sail the ten hours! You'll never make it," stated Cathy.

"No," answered Marks. "But I am going to raise the genoa and get as much assistance as I can from the wind. It'll save fuel in the long run, and *Strider* can make a half a knot faster when the head sail is lifting the bow out of the water. When she's just under engine power, the propellers have a way of making her nose dig into the bow wave slowing her down."

"Promise that you won't hang around here very much longer!"

"I promise," said Marks. "I just need to scrounge a little more fuel if I can. We weren't really able to stock up at Sodus Point after your little run-in at the gas station."

"Do you expect it to be better here?"

"No," he answered. "I expect that anyone who lives through winters in Watertown, New York, wouldn't leave his gas tank very empty, even if there's an unusual break in the weather."

"Jeff Koenig's car," said Pearson with growing awareness. "No wonder you wanted him to leave."

"What I have to do may not be pretty," warned Shrader. "I've been thinking about this all morning. I'd like to siphon the gas, but all I have is a garden hose, and I don't think that I'll be able to get it past the baffle in his car's fill tube."

"So, what will you do?" asked Cathy.

"Well, I thought about taking a gaff and smashing out the baffle, but then I looked under his car. He's got a fuel filter that runs right along the driver's side wheel well. I'll cut the line then slip the hose over it with a stainless steel clamp at the filter end and an old seacock at the other. It'll give me a spigot and I can drain off a gallon at a time."

"Into what?"

"That's the problem. I do have an empty milk jug, but I need something with a larger capacity, so I'm going to dump one of my water tanks."

"You're going to do what!?"

"It's the only way, Cathy. I have thirty-five gallons of drinking water under the v-berth. Ranger 30's also have a second water tank in the stern—fifteen gallons. I'll drain that, isolate it from my fresh water system, and use it as a fuel storage tank."

"But what about your water supply?" she asked.

"I'll just have to ration it more carefully. If I run out too soon, I'll try something else. Eventually, we'll all be collecting rain water anyway, and I could always run river water through those backpacking filters that we brought along. Improvising is the name of the game."

"Sooner or later, we all have to do it," said Philip, who seemed to have joined their conversation out of nowhere.

"Philip!" said Cathy, "Where'd you come from?"

"From a short walk in preparation for a long sail," he said with a cheery tone that made Shrader and Cathy look at one another. "Guess the spirit of adventure is finally catching up with me. Are the boys on board?"

"Yes," said Cathy. "They're anxious to get going. I think that they like Ashley and Kelly Barker and want to stay within sight of *Fairwinds*. I think they went below to dig out the code flags. Apparently, the kids have devised some sort of way to exchange messages."

"Good for them," offered Philip. "We can probably manage the lines without them anyway. How 'bout it, Admiral?"

Cathy gave another quick glance to Marks who seemed as puzzled as she. "Sure," she said as she began to free the dock line from the stern of the boat. Shrader had already gone forward to release the bow line. He held it loosely as Philip backed *Affinity* away from the dock in the same manner as *Fairwinds*. As the bow slipped clear, Marks flipped the line on to the foredeck. He watched the sleek boat turn. Cathy stood near the mast watching him. She didn't speak or gesture, but he knew what she was feeling.

"Good luck with your larceny," called Phil. He waved his arm as *Affinity* swung sharply around. Instinctively, Shrader waved back, then swung into action. He had a lot to do before his boat would catch up to the rest of the fleet.

40

"You seem cheery all of a sudden," remarked Cathy as she turned to Phil. "Why the change?"

"Do I have to have a reason for feeling good?" he quipped. "Maybe I just sense that things are going to start to turn around."

"What did you do?" asked Cathy sharply.

"Look, I'm just playing your game," he answered. "We left Shrader at the dock and he was just fine, wasn't he? Why do you suspect that I did anything? I wish him well. The guy has a lot of problems. There's just no reason why we should let ourselves get swept up in them."

Cathy had no answer to either his comment or her own suspicions. "I'm going down to check on the boys," she said at last. Philip made no response.

Down below, in the main cabin, Justin and Chris were looking at the colored reference pages in the ship's copy of *Chapman's Piloting*. "Hi, guys, what're you doing?" she asked.

"We're trying to find out how to use flag signals, Mom," said Chris. "Ashley Barker said that because you are the Admiral of the fleet that our boat is the flagship and we should be ready to read the signal flags."

"Yeah," chimed in Justin. "She said that we're lucky because our Admiral is a woman. She said that men and boys probably wouldn't even know what the flags meant."

"She was just rattling your chains," said Cathy. "Most people don't know what the signal flags mean."

"She does," burst out Justin. "She said that if we didn't know them, we were just little boys and not real sailors at all."

"Okay, let's give Ashley Barker a little test," offered Cathy with a smile. Chris and Justin brightened. "I don't know what all the flags mean, but let's send her a coded message and see if she gets it." She walked over to the navigation station and retrieved a slim, plastic-bound volume. "This book will tell us." She opened the pocket almanac to the international code section and scanned the list of two-letter signals. "Get out the flags C and S. CS is a question, and it means 'What is the name of your vessel?' If she answers, we'll know how much she understands."

"Thanks, Mom," chimed the boys in unison. They went back and forth to the colored pictures in *Chapman's* to make sure they had the correct flag. It was at that moment that a familiar voice came over the VHF radio.

"*Affinity, Affinity, Affinity,* this is *Major Blunder.*"

Cathy stepped to the nav station and answered the hail. "This is *Affinity,* go ahead *Major.*"

"Well, Admiral, I'm glad to report that you were wrong."

"Say again, Bert. What do you mean?" she asked.

"Your calculations were wrong," repeated Jenkins. "We've been motoring for about an hour-and-a-half at around six-and-a-half knots. We should be ten miles down river from you, but by my chart we are at Clayton, New York. That's about fifteen miles. You forgot to figure in the current and it must be running at about three miles an hour. At this pace, we should be at Red Mills in less than eight hours. It looks like Shrader will make it easily."

"Thank you, Major!" she said. "I guess I'm just a lake sailor and have forgotten about currents. It's nice to be proven wrong now and again! I'll pass the word on to Shrader."

"Just thought you'd like to know. This is *Major Blunder*, out."

41

Affinity was barely away from the dock when Shrader climbed over the lifelines and boarded his own boat. Once below, he stowed a partially used roll of paper towels that had broken free from the back of the galley. He opened the drawer under the sink and took out the sharpest paring knife he could find. The edge of the blade would not match that of the utility knife in his tool kit, but it was easier to retrieve, and time was of the essence.

Actually getting to the rear water storage tank was not an easy proposition. For a larger person, it would have been impossible, but Shrader managed to get the upper part of his torso through the access port in the quarter berth. He was now working behind the boat's engine in a low crawl space beneath the cockpit floor.

"Damn, I wish I'd brought a flashlight," said Marks to himself, but he wasn't about to turn back after getting so far into a hole that contorted every vertebrae. He could see the polyethylene tank plainly enough in the dim light. The problem was replacing the flimsy outlet hose with something more durable and fuel-resistant. Fortunately, he had about three feet of gas-line hose that would allow him to extend the drainage point to an area of the engine compartment where he could drain off a gallon at a time. He could then carry the jug outside the cockpit and pour the fuel into the main tank. It would be awkward, but it would work. It was a way to add fifteen hours of cruising time and increase *Strider's* range.

Shrader felt along the bottom of the tank until his fingers touched the hose and flange that protruded from its underside. "There you are," he said. He withdrew his hand long enough to retrieve the knife, then sent it back to the site of the outlet hose. Carefully he ran the blade back and forth along the edge of the tubing. He could feel cold water pouring on his fingers, and knew that the knife had found its mark. He gripped the tube and pulled. It stretched, then popped free. The water splashed out in a steady stream. He waited as the fifteen gallons drained, carrying a stream of engine dirt and grime down to the bilge.

It took some time for the water to empty. Shrader wedged himself to take the pressure off his straining arms. He found himself unconsciously holding his breath, waiting for something. At last he realized what it was. He was listening for the hum of the electric bilge pump. At last the water beneath the floor boards reached a depth to activate the automatic switch. The pump kicked on and he breathed a sigh of relief. The bilge could hold at least fifty gallons of water before reaching the floor boards, and the small electric pump would dump the fifteen gallons overboard in a few seconds.

At last the water stopped flowing from the tank, and Shrader was operating by Braille with regard to slipping the gasoline resistant hose over the outlet nipple. It was a bit of a struggle, but he was able to force the rubber hose into place.

"Dummy," he chastised himself. "That connection has to be clamped. It's no use having gasoline leaking into the bilge." It was then that he realized that the bilge pump hadn't cut out. In fact, the tiny motor of the submersible pump seemed to be humming in high gear. "What the...." His words to himself were cut off as he scrambled backwards out of the tiny tomb of an opening. His feet hit the floorboards with a soggy splash. The boat was filling with water! This was not the measly fifteen gallons from the tank discharge. It was lake water, icy cold.

"What now?" he said as his fingertips traced through the frigid waters to find the latch handle to the access plate on the cabin sole. He found the stainless steel ring and tugged. The wood flooring had already begun to swell. He jerked harder, and the cover broke free. It was too late to think about water temperatures or keeping his jacket dry. He reached down through the swirling water until his whole right arm was immersed in the deep bilge. Through the numbing cold he could feel the rapid inflow of water. It felt like the surge of a fire hose blasting out of the starboard side of the bilge. Quickly, Shrader spun around on his knees, sending a cascade of waves across the deepening water. He yanked open the drawer in the base of the nav station, nearly ripping it out. He rummaged past the flare gun and the signal flags to find another piece of emergency equipment, a wooden plug. His fingers gripped it, and he was back leaning into the bilge, his cheek pressing into the rising water. He pushed hard against the advancing flow, forcing the plug into place. The flow stopped, but Shrader was afraid to let up on the pressure from his arm for fear that it would pop loose. But the wood was already beginning to swell, and the plug held. He sat upright to survey the situation. In general, he knew what had happened. He just could not understand how it happened. Somehow the transducer on the boat's knotmeter had pulled out of the cylinder that protruded through the boat's hull. But it could not have happened by accident. The mechanism for self-sealing was simple and foolproof. The outboard end housed a little paddlewheel that would spin as the boat passed through the water. The spinning was converted to an electronic impulse which read out as a speed reading on the digital knotmeter in the boat's cockpit. The transducer was sealed with a series of O-rings and a bottle cap-type connection on the inboard end. Even if the sealing rings failed completely, the result would be a seeping of water through the threads of the end cap. For the whole unit to come out, someone had to unscrew the locking connection.

"Philip," said Shrader. It was the obvious answer. "But how, and why wasn't the floor wet when I came down?" He looked at the floating mess that surrounded him, and chilled him to the bone. The water looked strangely soapy and clotted with whitish fibers.

"The paper towels!" he exclaimed. Once more he risked the chilly water and began to fish the depths of the bilge until his grasp found the small battery powered bilge pump. He felt it vibrating in his grip. It was trying to work, but not pumping any water. He lifted the submersible unit out of the water. As suspected, the ribbed intake ports were clogged with soggy wads of toweling. He scraped them with his fingernails and lowered the pump to make contact with the water. It started immediately to gurgle and suck until more of the floating shreds dammed the inlets.

"That's why the water isn't going down," he said. He rose to his feet, and scrambled out on deck. He lifted the lid on the lazarette and withdrew a stainless steel rod which he slipped into a socket in the bulkhead. With determined effort he began working the lever, not unlike someone jacking up a car to fix a flat tire. Instead of a bumper rising, Shrader's action created a shooting surge of water from the stern of the boat. For all the ease of electric motors, nothing could match the effectiveness of a high capacity manual pump and a sailor on the verge of sinking.

At this point, however, sinking was not the issue. Drying out was. It was not long before the water behind *Strider* was sudsing and frothing with fragments of paper towels which passed easily through the diaphragm pump. There was also something else. A saltwater sailor would have dismissed it as the medusa of a small jellyfish, but at Cape Vincent in April that was a double impossibility. It was a small plastic bag, and the answer to the riddle. Philip had removed the transducer and replaced it with a plug of paper towels wrapped in plastic. The baggie would prevent the outside lake water from breaking down the toweling, but exposing the toweling on the inside of the boat would mean that water in the bilge would eventually destroy the integrity of the plug. To enhance the action he had added soap as a wetting agent and additional towels to take out the pump.

"I don't believe it," said Shrader to himself. "He meant for this to happen when I was out on the water when the bilge would get to sloshing. If I were at the wheel, I wouldn't even know the cabin was filling with water until it was too late to stop. At a minimum, I'd lose the boat. With electronics flooded and no ability to radio an SOS, I'd be into hypothermia in a few minutes. That bastard was trying to kill me without a trace."

It took a good half hour to clean the bilge and restore the systems. At its height, the water had risen to within inches of the batteries, but no damage was sustained. The flooring, however, was completely saturated, and Shrader was afraid to think about the mold and mildew that would soon follow. He still was not any nearer to having the gasoline he needed, but he was grateful that his draining of the water tank had sprung Philip's trap too soon.

Before he proceeded, he stripped off his wet clothes, dried himself off, and pulled on his wool cold weather gear. He prayed for a candy bar, but had to settle for a handful of spiced jelly beans that he had thrown on board. He felt as bulky as an Eskimo when he climbed back into the engine compartment to clamp the gasoline line. Still, it took a good forty minutes before he thought his body temperature was back to normal.

He still had to complete the sortie to the Koenig's family car with his length of garden hose. He hoped to scavenge at least ten gallons of gasoline, but before doing that, he went to the cockpit and uncapped the fill tube of the water tank which would now serve as his auxiliary fuel tank.

He took the cap back down below and proceeded to light the alcohol stove that was mounted in the galley. In summer temperatures lighting an alcohol stove is a feat. In winter, it becomes a miracle. The process requires directly burning enough fuel to heat a vapor chamber. Once the stove is hot enough from the initial burning, it is relit to burn vapors rather than liquid. Shrader was just glad to be striking a match, and did not seem to care about the fact that the burning fuel flared up in front of him. Into the flame he inserted the end of an ice pick. Once the tip was hot, he pressed it into the center of the screw cap that he had brought in from the cockpit. After several repetitions, he slowly melted a pinhole in the white plastic. "Perfect," he said at last as he squinted through the tiny opening. "A vented gas cap. Just what I wanted, small enough to release fumes under pressure, but not large enough to take on much water."

Surprisingly, the rest went very smoothly. By 10:00 a.m. *Strider*'s aft tank was full of fuel, and there were no discernable leaks. What seemed most odd to Shrader was the fact that he had seen no one all morning. He remained unchallenged and unnoticed throughout the whole process of draining the gasoline tank of a parked car. He pressed the starter and the motor came to life, bringing a smile to his face. He leaped to the dock, released the lines, and was back at the wheel before the boat could drift. He threw the engine into forward gear and slowly picked up enough speed to run in a giant arc back out into the channel of the great seaway to the Atlantic.

Shrader looked at his knotmeter. Philip would be distressed to know that it was working fine and reading 5.8 knots. When he raised the jib, the speed leaped to 6.3. He had not heard Bert Jenkin's transmission regarding the river currents, but Shrader was not concerned. He didn't need to calculate that he would be in Red Mills by 6:00 that evening. He knew that he would be there in time, and that he had survived the first test.

42

Cathy didn't think much of it when she was unable to raise Shrader on the VHF. "Forget it," said Philip after she had hailed *Strider* for the third time and to no avail. "What's so all-fired important that it can't wait?" he asked.

"I just wanted to share Jenkins' report on the river currents," she answered.

"It'll hold," he said. "He's a big boy and he can take care of himself, or he should be able to. Personally, I think he's been lucky to have made it this far."

"What do you mean by that?" asked Cathy who was still suspicious about the turnaround in Philip's temperament.

"Only that he's got an old boat, and already had an engine problem. There's no telling what will break down next."

"I think that's wishful thinking on your part," she goaded. "*Strider* is in very good shape. A spark coil is hardly a major breakdown. Happens once every decade or so."

"But he didn't have a backup part, did he?"

"No," she confessed.

"And this guy expects us to believe that he's prepared and has all the answers as to how to save us? Give me a break! You'd be a lot better off without him."

"I wish you'd try to get to know him, Phil. He's not a crackpot. If he wasn't too concerned about backup parts for his engine, it was because he knows that they're only of temporary value anyway. Once we're out of diesel, our engine will just be excess ballast. He'll be the first one to run out of fuel since he's burning gasoline."

"And it's more than three hundred miles to Québec! I've studied the charts, too. He can't really expect to sail much until he gets there, and then it's another five hundred miles beyond that. But let's suppose that he won't ever need his engine after Québec. He still has fifty hours of motoring. At a gallon an hour, he'll need a minimum of fifty gallons of fuel. How much do you think he's carrying?"

"I really don't know." answered Cathy, who was beginning to feel under siege.

"He's got a fifteen gallon tank on the engine. He had a five gallon jerry-jug, that's twenty. Even if he stowed another fifteen gallons, we're going to be saying goodbye to him at Montréal. He'll never make it to Québec. Unless..."

"Unless, what?" she said taking the bait.

"Unless we find a marina along the way that's open to sell us fuel. Of course that would mean this whole thing is a wild goose chase."

"It's not a wild goose chase," said Cathy, her face reddening.

"He's an egghead professor! And you're following him around like some wide-eyed co-ed who thinks that if you grovel enough, you'll get an 'A'. I got news for you. We'll be picking up his pieces on the way back tomorrow."

"Why would you say that? Have you done something, Philip?"

"Do you think that Dr. Shrader Mess-up is the only one with any intuition? Let's just say that I have a feeling about how this thing will play out, and this guy has been a fraud from the word go."

Cathy had nothing to add, and knew that it wouldn't matter. Philip's tone of voice and body language told her that the discussion was over and that he had won the encounter. It was the way most of their communications ended of late. Everything was framed as win-lose, and since he was the final authority, her role was to lose. Cathy climbed up on deck to look around, and to hide the frustration that clearly showed on her face. It was another adjustment that she had learned over the years. Always hide after an attack, because if Philip knew that he was getting to her, he would not let up. She scanned the horizon, looking for a distraction. Instead, she found herself worrying about Shrader. "Be careful, good friend," she whispered to no one. Her eyes wandered beyond her tears. She noted the green flasher that marked Feather Bed Shoal. Ahead and to the north was Carelton Island. In happier days they had talked about traveling there to see the ruins of Fort Haldimand, a British fort that was captured by the United States in the War of 1812.

Her senses began to return to her as she felt a gentle push of air against her cheek. She looked at the wind indicator at the top of the mast. It was pointing straight ahead, but she knew that it was a false reading. The wind was still blowing from their stern, but the forward motion of the boat was out-running the wind, making the *apparent* wind come from their bow. Overhead, there was a flutter of signal flags from the right spreader. She suddenly remembered the boys' signal to Ashley Barker on *Fairwinds*. She turned to look at *Fairwinds* which was motoring off the rear quarter of *Affinity*. Three small figures were gathered on the cabin trunk about to hoist a string of burgees.

"Chris, Justin, come here," she called. "Ashley is sending you an answer. Bring up that little book that I was using before and get the binoculars from your Dad."

The boys came from below decks. "What does it say?" chimed Chris.

"Well, I don't know," said their mother. "This flag thing is new to me. That's why we need the book."

"Oh," said Chris, who looked at Justin, who then went below to get the book. Cathy was just glad for the distraction of the moment.

"Put the strap over your head," Philip was saying to Chris. "And don't break them or it'll come out of your allowance!" In time, the boys and their mother were seated together. Cathy, who was in the middle, held the pocket almanac open to the color print of the code flags.

"The first one is yellow and red stripes kinda sideways," said Chris who was looking through the binoculars. The other two were squinting in the direction of the other boat.

"What do you mean, 'kinda sideways'? Can you show me in this picture?"

At his mother's request, Chris set aside the glasses, which were immediately pilfered by Justin who nearly strangled his older brother in the process.

"There it is," said Chris pointing to the code flag for the letter Y.

"The next one looks like an hour glass with yellow on the top and red on the bottom," offered Justin.

"Okay, you'll have to point that one out," said Cathy. Justin found it in the color drawing. It was the letter Z.

"All right," said their mother. "We have YZ. Let's see if that means anything." She turned to the next page in the reference book. She found the answer under the heading of two-letter signals. "Here's what it means: *The words which follow are in plain language*," she read aloud.

"What does that mean?" protested Justin.

"It means that there is another signal coming," said Cathy. "It will be spelled out rather than be in code." Sure enough, as the three watched, the YZ was followed by several other flags which they identified in sequence as F, R, W, N, D and S. "Good for them," she offered. "They've answered your hail very well." The boys looked at each other.

"But that doesn't spell anything," complained Justin.

"Sure it does," she replied. "You asked for the name of their vessel. They said, 'Here it is in spelling, F-R-W-N-D-S', which stands for *Fairwinds*. They just left the vowels out to shorten the message."

"But if we didn't know the name of their boat already, we wouldn't have been able to know that," protested Chris. "I don't think it should be counted as a correct answer."

"But you do know the name of their boat, so they figured that they could use just the consonants. They knew that the meaning would be plain language to you, but maybe not to someone who wasn't a part of our fleet. You can't put up a hundred flags at a time so you look for ways to shorten it without making it impossible to read."

"I still say it's not right," said Chris. "She thinks she's so smart."

"Maybe she is," his mother added. "If she's that smart, wouldn't it be good to have a friend like that on your side? Maybe you could work out your own codes to exchange messages faster?"

"Cool," said Justin.

"Like what?" asked Chris.

"Suppose when you're to spell out a message you use the letter *A* to stand for *Affinity*. We're the only boat that begins with that letter so that would be all you'd need to spell out the message."

"Okay, I get it!" A light went off in Chris' expression. "We could even use letters to stand for people, like using their initials."

"Sure. You could even write a code book for yourselves, but you'll have to agree with Ashley about it. The people at both ends need to understand." Cathy found herself looking back at Philip.

"Thanks, Mom," said Chris.

"Yeah, thanks, Mom," agreed Justin.

"Don't you need to give *Fairwinds* some sort of reply?"

"What do we say?" asked Justin.

"Well, the book says that the letter *R* can be used to mean 'I have received your last signal'."

"Okay, we'll send that," volunteered Chris.

"How about this instead," said Cathy. "We go below and call the *Fairwinds* on the radio. That way they can be working on codes, too. Tonight you may be able to get together and compare notes."

"Will Dad let us use the radio?" asked Justin.

"He'll probably get mad," answered Cathy. "But he'll be mad at me since I'll be helping you. I think the codes are a good idea. It's not for playing. There may be a time when we will really need to use them, and I'm counting on you kids to help."

"Ashley says that you are the Admiral. So Dad will have to listen to you," said Justin.

"I guess we'll find out. I guess we'll find out," she repeated.

43

Laura Romig was having an easier time of learning to sail than her husband John. Her good mechanical sense made the concepts easy to grasp. If she did not know the right terms for the various sheets, fairleads, and turning blocks, she at least knew that "pulling the red rope on the left side would fix the sail".

"No," repeated John, "it's not a *rope*, it's a *sheet*. We trim the port sheet to provide the optimum sail shape." His academic mind-set held him captive to the idea of mastering all the sailing jargon in one day.

"What was it that Shakespeare said about roses?" countered Laura. "Brittany, can you tell me if the boat is moving forward at the present time, and without burning fossil fuel?"

Brittany was at the helm, and smiled back at Laura. She knew that it was a question that didn't need an answer. For the Romigs, it was an old argument. The theoretician versus the pragmatist, but the contention was all in jest in a marriage in which each had a respect for the other. If *The Annapolis Book of Seamanship* seemed to be attached to John's right arm, they were both learning the language, and if Laura was the one to apply the muscle, John was quick to see the effects of her actions.

"Were those roses red or yellow?" asked John. "And didn't the seventeenth Earl of Oxford write Shakespeare anyway?" They both laughed.

Brittany Pearson loved it. The banter was quick and witty, and the affection was real. After a few hours, she was glad to be on *Mewtiny* with the Romigs rather than on *Affinity* where her parents' conversations left her feeling queasy and more eager to play with younger brothers than tolerate the adult company. More often than not, she hid herself in a novel.

"*Mewtiny, Mewtiny, Mewtiny*, this is *Major Blunder*," came a hail over the cockpit radio. John, who had read the chapter on VHF protocol, took the mike and answered.

"This is *Mewtiny*. Go ahead, *Major Blunder*."

"John, better have Brittany throw in the towel and turn on the engine. You're beginning to fall behind the rest of the fleet."

"We're doing almost six knots," protested Brittany.

"We're holding our own at around six knots," said Romig into the mike.

"I know," answered Bert Jenkins. "But the rest of us are pushing seven. You are dropping back by a mile an hour. I'd like you to close ranks some, or at least not fall off any more." Brittany stuck out her tongue at the radio.

"Understood, Major," said John. "We will engage the auxiliary and begin motor sailing."

"Wow. You sound like an old salt," commented Laura. "'Engage the auxiliary?'"

"He means he's going to turn us into a motorboat," whined Brittany.

"Yes, but Laura has been waiting for the smell of the diesel," said John. "And we've sailed a long way. With the shore line so close, there have been a few times when you haven't been able to keep much wind in the sails. We have been slowing down over the last hour. Major Jenkins is right."

"He just likes giving orders," said Brittany.

"Why do you say that?" asked Laura. "We aren't keeping up, are we?"

"No," she said begrudgingly. "It's just that my Dad says that he's on a power trip. Ever notice his wife?"

"Tiffany?" said Laura. "We just met her, but she seems nice."

"And she's young enough to be his daughter," offered Brittany. "My Dad said that's what these washout military types do. They get to the end of their careers and they realize that they're never going to make it to the top, so they latch on to some kid and start ordering them around."

John and Laura looked at each other before John answered.

"I don't know either of them very well, but it just seems to me that he's following your mother's orders. She gave him the orders to take the fleet on to Red Mills. If it's a male/female thing, it doesn't seem to fit with the fact that he's the one who dubbed your mother the *Admiral*."

"But my Dad says that real men don't need to find somebody younger or weaker to push around."

"Does he mean that you push around somebody your own age?" said Laura.

"Shhh," protested John. "That may be what your Dad thinks about Major Jenkins, Brittany, but what do you think?"

"My Dad is usually right," she defended. Laura rolled her eyes.

"That may be," countered Romig. "But what do you think?"

Brittany thought for a moment. "I guess I don't know," she said at last. "He has that uncool short hair, but he's always been nice to me."

"Maybe he married Tiffany because he loved her," offered Laura.

"And maybe it's our place to follow his orders at this point and start the motor," said John. Brittany, with practiced precision, fired the engine. The boat began to pick up speed until the sails dangled limply.

"I'll douse the sails," volunteered Brittany. "But someone will have to take the wheel while I go forward."

"How about if I help you?" asked John. "I need to learn this stuff. So far you've helped us convince everyone that we're old hands at sailing."

Laura stepped over next to Brittany and took the wheel. "You're a good teacher, Brittany," she said.

"Thank you," she answered.

"It's true," offered John. "You are a good teacher. You don't have to thank us for thanking you."

"No," said the girl. "I'm thanking you for not treating me like a kid."

"Hey, you're the captain when we're under sail," quipped Laura. "But when the engine is revved-up, I'm in charge! This is a male/female thing! And John is in big trouble." The three laughed deeply, and John and Brittany moved forward to furl the sails.

44

"How does it look, Ray?" said Gundersen into his handheld radio. Below him in the chamber of the Eisenhower lock was Ray Anderson in a Boston Whaler. The low power-craft had an oversized outboard on its stern, but Anderson carefully maneuvered it along every inch of the inner wall, inspecting the floating bollards where the smaller boats could tie off during a lock-through.

"Everything looks fine," came Ray's voice through the transceiver.

Gus pressed the small radio to his mouth and depressed the switch. "Okay, Betty, let the river take over."

In the control room, Betty Montgomery understood what he was saying. The two had worked together long enough that she knew what he meant. She initiated the sequence of events that would bring water from Lake Saint Lawrence, the upper pool, into the lock. It would take twenty-two million gallons in all to fill the chamber, and it would be done without pumps in only ten minutes. Ray Anderson looked like he was in a little rubber boat in a huge bathtub that dwarfed all proportion. Gundersen was also watching.

"This is where the river takes over," he said to himself as the water in the chamber began to rise. Here, at the lock, they let the river pass through one tub full at a time while the main body of the Saint Lawrence flowed through the Long Sault Rapids to the north. The Eisenhower and the Snell Locks were built on a manmade channel south of the original watercourse. The Wiley-Dondero Canal, as it was called, was the path around the rapids for Great Lakes shipping. Gus crossed over the catwalk that transversed the downstream gate. The lock chamber was eighty feet wide and nearly four hundred feet long. Below, in the rising chamber, Ray held his position against the internal swirling currents. When the water reached the level of the upper pool, Betty Montgomery opened the upstream gates. For Anderson, at water level, it was like a gigantic curtain drawing back on a long watery horizon. For Gus, on the walkway between the lock chamber and the lower pool, it was even more dramatic. It was like standing on the lip of an aquarium. On one side was a sheer drop to the river level. On the other, the water surface was more than forty feet below the river. If the gate beneath him opened, the surge would roll like a tidal wave, and the river would flow powerfully like the great cataract of Niagara.

There was an uncertainty in the air around them. Its presence was heavy, but word of it went unspoken. If the world were coming to an end, Ray, Betty, and Gus were clinging to the accustomed patterns. Testing the locking systems was a rite of the season, a ritual of familiarity to which they retreated for comfort. Though they knew full well that the events of the next few hours would be unprecedented, they practiced the springtime drill that marked the opening of the waterway to ocean traffic. There are times for thinking and times for doing. For these three, escape to the familiar was the only way to cope with what was otherwise unknown and unimaginable. They would follow their orders to lift ships to the safety of Lake Ontario's inland waters. It was a plan. Whether it was realistic or not mattered little, and if reality offered them something different, they would deal with that later.

45

Strider seemed grateful to be back in open water. She surged through the cold water, and Shrader realized that the speed indicated on his gauge was not an accurate predictor of his progress.

"There must be quite a current running," he said to himself as he settled back for a long day at the helm. The other boats were ninety minutes ahead of him, but he would have no trouble making the rendezvous point. The glowing digits of the knotmeter reminded him that he would have to deal with Phil Pearson at some point. He thought about what might have happened if Pearson's mischief had not gone off prematurely. If the plug had broken loose here in the seaway channel, Shrader wouldn't have had much of a chance. The boat slipped smoothly through the water as he sailed beneath the Thousand Islands Bridge. He was in the shipping channel and his depth gauge read one hundred and thirty nine feet. There was plenty of room under his hull to lose a boat, and unless he could make it to a nearby shoal, the cold water would have rendered him unconscious.

If this is a game of cat and mouse, thought Shrader, *I think that I'll just let him think his trap is not yet sprung.* He considered trying to raise *Affinity* on the radio, but dismissed the idea. *For the time being, he can keep guessing.*

Shrader turned the wheel to move *Strider* out of the main channel. In the shallower waters he hoped to find swifter currents. So far, he had managed to maintain a good speed without the aid of the engine. As the river narrowed, however, and the islands that he'd left behind became barriers to the direct force of Ontario's winds, his progress began to slow. Within an hour, he watched his hull speed drop to four knots, and it was time to fire up the "iron monster". As much as he hated motoring for long periods of time, he breathed a sigh of relief when the engine turned over and settled down to a steady purr. "Thank you, Jeff Koenig," he said in gratitude for a borrowed spark coil.

He throttled back the motor to a crawl and locked the wheel in place as he furled the genoa that was now luffing in the still air. Once the sail was down, he returned to the wheel and powered up the engine. He watched the speed increase to 5.8 knots. "That's about the best she'll do under power," he observed. *Strider* was already pushing a wall of water ahead of its bow and would not be able to surf over the wave that was made by its forward motion. Fortunately, the current was running with the craft, and Shrader knew that his speed relative to the riverbed was much faster than his instruments could measure.

As time passed, Shrader wished that he had a thermometer. The sun felt positively warm, and the winter-barren landscape was showing traces of red in the budding tips of the branches. If his calculations were correct, he was just north of Ogdensburg, New York, and perhaps ten miles from the rendezvous point. The others would be there by now, and it was past time to break radio silence. Still, he marveled that no boats were to be seen. Under normal circumstances, such a day would be an irresistible temptation to the diehard boaters along the river's edge. Was the news so bad that it eclipsed all else? Shrader wondered as he steered *Strider* into the center of the channel. He was going to try a new strategy for his single-handed radio calling. He put the engine in neutral and allowed the boat to drift freely in the current. Like a leaf on a puddle, *Strider* would float slowly in the right direction, more or less. He looked again at the chart to make sure that he was not coming quickly upon a rock or shoal, and then he went below and switched on the VHF radio.

"*Affinity, Affinity, Affinity*, this is *Strider*." He waited for a response which did not take long.

"Shrader, are you all right?" Cathy's voice was excited, and radio protocol slipped aside.

"Yes, I'm fine," said Shrader who was trying to imagine the look on Philip's face. "The river hasn't given me much of a chance to use the radio," he added. "The knotmeter has gone out so I can't report my speed, but I make my position at Ogdensburg."

He lied about the knotmeter, but figured it would offer some false hope to Pearson.

"You've made good time then," remarked Cathy. "We are rafted up just east of Red Mills. The water is deeper than the charts indicate, but the current is running pretty strong. I wouldn't trust the raft to hold up over night."

"It won't have to," answered Shrader. "We've got to move on through the Iroquois lock."

"I know," she agreed. "We held a captains' meeting and John Romig has us all pretty worried. He says that the only way that the atmosphere could be this warm is if there is a lot of volcanic activity along the major oceanic plates. You've got some scared people over here, but most of them are willing to go forward, rather than to do nothing."

"We're going to be okay, Cathy," assured Marks.

"I'm glad you think so. What if the locks aren't operating?" she asked.

"What?" replied Shrader who had not considered that possibility.

"Haven't you noticed," she continued, "there's no one around? I can see the shore highway and a moving car is a rarity. As for other boats, I don't think I've seen one all day."

"Yes, I noticed that," said Shrader. "Whatever is coming over the airwaves must be giving everyone pause. Maybe it's good that we aren't following the news too closely."

"But what if the locks aren't operating?" she asked again.

"They are," said Shrader with certainty in his voice. "Don't ask me how I know, but I don't see us being stopped. There will be dangers, but the way is open, I'm sure of that."

"I guess I'll have to leave that part up to you," she answered. "I've had a few problems over here."

"What happened?" asked Marks. He imagined the possibilities of mechanical failure or accidents. "Has anyone been hurt?"

"No, nothing like that," she said reassuringly. "It's just that the troops are getting restless. I wanted to wait until you got here, but decided that I had to call a captains' meeting without you."

"Did you come to any conclusions?" There was a pause before Cathy answered.

"This isn't the place to talk about it in any detail, but John Romig gave us his theories on what might be happening. It opened a few eyes. In the end, we took a vote on whether or not we should continue forward, and the majority favored at least locking through the Iroquois tonight and talking about it again tomorrow."

"You put it to a vote?" asked Shrader. "Was there much dissent?"

"It was close, Shrader, but everyone agreed to stick with the majority, at least this time. No boats will be heading back, at least not right away."

"Were some thinking of bailing out?" asked Marks. "Was it that close?"

"Yes," said Cathy with a pause which indicated that the topic was too sensitive to discuss. "My vote decided it," she added in a low tone.

The airwaves went silent as Shrader considered his response. "We'll have to move on as soon as I make the meeting point, but maybe we could talk about it later. You could brief me on the details," he stated.

"Will do," she said as though a weight had been lifted from her. She quickly logged off the radio. Shrader was left alone with his thoughts. It was clear that there would be more obstacles to this voyage than those provided by the elements. But something even more bizarre was going on within him. He found himself wishing that he could just lie down and sleep. The feeling was more than could be explained by the exhaustion that was creeping up within him. Something was lurking just beyond the edge of his consciousness, and he wanted to open himself to his dreams. It was an awareness that startled him. Two weeks earlier, he avoided sleep at all costs. Now, he longed for it.

His dreams had been the knife that struck at the heart of his weakened marriage. His thoughts turned to Lynn. He wondered what she was thinking of him. Did it even matter? In the cycle of the world, everything had changed. Familiar ways and places were now foreign and beyond recapturing. For all he knew, none of those places existed anymore and never would again. To look back would be to go insane. Then again, the way ahead provided little comfort. Perhaps it, too, would lead to insanity. Shrader looked back over the transom of the boat where the water coming off the sides of the hull met in small eddies like miniature whirlpools that flattened out into calm water that trailed behind like footprints that had not yet been erased by a rising tide.

Suddenly, the tranquil image deserted his senses as his mind began to transform sight to a deeper vision. The line in the water that trailed behind the boat became a corridor, bounded by walls of thick cloud. From out of the mist he could hear cries for help and the roar of a furnace. As quickly as it had appeared, the image flashed away, and Marks found himself staring at brown water and clearing blue skies.

46

"Gus, you'd better get up here." The tone of Betty's voice told Gundersen that something was wrong.

"What's the matter?" he asked speaking into his handheld radio.

"Just some distressing news out of Montréal," answered Montgomery.

"I'll be right there," said Gus. Ray Anderson had been listening on the same channel and turned back toward Gundersen in time to see him crossing the catwalk toward the traffic control center. He waved in recognition and continued motoring along his inspection tour of the Eisenhower Lock.

"What's so all-fired distressing?" said Gus as he entered the control cabin.

"We're getting word from the Canadians that the water levels are rising dangerously."

"It's probably just the fast ice-melt in the upper Great Lakes," he responded, blowing off the comment.

"No," answered Betty. "You don't understand. The water is rising downriver at Montréal. The ocean levels are rising and the flow of the Saint Lawrence is reversing."

"What?" exclaimed Gundersen.

"Just what I said," argued Montgomery. "Water is rising out of the Gulf of Saint Lawrence, and it's rising fast. They've opened the Saint Lambert and Côte Sainte Catherine Locks."

"To counter the flow?" asked Gus.

"No, that's just it," remarked Montgomery. "They're breached. The water is flowing upstream through them and still rising."

Gus Gundersen dropped to a chair to ponder the unimaginable. "That's more than forty feet," he said at last.

"And still rising," she added.

"What's happened to Montréal?"

"Evidently it is becoming a very small island. The water rising has left Mount Royal as one gigantic evacuation center," she said. They both paused to envision the great city awash, but couldn't.

"It can't get too much higher," repeated Gundersen as if to convince himself. "What about the flotilla that was headed this way?" he asked.

"They're still moving this way. In fact, the orders have come through that we are to open any lock if there's a chance that high water will mess up our operations."

"What the fuck kind of order is that? Just what is so damn precious about those boats that they haven't turned aside to help with rescue, and we're supposed to risk the lock system so that they can come upstream?"

"I don't know," said Betty trying to calm Gus' sudden flare-up. "They're probably just too big to help with any kind of rescue that would take place in the city. They'd need small boats to move between the buildings."

"You're right, but it still doesn't make sense. Do we have any descriptions of those ships?"

"It's sketchy, but it seems like a mixture of small tankers and bulk cargo ships, and military vessels."

"Food, fuel, and nuclear weapons," said Gundersen, "the three necessities of modern life. Wait a minute! The airports, are the airports flooded? Oh, shit, it doesn't matter, the poor devils."

"What are you muttering?" asked Betty.

"I was just thinking about a chain of events. Once the water is high enough to flow over the containment areas around the oil and chemical storage tanks, well, there's going to be quite a slick on the water. If enough of it is really volatile, like gasoline or naphtha, then the whole place is a spark away from hell."

"*Poor devils*, is right," agreed Montgomery who was always astounded by Gundersen's wealth of knowledge. "Is there anything we should be doing?"

"We play the waiting game," said Gus. "If we get any traffic coming up from Montréal, there will be no telling what kind of shape they'll be in." They went silent for a moment, but the quiet was disrupted by the whirring and clicking of an incoming fax.

"What now?" asked Betty. "That thing has been the bearer of bad news all day." Gundersen scanned the copy as it emerged from the machine.

"Great!" he said. "That's all we need. What a shithead!"

"I'm afraid to ask," interjected Betty.

"Oh," said Gus. "It's nothing about the troubles downstream. It's that ignoramus who calls himself a lockmaster at the Iroquois. He says that he has to warn us. Listen to this." He lifted the paper. "'With recent reports coming from Montréal, I thought it best to warn you that eight sailing vessels have entered the Lake Saint Lawrence basin. They have done so with full compliance to all Seaway regulations.'"

"Of all the dumb shit," continued Gundersen as he looked at the curling paper in his hand.

"He's just covering his tail because he knows you were right about stopping all the downstream traffic," agreed Montgomery.

"*Full compliance to Seaway regulations.* You know what that means, don't you?" he asked.

"Yep," said Betty. "They each put a few bucks on a clipboard to cover their line-handling fees."

"You got it," he agreed. "But we'd better warn them. Betty, get through to Ray on the VHF. He or I or both of us needs to take out the Whaler and try to intercept those boats. Hopefully, they're together and not spread out all over the place. While you're doing that, I want to make a phone call to a certain lockmaster to get some clarification on Seaway regulations." His look was not playful; this was not his usual manner.

"With what's going on downstream," she answered. "I think you need to make him squirm a little."

"Well, that's what worms do best, isn't it?"

47

Rafting sailboats together can be a tricky proposition, especially in windy weather, but the winds were light on that Saturday evening when the eight boats gathered in the protective waters of the man-made lake. Behind Ogden Island, they were protected from the current, and *Affinity* dropped its oversized plow to anchor the raft in place.

The first pair of boats carefully maneuvered into place on the port and starboard sides of the Pearson's craft. Then, one by one, the boats tied off to each other. Each was met with a scramble as the crews dropped rubber fenders between the hulls and pulled the boats together snugly. At last the eight yachts were in a row like a floating island on a tether suspended from the centermost boat.

On board, the mood took on a holiday spirit. After being tied to one boat for twenty-four hours, the expanse of eight decks lashed together seemed like a football field. The children disappeared first. After the hail of shouts from parents worried about someone falling overboard, they seemed to opt for being not seen nor heard. In point of fact, they took refuge in the cabin of *Fairwinds*. At fourteen, Anthony Ragni was the oldest, tallest, and most outspoken of the group. Brittany Pearson, who was the same age, had opted to stay with the Romigs aboard *Mewtiny* and posed no threat to his position as leader-by-default. Around the edges were Allison and Sandi, the Koenig's grandchildren, and

Cameron and Ben Romig. These four were the newcomers, the relative outsiders who were most likely to get motion sickness. They tended to watch from the fringes as Ashley Barker explained her system of flag codes. The rivalry between her and Chris and Justin Pearson had evaporated. The three were now fast allies in a plan that had become more than a game.

Before long every boat was being raided for pencils and blank paper. The parents were grateful for quiet activity and gladly surrendered legal pads and spiral notebooks. Once again, the kids cloistered themselves in the depths of *Fairwinds* like monks carefully copying texts of holy writ.

"For now, this is highly secret stuff," warned Anthony Ragni. "Isn't that right, Ash?" he continued, turning to Barker whom he was now addressing with casual familiarity.

"Yes," she answered. "Our first loyalty is to the Admiral, and I think that we should test this code before we tell anyone."

"And she'll be the first that we tell," chimed in Chris Pearson.

"That's because she's your mother," accused Teresa Ragni who was feeling upstaged by her older brother.

"No," stated Ashley unequivocally. "It's because she is the Admiral and that's all there is to it. Does everyone agree?"

"Well," bullied Anthony. "You heard her. Let's vote. All who agree raise your hands." When all hands went up except Teresa's, all heads turned to her.

"Okay," she said as she reluctantly raised a hand. "I won't tell."

"You, sure as hell, better not," warned her brother.

"And you'd better stop swearing and trying to act tough or I'll tell Mom," came the quick reply.

At the other end of the flotilla, *Strider* was moored. In the dimly lit bowels of the ship, three figures talked in low tones. They did so for good reason. Aboard small cruising vessels there is no such thing as auditory privacy, and the three did not want to be overheard.

"I didn't want to say this when we had the captains' meeting at Red Mills," said John Romig, "but the situation has to be critical on a planetary scale. Shrader has been right from the beginning. We're headed for an ice age."

"But why is it so warm?" asked Cathy.

"It's deceptive, isn't it?" agreed Romig. "To get the temperature increases, there must be tremendous volcanic activity. Heat from the earth's core is being pumped into the atmosphere."

"Along with ash," added Shrader.

"Yes, and that's critical," stated Romig. "For a while we will get a tremendous warm-up, but then it will tip the other way. Once the outer levels of the atmosphere get inundated with ash, it will be like drawing a window shade on the sun's radiation. It will get cold, real fast."

They sat in silence for a moment. In the pale light the teak bulkheads of *Strider*'s interior took on sinister shapes in the wood grain. In Shrader's mind, they began to swirl and leap like the flames of a roaring fire. He watched with fascination as though mesmerized by a dimension of sight that the other two could not see.

"I think Shrader is dead," said Cathy to Romig.

"I'm sorry," said Marks. "I know that this is important, but I can't keep myself awake."

"Go to bed," said John. Shrader didn't need convincing. He started to sink down on the settee berth. Cathy got up and went into the forward cabin. Almost immediately, she returned.

"The v-berth is open," she said. "He'll be more comfortable forward where there's more room." She and John coaxed Marks to his feet, and he stumbled through the narrow passage that led to the wide berth in the bow of the boat. Under sail, the bunk would pitch and roll with the movement of the waves, but here, at anchor, the expanse of the deep mattress welcomed his overtired body. He was almost asleep when he felt Cathy pull off his boat shoes and throw a quilt over him.

"He's pretty much had it," said Romig softly. "I'll bet he's not eaten either."

"He lives on peanut butter," added Cathy with a gentle smile. "I'm going to brew some coffee. I think I'll take his thermos and fill it."

"I'll bring some sandwiches, but not peanut butter," offered John.

"Not peanut butter," repeated Cathy as the two made their way aft toward the companionway exit.

48

The buds of the trees were thickening, and already there was a trace of color as the swollen red stems prepared to burst into leaf. Cathy was not conscious of the early signs of the changing season. She sat quietly on the foredeck of *Affinity* with her back propped against the mast. Behind her, in the boat's cockpit, a small party had erupted. Long hours of sailing had left them all more fatigued than their minds would allow them to believe, but they quickly kicked-back, and it didn't take long before spirits ran high. Cathy was glad for the familiar clamor which sounded more like the day's end during a summer cruise than the din of a refugee fleet. As for herself, thought turned inward. She tried to imagine the next leg of the journey by visually translating the two dimensional renderings of nautical charts into a scene of three dimensional reality.

They were rafted in Lake Saint Lawrence, an artificial pool created by the Long Sault Dam to feed the turbines of the Moses-Saunders Power Dam. Tomorrow, they would follow the shipping channel south to enter the Wiley-Dondero Canal and finally to the only two locks under U.S. control. The thought of locking through the Eisenhower made her apprehensive, but Shrader had seemed confident that it wouldn't be a problem. Her greatest concern was for the boats themselves. They would need adequate fenders and all hands to hold off possible collisions between the sheer walls of the lock chambers and the fiberglass hulls.

She was deep in thought when a familiar sound buzzed into her consciousness. It was the sound of a powerful outboard revved to a high pitch. She scanned the horizon to find the source of the reverberations. It was a craft which rode low in the water, not the familiar shape of a cruiser. What's more, it seemed to be headed directly for the rafted sailboats. Cathy watched as the indistinguishable dot grew in size, and transformed from a tan blur into the image of two men in a Whaler. One sat at the console, steering the craft. The other stood beside him, vested in an orange life jacket. The standing man pointed toward the flotilla as the boat continued on a collision course.

Cathy rose to her feet before the voices in the cockpit quieted.

"What is it, Cathy?" called out Vince Ragni.

"I don't know," she said. "But it looks like they want to talk to us." She wished Shrader was with her and thought about trying to arouse him. There was no time, however. The fast boat was just beyond the scope of *Affinity's* anchor line. The engine droned to an idle, then turned to stand off within hailing distance.

"Ahoy, sailing vessels!" called one of the men, the one standing in the boat. He was a large man in his early to mid sixties. His thinning gray hair was clearly askew from the high-speed ride. He brushed it back with the palm of his hand. As he did so, Cathy moved forward to the bow pulpit. Her movement caught his eye, and he began again. "Pardon me, Ma'am," he said politely. "My name is Gundersen, and I am the lockmaster at the Eisenhower. We have been trying to raise you on the radio for more than an hour. What channel have you been monitoring?"

"We're settling in for the night," said Cathy calmly. "We've turned off the radios to preserve our batteries."

"Well, I have to ask you what your intentions are and warn you against trying to continue through the Seaway," replied Gundersen.

"Warn us?" responded Cathy. "We are taking advantage of an early spring," she added coyly.

"Well, it's a dangerous business right now," answered Gus in a serious tone. "The Seaway has been closed to downstream traffic, and I expect that very soon the shipping channel will be full of commercial freight coming in from the Atlantic. I don't think you'd want to be in the way."

Without knowing what to say, Cathy repeated a courteous conversation stopper. "Well, thank you for the information." The man turned to his companion seated at the control console and said something that Cathy couldn't hear.

"I'm not sure you understand what I am saying," said Gundersen. "You need to head back to where you came from. The situation is extremely critical and you would be better off in your own homes."

"We are aware of that," answered Cathy to his surprise. By now the boats' population had come up onto the decks, and the two men in the Boston Whaler felt overwhelmed by the stares of the families. Gus cleared his throat and put on his most dispassionate, professional voice.

"Well, it's my duty to warn you that you need to move back up the Seaway. By tomorrow there will be a lot of commercial traffic passing through, and there will be no telling when you will be able to lock back through to Ontario."

Cathy studied the man for a moment. Behind the official khaki exterior, she could sense his intensity. "Thank you for the warning," she said. "You have done your duty."

Gus' look turned to exasperation. "Lady, do you understand what I have said? Is there anyone in charge here?" This time it was Cathy's reaction that drew all eyes.

"I know quite well what is happening, perhaps better than you," she answered coolly. There was steel in her eyes as she continued. "You have done your duty. You have spoken to the person in charge, and what I am telling you, I will say plainly. These boats are not going back through the Iroquois lock."

A red-faced Gundersen fought back an explosion, "And you're damned sure not going out through the Eisenhower. You have reached a dead end."

"Perhaps," she said. "Then again, where we go and who goes with us may already be beyond your power. Look over there," she said pointing to the eastern sky. Gundersen turned to follow her gesture.

"Holy shit!" he cried. The darkening sky glowed like the aura around a great city, and above it all a huge swirling cloud of multi-colored smoke. He grabbed the handheld VHF that was set in a bracket on the steering console. "Betty, what the hell is happening?" he shouted into the transceiver. Turning to Cathy, he said, "Stay put!" He turned his attention back to the radio and gestured to Ray to turn the Whaler around. The engine surged as the bow of the speedy boat lifted, and the craft climbed over its bow wave and came up to plane.

Cathy watched the boat skimming across the water like a skipping stone bouncing from ripple to ripple. "We'll see," she said under her breath. She turned to the blank faces of her companions. "Get your boats ready to move," she barked. "We'll be motoring, so get your sails well furled, and lash everything down, below decks, too." To her surprise, there wasn't a single challenge. People scurried everywhere. "Shrader," she said to herself. "I've got to talk with Shrader."

49

"Damn it, Betty. Answer me!"

"Gus?" came a weak reply.

"What the hell is going on?" he asked.

"We're losing contact," she said slowly. Her voice trailed off to silence.

"You mean my radio signal is breaking up?" he asked. She didn't respond. "Betty, do you read me?"

"I'm sorry, Gus," she said at last. "I can hear you just fine. I just don't know what's going on. I've lost contact downstream. All our communications seem to be wiped out to the east. I think something terrible has happened."

"Okay, Betty, calm down," said Gundersen. "Why do you think something terrible is going on?"

"I was on the phone talking to Jean Marsett at Melocheville Lock. I figured that it would be a good idea to keep a line open. I thought he'd be able to figure out what's going on now that we know that the Ste. Catherine has been breached." She paused as though trying to remember something better forgotten. Gus could sense her stumbling speech.

"You're doing fine," he encouraged. "What did he say?"

"He was like, real calm. He had someone out on the downstream gate relaying the depth readings."

"You mean the water was still rising?" interrupted Gus.

"Yes," she confirmed. "I think he was glad to have me on the line because he was scared, too. Did I tell you that they opened the lower lock?"

"No, you didn't," said Gundersen. He made a quick calculation. To render the Beauharnois Lock useless, the water level must have been around a hundred feet over normal sea level. "Was the water so high that they thought the lock would be submerged?" he asked.

"No," said Betty. "Not when I was talking to him. They opened it to allow the traffic to move through freely. They figured that by opening the gates, which were pretty much useless at that point, they'd be assuring an open channel. The other way, the gates would become a dam if the rising water took out the power and they were closed."

Gus had to admire Marsett's ingenuity. No order would have come down from on-high that would have been that gutsy. "Good going, Jean," he said under his breath. "Maybe you were cut off with a power failure."

"No, Gus, something happened!"

"How do you know that?" Gus pushed the handset closer to his ear. The noise of the engine was beating his brain. He covered his left ear with his free hand.

"It's what he said, Gus. We were talking; like I said, he was calm. Then all of a sudden he broke into French. You know, we were speaking English and something threw him into French. He said, 'Mon Dieu' which is easy enough, but then he said something like 'se nommez' and then it went dead. What does that mean?"

"You've always been better at parleying with the Québecois than me."

"Well, I can't figure it out. Somebody 'naming himself', but it's wrong. Something's happened, Gus and it's coming our way."

"I'll be there in a few minutes. Just hold tight, Betty." Turning to Anderson, he asked, "Any chance that we can get more speed out of this?" Ray didn't answer. Instead he tapped the chrome lever that controlled the throttle. It didn't move. It was already at the highest setting.

Gus turned his gaze forward toward the horizon. The gathering cloud was more ominous than any storm. He found himself repeating Betty's last communication. He knew that Ray would not have been able to hear Betty's conversation. He leaned toward Anderson and shouted over the high-pitched roar of the engine. "What does '*se nommez*' mean?"

Ray broke into a half smile. "Is this a joke?" he bellowed. "Okay, I give, what is a tsunami?" Gus blanched.

"Shit!" exclaimed Gundersen. He left Ray in a fog of confusion as his brain did a cartwheel. "We're a thousand miles inland. There couldn't be a tsunami here," he consoled himself. "But could there be a surge from the Atlantic that would appear like a wall of water?" He had no answer, just fear. He set his jaw and stared straight ahead. His eyes were open, but he saw nothing.

50

"Shrader, wake up," said Cathy. He was sound asleep and obviously not affected by the hubbub that was taking place above the decks.

"What's the matter?" he asked, groggily.

"Something's happening. While you were asleep, two men came out from the lock to say that we had to turn around, that we'd not be allowed to go through the Eisenhower. But something else is happening. The sky to the east is very strange." Shrader slid out from under the blanket. The cool cabin air made him shiver. He stepped into his shoes and was mounting the companionway steps before Cathy could make another comment.

The sun was in the west and throwing long shadows across the waters. Marks stepped out on deck. Cathy watched him from the cockpit. He seemed entranced, staring blankly into nothingness, or perhaps seeing things that others could not. He clutched the whale effigy that hung from his neck, and Cathy thought she heard him talking or chanting.

"Shrader," she said calling out to him, but he could no longer hear. Other eyes turned to look at the solitary figure. Cathy was aware that there were murmurings. "Do you have everything battened down?" she asked to divert attention.

"Cathy," said Shrader with a wild intensity in his voice. "We're going to have to go through the Eisenhower right now."

"But the lockmaster said..."

Shrader cut her off. "The water will be turbulent. You will need to take *Affinity* through first to give the others courage. Steer hard to port, there's a hydraulic that will try to throw you to starboard."

"Won't we lock through at the same time?" she asked, still confused.

"No! Listen!" It didn't sound like Shrader Marks. "You will fly through the canyon in white water. Steer hard to port. I have to come through last. Ride the ribbon of water and do not turn back for anything. Do you understand?" Clearly she didn't, but it was not the time for explanations.

She turned to meet a line of faces with looks more blank than her own. "Hang your fenders out over the sides. We're going to be motoring straight through the lock. I'll lead the way in *Affinity*. Leave a couple of boat lengths between each other, but stick together. Any questions?" She hoped against hope that there would be none, for she had no answers to give in any case. None were asked, however, and no one was willing to choose that moment to challenge her. They wouldn't, for they had crossed the line that represented the limits of any reasonable experience. In that moment, riding into the thickening smoke seemed no more insane than trying to outrun it.

51

"Betty, listen to me," said Gus into the VHF radio. "What I'm going to tell you to do is against every sensible thought you ever had. Open all the gates on the Eisenhower and the Snell."

"But...," she stammered.

"No, Betty, just do it. There is no time for an explanation."

"Should I ask..."

"Don't ask!" he shouted. "Just do it now! A surge of water is going to hit you in a minute; you've got to break it by throwing the whole force of the river toward it. Do you understand? Oh shit, I don't care if you understand, just do what I said." Gus turned off his handheld to put an absolute end to the discussion. There was no time to talk, and little in which to act. He also gambled that Betty would quickly toss aside consequences in favor of loyalty to a long time friend and colleague. He was right. She opened the gate to the lower pool, and then overrode the safety parameters in the computer to crack the opening in the upstream gate. The water leaped and spewed with such force that it nearly ripped away the steel and concrete like a paper towel. In a moment she was talking with the operator of the Snell who could see a wall of fire rolling toward him across Lake Saint Francis. He needed no convincing to do the unthinkable act of giving control of the water back to the river. It was like trying to push the flow of the Niagara backwards with a fire hose, but desperation does not need the confirmation of logic. In a panic, even a reasonable person would raise an arm to fend off a bullet.

Gus could feel the river leaping beneath the hull of the Whaler. In a strange way, he felt an excitement, not unlike a father touching his wife to feel the first kick of their unborn child. Careening along at high-speed, and having to brace himself against the bucking and bouncing of the now churning waters, lines from a book long forgotten came to his lips. It was something he'd memorized in his boyhood when the Eisenhower was dedicated. They were words he had always believed, but were now startlingly affirmed:

> "Did the river hear the faint scratching of the pens? Was the sound of cameras perceptible beside the fall of the Niagara, in the whirlpools, eddies, and rapids? No, the River only smiled that morning and went about its spring business of breaking the winter's ice, for it knew that men would never tame it."

He looked back at his friend, Ray Anderson, who was at the wheel with a look of serious concentration on his face. He skillfully threaded the boat toward the lock. Ray returned his glance. It was as though the years had fallen off his face. They each turned their gaze back to the river as they raced forward toward the unknown. It was the last time they would ever see each other.

52

Breaking up rafted sailboats can be as tricky as the initial setup. In a hastily called meeting, Cathy reminded everyone of the process.

"We have to keep the raft balanced so that *Affinity*'s anchor doesn't break free. That means the two outside boats will have to peel off first."

"That would be *Strider* and *Wave Chaser*," observed Vince Ragni from *Dream Dancer*. Cathy was glad to see that he had his wits about him, for he seemed the most affected by the early happy hour.

"That's right," she agreed. "Now stay in close, because I'll be the last one off, but the lead boat when we get under way. You'll have to allow us time to retrieve our plow." She was referring to the deep-setting anchor that held the string of sailboats in place. "From what Shrader says," she continued, "it's going to be a wild ride through the lock."

"Steer hard to port," said a sullen Shrader who sat at the edge of the group. All eyes turned to him. "The current will try to push you against the right wall." He seemed exhausted and diminished.

"How the hell would you know?" barked Phil Pearson.

"He sees things that we don't," chimed in Cathy. She could see questions wash over the faces of the others and tried to divert them quickly. "When we clear the other side, we'll rendezvous."

"No!" came a booming voice that Cathy would not have recognized. It was Shrader. He was on his feet, and seemed a menacing power. It was a remarkable transformation from the passive shape of a moment earlier. "There will be no rendezvous. You must follow and not look back. Ride the ribbon of water and do not turn back for anything." His breath was heavy and his eyes glinted with a wildness that made the others look away. It was Cathy to whom they turned.

"I will lead you through," she repeated. "Follow in line. If you get in trouble, I will not be able to help. Shrader will come along last. He may be able to give assistance if you have a problem." All eyes went back to Shrader, but he was not there. He was moving across the decks of the rafted boats toward *Strider*.

"Shrader is right," called out Cathy. "We don't have much time; we have to break up the raft. Let's get to it."

At her words, people began to scurry over the decks. They broke into two teams and moved to the outside edges of the raft. By the time one team got to *Strider*, Shrader had already started the engine and was loosening the lines that secured him to the next boat.

"Here, I'll get that," said John as he took hold of the bitter end of the stern line. Shrader said nothing. "Are you all right?" asked Romig. His question was met with a forbidding look that cut off all potential conversation. He tossed the line to Shrader who coiled it and threw it into the cockpit lazarette.

"I'll see you on the other side," said Marks without making eye contact. "Be careful," he added.

"Wait!" called a voice from over the decks. It was Cathy. "Take this with you, Shrader," she said as she tossed him a black, handheld VHF radio. "We have a radio mounted in the cockpit. You won't be able to go below to get to yours."

Shrader nodded as the drift between the boats increased. Marks engaged the gears and *Strider* began to pull forward. Already, hands were busy uncoupling *Rol's Royce* from the rafted flotilla.

"Better abandon ship, Admiral," said Marty Koenig.

Cathy looked around and realized what she had meant by the comment. In a moment, the boat would be free from the raft and

Cathy would find herself on the wrong side of a water gap. "Thanks for the warning," she said automatically as she hopped over to the next boat which was *Mewtiny*. She found herself next to John Romig. "Is Shrader okay?" she asked.

"I don't know," answered Romig. "He seems real distant." They felt the diesel engine fire beneath their feet. They could feel the vibrations of the motor through the cockpit sole. Brittany was at the wheel. She nursed the sputtering engine to a steady idle speed.

"It looks like I need to move over to my boat," she said stepping over the lifelines onto *Affinity*. She moved aft to the cockpit and engaged the engine. Phil and the boys were casting off the lines that held *Mewtiny* in place. She looked over at the other boat and her gaze fell on her daughter. Brittany looked, for all the world, like a woman and not a fourteen year old. She stood confidently at the boat's helm. Cathy was overwhelmed by conflicting emotions. She wanted to take Brittany by the hand and lead her to the safety of her own boat, but she knew that safety was a gift that she could not give. Instead, she turned to her and spoke softly, "How are you doing, Kid?"

Brittany smiled broadly. "John and Laura are really nice," she said.

"Well, take care of them," said Cathy. "And take care of yourself. I love you."

Brittany looked at her mother. "Thanks, Mom," she answered, "I love you, too." She hesitated, then added, "you know everyone here thinks you are amazing the way you make everyone feel confident. I guess I feel that way, too."

Cathy felt a constriction in her throat. "Thanks, Baby," she managed to say. To herself, she wondered when her daughter had become a woman. The two sailboats were separated, and Brittany slowly pulled her craft away from the anchored *Affinity*. Cathy stood as though in a dream as Brittany and the Romigs seemed to fade from her line of sight.

"It goes around clockwise," a man's voice said from the bow. "Can't you do anything right?" It was Philip who was trying to get Chris and Justin to raise the anchor with the help of the electric windlass mounted on the foredeck. Eventually, he pushed them off and took hold of the line. "If you guys are going to act like wimps, you might as well go back and sit with your mother," he chided.

The two boys slinked back to the cockpit. Cathy saw the hurt and anger in their faces. "It's okay, fellows," she offered. "It's hard to raise that anchor, even with the windlass. Your father needs to do it himself."

"It's Brittany's fault," barked Chris. "It's her job, and she should be here. She's lazy like Dad says."

"No, she's not," defended Justin, who could barely get the words out before breaking into tears.

"Both of you, get your lifejackets on," said their father, returning from the bow. The boys vanished below decks. Cathy had already eased the transmission into forward and was bringing the boat to full power. "Let me take the wheel," he said to Cathy. "This could get rough."

"I know," she answered, "which is why I will stay where I am. You'd better get out the harnesses and make sure the boys are wedged where they can brace themselves if need be."

"It's Shrader, isn't it?" he said.

"What?" asked Cathy.

"Shrader is filling your mind with wild ideas and making you think you can pull this thing off. But you're not that good, and neither is Shrader. He's going crazy."

Cathy studied her husband's face. For the first time, he seemed diminished in her eyes. With cool indifference, she answered. "I tell you that Shrader Marks is not crazy. He is, in fact, the most sane person here, and the test of our sanity is our willingness to do what he says."

Philip blew off her statement with a huff. "It doesn't matter what you think anyway," he said. "That old boat of his will fall apart before this trip is over."

"What?" interjected Cathy, who was remembering similar comments when they left the dock at Cape Vincent. "Have you done something to his boat?"

Philip smirked, but said nothing. Cathy threw the on-switch to the cockpit VHF. "Shrader, I think Philip did something to your boat," she said, disregarding all radio protocols. She did not expect to hear laughter through the deck-mounted speaker, but she did. Philip heard it, too, and his face grew hard.

"Tell him that my knot meter is reading out at 4.8 knots," said Shrader. Cathy didn't need to say anything to her husband, for he heard it plainly over the speaker. His only reaction was a clenched fist and a beet-red face.

"What does that mean?" she said to Philip without realizing that she had depressed the call button on the microphone.

"It means he can fry in hell," came Marks' voice over the radio. "And you both will very quickly if you two don't prepare to get through the lock." Shrader's words and tone wrenched Cathy back to the tasks at hand. "Hang as many fenders from the lifelines as you can find," she commanded. Philip opened the cockpit storage compartments and found three additional fenders to add to the four already deployed. His rage over Shrader's comments kept him from questioning Cathy's orders. She opened the throttle and soon *Affinity* was approaching eight knots in relation to the water. The others were following suit. She could see Rhonda Ragni and her son Tony hanging out fenders on *Dream Dancer*. Bill and Connie Morgan on *Wave Chaser* were untangling their harnesses and attaching them to the lifelines. All the boats deferred to Cathy and fell in line behind. In her mind, she rehearsed the warnings of Shrader Marks. They were cryptic words that she didn't fully understand, but she hoped that their meaning would become clear in time.

"Ride the ribbon of water, and don't turn back," she found herself repeating out loud.

They had been anchored behind one of the river islands and out of the current, but as they rounded the point of land, Cathy sensed a change. The first sensation was the breeze in her face. Initially, she thought that the wind had picked up, but then she turned and saw that the other boats were falling off quickly behind her. The others had not yet entered the current of the main channel, and the gap between them widened. It was as if they had sailed over an invisible mark on the water and were now being hurled forward.

She had no way of judging the speed of the boat in relation to the land, but within the flow of water, *Affinity* was nearing its hull speed of nine knots. She looked ahead and saw that they were rushing toward the narrows that led into the Wiley-Dondero Ship Canal. She pulled back on the throttle to try to slow the boat. The engine noise subsided, and Phil looked up at her, then down at the knotmeter which was falling off.

"If you're in such an all-fired hurry," he said, "why are you slowing down?"

"Look," she said pointing to the shoreline. He hadn't noticed that they were now traveling at breakneck speed. She set the engine at near idle with just enough forward speed to maintain the helm. Ahead she saw what looked like two pillars rising out of the water like the incisors of a great gaping maw. She knew at once that she was looking through the Eisenhower Lock, and it was alarming. Both the upper and lower gates were open, and the mystery of the racing current was solved. The lock walls, the revetments, became channels for the running water, and the sound of the newly formed rapids began to wash over them.

"Oh, shit," murmured Philip. "Turn back!" he shouted. But Cathy held her own. She knew it would be pointless to attempt to turn off. Even at full power the engine could not give the boat any headway against the current. They were committed to passing through the eye of this concrete needle, or die trying.

"Check the boys below," she said with command in her voice. Philip's quick response surprised her. "Batten down all the hatches," she added as he disappeared below. Even against the growing thunder of the water, she could hear Philip throwing the latches on the deck hatches. She drew the microphone of the radio to her mouth and spoke clearly into it. "I am approaching the lock," she said calmly. "It is coming up very quickly and it's a powerful sight. Hang back as best you can until I am through. Once you are into the channel, you'll not be able to fight the current so try and angle toward the edge of the flow until I give the all clear. Keep your engines in gear just in case you need to throttle up for steering power."

She hoped that her transmission was received as she returned the microphone to its clip. In any case, she would not take her hands off the wheel until the course was run. From below, Philip inserted the lap boards in the companionway and drew the hatch closed. He had made his decision to ride this out below decks. Cathy was at the helm with ten tons of boat in front of her. She pointed the bow to shoot through the eighty foot gap of churning water. On her left, a concrete wall narrowed the approach passage. She was in the forebay, and she could feel the growing turbulence through the vibration of the wheel beneath her grip.

Suddenly, the boat dropped as she cascaded over a standing wave that threw her sideways. She steered hard to port, but the starboard revetment loomed as the boat slipped sideways. Instinctively her hand went to the throttle and pushed the engine to full power. She heard the surge, but feared the worst. Her arms were heavy as she fought to hold the rudder. The boat kicked out beneath her. It felt like a wave breaking beneath a dinghy, but the scale was all wrong. Now the current reflected off the wall and sent her hurtling in the opposite direction. She spun the wheel clockwise, throwing her body weight against it to keep from being tossed aside by the water pressure against the rudder. When she thought she could hold it no longer, the lock spit her out into the lower pool. Still running at speeds to make a power boater envious, she felt the pressure lessen and she let the wheel spin back to a more neutral position. She reached for the radio.

"This is *Affinity*," she said, trying unsuccessfully to block the adrenaline that was still pulsing through her veins. "Shrader was right! You *will* have to steer to port. The current will try to push you into the starboard wall. Gun your engine to get through it. It's quite a sleigh ride," she added. Looking back through the lock, Cathy was startled. From downriver it was a seething, frothing water course. At the upper end, she could see a mast dipping and careening as it entered the downhill ride. It was *Dream Dancer*. It bounced like a Styrofoam fishing bobber rather than a heavily ballasted hull. Cathy held her breath as it traveled the nearly eight hundred feet of white water. It steadied as it passed the portal of the downward bay, and was cruising in the channel. Cathy realized the second truth of Shrader's warning. The current was still so strong that she could not turn back and give any aid.

"Mayday, Mayday, Mayday," came a voice over the radio. Cathy jumped to hear the words that every boater knows, and hopes to never use. It was a woman's voice, one that Cathy couldn't identify. "Mayday, Mayday, Mayday. This is Eisenhower, Eisenhower, Eisenhower." Cathy realized that the strange message was coming from shore, and not over the normal channel.

"Mayday. Eisenhower, Eishenhower, Eisenhower. This is *Affinity, Affinity, Affinity*. Received Mayday," answered Cathy in textbook style.

"I saw you come through the lock," said the voice, all protocol vanished instantly. "There's a boat overturned in the water near your position," she continued. "It took me awhile to find what channel you were monitoring, but I can see you, and you are approaching the boat. It's near the shore on your right."

Cathy scanned the fast moving water's edge. She picked out a tan shell floating on the surface. Two orange objects were floating at its side. "I see it," she said into the radio. She turned the wheel to try and intercept the overturned hull.

"It's not right for me to make the Mayday call, but they can't do it for themselves and they're friends of mine," said Betty Montgomery.

The water was moving swiftly. Cathy tried to cross the current at an angle that would let her intercept the capsized Boston Whaler, but it was no good. The small boat, which had been drifting, suddenly stopped. It was hung up on something, and the river started to roll over it and push it down. Cathy could only watch as she sped past the derelict craft.

"I'm sorry," she said. "Maybe one of the others..."

"Did you see any sign of Gus or Ray?" said Betty, cutting her off.

"No," Cathy answered. "At first I saw two orange shapes which could have been lifejackets, but when the boat got snagged... Well, I don't see anything else now." The channel went dead. "Maybe one of the other boats can get closer," Cathy continued apologetically. "But the water is pretty cold."

Betty understood the last comment. A person in the water would not have much time before hypothermia would become fatal. She slumped down in her chair, put her face in her hands, and began to sob.

Cathy could not see or hear what was happening in the control cabin, but she hailed Shrader who was still cruising in the upper pool.

"Did you hear that?" she asked him. "There's a boat capsized down here."

"It's not your concern," answered Marks with no hint of emotion. "Keep headed out, you've got to stay in the current." There was no satisfaction in what she heard, and her stomach churned as she looked back at the disappearing speck on the water that represented two lives. At that same moment, her eyes were drawn to the sight of another mast careening through the sluice gate. A quick count told her that five boats had now navigated the rapids safely, if that word could even be used. One of the boats was *Mewtiny*, and Brittany was at her helm. The idea lifted her spirits, and she turned her attention to her forward course.

Above the lock, Shrader's attention was turned to the pair of boats that had not yet entered the turbulent waters of the lock. The energy of his dreams came back to him. He remembered the sensation of white water rafting through a steep canyon and seeing the boat behind him scraping the sheer wall. If it was a vision of this moment, he would prevent it from happening by being the last boat through the lock. Still, he could not be sure if this was, in fact, the canyon of his dream, or another. Down river was a second lock, the Snell. The journey through this passage would be a prelude to the next, but he would not take any chances. *Strider* would be the last boat to enter the Eisenhower.

Ahead of him and slightly to port was another sloop. Shrader did not have to look at the hull graphics to know its identity. It was *Fairwinds*.

"Just stay in front of me," said Shrader to Jim Barker who could not have possibly heard. By now the roar of the water through the lock was reaching his ears, and his focus turned to his own course. He was gaining on the Barkers' boat so he reversed his engine to slow the boat. There would be no halting of his forward progress. The boats were all at the mercy of the current, and would be swept in order through the narrows.

Suddenly, Shrader saw something white in the water directly in the path of *Fairwinds*. His first impulse was that it was a gull floating with the current. But the boat was overtaking it. A bird would not be able to remain stationary against the rapid flow. He looked closer. Whatever it was, there was water rushing over it, partially obscuring its bulk.

"What the hell," he found himself saying out loud. Then recognition swept over him. It was a mooring buoy. Whether it belonged in the channel or was swept there by the flood, he didn't care. Beneath the floating marker was a length of chain.

"Watch out!" he yelled at the top of his voice. But against the backdrop of noise, there was no chance of his words being heard. There was no time, either. As though everything suddenly dropped into slow motion, he saw the bow of *Fairwinds* eclipse the floating ball. Shrader held his breath, hoping that the hull would ride over the mooring chain. One, two, three, his heart pounded as the other boat glided smoothly along. Then suddenly its bow dipped as the sloop's long keel tangled with the submerged tether. The boat stopped with an abruptness that sent Tish Barker flying against the cabin trunk and Jim into the wheel. A sudden grounding is always alarming, but this one held a double impact. With the sudden loss of forward momentum, the stern of the boat became victim to the current and began to rotate around the pivot of the keel. It careened counter-clockwise until it lay broadside to the rushing torrent. At that point it broke free, still spinning until it was drifting stern first.

Shrader stood by absolutely helpless as *Strider* glided past the hapless vessel. He could see everything very clearly. Blood was flowing from Tish's forehead where she had caught a winch just above the right eyebrow. Jim was doubled over at the helm, the wind knocked out of him.

"Mind your helm," he shouted. Through the paroxysms of trying to catch his breath, Jim gave a look of comprehension. He leaned on the wheel, turning it to complete the 360 degrees. *Fairwinds* came about and fell in line behind *Strider*.

"Steer hard to port," Shrader called to himself as if out of his own dream. He turned from *Fairwinds* to find himself entering the swirling rapids of the wide-open lock. The canyon of his nightmare closed in around him. A wall loomed up in front of him as he steered desperately to avoid a collision. He turned the wheel to its limit and prayed that the helm would respond. Still, he was pushed closer by the seething water until he could touch its slimy coarse surface. In a futile gesture, born of instinct and not reason, he reached out to push off the revetment. The forces at work could have easily snapped his arm, but his reach fell short as the boat suddenly lifted on the crest of a standing wave and surfed forward, turning sideways within the lock. Once through the lower gate, the waterway widened, and *Strider* continued its spin until Shrader found himself facing the lock and drifting backwards. He opened up the throttle to the highest rpm's the old gasoline engine could muster. Motoring against the current was a losing battle, but his Atomic IV had more horsepower than a comparable diesel. In reality, the motor was a modified tractor engine, and Shrader was counting on slowing his backward drift to manage the next part of his dream. It did not take long to see what he would be facing. *Fairwinds*, not fully under control from the ordeal in the upper pool, crossed into the watery chaos of the lock chamber.

Shrader could see trouble from the start. The boat did not begin in the center of the channel, but came in closely parallel to the left wall. In an instant it would hit the hydraulic, and be pitched further aside.

"Keep left! Steer to port," he called out. But even if his words could have been heard, no maneuver in the world would have been effective against the power of the water.

Shrader heard the rasping tear as the hull scraped against the revetment. For a moment, he thought that he could see sparks flying where the heavy, metal chain plates sheared off, and the wire shrouds that held the mast sprung free like guitar strings popping. With that, the mast began to wobble under its own weight. Shrader feared it would snap, but the river was not yet through with its mischief.

Fairwinds rebounded off the wall with such force that turned it sideways to the current. The standing wave which had hurled the other boats out of the lock now met the beam of the vessel. Its force rolled the craft ninety degrees, pushing it out of the lock, mast first. Shrader could see the whole thing as his motor strained against the current. He found himself looking down on the top of the cabin. Jim and Tish Barker were both thrown against the lifelines. He could see that Tish was holding fast to the rail, struggling for a toehold in the sideways world of a knockdown. Jim was over the lifelines. Shrader could not tell if he was conscious. He was in the water, dangling by a fire-red tether attached to his harness.

With a loud cracking sound, *Fairwinds* righted itself. Shrader realized that the noise was the final price exacted by the Eisenhower. In a parting gesture, it grabbed the boat's stern rail, ripping away the backstay and severing the rudder stock.

The boat was totally adrift, and Shrader found that time was again slowing before his eyes. Everything seemed now to move at a decelerated pace. The mast, already weakened by the loss of support, began to fold on itself. It began to bend, slowly at first, then it came down, crashing like a tree broken midway up its trunk.

Rudderless with the propeller still turning, the boat began to careen toward *Strider*. Shrader tried to angle away, and narrowly escaped a collision as *Fairwinds* passed. It was moving on a collision course with the southern bank of the channel. Marks surveyed the hapless craft as it passed. He saw that its deck had been pierced by the fallen masthead. He saw some movement in the cockpit, and turned his focus to see Tish beginning to move about, her head now caked with blood.

"Kill your motor," shouted Marks in what he thought was a hopeless gesture. To his surprise, Tish turned with practiced skill and threw the kill switch. The boat, still captive to the current, continued to move, but it began to slow to the forward speed of the water.

It was then that Shrader saw the limp form of Jim Barker emerge from what looked like a spouting wave running parallel to the boat's course. He was being dragged by his tether. Under the best of circumstances, getting an unconscious victim out of the water is a monstrous feat, and Shrader racked his brain for a strategy. He felt sure that he could overtake the boat now that it was downstream and drifting. He would use *Strider*'s engine to outrun it. He turned the wheel to come about. He was ready to shout again, but Tish had turned away. She was frantically working to open the companionway hatch which was partially blocked by the fallen spar and rigging.

The children, thought Marks, *they're still below*. The hatch opened and three small bodies leaped out to their mother. By now, Shrader was nearly alongside the other vessel. He feared getting too close and crushing Jim between the hulls. But something else was happening. *Fairwinds* was shrinking.

Marks' mind raced to understand what his senses were telling him. Was he having another damned vision? Then it struck him. *Fairwinds* was taking on water. It was sinking. He looked at the three children. They were soaked. The cabin was already partially full. He had to act. He wheeled the bow of his boat close to the other craft hoping that he could keep an open space between the aft quarters. He threw *Strider* into neutral to stop the propeller and keep it from being fouled by floating lines, or worse. In a moment the spinning blades could shred an arm or leg.

"Step across!" he ordered with no room for argument in his voice. Tish pointed, and Ashley, Kelly, and Aaron obediently stepped over the lifelines onto the other boat. Tish followed behind.

"Where's Jim?" she shrieked with sudden awareness.

"I've got him," answered Shrader. His only hope was that she would believe the lie. She gave him a puzzled look, and started to step across. When she looked down, she saw her husband dangling lifeless in the water between the boats. Her hesitation made Shrader erupt.

"Get the hell over here and I'll be able to get him out of the water." It was a lie, and Shrader knew it. But it was a lie that was worth the risk. Tish crossed over, and Shrader disconnected the tether of his own harness. He stepped up to the cockpit coaming with only one hand on the wheel.

"Take this," he said as he let go of the wheel. Tish jumped quickly to take the helm, and Marks was over the side. *Fairwinds* had only a foot of freeboard left. Already the cockpit was flooding with water flowing in through the scuppers. There was not much time left. If the boat went down, it would pull Jim with her.

Shrader shackled the loose end of his tether to one of *Strider's* lifeline stanchions, and unhooked the end that attached to his own harness. He looped the shackle over the taut line that was Barker's only link to the boats. Shrader still had to release the shackle that attached Jim's tether to *Fairwinds*. He pulled with all his strength to get some slack to release the shackle, but it was like trying to pull against a straining horse. He braced himself against the cockpit coaming and used the strength of his legs to push off. The nylon webbing of the strap cut his palms, but still he pulled. Slowly he felt himself pulling away. In a quick motion he opened the shackle and let the trailing weight of Jim Barker draw back against his hard-earned slack. The tether slid back, attached only to *Strider*. Shrader did not release his grip, and the release of the shackle would have easily yanked him overboard, but there was no longer any boat beneath him.

Fairwinds slipped beneath the water with a great gasp as the last air from the flooded cabin erupted into the twilight. Once the bubble escaped, the boat went down quickly under the ballasted weight of its lead keel. Shrader was pulled downward by the sinking craft whose plummeting bulk created a vacuum that sucked him beneath the surface of the cold water. He nearly gasped at the sudden grip of the frigid water, but he managed to steel himself against the shock that would rob his breath and flood his lungs. He was carried beneath the water. He kicked with his feet in an effort to overpower the downward pull. He wondered if his numb fingers were still clutching the tether. He could not tell. Finally, he reached the limit of his buoyancy and began to rise. When he broke through the surface, he found himself trailing behind *Strider*. Tish was at the wheel, and the faces of her three children were staring behind him at the floating form of their father.

Ignoring his growing weakness, Shrader worked his way back along the tether until he reached Jim Barker. He was floating upright in his bright orange PFD. His eyes were closed.

"Jim," said Shrader. To his surprise the man's eyes opened momentarily at the sound of his own name. "He's still alive," Marks called to those on the boat. He took a mouthful of water for his efforts. "Pull us in!" He had realized that his own strength was dissolving quickly in the chilly water. On board *Strider*, Tish and the children began to tug at the woven tether, but to no avail.

"Put down the swim ladder," Shrader said, realizing that he needed a change of strategy. Tish switched her attention to unfastening the latch that held the transom boarding ladder in its upright position. She fumbled momentarily, then managed to free the stainless steel ladder and swing it down on its hinges so that the lower two rungs reached beneath the water's surface.

Shrader tried his best to maneuver himself toward the boarding ladder, but he felt himself drifting off to sleep. *This is crazy,* he thought. He knew that even if he could manage reaching the boat, he would be lucky to be able to haul out his own weight. He would never be able to get Jim out in time. Barker was unconscious now, and Marks could not elicit any response from him.

Strider was drifting sideways to the current. In the panic of the moment, the helm was left unattended, and the boat was no longer facing downstream. Marks and Barker were dangling fifteen feet off the boat's stern, but also in clear view of the river ahead.

Something caught Shrader's eye. Just ahead was a tan-colored pontoon of some sort. It was obviously anchored to something because it was not moving along with the flow. They were approaching it quickly. It was the overturned Boston Whaler that Cathy had warned him about.

In an instant Shrader was kicking out away from *Strider* in order to stretch the tether to its greatest length. Even if it took his last ounce of energy, it would be worth the effort. He wanted to catch the Whaler between himself and the sailboat. He kicked three more times and positioned himself for an impact. He kept

Jim behind him, and slipped his left arm over the tether. Leaning back, he could feel Barker's bulky life jacket against him. Shrader shivered and wished that he'd worn a PFD along with his harness. It would have helped preserve his body heat and absorb some of the impact that would soon be crushing him. As it happened, however, the collision was not jarring. He reached the exposed part of the overturned boat and worked his way long the hull on the opposite side from where *Strider* was passing. The tether rode up over the stern of the capsized boat. As *Strider* glided past quietly, Shrader could feel the line tensing under his arm. He reached beneath the waterline for some handhold for what he knew would soon follow.

When the drifting boat reached the limit of the line, it pulled taut. Shrader gripped tightly as he felt the strap cut into his armpit. His cheek and face were crushed against the hull as he fought the pressure that would drag the two men up over the top of it. Shrader held on, squeezed between the fiberglass and the inanimate body of Jim Barker.

Suddenly, pain raced through his shoulder as his arm popped out of joint. Instinctively, he reeled away, and felt Jim slide up past him. He grabbed with his right arm, and caught a leg. He also would have been carried over the top, but at that moment the overturned launch broke free of whatever had snagged it. It began to drift, and the force that had threatened to drag them back into the water now lessened. In point of fact, Jim was now completely out of the water and lying on a fairly stable platform just a few feet from *Strider*'s stern rail.

Shrader moved as quickly as he could working his way around the boat toward the sailboat's boarding ladder. He feared Jim's being pulled off the precarious perch.

"Get me a line so that I can tie off the boat," he cried. Tish just looked confused. "Hand me the end of the mainsheet." She understood what he meant and immediately began to uncoil the long strand of rope that controlled the mainsail. She tossed the free end to Shrader. After three attempts, he managed to snag the line and began to work his way along the gunwale of the overturned powerboat. His hands searched anxiously beneath the waterline. He was trying to find a place to tie off the line that could secure the two vessels to each other.

His fingers touched the upholstered grip of a pedestal chair. He gripped tightly and pulled to see if it would hold, but it didn't. It came free in his hand. He let it go, but something clutched back at him. A wave of panic raced through him as he struggled to pull his arm free. Instead, a head emerged from the water next to him.

"Who the hell are you?" he heard himself say to the sputtering face.

"We've got to get out of this water," came the reply. It was not the time for an argument, and Shrader knew that it was true.

"I've got an unconscious man here!" Shrader barked.

"I know," said the stranger. "Between the two of us, maybe we can do it quickly." They worked their way around the hull until they were between the sailboat and the capsized Whaler. The nameless man reached for *Strider's* boarding ladder and stepped up onto the first rung. "All of you, take hold of the lifeline and pull when I tell you," he said to the stunned family members who were watching from the cockpit.

Whoever this interloper was, he took command easily. Shrader was glad as he contemplated the futility of his own efforts. The man turned back toward Marks. "When we pull, just help guide him toward us and give him a boost if you can."

Shrader didn't have time to protest even if he wanted to. The man had Tish and the children tugging on the nylon tether. It was of no avail until he set his hand to the task. To Marks' surprise the gap between the two hulls began to lessen, and then, Jim's body began to shift.

"Pull hard," cried the man. The powerboat seemed to be falling off, and Barker seemed suspended. Shrader thought he'd be crushed by the falling weight, but Barker did not fall. Gundersen's massive hand took hold of him by the harness and flew him over the widening fissure between the boats. Barker's limp legs brushed past Marks, kicking against *Strider's* transom.

They had him aboard, or at least his torso. It was a simple thing to haul his legs in. Shrader felt a rush, forgetting that he was still in the water.

"Do you need help?" came a voice from overhead.

"What?" asked Marks.

"Getting aboard," said the man.

"Oh. No," said Marks, unsure of his words as they came out of his mouth. For a moment a strange thought shot through his brain. What if he just let go? What if he gave himself to the river?

Somewhere, either in his brain or in his ears, he heard a call. It might have been his name, and it might have been Cathy's voice. But there was a part of it that was deeper and wilder, and it said "Whaleman". He tightened his grip on the ladder and tried to pull up his own waterlogged bulk. Then another hand was on his shoulder, pulling to lighten his ascent.

53

Cathy's last communication with Betty Montgomery left a hard knot in her stomach. The fact that she couldn't help the people in the overturned boat made her realize that they had crossed the line between a pleasure cruise and survival. Some would not survive. The river, however, would not let her dwell on the possibilities. The realities were enough. Already ahead she could see the Snell Lock. It, too, was wide open. Beyond it was sixty miles of river and the close approach to Montréal.

She stood at the wheel of *Affinity* and braced herself for the race through the second sluice gate. She wondered if the water coursing through the lock would behave in the same manner as the previous one. She knew that she was not in charge; the river had taken complete control and she could only stay alert and react. Cathy wondered what lay beyond the lower pool, but her vision was shielded by a wall of dark clouds beyond.

The boat was approaching the softnose that marked the entrance to the forebay of the great lock. Philip stood in the cockpit, bracing himself on the cabin trunk.

"Better tell the boys to lay low and hold on," warned Cathy. Phil called down below to warn Justin and Chris. It was then that they caught the first reek of smoke. Neither said anything. It was too late for speech, and too late to turn back.

Cathy steered for the center of the channel. The boat hit a standing wave at the first gate, and dropped as though the bottom had fallen out of the world. The hull hit hard, like a breaching whale. It rolled as it regained its center of gravity, and surfed straight and true toward the lower gate. They were out. Cathy broke her radio silence to let the fleet know how to handle the flood through the Snell. The Ragnis in *Dream Dancer* had remained behind them the whole way and were already into the lock before Cathy could offer a warning. The second boat tracked as true as the first, and in a short time a line of masts followed behind *Affinity*. Only *Strider* and *Fairwinds* were left unaccounted.

Cathy could not let her fears for Shrader and the others divert her attention from what was ahead. The water in front of the bow was on fire. It was an image too absurd to register as real. She turned aside to look at the thing that she couldn't understand, but the answer was simple. They were motoring into a burning chemical spill. The dark smoke was held at bay by the prevailing wind, but even now, the stench was becoming pervasive.

The current was in control, and Cathy could only hold her course as the boat flew toward a solid wall of smoke and flame. Whatever had caused the calamity had created a backwards surge up the river, pushing back the Saint Lawrence with its fiery flow. They were still in the Wiley-Dondero canal and running on the torrent that had been unleashed by the opening of the locks. Ahead they would join the main body of the river, but it had become a river of flame. The tidal surge which carried the burning slick had already carried its deadly discharge upstream; only the force of the current kept the canal free of the blaze.

Cathy strained her eyes to watch the waters ahead. She was riding on the forward edge of the locks' effluence. In a matter of minutes, *Affinity* would cross what should have been an imaginary line where the waters of the canal would meet the waters that spilled through the Long Sault Dam along the river's ancient course. The line was no longer imaginary. It was billowing with gray and black smoke.

"Turn back!" shouted Philip, who blanched at the sight. But Cathy held firm on her course. From within her emerged an inexplicable confidence. She centered her mind on Shrader's insistent command, "Ride the ribbon of water and do not turn back for anything."

Philip turned to her with terror in his eyes. "You can't go into that," he said. "The fiberglass will go up like a flare." He took a step toward the wheel, but Cathy waved him off.

"Wait," she said. Her eyes strained to see the leading edge of the water washing out the mouth of the canal. Then it happened. The rushing water split the inferno, cutting a swath through the burning slick. "Look," she said, pointing to what was happening.

"It won't hold," complained her husband.

"Shrader was right," she continued. "He said that we would ride on a ribbon of water. Get on the radio and tell the others. Tell them to close the gap between the boats since we don't know how long this surge will continue."

Philip took hold of the microphone on the cockpit VHF and warned the others. Within, however, his fear was turning to rage. He looked at Cathy and hated her for being right. For her part, she could sense his emotional shift. It bothered her less than in the long years of their marriage when she took responsibility for his moods. She now knew the truth. For Philip every emotion eventually distilled to rage, but now she was no longer afraid.

One by one the boats in the fleet responded to *Affinity*'s broadcast. The Ragnis aboard *Dream Dancer* were already shortening the distance between them when *Rol's Royce* and *Wave Chaser* came on the air waves. Behind them were *Mewtiny* and *Major Blunder*. Cathy breathed a sigh of relief at the sight of *Mewtiny* with Brittany at the helm. She waited for two other signals, but they did not come.

"Can you see *Strider* and *Fairwinds*?" she asked.

"I can't see anything," said Philip. "Shrader might have been right about the water, but not about the smoke."

Pearson was right. When Cathy turned back, she could see the dense smoke wafting between the hulls and the rigging. It choked her and she tried to cough it off.

"Better warn the others. If they have dust masks or handkerchiefs, they should use them." Philip was back on the radio, but the warning was unnecessary. The others had all seen the danger.

"*Affinity, Affinity, Affinity*, this is *Major Blunder*." Cathy recognized Bert Jenkins' voice.

Only a retired Major would worry about proper radio protocol at a time like this, she thought to herself. Philip answered the hail.

"What is it, Bert?" he asked.

"It's the cabins," he answered disregarding radio etiquette. "The fumes will collect down below. Make sure all the hatches are sealed. If there are people below, they shouldn't lie down; the bilges will fill up first."

"You're right, Major," answered Philip with an air of icy control. "Since you are the last boat in line currently, I'll put you in charge. Anyone experiencing problems should report to Major Jenkins, who will be in the best position to reach you. Any questions?"

There was an awkward silence before Jenkins spoke. "I'll be glad to give assistance as needed. If it's all right with the Admiral."

"She's standing right here," said a red-faced Pearson. "Do you have to hear it from her own mouth, Jenkins?"

Cathy suddenly felt sorry for her husband. In corporate America he was used to being obeyed, and now he was betrayed by a circumstance that he could not manage or control. She nodded her head. "It's a good plan, Philip."

"Didn't mean to set you off," came the reply over the radio, "just making sure of the chain of command. This is *Major Blunder*. Out."

"He's the major blunder," coughed Philip as he returned the microphone to its bracket. "I'll try to find a mask or something," he added.

"Check the boys, too," said Cathy. Pearson nodded his head rather than take in enough air to mouth the words. The air was thick and the heat was beginning to intensify.

Cathy throttled back her engine for fear of outrunning the surging river. The knotmeter showed that she was almost dead in the water, running at 1.25 knots in relation to the water, but she knew that they were traveling much faster. In relation to the land, they had to be moving at fifteen to twenty knots as they were carried with the fluid mass of the rolling flood.

"Where are you, Shrader?" she asked out loud. The price of her words was a cough that made her feel like her lungs were turning inside out.

54

Shrader looked at his knotmeter and took another sip of his coffee. The gauge read 6.28 knots, and he had no idea how the coffee got into his thermos. He had no idea about a lot of things that had happened in the last half hour, but his wits were coming back to him.

"This coffee has probably saved our lives," he said to a quiet stranger who was seated in the cockpit.

"Let's hope it does the trick on *your* friend," he answered, "but *my* friend is still out there." Gus gestured toward the expanse of water behind them. "If you can get me near the shore, I'm sure I could make it," he pleaded.

"Not in this water, and not in this current," said Marks.

"But I could get a search team, and we could find Ray."

"Ray didn't make it. I'm sorry."

"How do you know?" asked Gundersen.

"I can't explain it, but I would just know," answered Shrader. "Think about it. He was in the water longer than Jim, and he's in bad shape. You survived by getting up inside the hull. Your friend wasn't so lucky."

"But he could have made it to shore."

"Then he'll have a chance to make it on his own, but we won't if we don't catch the others." Marks looked ahead at the smoky mass into which he had seen the last boat disappear.

"Are you people part of some crazy religious group?" asked Gus. Shrader laughed out loud, and Gundersen wondered if he were indeed in the presence of a madman.

"Maybe we are," he said at last. "Look, I wish I could find your friend. I wish I could let you off somewhere safe. But there is nowhere that's safe, and we're going to need each other to get through that," he said, pointing to the fiery boundary that they were fast approaching. He opened the lazarette compartment next to the wheel, and withdrew the handheld VHF. "I almost forgot about this," he said handing the radio to Gus. "See if you can call your friends at the lock."

Gus didn't need any further instruction. He set the radio to channel 12 and spoke excitedly into the small radio. "Betty, this is Gus. They picked me up in one of the sailboats, but we can't find Ray."

"Gus?" came an unexpected reply. "Are you okay?"

"Yes," he said, "but listen! We couldn't find Ray. Maybe he made it to shore. Can you send someone out? He'd probably be on the south shore, but maybe he's ended up on Barnhart Island. Can you do that?"

"I don't know. Sure. Yes, I'll go myself if I have to. What about you?"

"For the time being I'm at the mercy of my host," he answered. "And we're both at the mercy of the river. Just look for Ray, okay?"

"Sure, Boss," she said. "Hang in there."

"You know me, Betty," he said with as much confidence in his voice as he could master.

"Yeah, I do, Gus. You're the best."

"And you're in charge until I get back," he answered.

"Just hurry, then," she said, and the radio went silent.

"Switch to channel 68," ordered Shrader. "It's our working channel," he said as Gus hesitated. "Call *Affinity*. We might be able to get a report if they're still on the air." Gundersen held out the radio to see the LED readout. He held down the select button until channel 68 appeared on the display.

"He's having a lot of trouble breathing," came a woman's voice over the radio.

"Get him down below as quickly as possible, but don't leave any hatches open any longer than you have to. Use a wet handkerchief as a mask," answered a male voice that Marks recognized as Bert Jenkins.

"It's a good thing that Jeffrey is here to handle the wheel," returned the first voice. Shrader realized that it had to be Marty Koenig.

"Is something wrong with Rollie?" he asked, breaking into the conversation.

"Is that you, Shrader? He just can't breathe, and I'm really worried about his heart. It's the smoke; it's really bad, but worse for him."

"Tell him to hang on a little longer, Marty," said another woman's voice. Marks knew it was Cathy. "*Affinity* has just broken out of it. It should be just a few minutes until the air freshens up. Welcome back, Shrader. Is *Fairwinds* with you?"

"The Barkers are here," answered Marks not wishing to broadcast the news of the loss of the boat. "We also took on a passenger from the overturned powerboat." Shrader looked at Gus Gundersen. "The fire is still raging back here. I can't believe that it's not burning the whole length of the river."

"We're not in the river," answered Cathy. "We've broken through to Lake Saint Francis. It's huge. I'd guess that the slick burned off more quickly than in the river."

"It's not that much bigger than the river," argued Gundersen. "Unless..."

"Unless, what?" asked Marks.

"Unless, the Frenchman was right about the tsunami. What does her depth gauge read?"

"Cathy, what is the reading on your depth indicator?" Shrader repeated.

There was a pause before Cathy spoke, "One hundred and twenty-six feet," she said.

"What is the chart depth for the waters there?" asked Shrader, turning to Gundersen.

"Not that deep," he said, "not nearly that deep. It's been a while since I've seen a chart, but I'd say it should run at about eighty feet. Unless, well, I guess she could just be over a deep place in the channel or something."

Shrader put the handheld radio to his lips and spoke again, "Watch your depth meter for a while, Cathy. I'll call you back." He turned back to Gus and asked, "What did you mean when you said something about a tsunami?"

"When we left you guys at the boat, Betty, the lock operator, said that she was on the phone with one of the Frenchmen at the Melocheville Lock when communications were knocked out. He used the word 'tsunami', just before things went ka-flooey. I figured that some kind of surge came up the river pretty fast. That's why I had the gates opened on the locks. I figured if the river hit the surge hard enough, whatever was coming back at us wouldn't wipe out the hydroelectric plant near Cornwall."

Shrader did not know the stranger who was sitting with him, but he was impressed with his mental quickness. Long years of education could not replace innate intelligence or practical wisdom. Gundersen had both. While Marks could not follow everything that Gus said, he understood enough. "How high are we above sea level?" he asked. It was a question which would stymie the average person, but it didn't faze Gundersen, who spent his life lifting ships from Lake Saint Francis to Lake Saint Lawrence.

"Francis is one hundred fifty-two feet above sea level. Larry is two hundred forty-two," he said using the lakes' familiar names.

Shrader let the math run through his head as he spoke. "Cathy's gauge is reading one hundred twenty-six feet. It should be reading eighty. That's a difference of forty-six feet. Forty-six plus one hundred fifty-two is one hundred ninety-six. Am I right?" asked Marks. "The ocean level has risen by one hundred and ninety-six feet," he said, not waiting for an answer.

"Couldn't be," protested Gundersen. "We're still five hundred miles from the ocean."

"There's another way to check," assured Shrader. He raised the handheld radio to his lips and spoke into the transceiver. "Cathy, can you reach the water to get a sample?"

"Sure," came the tentative reply. "Why?"

"Taste it," ordered Marks.

"It's salty." An unidentified voice broke into the silence between transmissions.

"Is that you, John?" asked Marks.

"Yes," said Romig. "When we broke through the smoke, I thought the air smelled saltier. I thought I was back in Labrador for a moment."

"I've got a rough calculation," Shrader advised. "I figure that the ocean is up about a hundred and ninety-six feet. You're the expert in earth science. Is that possible?"

"Theoretically," answered Romig.

"John, we aren't in a lecture hall. The theoretical is out the window; what does your depth gauge read?"

"Okay, it's possible. But I hesitate because that's more than what a total meltdown of Antarctica would do. That's pretty close to the limit of what all the ice melt on the planet could do."

"Maybe the Arctic cap has melted, too?" asked Shrader.

"There's a lot more ice in Greenland than there," corrected Romig. "But I can't imagine how things could have gotten that bad."

"I think realities have gone beyond where imagination can lead us," remarked Shrader. "But it's getting hot and smoky here," he added with a cough.

"Get a mask on," warned Cathy. "Once that stuff is in your lungs you won't be able to stop coughing and that just makes you gasp for more. Is the pathway holding?"

"So far," said Marks. "But as the water levels equalize, I figure the fire will start flowing back at us." There was a long silence before Shrader spoke again. "Cathy, it'll be dark soon. If the current isn't so strong where you are, can you raft up the boats? I think we need to talk about what comes next, and maybe work out some sailing arrangements."

"What do you mean?" she asked.

"I mean I started the day sailing solo, and now there are seven of us on board."

"Enough said," she answered, but Shrader couldn't hear. His body was racked by a coughing spasm. Gundersen had pulled his t-shirt collar up over his nose and was doing a little better. Marks signaled to Gus to take the wheel as he went below to check on the others and to retrieve several dust masks that were with the paint and fiberglass supplies.

55

"Dad isn't doing very well," said Jeff Koenig to Cathy. "Mom's saying that it's just another one of his angina attacks, but I think it's more than that."

Cathy felt a wave of helplessness wash over her. What could she do to help? In spite of her insecurities, the words that came out of her mouth sounded reasonable and confident. "Does anyone aboard the fleet have a medical background?" she asked calmly.

"Laura Romig is a nurse," said Brittany, who had sought out her mother when *Mewtiny* joined the raft. "She talked to me about putting John through graduate school."

"Brittany, would you ask Laura to go over to *Rol's Royce* right away and see how things are going?"

"Sure," answered the girl who moved quickly away over the decks to the Romigs' boat.

"Well, that's a real kick in the pants," said Bert Jenkins. The Major had come to talk to Cathy in private about radio transmissions that he was monitoring on his single-sideband radiotelephone.

"What do you mean?" asked Cathy.

"Only that I've been doing a little undercover intelligence, and I just got beat out by a teeny-bopper."

"Huh?"

"I just figured that it would be good to have some sort of profile on everyone. When you asked about who had a medical background, I was ready to tell you about Bill Morgan on *Wave Chaser*. He's a dentist," offered Jenkins. "I'm not sure that's much help, but it's in the medical field. But before I could say anything, your daughter has better information."

"Well, don't be too hard on yourself, Bert," assured Cathy. "She's been ahead of me for years, and remember, she's been in close confinement with the Romigs all weekend."

"Is that all the longer it's been?" asked Jenkins. "It feels like we've passed through hell and back."

"I think we did," she answered. "I wish *Strider* was accounted for."

"Shrader can't be that far behind us," consoled Jenkins. "I'm sure when he clears the smoke, he'll call us. You know how difficult it was to breathe in there. I don't blame him for not calling on the radio."

"But it's dark," said Cathy. "He could easily motor right past us, and we'd never know."

"The whole raft is lit up like a Christmas tree," offered Jenkins. "Every running light, every anchor light is burning, and I even have a spotlight rigged in case we hear anything."

"Thanks, Bert. I feel way over my head in all this. The crews and captains may look to me for decisions, but Shrader is the one with the answers."

"*Affinity, Affinity, Affinity*," came a woman's voice over the radio. "This is *Strider*."

Cathy breathed a sigh of relief, and took the microphone on her boat's binnacle-mounted VHF. She wanted to cry out, "Is Shrader safe?" but she didn't.

"Go ahead, *Strider*, this is *Affinity*," she said. Her voice was steady even if her emotions were not.

"Cathy, this is Tish Barker. Shrader asked me to call now that we're through the smoke."

"Is everything okay?" asked Pearson.

"Jim is pretty sore, but he's resting," offered Tish. "The children were scared really bad, but now that their father is alert and talking, they've settled down."

Cathy and Bert looked at each other with more questions than they could hope to have answered. She settled for, "Where are you?"

"The fire is behind us, and Shrader wants to know where we should start looking for the rest of you. He'd talk to you himself, but the battery is dead in the little radio." The last comment consoled Cathy as much as anything.

"Tell Shrader that we are anchored off the south shore of the river. I don't see any lights on shore. My guess is that the electricity is out, so we should be easy to spot. We're in thirty feet of water. We'll be watching for you, so make sure your running lights are on. Bert Jenkins has a spotlight rigged, so we can guide you in, if need be." There was a pause before the reply, and Cathy assumed that Tish Barker was relaying the conversation to Shrader before answering.

"Shrader asked me to ask you how long and how fast you traveled once you were past the dense smoke."

Cathy looked at Bert. "I'd say we went for about forty-five minutes to an hour at 4.5 knots," he said.

"That's about right," agreed Cathy, who transmitted the message to Barker. After that, the radios went silent.

"I told you that they'd be all right, Admiral," said Jenkins with a wink that was meant to urge a smile from her face.

"And you were right, Bert," she answered without picking up on his cue. "Can I ask you a favor?"

"Name it."

"Would you look in on the Koenigs? I don't think that I can face Marty right now. On second thought, I have to," she said as if talking to herself. "I'll check on Roland, and then I'd like a little time to myself. Would you be willing to handle the questions until Shrader makes contact?"

"No problem, Cathy," answered Jenkins. There was something in the way that he said her name that penetrated her exhaustion and startled her, but she could not name it. It passed over quickly.

"Thanks, Bert," she said. "You're a life saver."

56

The red, green, and white lights of the sailboats were matched only by the brightness of the sky above. A full moon cast shadows against the black water. Inside the cabins, the lights were out. Most were asleep, driven either by exhaustion or by the need to escape the waking memories of fire and smoke.

Lights were still glowing in one cabin. Cathy could see their luminescence through the forward port of *Rol's Royce*. She knew the scene in that cabin. It was one she could not erase from her mind. Roland Koenig was adrift in some netherworld between consciousness and coma. Laura Romig had quietly noted his blue lips and fingernails. Marty was beginning to finish her husband's sentences when they drifted into nonsense. "Oxygen deprivation" was the phrase that was whispered on deck.

The night air wrapped itself around the rafted line of sailboats, and Cathy found herself sitting out on the bow of *Affinity*.

"Shrader, what have we done?" she asked the darkness without any hope of an answer. She sat in the pulpit and let her legs dangle over the left side of the boat. The red glow of the bow light drained all the color from her faded jeans.

"We have to push them harder," said Shrader. Cathy turned to see her friend sitting next to her on the foredeck.

"But they've come through so much already," she protested. His presence seemed so natural that she was not surprised by the suddenness of his appearance.

"It's more dangerous here than you can imagine, and it will be worse as we approach Montréal," argued Marks.

"You mean more fires?" she asked.

"No," corrected Shrader. "There are wolves along the river, and they are the kind that will kill out of fear rather than need. They will follow us until we are out of the St. Lawrence."

"But there can't be that many wild animals here," protested Cathy, who had not understood Shrader's image.

"They are human wolves," he said, correcting her confusion. "They have seen horrors that are unimaginable and are fighting back at an imaginary enemy. That's why they are dangerous, and that's why we have to press on before the daylight exposes us to their eyes."

"But, what about Roland Koenig?"

"Our staying here will not help or hinder his condition," said Marks. Then he added, "He is already beyond our help."

"You mean he's going to die?" Her words fell to nothing, and he did not answer. It was a soft rhythmic thumping against the hull which actually awakened her. She looked around and saw that she was alone.

In the water beneath her feet, she saw a snag gently rocking against the hull. Gripping the stainless steel rail of the bow pulpit, she extended her body down toward the water to push the floating log away from her boat. With the tip of her toe, she managed to reach it and push off. It yielded against her touch and rolled out in front of the boat. In the moonlight she caught a quick glimpse of a charred and bloated face as the body rocked and settled back to its facedown position.

Cathy must have cried out because Bert Jenkins was quickly at her side. No one else heard, and only his eyes saw as she pointed to the corpse.

"Keep your voice down," said Jenkins. "I'll take care of it." He went back to *Major Blunder* and returned with a gaff. Cathy watched in shock as he hooked the corpse and drew it back into the shadow of the hull. "In cold water like this a body will usually sink pretty fast," he said as if talking about a can of tuna fish. His coolness seemed brutal to Cathy. "Here's the problem," he said to himself. "The bastard is wearing a life jacket." He reached into the pocket of his dungarees and pulled out a rigging knife. Its serrated blade made quick work of the nylon straps that held the PFD in place. "And just in case his lungs are still full of air…" He did not finish the sentence which was not meant for anyone anyway. Quickly and quietly, he slashed open the man's throat. Cathy heard a release of air, then a gurgling, then nothing.

Cathy did not know whether to scream or cry, and felt guilty that she felt better when the thing sank out of sight. Then she felt guilty for thinking of the body as a thing. "Who was he?" she asked.

"A person in the wrong place at the wrong time," said Jenkins without an ounce of inflection in his voice. "That must be Shrader," he added, pointing out across the water.

Cathy looked in the direction that he indicated, but could not see anything except the stars. It was then that she noticed that one of the stars was moving along the horizon. It was *Strider's* masthead light.

"Thank God," she said.

"I'll go wave him in," said Bert as he moved off over the decks of the rafted boats. Beneath his feet, the sleepers tossed in their bunks.

57

"I'm surprised you aren't complaining more. It's definitely broken," said Bill Morgan as he examined Jim Barker's throbbing right forearm. "How do you think we should handle this?" he added, turning to Laura Romig. The two switched places within the confines of *Strider's* main cabin. Laura was now seated opposite Barker who extended his arm across the drop-leaf table. Gently, she touched his fingers. They were cold to the touch.

"Can you rotate your wrist?" she asked. Slowly, Jim Barker rolled his hand. Laura could see him wince as the sweat broke out across his twisted face. "Would you let me touch your arm?" she asked. Barker nodded, but she could see his fear. He closed his eyes in anticipation of the pain, but her touch was skillfully light and over before he could react. "Thank you," she said. "Dr. Morgan and I need to talk. You should rest if you can."

Out on deck Laura Romig and Bill Morgan held a consultation. Soon they were joined by Shrader Marks. They acknowledged him with a shake of the head, but continued their debate.

"We really need to get him to a medical facility, and have it x-rayed," argued Morgan.

"I agree," offered Laura. "At least I would agree if we were under normal conditions, but that is not the case here. He has a compound fracture. There's no break in the skin, but I'm sure the bone has torn up some tissue inside."

"Which means there's a pretty good risk of infection," added Morgan. "Okay, I agree. We will have to do the reduction as best we can. If we can get help later, it can be x-rayed and reset. I might be a dentist, but this is medical practice out of the last century at best."

"What are you going to do?" asked Shrader, who had been taking in the conversation.

"The bone is broken and out of place, so we can't just splint it and allow it to heal," explained Bill. "We're going to have to move the bone back into place and then splint it."

"Can you do it?" asked Marks.

"There's some guessing involved," said Laura. "We will not be able to tell if it's exactly right without an x-ray. There's a chance that we could be off a little when it's set."

"What will that mean?"

"Some limited motion, perhaps," said Romig, "maybe some noticeable deformity."

"I think the possibility of infection is the short-term worry," added Morgan. "I wish we had some antibiotics to start with."

"We do," offered Shrader. "I have a supply of tetracycline."

"It wouldn't be my first choice," said Morgan. "But it will have to do. It isn't old, is it? Outdated tetracycline is extremely toxic."

"No, it's fresh and in the original packaging. I'll go get it." Shrader disappeared as the two discussed pain control.

"Unless Shrader has something else tucked away, we'll have the options of the mid-nineteenth century. This is pathetic," said Bill Morgan.

"I'm sure that we can find enough liquor to provide some relief," offered Laura.

"Or a rawhide strap to chew on," added Morgan. "Like I said, it's pretty lame. The alcohol will diminish the effectiveness of the antibiotic, so there's no point in starting that until we get the thing set."

Even in the dark, they could see Shrader was coming toward them over the decks of the rafted boats. As he reached them, he held out his hand and offered a package to Morgan. "Here," he said. "It's the best we could do on short notice."

"What in the world?" asked the dentist. He looked down at the blister pack that Marks had placed in his hand. He read the label that was imprinted with brightly colored aquarium fish. "This is for tropical fish tanks!" he said incredulously.

"I know," replied Marks. "I told you that it was the best we could do for an antibiotic. It's marked in U.S.P. doses. It should be okay."

Bill Morgan looked at Laura Romig. He handed her the package. "It is tetracycline," she remarked. "It could work."

"But it wouldn't be my choice," sighed Morgan. "Then again, we seem to be moving into a world without choices. We'll do our best."

"That's all anyone could ask for," remarked Shrader. Marks had certainly underestimated Morgan; everyone had. There were not many African-Americans in the sailing community. Shrader had known a few and found that each had a distinct story. One had been the son of a fisherman who was practically born in the water. Morgan was a graduate of the University of Pennsylvania and obviously a lifesaver.

58

By the time Cathy and Shrader could find a quiet place to talk, nearly everyone on the raft was awake and restless. The unease began with the screams of Jim Barker. The scotch that was meant to lessen the pain at the setting of his broken arm managed only to loosen his inhibitions for yelling. After that, what sounded like gun shots were heard from the shore. The adults told the children that they were nothing more than firecrackers, but Major Bert Jenkins had a tuned ear for the report of a rifle, and warned Cathy.

"Jenkins says that's gunfire in the woods," said Cathy to Shrader in low tones.

"I already told you that we can't stay here tonight," offered Marks. "We've been here too long already. We need to get beyond Montréal before the cover of dark is taken from us."

"What about Roland Koenig and Jim Barker?" asked Cathy.

"We've done our best for Barker, and Roland is beyond anything we can do."

"I'll call a meeting of the captains, and we can discuss the options," said a frustrated Pearson.

"No," protested Shrader. "They don't have any options, and neither do you. You need to tell them that we are moving on tonight. Let Jenkins tell them about the gunfire or about the floating body that you found earlier. We are beyond the point of choices."

"How did you know about the body?" she queried.

"I see a lot of things that I can't explain. I also know that we'll sail through worse; the darkness will be a friend tonight."

Cathy studied Shrader's face. He looked gaunt, with dark circles and deeply cut lines. Only his eyes seemed alive, and they flashed with a wildness that frightened her.

"I'll get Jenkins to help break up the raft," she answered, but Shrader's gaze was out across the shadowy waters. He did not acknowledge her comment.

Marks had been right about playing to the fears of the crews. No one wanted to pull up anchor in order to sail in unfamiliar waters. When Jenkins confirmed the gunshots and told of the floating corpse, however, all hands made themselves busy. Still, there were grumblings by a few. Phil Pearson had openly challenged his wife's orders and twice referred to the conspicuously absent Shrader as the "wild man". In the end, Cathy's directives held. Her last coup was to make new boat assignments.

"I don't need to tell you that we've lost *Fairwinds*," she began. "*Strider* is the smallest boat in the fleet, and right now it is carrying Shrader, the Barker family, and Mr. Gundersen. That's seven people, one of whom is hurt, and they're in a boat that will sleep five at best."

"What do you propose?" The question came from Bert Jenkins who was developing the ability to make Cathy's orders sound like answers to the group's requests.

"Well," she began. "Let me start by asking a few questions. Jeff," she turned to face the Koenigs' son. "Can you and Carol manage to sail *Rol's Royce*?"

"Sure," he answered. "We've used the boat ourselves in the past."

"Great," she replied. "I'd like to move your mother and father over to *Mewtiny*. Laura is a nurse and can keep your father under observation. That will put six on board *Mewtiny*, but the Romig boys are small and can double-up in a berth if they have to."

"What about me?" asked Brittany, who had slipped into the fringe of the group.

"I need you back on *Affinity* to help your father." Her choice of words made Philip perk up his ears.

"Where are you going to be?" he asked.

"I'd like to keep the Barkers together as a family, so they'll come onto our boat."

"Where are you going to be?" repeated Philip.

Ignoring him for a second time, she turned to Bill and Connie Morgan. "Would you be willing to take our boys, Chris and Justin, aboard *Wave Chaser*?"

"Sure, but wouldn't they be happier with their family?" said the dentist.

Cathy caught Philip's eye. Her words were measured out carefully. "I'm more concerned about the trauma that the Barkers faced and what the kids saw when their father was in the water. My boys will be fine. They'll probably sleep through most of it. These changes are only temporary. We can reassess when we get past Montréal."

She turned her gaze to her husband. "I'll be sailing aboard *Strider* with Gus Gundersen and Shrader Marks." She saw his eyes grow cold, but she continued. "Shrader has not had any relief and needs to rest. Gus has as good a knowledge of the St. Lawrence as anyone here. We'll sail out first. I'll be relying on Gus' familiarity and Shrader's intuition. Bert and Tiffany Jenkins will follow last in case any boat in the fleet has problems. Are there any questions?"

If there were any, people were too polite to ask. The one exception was Philip Pearson whose reaction did not bear any relation to politeness. It was inner-rage that sealed his lips. Cathy could see it in his manner, and in an instant decision, resolved not to go back to get anything from below decks on

Affinity. She did not want to be alone with him. Instead, she busied herself with helping those who were switching their accommodations. The most difficult part was seeing the drained body of Roland Koenig being lifted out of the cabin of his boat. He made the journey over the decks to *Mewtiny* without any hint of complaint, but his pallor gave him an unearthly appearance matched only by the distress on Marty's face.

The Barkers were easier to move. They had nothing. All their possessions had gone down with *Fairwinds*, but as they walked across the rafted decks, they were offered gifts from the others. The Romigs offered a change of clothes from their boys who were close in age and size to Kelly and Aaron. Cathy smiled when Brittany offered some of her own clothes to Ashley who was only two years her junior.

"Don't you think that I deserved to be consulted about these arrangements?" hissed Phil as she passed over the deck of her own boat on the way to *Strider*.

"I'm sorry," she offered. "There wasn't time, but I promise that it'll only be until we can get past Montréal. I need to hear what Shrader has in mind, and it was the only way that I could come up with."

"Convenient, I'd say," griped her husband. "Are you going to stick Gundersen behind the wheel while you two get friendly down below?"

Cathy held her tongue and gave him an icy stare. "That's not worth a reply," she said at last. "I promise you that I'll come back when we've made it through Montréal. Shrader feels this is the most dangerous part of the journey."

"If he crosses me, he'll find out what danger is," warned Pearson. Cathy gave him a last sideways glance and continued toward the boat on the end of the raft. Gus was already there. He stood in the cockpit looking toward Cathy as she approached through the dimly lit haze.

"Is he all right?" asked Gus.

"Who? Phil?" responded Cathy.

"No, him," said Gus pointing toward the foredeck. There, the dark outline of Shrader Marks stood like a shadow. He seemed to be talking to someone unseen and unheard by the others. Cathy could not make out most of the words, but several filtered through. He seemed to be arguing about bridges and staying in the channel. Cathy gave Gus a reassuring glance, then stepped out of the cockpit and moved forward along the cabin trunk. Shrader did not seem to notice her presence as she approached. She was close enough to touch him, but still he did not regard her.

"But how will I recognize you?" he asked of the night. Cathy was confused, but held her silence. "Yes," he said. "Brothers will know."

"Shrader?" said Cathy cautiously. He did not answer immediately, so she spoke again, "Shrader?"

As if returning from a great distance, he turned to her with a calmness that caught her off guard. "Cathy," he uttered in a low tone. "When did you get here?"

The question threw her. Something in the tone of his voice left her wondering what the words meant. Did he mean, "When did you come on board?" or "When did you arrive in that moment?" It was as if he were in another dimension that had only briefly collided with reality.

"I had to get the others settled," she said at last. "We're ready to break up the raft and can set sail whenever you think it best." she offered.

"Great!" His response seemed out of character with the haggard wild man that she had encountered a half hour earlier. This man seemed rested and anxious for the adventure that lay ahead. "You're right about setting sail. We've motored enough. We want the silence of the wind and the cover of the darkness. Tell the others to hoist sails and to kill all the running lights. The only light to be kindled tonight will be on *Strider*'s masthead. It'll give everyone else something to steer by."

"Gus and I will be with you tonight," Cathy added.

"Sure. Why not?" he agreed. He turned back to the night and spoke in low tones to someone else. Cathy felt as though she had been left behind, that their separate realities had shifted again. They stood together, but alone.

"I'll tell the others," she offered, but she was talking to herself. She worked her way aft where Gundersen stood patiently.

"Well?" he asked.

"I think he's okay," she assured. "But we have to tell the others to switch to sail as soon as they can and to run without lights."

59

Gus was not a sailor, but he proved a steady hand at the wheel. Cathy had shown him how to read the wind point gauge that was mounted by the companionway. The wind was out of the southeast, so the sails were set for a beam reach. Cathy kept them trimmed, and *Strider* responded to each adjustment by leaping ahead in a race with the wind.

Gus estimated that they were at least twenty miles from Montréal, thirty at the most. Cathy figured that it would take as many as four hours to reach the island of Montréal and another three to sail past its shores. Shrader was silent on the foredeck, brooding, Cathy thought.

"I don't think we should have any trouble in Montréal," said Gus, who seemed anxious to fill the silence of the night with words.

"I'm sorry," said Cathy. "I must have missed something."

"Getting past the bridges," he offered. "It shouldn't be much of a problem. When the Seaway was built in the fifties, all the bridges in Montréal were raised to offer a minimum clearance of a hundred and twenty feet. Even if the water is up fifty feet, we should have seventy feet overhead. That would be enough, wouldn't it?"

Cathy paused. Her mind was still on Shrader and not in the present conversation. She must have looked blankly at him, because he rephrased the question. "No one has a mast height of greater than seventy feet, do they?"

This time she heard the question and began to calculate. "*Affinity* is one of the longer boats, and our mast is about fifty feet above the water. That's not counting the radio antenna, but even with that you're right. We should be okay."

"Then why is he so nervous about getting through Montréal?" he asked.

"I don't know," answered Pearson. "I risked my husband's rage to sail with you two. I thought I'd get the chance to find out what's going on in Shrader's mind, but I'm not sure that he knows yet, either."

"When he pulled me out of the water, he seemed pretty level-headed."

"You mean 'normal'?" corrected Cathy.

"Yeah," continued Gus. "But when we joined up with the rest of you, he kinda' went dotty, if you catch my drift. Is he okay?"

Cathy offered a smile that betrayed both her compassion and her fatigue. "This must all be very confusing to you, and I've been too preoccupied to help you understand anything. Shrader is okay. He's just overwhelmed, as are we all," she added.

It was Gus' turn to let down. His eyes softened, and his face was washed over with a sadness that Cathy could not penetrate. "You're not a captive here. At the first opportunity, we'll let you off. Or, if you decide that we're not absolutely weird, you can choose to stay. Is that what's bothering you?"

"No," replied Gundersen. "It's not that, but we didn't start out on the best footing when we met out on the lake. I thought that you had to be the most stubborn people that I'd ever met. I was trying to warn you off, and you were acting like I was some pesky fly buzzing around your head."

"I'm sorry about that. It's just that we were on a mission, so to speak."

"And as it turned out, you knew more than I did."

"I'm not sure we knew or know anything really," she confessed. "I trusted Shrader when he said that we'd be able to get through the locks."

"And that was the one thing that I knew would not happen. There was no way that these rich, overindulged, yacht owners were going to screw up my Seaway."

Cathy smiled. "You were pretty intense, and I was being pigheaded." For an instant the two quieted before Cathy spoke again. "Was the other fellow a friend of yours?"

Sadness came over Gus' face. "Ray Anderson was the best friend any man could have. Oh, shit," he added as his words stopped short.

"What?"

"It's just that all night I've been saying to myself that Ray is okay, that somebody probably picked him up. But I just said 'was'."

"You could be right, about somebody picking him up," she said trying to console him.

"No, I'm a complete blank about what happened in the water. I remember telling Betty to open the locks, and I remember getting caught in the current and sucked through. I yelled to Ray because we were going to bottom out in a standing wave. I turned toward him, but after that, nothing. I can't remember anything until I was huddled up in the boat after it turned turtle. That's when I heard Shrader scrabbling around the hull."

"A lot of things must have happened very quickly. It's no wonder you can't remember every detail."

"But why didn't I look for Ray? He would have looked for me."

"You were in shock, that's all."

"No," he added slowly. "There was something else." His words were deliberate as his mind raced to remember the thing he had forced out of consciousness. A look of terrifying recollection came over his face. "He wasn't there," he blurted out.

"What?" asked Cathy.

"When I looked back to warn Ray about the wave, he wasn't there. The wheel was just running loose. He must have been thrown from the boat, and I didn't even know it." Gundersen had tears streaming down his face as he spoke. The sails began to luff, telling Cathy that the boat was pointing too close to the wind. She got up and took the wheel.

"Why don't you rest for a bit?" she offered, and Gus did not argue. He wedged himself against the cabin trunk and stared blankly into the shimmering, watery night.

60

The breaking of the raft had proved more of a danger than anyone thought. As the boats peeled off and raised their sails, the shots from the shore became more distinct, like a line of thunderstorms drawing nearer. Sailing in the dark heightens the senses of a mariner, and never feels routine. Those on the decks donned harnesses as a precaution against going overboard. Though the weather was pleasant and the waters relatively calm, all were aware of the fact that going overboard in the dark made rescue all the more difficult, if not impossible. Night sailing has a way of reducing vision to a secondary sense, less acute than hearing. Those at the helm would know their speed by the sounds of rushing water, and the closeness of another boat by sounds echoing off sails. Only *Strider* was running with any lights, and that was only an all-around anchoring light at the top of the mast. The light radiated from a point like the beam of a guiding star. Unlike a star, however, the sails flying beneath took on a soft glow. The boat appeared like a gossamer guide carrying a small spark in upraised hands. One by one, the other boats joined the silent procession into the darkness.

As planned, Bert and Tiffany Jenkins were the last to join the line of boats that sailed off toward Montréal. As soon as they hoisted sail and shut down the engine, they were discovered by someone on the shoreline. There were two quick pops, and the Major realized that they were under fire. He quickly dismissed as harmless the high-pitched report of the .22 caliber rifle. He thought them random bursts into the darkness, but the shots were meant for *Major Blunder*. They had been spotted and followed. Keen eyes accustomed to the darkness had taken aim, managing to punch two holes in the foresail. It took a while to realize the damage. The genoa caught the wind and took the correct shape of a giant airfoil. Weakened as it was, however, the freshening air used the tiny bullet holes to start a tear that quickly transformed the Dacron into shreds. The remnants of the sail flew like streamers.

In an instant, he realized what had happened, but there was little that could be done. He told Tiffany to stay below, and they sailed on the main alone until he could risk going out on deck to pull down the fragments of his best jib.

Damn, he thought. His mind raced through the inventory of sails that were stowed about the boat. There was nothing to replace the 155 which now fluttered like a flag in a hurricane. He would have to go to a smaller foresail, which meant that he would lose performance, and, over the long haul, speed.

A half hour passed before he felt secure enough about their distance from the shore. His military training made him cautious, and he thought of all the sophisticated scopes and heat sensors that would *see* a person moving about on the deck. *Naw,* he assured himself. *A shooter with a night scope wouldn't be using a .22.* With no lights along the shore, he knew that whoever was there would have to follow their downriver progress on foot and in the dark. *Not likely,* he thought. In spite of his reasoning, he held onto his doubts longer than required. His internal argument lasted beyond necessity, but waiting patiently under cover was also a part of his survival training. He assuaged his paranoia by slowing down his pulse. *Part of winning is knowing how to wait,* he said to himself as though it were a mantra. It was a truth that he was learning to live with.

"Tiffany," he called out to his wife who was in the cabin below decks. "It's all clear. You can come up now."

"I'm scared, Bert," she said as she emerged into the cockpit.

"Nothing to be scared of, Baby," he responded. If at times he treated her as a child, it was because he saw her that way. After three years of marriage, at age twenty-five, she was still narrow-hipped and slender with a prepubescent manner about her. He had been forty-five when he first spotted her working at the reception desk in the base hospital near Seoul. At that time, he did a quick background check on her. He found that she had been married at eighteen, beaten regularly by an alcoholic husband, and abandoned after two years. Their courtship was fast and furious. At forty-five and in the uniform of an Air Force major, he had seemed like a rescuing prince. It was a role she wanted him to play, and one that he always enjoyed.

"I'm going to go forward to change the jib," he said to her. "Do you feel up to steering into the wind, or would you like me to set the autopilot?"

"If you trust me, I think that I can steer," she offered.

"You're being brave," he consoled. "If you get scared, just call." He kissed her gently on the forehead, attached the tether of his harness to the jackline that ran the length of the forward deck, and stepped out of the cockpit. At the mast, he released the jib halyard, and called back to Tiffany to begin the maneuver to turn *Major Blunder* into the wind. He sat down and scooted to the bow of the boat. When he felt the wind in his face, he pulled on the shredded fabric which had been the forward edge of the sail. Hand over hand, he pulled until he had the halyard shackle in his grip. He disengaged the clip from the sail and fastened it temporarily to the bow pulpit. As he crawled back toward the cockpit, he bundled the splintered material ahead of him until he pushed it into a heap on the cockpit sole.

"There," he said to himself more than to Tiffany. "The job's half done." He scanned the dark water to try to determine the boat's position. In the moonlight he could see the ragged edge of the trees, jet black against the speckled glimmer of the clear night. "We're closer in than I thought," he said, stepping behind the helm next to Tiffany. His wife let go of the wheel as he reached to grip its gleaming stainless steel rim. He throttled-up the diesel and turned the boat back to a more northerly heading. "Can you make out the location of the rest of the fleet?" he asked.

Tiffany scanned ahead in the darkness. "No, I don't see anything," she said finally.

"This is really weird," remarked Bert. "There are no shore lights, nothing to really use as a reference point." He looked at the stars and picked out the familiar constellations. "This is ridiculous," he said as he reached for his handheld GPS. He depressed the on/off switch with his thumb, and the LED screen came to life. In a moment he would be able to read his latitude and longitude from a global positioning satellite. "This is no good," he said as a new realization struck him. Tiffany looked at him. For the first time, Jenkins realized that his technological advantage offered him no help. "Even if I pinpoint our position," he explained, "none of our charts will show us the coastline or the underwater hazards. We're sailing in waters that weren't here yesterday. Have you found *Strider* yet?" he asked.

Tiffany had not been looking, and quickly turned her eyes to the horizon. She caught the faint glimmer of a sail and pointed toward the northeast.

"That's where we're headed, then," said Bert as he corrected his course toward the muted glow. "I guess we have no choice but to throw our lot in with the crazy man, at least for now. Take the wheel," he said to his wife. "I have to finish changing the head sail."

61

It was an odd sensation for Shrader to be out on *Strider*'s deck while the boat was under sail, especially at night. There was no mistaking it; the day had been a strange one. He had ridden a wave of reaction to event after event, with no time to assimilate the meaning of anything. Now, in the darkness, his thoughts caught up with his body. The starry sky opened up before him; he felt as though he was the first man to see them and wonder.

Strider, he knew, was no longer sailing out the Saint Lawrence; she was sailing out of time. Everything that came before was a dream, or at least a reality that was past retrieving. His thoughts turned to his wife, Lynn. Where was she? What was she thinking? Now that the comet had committed its treachery, did she think better of him? Did any of his questions matter? Not one would ever find an answer. Still his mind circled on them.

"My life is defined by the questions that I cannot answer," he said out loud. Hearing his own voice surprised him almost as much as the tear that suddenly rolled down his cheek.

"And by the questions that you never ask," came another voice. Shrader had heard the stranger before, mostly in dreams, but also in waking moments. He reached to clutch the whale effigy that was still hanging around his neck. Without panic or fear, he addressed the night.

"You sound close," he said.

"Because you are getting nearer," came the distinct answer. Marks turned around to see Cathy dimly lit by the light of the compass binnacle. She seemed to be dozing at the wheel, oblivious to any voice except wind and water.

"How do you know me?" he finally asked.

"Our people do not soon forget our friends," came the answer. "You wear the token of our little brother, Muoshti, and you heard us when we called to you."

The words were a puzzle to Marks, but there was something in their tone that gave him a strange comfort. It was a comfort that comes of being drained of all energy and finding that you are still known to someone, even when you are no longer known to yourself. It was then that he understood. The only power that he had left to wield was the power to put himself in the care of another.

"What should I do?" he asked.

"Listen," was the brief reply. Then almost as an afterthought, the voice added "Sing."

"Sing? Sing what?" The request caught Shrader by surprise.

"It does not matter, *Whaleman*. Sing the words that are true and we will know that you are also our brother."

Shrader thought a long while about the songs that he liked and the tunes that he had hummed to himself over the years. A lot of them were about sailing, and a Jimmy Buffett lyric about "Mother Ocean" popped into his mind. The words that came from his mouth were quite different, however, and yet not so different:

> You fearful saints, fresh courage take;
> the clouds you so much dread
> are big with mercy, and shall break
> with blessings on your head.

It was a hymn from his youth, a metric psalm, to be exact. He could not recall the name, however, or how it now so easily came to mind.

"We understand your song," said the voice.

"Then could you explain it to me?" answered Shrader.

"In time, you will understand, *Whaleman*," came the reply. "We will meet you soon."

"Where?" asked Marks.

"Beyond the fires, along the path of your dreams, on the way to the *Inuksuk*." The statement was cryptic, but spoken as a final thought. Shrader knew that he could not follow with any more questions. It was as if the party on the other end of the line had hung up the phone, and he was left holding the receiver. He listened, but the only sound to greet his ears was the rushing of water. Overhead, the stars performed their nightly dance around Polaris, and he remembered living this experience in an earlier dream. He strained to recall to consciousness the voices of his restless nights, until, in the midst of his struggle, he let it go. He listened to the rhythm of the waves washing against the bow of the boat. Beyond that lulling sound was a deeper silence than he had ever known. Shrader found himself in a place between time, between present and future. In the vacuum of the 'not yet', he stood in expectation of words that lived beyond all syllables.

In that place there was no sky, or it was all sky with no stars, or the spaces between the stars were so vast that he could not see another point of light other than his own. And then, he was not there either. He was in a place without himself, the center of all things, the center of nothing.

Shrader Marks, the anthropology instructor, would have demanded an answer, but he was no longer that person. Whoever he had become at that moment, he did not need to understand any of it. His curiosity about the emptiness became the shadow of someone else, so great was the feeling that he knew that he was understood by the Nothing.

"Shrader," came a voice and with it, the sound of the water and the overcast shadows of the stars. It was Cathy's voice. She was up on the deck, making her way forward. He turned to her for a second, trying to get used to his own shivering skin.

"What is it?" he answered.

"We've been motoring for two hours," she pleaded. "I don't think that my nerves can take it. Every minute I think we're going to run aground and rip off the keel, or slam into something. Can't we hole up somewhere until we have some daylight?"

"No," said Shrader. "That is the one thing that we can't do."

"But we need a compass heading, or a reference point."

Shrader did not answer immediately. He strained his eyes toward the horizon. In the distance, off the port bow, he saw dark shapes which blacked out the stars like spiked pinnacles rising out of the water.

"There's your mark," he said at last, pointing. "They are standing stones. They were placed there to guide mariners, to guide us."

Cathy looked in the direction indicated, but hardly knew what she was supposed to be seeing. She turned back to Shrader. His face had softened. He seemed both relaxed and confident; his eyes were seeing things that she could not. Again, she followed his gaze and watched patiently until she saw black shapes against the star bedazzled night sky.

For a moment she wondered what she was seeing, and remembered Shrader's description of the standing stones used in archaic maritime cultures for navigating the North Atlantic coast. But what were they doing here on the Saint Lawrence so close to Montréal? Then the truth hit her. What she was looking at was Montréal. The skyline of the entire city had become a lifeless shape against the distant horizon. Iciness gripped her for a brief moment. This was her course, her point of sail, but what would be waiting for them when they got there?

62

The distant skies glowed pink, but the sun had not yet risen. The only sound was the low-throated chugging of seven sloops. With their sails furled, the boats motored down the Saint Lawrence River. They moved smoothly through the water in single file like a silent funeral procession moving through dark shadows. None of the people on the boats could have known what to expect. Those who had given it some thought, found their assumptions faulty. Gus Gundersen had promised Cathy that there would still be seventy feet of clearance under the highway bridges, but he was wrong. He had forgotten to calculate that Montréal proper was much closer to sea level than Lake Saint Francis. Though more than five hundred miles from the Atlantic, the normal water level of the Saint Lawrence is only twenty feet higher than the ocean. Here, the bloated sea had taken hold of the city and the skyline had melted into the waterline. Still, portions of the island city were above the water. The scattered hills became small islands in their own right, the largest being Mount Royal which rose out of the center of the city. Fires still burned on the heights creating an eerie glow as the procession slid through on the swift running flow.

The boats maintained radio silence except for a brief exchange between Cathy and Bill Morgan who was aboard his boat, *Wave Chaser*. Morgan had held off giving Jim Barker the tetracycline as a precaution against infection in his broken arm.

"Barker's temperature is going up," said Morgan. "I'm sure there's an infection setting in that arm with all the internal damage."

"Aren't the antibiotics working?" asked Cathy.

"I'm not going to let them be used. In fact, I've fed them to the fish already," answered the dentist.

"But they could have made all the difference," she protested.

"They could just as easily have killed him, too. Give me some credit, would you?" Cathy could hear the tension in his voice. "I might be *only* a dentist, but I do know a few things about medications. What Shrader gave me were tablets for a fish tank. I was not about to give them to Jim Barker or anyone else."

"But they are all we have!"

"Then he'll just have to take his chances with an untreated infection."

"Bill," said Cathy in her most soothing tone. "Would it have hurt that much to give it a try?"

There was a long pause before Morgan spoke. "I don't know," he said in a sarcastic tone. "How painful is dying of kidney failure?"

"What?" she asked.

"Outdated tetracycline is nephrotoxic. It destroys the kidneys. It's called Fanconi Syndrome. I do know what I'm talking about," added Morgan. "Barker might survive the infection, but he won't survive a bad dose of medication."

Cathy couldn't carry the argument any further. "Let me talk to Shrader," was the best she could manage.

"Fat lot of good that will do," came the answer, "he's the one who brought the fish food."

"Bill, can I ask you something?" she asked. "How do you know that Jim's fever is up? He's aboard *Affinity*."

"Actually, Justin told me. There was some kind of signal sent from *Affinity*; I assumed that you had worked out the system."

"Yes," she said as a cover. Then she thought about the children's playing with the code flags. *This is getting pretty sophisticated if they can give temperatures,* she thought to herself. Her answer to Bill Morgan was less revealing, "Hail *Affinity* on the radio and have Phil or Brittany give you a current reading. I'll speak with Shrader, and get right back to you." She did not bother waiting for an answer or radio protocol. Her concern was for Jim Barker who might be their first casualty, succumbing to a broken arm, of all things. What was even odder was that she was going to ask advice from a brooding Shrader Marks.

"What do you think, Gus?" she said, nodding toward Shrader who sat in a somber heap on *Strider's* bow. Gus was at the helm, but didn't give a second glance toward Marks.

"He is a strange one," was his only comment. If she had had more time to reflect, Cathy might have protested, but it wasn't worth arguing. She climbed over the cockpit coaming and made her way forward past the steel shrouds that supported the boat's mast.

"Shrader," she said gently. The man did not move. "Shrader," she repeated.

"They are very near," said Marks softly.

"What?"

"Soon we shall have better help and counsel than I can give," he said with sudden clarity.

"Bill Morgan has thrown out the tetracycline." Shrader did not respond.

"Did you hear?" she asked. "Jim Barker is running a fever, and we have no antibiotics."

After a long silence, Shrader turned to her and said, "tell Morgan that I will give him what he needs to treat Barker after we get through Montréal." There was not an ounce of inflection or emotion in the flat tones of the response.

"Are you okay?" she asked.

"No," was the monosyllabic response. It was spoken in such a way as to stop all speech. Shrader's gaze went forward and away from the discussion, away from the whole world.

63

After a brief radio conversation with Bill Morgan, Cathy sent an announcement to the fleet ordering that the children be sequestered below decks. The command was the result of her noticing a gull on the water picking at its meal. It is a common enough sight, but the bird was not feasting on a dead fish. Its carrion was or had been distinctly human.

For some time they must have been motoring over what would have been homes and neighborhoods. None of them could imagine the changes in the terrain, or lack of terrain. In less than twenty-four hours a great city had been swallowed by the sea. Beneath more than a hundred and fifty feet of water lay an Atlantis to be discovered by some future civilization. Those who might have survived the tidal surge did not survive the firestorm. Fueled by the floating petroleum of compromised storage tanks, it had raged over the waters. Everyone on deck was struck by the silence and by the awesome devastation.

It was Shrader who guided them precisely as if by an unseen force. He cared not at all for the floating jetsam, and gave a harsh look at Cathy when she changed course to avoid a snag. "No," he cried waving his arm to starboard, "Over here!" Cathy could not see any reason to follow his command, but neither did she wish to argue the point.

They were well outside what would have been the normal watercourse. Only the tallest of the buildings stood visible like charred monuments jutting out of the water. Slowly, the boats twisted their way through the path of these standing tombstones that had once been the high-rise buildings along Dorchester Boulevard in the heart of the downtown.

The reactions on each of the boats varied. Most were numb. Those at the helm focused on the transom of the boat directly ahead of them and never looked toward the smoke billowing above Mount Royal or the morbid sludge of the river. Aboard *Major Blunder*, Bert Jenkins stood at the wheel. Tucked in his belt was what he referred to as his "security system," a stainless steel Smith and Wesson 632 Power Port. John Romig on *Mewtiny* was putting his academic detachment to the test. He concentrated on mental calculations of geological scenarios which would explain the extremes of the high water. Below deck, Marty Koenig maintained a vigil at her husband's bed in the aft compartment. The two had earlier transferred to *Mewtiny* so that Laura could watch him, but Roland was already too far gone. In the end, his heart gave out. His last hours were characterized by hallucinations, though, at the very last, he seemed suddenly lucid. He sat up and turned to his wife. "Marty," he said. "I'm not going to be able to go on with you. I love you."

Marty Koenig was standing next to Laura at the time. She took her husband's hand, and thought he was going to say something else to her, but he turned and focused on the empty space between the two women.

"They're waiting for you, Shrader," he said. "They know the way and are close by. You'll meet them soon."

"Shrader isn't here, Darling," responded Marty.

"Sure he is," came the answer along with a look that told her not to be ridiculous. Turning back to the empty space between the two women, he said, "I leave them in your care, Shrader. Take care of my family."

Marty and Laura were still puzzling over Koenig's insistence on Shrader's presence when they realized that his breathing had stopped. It had happened so silently and softly, that they could not tell the moment of his passing.

"Rollie," said Marty speaking gently to her husband, but he was gone. She turned to Laura with a look of disbelief. Laura, who had already had her hand on his pulse, met her eyes and slipped her arm around the older woman. They stood in silence for a long moment. Marty leaned over the body of her dead husband, and gently stroked his still warm cheek.

"Laura, could I be alone for a moment?" she asked at last.

"Of course," she answered. "I should have asked."

"No," said Marty. "You have been very kind. Thank you." Laura quietly slid through the narrow passage that separated the aft cabin from the yacht's main saloon. There she met the faces of her two sons, Cameron and Ben. She hesitated, trying to think of the proper words, but none came to her. Instead, she said only, "Mrs. Koenig wants to be alone. We have to be especially quiet."

"Isn't Mr. Koenig in there with her?" asked Ben, a six-year-old who couldn't follow the subtlety of Laura's words.

"No. He's not, honey," answered his mother. The sounds of soft weeping came through the narrow passage from the aft cabin.

64

There was no private way to let Jeff and his family hear of his father's death. The news came over the VHF in the form of a radio call from his mother. He detected her overwhelming grief in the tone of her voice, and wanted, at once, to both hold her and to shout down the voices of consolation that immediately came from the other boats. *This should have been a private time*, he thought. His anger kept him from lifting the mike and answering her hail, but his grief made him swerve from his course. By the second time his mother pleaded to him for an acknowledgment of her message, he was maneuvering his boat alongside *Mewtiny* so that she could step across and join her family. Once his mother had boarded, he was free to speak his heart, though his wet eyes said enough in their silence. Onboard *Rol's Royce*, mother and son watched the gap growing between the two boats as *Mewtiny* pulled away. It was like watching an ancient funeral barge drifting off into the deep as they left Roland's lifeless body in the berth where he died.

By now the fleet was moving through the streets of Montréal, motoring quietly in procession between the buildings that stood like cemetery markers. In point of fact, the city had become a grotesque graveyard where corpses appeared in the dim light as though disinterred from the bowels of the earth. Those on the decks of the boats began to notice more bodies floating in the river. The sea gulls picked at the lifeless forms as though they were huge bloated fish that were cast aside by a fisherman or caught in a propeller. They saw no one alive, and soon hardened their minds to see the dead like any other piece of flotsam. Sometimes the bodies were so dense that they jostled against the sides of the hulls as the boats passed. Below decks, blunt thuds against the fiberglass made pulses leap in fear of being holed by a log or a snag, but more often than not, it was the skull or foot of one of the victims of the water's treachery.

If some got through that sordid morning by ignoring their eyes and retching guts, there was no such luxury for those on *Rol's Royce*. Jeff was at the wheel, and each body became a reminder that his father had died in the night. He wondered now if there would be a time to bury the man, or whether his remains would join the mass of the unidentifiable which now belonged to the river. It was at that moment that he realized that he was moving toward the head of the flotilla. On his right, he was parallel to Phil Pearson aboard *Affinity*. Ahead, at the very front of the procession, was *Strider*, with Gus Gundersen at the wheel. Shrader Marks stood in the bow pulpit looking like a figurehead carved in a forward-looking pose. Jeff turned to look at *Affinity* which was running alongside of him.

The sound of the diesel was drowned by the churning waters of the bow wave. Brittany Pearson was at the helm, and her father was seated in the bow pulpit with a rifle across his lap.

Periodically, he would raise it as if taking aim at the male figure on the deck of *Strider*. Shrader, who was on the other end of the gun site, never noticed, or didn't care; he did not let his gaze shift from ahead. Then, without warning, Shrader turned to face Jeff, and the distance between them seemed to melt. It was as if Marks had been transported to his own boat.

"He will be honorably buried," said Shrader in a clear and distinct voice.

Jeff reeled in the shock of hearing the answer to a question that he had not yet voiced. "How did you do that?" he asked, but Shrader's image appeared mute. He looked into the eyes of the apparition and saw only certainty in their depths. The moment passed, and Shrader Marks once more became a figure in the distance. Cathy was out on the bow with him, and Marks was pointing toward the buildings jutting out of the river flowing in spate.

As he watched, Cathy raised a handheld VHF to her mouth and spoke. Her voice came through the cockpit speakers on *Rol's Royce*. "This is a general announcement. Major Jenkins will take over leadership of the fleet. His orders are to cruise downriver at three knots. *Strider* will join you soon after. Stay together and keep moving."

The last words were clipped short, and Jeff noted the use of Jenkins title. *So much for democracy in action,* he thought. He suspected that from now on everything would be a matter of chain-of-command.

Just then, *Strider* broke ranks with the others, swinging wide to port. It was a move that brought a swift reaction from Phil Pearson on the bow of *Affinity*. "Where the hell," he shouted to no one. Then turning to Brittany who was at the helm, he barked, "Follow them!" To her credit, she did not budge. She reduced throttle to three knots and proceeded with the main body of the fleet. Her mother, on the other hand, opened up the power on *Strider's* gasoline engine. The smoky exhaust hung suspended in the light air as the craft pulled away at increasing speed.

Cathy radioed no explanation for their desertion. She had none to share. Shrader had insisted. "They are in the clear," he said. "We need to turn back into the danger." As before, he directed their path with simple gestures from his position on the bow. Now, as they pulled away from the others, Cathy felt as though there was another presence in the waters, and her imagination caught images swirling through the murk. To squelch her fears, she chatted with Gus. As if unwilling or unable to deal with the reality of the present, they spoke only of their pasts.

It was Gus whose thoughts crept back to the moment. "Has he always been like this?" he asked, gesturing toward Shrader.

"Not at all," she answered. "Not even forty-eight hours ago. I confess that I can't pretend to know what he's thinking or why he's acting so strangely."

"Has he cracked?"

She thought for a while before speaking. "I don't think so. I mean, the last two weeks we've been putting this together, and..."

"Two weeks? How could you have known about any of this?"

Again Cathy was forced to consider how to answer this man, who was still a stranger, even after passing through so much with him. She decided to provide a reasonable explanation for the time being, and avoided the truth. "Shrader and John Romig are, or were, professors in Syracuse. I think they had access to sources of information that were kept out of the media. When Shrader talked to me, we set up this little cruise as a kind of escape hatch if things really got bad."

"They sure did," said Gus. "But that doesn't explain this kind of..." He had trouble finding a word.

"Weirdness?" she volunteered. "No, I guess it doesn't. There is something going on in him, like he's gone so deeply into himself that he almost can't get out."

"But is he mad?"

"If I were you, I might think so, but remember that day you came out to us when we were all rafted-up. God, that seems like months ago. When was that?" But neither could recall with any certainty.

"Anyway," she said recovering, "you said that we would not be allowed through the locks, and Shrader said we would. We were in position to go through because he sensed when they would be opened."

"Even I didn't know that," said Gus.

"He knew we would lose a boat, and he knew which one. He knew that the opening of the locks would create a brief path through the fire. Everything he's told us has happened. Is he crazy? Honestly, I don't know, but out here he seems to know more or sense more than anyone else can guess."

Gus sat silent for a long while before speaking. "Where are we going now?"

"Wherever Shrader tells us."

The fact is that Shrader never said. Half an hour later, he stood up straight on the deck and pointed to what appeared to be a floating island of flotsam. "Over there," he said wildly. Cathy swung the boat to port and throttled back the engine. Strider's five tons of bulk glided along by inertia. Very slowly the speed began to drop off.

Gus and Cathy could not make out what Shrader wanted. They knew the direction, but they did not want to navigate too close to the snag. It appeared to be a tangle of trees that had locked together during their drifting.

"Move in closer!" shouted an animated Marks. Cathy now realized that he meant to rendezvous with the mass of logs. She looked at Gundersen.

"I sure hope there are no surprises under the water," she stated as she turned the boat toward the snarled mass.

"Me too," agreed Gundersen. "I've been in the water enough." They both knew that a log penetrating the hull would send the boat to the bottom in just a few seconds. Cathy jumped as the water on the starboard side swirled suddenly and a telephone pole-sized log leapt clear of Strider's hull.

"That came close," she said. "Funny, I don't think we hit it, but it rolled away somehow."

"I think we would have heard it hit the side," responded Gus, "but then again, I've been trying to not pay attention to the sounds of what has been bouncing against the boat." Cathy knew very well what he meant. Normally, the hollow thud of an object striking the boat would raise an alarm, but there had been too many painful surprises to greet the eyes of the curious. It wasn't just the bodies. In particular, she remembered a sodden teddy bear. She closed her eyes tightly as if closing her vision would erase the memory. It probably wasn't the smartest thing to do, but by now, *Strider* was dead in the water. She let go of the wheel, with the engine in neutral, and, with no forward progress, a turn on the helm made no difference. They were bobbing in the lightly rolling water. She looked to the foredeck to see what Shrader wanted, but he seemed to take no notice. To her surprise he swung himself over the side of the boat.

"Gus," she gasped, "he's gone in." In a moment, however, his head emerged above the sheer of the bow.

"What the," answered Gundersen. He too had seen Marks' acrobatics, but was now incredulous at the sight of Shrader moving away from the boat, apparently on foot. Gus quickly stepped up to the cabin trunk, and a broadening grin replaced the look of astonishment that had gripped his features. "He's out on that floating crap," was his only reply. Cathy understood instantly. At the bow, Shrader had jumped onto the floating mess in the familiar manner of stepping off onto a dock.

"Shrader, it might not hold you," she warned.

The reward for her concern was a glance that said, "don't be silly." Still she watched as he boldly made his way through what appeared to be the snarled boughs of a floating forest. He moved swiftly, confidently, and with a purpose that surprised the two. At one point he disappeared from sight, dropping behind a massive trunk that seemed to be at the center of the snag. Just as quickly, he emerged with something white clutched in each hand. With hands full and perfect balance, he made his way back to *Strider*.

"Get a garbage bag," he ordered. "There's more here than they said."

Gus and Cathy looked at each other, each stretching for a context to understand the remark. "There's a roll of bags on the shelf behind the galley," continued Shrader. The instruction set off an image in Cathy's mind, and she descended the steps into the cabin. When she returned with a plastic bag, Marks was leaning over the cockpit coaming. He set two plastic bottles on the seat. His presence made such an odd picture. His standing outside the boat and leaning in was so distracting that Cathy could not focus on the bottles. "Thanks," he said taking the limp polyethylene from her outstretched hand, and then he was gone, moving back over the floating raft. Now she dropped her sight to examine his salvaged booty.

"It's medicine," she said. Gus moved next to her, and she held out one of the bottles. Printed on the label were the words, "Beckley Laboratories, Amoxicillin 500 mg." The second read, "Omega, Lisinopril 10 mg."

"Well, I'll be damned," said Gundersen. "How did he know?"

When Shrader returned, he tossed a lumpy sack over the lifelines and used a stanchion to vault himself back into the cockpit. "What do you say to putting up the sails and dousing the stinking motor?" he said as if nothing unusual had happened. Cathy just stared at the lifeless sack with its knotted top. She assumed, as did Gus, that it held the contents of a small pharmacy.

"How did you know?" she repeated Gus's question.

"Know what?"

"Know that you'd be able to find those medications, walk on those logs, everything!"

"Just seemed obvious," was the simple reply. "Is anyone else hungry?" he asked as if nothing had transpired. He climbed down the stairs to the aft galley. "I know I have some bread left, and peanut butter. Any takers?"

"Sure," said Gus. He turned toward Cathy who was as confused as he was about the turn of events, and Shrader's unwillingness to give any explanation. Their eyes met with the recognition that if something important had just taken place, they were not going to be made privy to it.

For the next two hours, the three took turns at the helm. At some time during the voyage, distant masts came into view. "The Major has kept their pace to a crawl," observed Cathy. "We ought to overtake them in an hour or so."

"I don't think the Major is responsible for the slower pace," responded Shrader. "Our knot meter shows we're going 7.5 knots; that's about top speed for *Strider*. I figure that we've gone over five hundred miles in the last fifteen hours. That means between the backwash from the surge and the open locks, the water under the hull must be carrying us much faster than the wind. Here the river has widened; we're still in the fast flow, but they're over the crest."

"But if we've gone that far, we would have passed through Québec City," protested Gus.

"Would we?" suggested Marks.

As Cathy considered his words, Shrader looked skyward. "It's quite a beautiful day, isn't it?" He was right. In spite of all the tension and trauma of the past days, the sun had painted the sky ahead of them a deep blue.

"Let's go back and sit down," she said, taking his hand. They took seats opposite each other in the cockpit. Gus was standing behind the wheel. She knew that Gundersen was having a difficult time understanding Shrader Marks, the man. His only experience with him was with a brooding, reclusive presence, but the awareness of the day had turned him back to his old self, bright, articulate, and affable. Most surprising was the ease of his laughter. Cathy, too, had changed. She had softened with the friendly banter and was at ease.

After a brief volley of jokes, Gus found himself asking a surprising question. "Are you sure you two aren't married?"

Both Shrader and Cathy blushed, but said nothing. Gus didn't know why he had said what he did. He knew that they weren't a couple, yet something within the banter reminded him of quiet moments lying next to Cassie, when playfulness deepened into the silence of touch.

65

"Shrader says that we have to be careful about anything that looks like a shoreline." Cathy was speaking into the handheld VHF radio. "There are a lot of snags just beneath the surface. Put someone out on deck to watch as you move toward shore. Use the boat with the shallowest draft."

A reply came from Bert Jenkins, but the signal was too weak for Gus or Shrader to hear distinctly. "You should be able to see us pretty clearly on the horizon," she continued, "we're using the genoa." Cathy turned and looked at the sky astern. "Maybe not," she replied, "the sky is closing in back here, but we can see you. Keep an eye out for a place where you might be able to put down a hook. If you find some reasonable anchorage, raft up the boats and we should be able to join you in an hour. If the raft holds together, we'll stay put for the night. I know, Bert, I know. I'll check back in thirty minutes." She turned a knob on the small box and there was a solid *click* amplified by a burst of static. Gus turned toward her with a look of expectation. Shrader was withdrawn and was staring out over the water.

"Well?" asked Gus, "What's the story?"

"They haven't spotted us yet. Jenkins said we're probably blending with the clouds. They are pretty thick to the west." Gus looked back to see a wall of dirty-white which extended out to the horizon.

"They're approaching a pretty large island," continued Cathy. "They thought it might provide some shelter, so they're going to look for an anchorage before it's too dark."

"That island," remarked Gus, "is probably a lot further off than they imagine."

"What do you mean?" she said.

"Only that it has to be Île d'Anticosti. As big as it looks from here, it's a lot larger than that. The whole lower half has to be hidden by the horizon."

"Or under water," added Marks.

"What do you see, Shrader?" asked Gundersen.

Marks made no comment. Instead, he shivered and crossed his arms as though attempting to ward off some imaginary chill. Gus and Cathy did not pursue any further response, nor did they question Shrader when he made his way to the foredeck and squatted down in the shadow of the massive jib. After about ten minutes, Cathy turned to Gundersen, "Would you take the helm, Gus?" His answer was to step around the pedestal and place a hand on the wheel. Cathy moved forward to where Shrader had taken his position. She said nothing as she sat next to him, but tried to follow his gaze toward some unmeasured distance. Before she could say anything, he spoke to her in clear, soft tones.

"We're sailing into trouble."

"What do you mean?"

"I'm not exactly sure, but we are getting close to the place we dreamed about."

Cathy's stomach jumped at the words so calmly spoken. The remembrance of terror gripped her instantly. "Are you sure?"

"Yes."

A long silence passed between them. Cathy spoke first. "Do you know what it means, or what is going to happen?"

"No," answered Marks, "what was happening to you wasn't a part of my dream. Somebody was coming at you. With a knife, I think, but I never got a clear view as to who it was. Do you remember? You were looking at him as you called."

Cathy closed her eyes, trying to go to a place in her memory that she had locked away. The door was shut fast, but one image flooded her mind. It was Bert Jenkins slitting the throat of a floating corpse. She started to speak, but stopped.

"What?" he asked.

"Only something I remembered from the night when we heard the shots being fired. Bert Jenkins has a rigging knife and used it to sink a body before the children noticed."

"That was the first body, when we were all innocent," remarked Shrader. "Then be careful of him."

"But I don't know if it was him, or not."

"It really doesn't matter," contested Marks. "All I know is that I tried to change a dream sequence back when we were going through the lock. I wanted *Fairwinds* to pass through before me, so it wouldn't be like the dream. But, in the end, I couldn't stop it from happening."

"But why would Bert want to hurt me?

Shrader shrugged his shoulders. "Why does anything happen?"

66

Bert Jenkins ordered Phil Pearson to drop the anchor on the bow of *Affinity*. One by one, the other boats were lashed to starboard and port of the central craft. In time, they had successfully managed to get the six boats together without tangling the standing rigging. The result was a floating island where the crews could cross over to the other boats. *Mewtiny* was tied on last so that no one would have to walk over the deck above Roland Koenig's shrouded body.

Whether it was the presence of death or the numbness brought on by hours of unspeakable trauma, the raft was nearly silent as *Strider* approached. The unnatural warmth of the day was giving away to a chill as the sky seemed to close over like a blanket.

"I thought it was supposed to get warmer when you pulled up the covers," said Cathy to no one. They were less than five hundred feet from the raft before they were noticed.

"It's Mom!" said a startled Brittany who was coiling a line in the cockpit of *Affinity*. With that, it was all hands on deck, with a few exceptions that Cathy noted in her mind. Absent were Marty Koenig and her son, Jeff, Jim and Tish Barker, and Laura Romig. Cathy quickly pieced it together. Marty was with Roland, and Jeff was consoling his mother. Laura was reassuring Tish that her husband's fever would break. All the while, she wondered whether she should have given him the "fish tank" antibiotic.

With the engine running and sails furled, Gus steered *Strider* along a course that would bring them parallel to the transoms that formed the boundary wall of the raft.

Dr. Bill Morgan was already straining over the stern rail. "His temperature is going up quickly," he announced. Cathy's wordless answer was to take hold of the garbage bag that Shrader had filled with his drug store flotsam. She held it up with two hands. Its weight took her by surprise.

"Just what the doctor ordered," she quipped. She didn't expect that Morgan would reach out and snag the sack from her hand, but he did. Quickly he ripped open the bag and dumped the contents on the white cockpit cushions. Without much need of examination, he recognized the canisters.

"How in the world?" he queried.

"I don't know," she replied, "Shrader seemed to know where to find them." Both of them turned to look at Marks who stood in *Strider's* bow pulpit. His gaze was directed toward the fading image of the island. Instinctively, Cathy followed his line of sight. Even in the dimming light, something seemed different about the land mass. Suddenly it struck her that there was no shoreline. In this part of Canada, the beaches were covered with water-worn rocks. She would have expected to see waves running up to stones blackened by the surging rush. Instead, the waves were dampened by what looked like a stand of small Christmas trees. The line of trees was backed by taller trees and these by taller still, as if some nature photographer had set the forest in rows with the shortest trees in front.

At first, she didn't know what she was seeing; then, it dawned on her. The small trees in front were every bit as tall as the ranks behind them. The apparent gaps between them gauged the massive trunks and canopies that now extended to the lake's bottom. Gus, who had seen Cathy turn aside, gave a low whistle.

"I'll be damned," he said, "it is under water, at least a third of the island. We're sailing over a friggin' pine forest. No wonder I thought we were so far away."

"You were right about the island, Gus," she said. "It wasn't your eyes playing tricks; it was the river taking over."

The reunion was suddenly animated and loud. The children wanted to use their flag codes to signal the homecoming. Anthony Ragni suggested spelling out "*Strider* is back," but his sister, Teresa, said it would take too many flags.

Cameron Romig was looking at the pocket guide and said, "What about just C-K? It means, 'assistance no longer needed'." In the end they settled on that, raised flags, and dared the adults to figure it out. With everything going on around them, they didn't find too many grownups who were willing to play, but this group of mutineers was determined. In the end, Marty Koenig went back to *Rol's Royce* to find Roland's code book. In the dim light of the cabin, she sat down and opened the vinyl-jacketed book. Before she found the page, she sensed the space around her. It was full of Roland and their life together. Mounted on the bulkhead was the engraved brass bell that she had given him during Chanukah the year after they got the boat. His foul weather gear and boots were in the wet locker next to her. The book in her hand had been a gift from Jeff, and the words "Smooth sailing" were inscribed on the frontispiece. She wept as she opened the pages to the section on code flags. In that version, the flags' description read: "assistance no longer required by me."

"Roland," she said in the silence, "I know you can hear me. I don't know what is coming next, but we'll make you proud. Goodbye, Darling, I'll see you again." The holy reverie was broken by steps on the companionway.

"Mom, are you all right?" came Carol's voice.

"I'm doing better, honey," she said to her daughter-in-law, "much better. Assistance no longer required by me," she continued.

"What?"

"C-K! The code flags. They mean, 'assistance no longer required by me.'"

"Oh," said Carol, who was now in the compartment. "I didn't understand what you meant." Marty stood up and took a deep breath, filling her lungs with the cabin air.

"Let's go break the news to the fleet," she said taking Carol's hand.

When the two emerged from the cabin, Marty called everyone to attention. "Just so our young crew members don't think we're all a bit dotty, we've broken the code. All it took was a little life experience, the wisdom of age, and the last code book that hasn't been absconded by pirates!" With this she raised the book over her head to a chorus of cheers from the children as well as the adults. "Assistance no longer required by me!" Cathy noticed that she exchanged glances with Jeff and Carol who smiled back.

Carol mouthed the words, "We love you, Mom." Marty misted over, but it soon passed.

"Tomorrow there's going to be a funeral," said Shrader moving to Cathy's side. "I'll take a burial detail to the island."

67

"I don't want to be disrespectful, but we have to do something with Roland's body." Shrader turned to face his old friend John Romig who was speaking.

"I know," he said. "I don't want to put him in the water, not with all that we've seen. I don't think anyone could handle that, especially Marty. I thought we could move him to the island."

"Well, we need to do it soon. Laura can't stop playing the nurse. She cleaned him up pretty well for the family, and, as expected, *rigor mortis* set in. She checked on him a bit ago, and his muscles have relaxed; he's no longer rigid. It won't be long until he's going to begin to bloat up."

"Can you and Laura do me a favor?" asked Shrader. "I have some plastic foul weather gear. Would you put it on him while I talk to Jeff?"

"Sure, we can do that," answered Romig. Shrader went below and quickly returned with what looked like two bright yellow rolls of plastic.

"Here," he said, "they should fit pretty loosely, and he'll look like he's ready for any storm." The men parted. John scrambled back with his bundles, and Marks moved over the raft toward *Rol's Royce* where he could see Jeff coiling a length of nylon anchor rode. Jeff looked up as he approached, and Shrader lowered his voice when he said, "Jeff, we have to move your father. I thought you'd want to help."

"Where to?"

"I thought the island, if that seems okay to you."

Jeff's features relaxed, and Shrader knew his thoughts.

"Sorry," said Koenig, "there have just been too many bodies in the water. I don't want Dad to be one of them."

"Nor do I. I've got an old inflatable raft on-board *Strider*. I thought that we could put your Dad in it and tow it over into the trees. We ought to be able to move to higher ground where we can make a proper grave."

"We have a dinghy on the *Royce*. I could get Mom and the family over to the island."

"I was counting on that," said Marks. "Could you also tow the inflatable over, too? I don't think I could row it with your Dad inside. How soon can you launch it?"

"It's been a while since I did it, but maybe forty-five minutes."

"We probably won't need it until early tomorrow morning, but if you can get it in the water tonight, that would be good! Right now, John and Laura are getting everything ready on *Mewtiny*. Maybe you'd like to get your family over there to say your 'goodbyes'." Jeff nodded.

"Shrader, I think we all want to be there on the island to see the spot and all that."

"I'll do my best," he answered. "Could I borrow that anchor line you just stowed?"

"Sure," said Jeff, "What for?"

"I'll use it to mark the way to the site so that we can all find it in the morning." With that, the two took to their separate tasks. Shrader used a foot pump to blow up his four-person raft. After checking with the Romigs, he recruited John and Gus to go with him onto the island. By now, it was dark and colder than it had been in the past few days. The three took an ax and several folding shovels from the stores in *Strider*. They found a propane lantern aboard *Mewtiny*, and took it along with two hundred and fifty feet of line from *Rol's Royce*. Tiffany Jenkins surprised them with a thermos of coffee as they got ready to shove off.

Shrader left the anchor light lit at the top of Strider's mast so that they could find their way back. They set off, looking for all the world like a painting of Washington crossing the Delaware. Gus stood in front with the lantern, John was seated in the stern, and Shrader at the oars.

When they reached the first of the trees, Romig tied off one end of the nylon line to an outer limb and let out the rope as they drifted in deeper. Soon the oars were of no use, and Shrader and Gundersen pulled the small boat through the brush by grabbing on to the sticky spruce boughs. Gus put out the lantern for fear of setting the canopy ablaze. John produced a small flashlight and did his best to shine it forward to light the way. Suddenly, the branches stopped brushing over them. They were under the trees. Gundersen fumbled in the dark with matches and relit the lantern. As he trimmed the flame, they saw the shining black water. Overhead was a dense tangle of tall white spruce. They were now in the space between the forest floor and the lowest boughs. Vertical tree trunks stood like endless pillars supporting a great roof. Behind them was a wall of needled branches that had closed in. The only sign of their passage was the nylon hawser that had been threaded through John Romig's fingers.

Even in the dark, they could tell that they had entered a large cavern which was defined by the forest. The three sat quietly, like pious pilgrims in a shadowy cathedral. At last Shrader took one of the oars and used it like a paddle to cover the last twenty or so feet until the rubber raft lightly touched ground. His first step over the bow proved precarious. He ended up sprawled in a thick bed of short, sharp needles.

"Looks like you need to find your land-legs, sailor," laughed Gus.

"No," protested Shrader, "it's not that. The needles are deep. I'm not sure anyone has ever been here before." When they stepped out, they understood his meaning. Tying off the line to a nearby trunk, they took the lantern and the shovels and made their way up the hillside, treading as in deep snow. They did not go very far when Shrader stopped.

"This looks right," he said. Hanging the lantern from a dead branch, he began to scrape away the blanket of needles with the side of his foot. The spot was in a relatively flat space where the roots of a great fir spread out protecting the soil from erosion.

"If we dig here," he said, pointing to the ground, "we can use the root structure to support the walls of the crypt."

"Crypt?" asked Gundersen.

"He's an anthropologist," began Romig. "He's used to talking about the graves of Stone Age peoples."

"That's what we are, aren't we?" offered Shrader.

"I guess we are," said Romig who followed Marks' lead and began to clear the site. They found a good many flat rocks beneath the layer of needles. These they set aside. When the actual digging began, the soil was rich and black and loamy. Aside from an occasional boulder, opening a shallow grave proved an easy task.

The three carefully lined a canoe-shaped trench with boulders and flat rocks. Shrader kept aside the widest of the flat stones. "I'm going to lay these across the crypt so that there's a chamber for the body," he explained.

"It's pretty shallow," questioned Romig. "What about animals digging?"

"I say we raise a cairn over the spot with all these extra rocks. That should be enough. Maybe we should burn some of these needles and twigs around the edges. The burnt charcoal might put off a foraging pest, at least for the time needed." As he said this, Shrader could feel the whale effigy beneath his shirt. An odd feeling came over him, like he had been in this place or a place like it before.

They traced their way back to the inflatable, clearing a path as best they could. Tomorrow, Marty Koenig and others would make their way back along this route, but no one wanted them to experience Shrader's rough landing.

Though the night had grown cold, the three were hot and sweaty when they reached the water's edge. With towels they had stowed in a garbage bag, they rinsed off in water they drew out with a bucket tied to a lanyard.

They used the anchor rode as a lifeline through the spruce. With no need to row, they set themselves to hacking and sawing through the small limbs, creating a path as wide as a dinghy.

When they cleared the last boughs, they saw the light from *Strider* and the dark silhouette of the rafted flotilla. All three were asleep as soon as they hit their bunks.

68

Shrader was awakened by a soft thud against the hull. The voice he had heard so many times before echoed through his half-conscious mind. "We must meet tonight."

"Okay," said Shrader like a man who had just resigned himself to a task long postponed. "Tonight, I will put to sea alone. Come to me then." There was no fear in meeting the voices that had guided him through the locks and to the stash of pharmaceuticals that, even now, were bringing Jim Barker back from the edge of death. Nothing in the past led him to believe that the voices from within were untrustworthy. His growing apprehension was that they were simply that, voices from within. A delusion which proves helpful in the first instance may betray in the last. At sea, and alone, the voices would have to come to him or leave him to himself.

He got out of his berth and noticed that the air was cooler in the cabin. He gave a tap to the brass thermometer. The temperature needle dropped to forty-eight degrees. The barometer next to it had fallen, too. It was about 6 a.m. Gus was still asleep in the quarter berth. He leaned toward the sleeping man, "Gus, up and at 'em. Meet me aboard *Mewtiny* in a few minutes; we need to move Roland up the hill."

Gundersen mumbled something inaudible, but Shrader knew that he had heard the message. He'd be there. In spite of their short acquaintance, Marks knew that Gus was one of the good guys.

Out on deck, the flotilla was still resting peacefully. The rubber inflatable bobbed gently against *Strider*'s hull. Was that the sound that had awakened him? Shrader didn't want to think about it. He rustled through the contents of the lazarette until he found a small canvas canopy that he normally used over the boom for a sunshade. He also took a fifty foot length of half-inch nylon line, an aluminum gaff, and a snap shackle. These he threw into the rubber raft. They hit the floorboards with a soft plunk.

He then slipped over the side and into the raft that wanted to slip sideways in the water. He tamed its slide by hanging onto the gunwale of the larger boat. In a quick motion, he released the short painter from its cleat and dropped to his knees. In an instant, a paddle was in the water, and Shrader was moving the small craft across the sterns of the rafted fleet toward *Mewtiny* which was on the far end.

The sound of the raft scratching the sides of *Mewtiny* echoed through the hull and brought Laura and John Romig to life. John was still getting used to living inside a drum, for that's what the plastic hull seemed when it amplified the vibrations that traveled through the water. He quickly went topside. His faced showed his relief when he saw Shrader's head pop up over the gunwale

"I thought I was getting rammed by a floating log."

"Sorry," replied Marks, "I just thought we should move Roland before everybody starts stirring. Gundersen is on his way. Why don't you go get Jeff? I think the four of us can handle it." Romig nodded as he slipped down the companionway for a jacket, and then set out across the boats to *Rol's Royce*. Shrader snapped the shackle to the end of the boom, threaded the nylon line through the pulley, and tied it to the center of the gaff. By the time Gundersen arrived and Romig had returned with Jeff, he had spread out the canvas on the cockpit seat.

The others immediately grasped what he was doing. They would set the body on the canvas. By tying loops through the corner grommets in the canvas, they could hoist Roland over the side and lower him down to the raft.

They used a blanket to get the body through the cabin. Laura had to help as they lifted him up the cockpit steps and through the companionway. Once the loops were slipped over the ends of the gaff, it was an easy job to hoist the body and swing it out over the small boat. The line went slack when the weight rested on the wooden floor. With a few twists, the loop ends were freed from the gaff and the boom was pulled away. Jeff looked down on his father who seemed to be lying comfortably in the floating raft.

"Bring your dinghy around so that we can tow it to shore," said Shrader, placing a hand on Koenig's shoulder.

"Sure," said Jeff, "I launched it last night." He brought the small rowboat to the stern of *Mewtiny* where Gundersen and Romig joined him, taking seats in the stern. Shrader lowered himself into the raft next to Roland's body. He handed the bow line to John as Jeff rowed alongside. There was a slight jolt when the short painter reached its limit and the dinghy began to pull the inflatable forward. Jeff Koenig strained at the oars, but declined help when Gus offered to take a turn.

It wasn't very far to the path through the trees. Once they reached the outer edge, Koenig shipped the oars and followed Gus' and John's lead as they pulled their way, hand over hand, through the prickly branches. In the trailing boat, Shrader pushed out, fending off the stiffer boughs. Once they passed under the canopy of the trees, Jeff Koenig stopped pulling and sank to his seat.

"This is a wonderful place!" He said to no one. "Thank you," he said, turning his glance to the three men in succession.

"Gus, John, why don't you show Jeff the way up the hill? I'll get things ready here," suggested Marks. The two nodded. After beaching the two dinghies, the three walked quietly up the slope while Shrader slid the gaff through the front loops of the canvas. When they returned, Shrader gestured for John to take one end of the gaff. Gus took the other. Marks and Romig each grabbed one of the loops on the back edge of the tarp.

After a few steps the two in the rear couldn't go much further as the ropes cut deeply into their hands. "Just a minute," gasped Romig. They lowered their bundle and John grabbed a fallen limb that lay in the needled carpet. "This will help," he said slipping it through the rope loops. With this adjustment, they quickly managed to move the body to the crypt. After laying down a bed of needles, they transferred the body by hand from the canvas sheet.

The four stood in silence. Jeff was the first to speak. "How do we cover him up?" His voice quivered with the words.

Romig answered, "We'll lay those flat stones between the upright ones we used to line the pit. They will make a bridge and form a small chamber. Then we can mound up the soil we removed. Shrader wants to burn some of the needles for a layer of ash and then pile boulders to make a mound. That will mark the grave as well as protect it from animals."

Jeff seemed lost in thought. "I just didn't want to think we'd just put the dirt over him around his face. This is good. Thank you. Again."

"Do you think your mother would want to come see this before we close it up?" asked Gus.

"I know she would! So would Carol and the kids."

"Why don't you and I go get them in the boats? John and Shrader can wait here until we get back." The four agreed. The plan was well underway when Romig and Marks helped shove off the dinghy with the inflatable trailing behind.

As they waited, Romig and Marks began to talk quietly.

"Are you all right, Shrader?" asked John. Shrader just looked away. "Look, we've been running for three days or forty years, I can't remember which. A lot of this fell on you! Are you holding together?"

Shrader laughed, "You and Laura have been shipmates with a dead man for two nights, and you're worried about me?"

"Does sound odd, doesn't it?" replied Romig. "But as things have been going, that's pretty tame." The quiet tone brought them back to the place established by years of friendship. Marks told him about the voices and about the meeting planned for later that night.

"Am I crazy? Are these voices in my head like a psychotic who has stopped his medication? Or are they real? I can't say which would be more alarming."

"I've known you a long time, and I don't think you're crazy. In fact, as an outsider, you've been brilliant getting us this far. This burial is a page out of one of our digs. It could be written into a how-to handbook of Neolithic mound building. I've studied it, but never would have thought of using it."

"That's the thing," said Shrader. "I didn't think about using an ancient technique. I just wanted our brother to face the sea so that he could watch for our boats." There was a long silence.

"Do they trust me?" he asked, finally.

"Trust?" queried Romig. "Some do."

"Who, then?"

"Cathy trusts you, and Laura and I do. I guess Laura trusts you because I do. I think Gus trusts you, but thinks you're quirky. The Koenigs and the Barkers are so grateful that they'd do anything to protect you, but I don't know if that translates into trust. The Ragnis don't say much at all, I don't know; they might be totally overwhelmed, and the Morgans are still in awe about those jars of antibiotics. I don't think the kids know you're here. They're oblivious, except for Brittany who's pretty well in tune with her mother."

"What about the Jenkins and Phil Pearson?"

"I think Tiffany Jenkins isn't allowed too many opinions, so she's hard to read. Bert is military all the way. To him, you're a loose cannon, but he's not afraid of you. He doesn't seem to balk at following orders, but there are times, I think, when he'd like to be giving them."

"And Phil?"

"That one is easy. He just plain hates you! He wants you dead, preferably by some slow and painful means." They both laughed.

"I know it's not funny. He even tried to kill me once. Okay, maybe 'kill' is too strong a word. He tried to pull the plug on *Strider* while I was aboard. What have I ever done to him?"

"Oh, nothing, except, you stole his wife out from under his nose!"

"Cathy? How? We've never even. . ."

"Had sex?" Romig interrupted. "You didn't need to. You did worse that that. You treated her like a competent leader. You and she made a plan and she is playing her part perfectly. His wife is supposed to do what *he* says. Now he has to do what she says, and it's all your doing! That's why he hates you."

"What about Cathy? Aside from Phil, what do the others think?"

"The kids said it all! That *C-K* wasn't for you. Everyone breathed a sigh of relief when they saw that she was back. Actually, they were all pretty bummed with Jenkins at the time. Evidently Cathy told him to keep the boats together and he took his command a little too seriously. He kept barking out orders to keep all the boats in some sort of formation. Kind of funny really, as long you knew it wouldn't go on forever."

"So," said Shrader, "everyone seems to trust Cathy, but they think I'm a little short-circuited in the head."

"Pretty much, but I think there are some who think you're behind everything Cathy does."

"Like Phil."

"Like Phil, and maybe a few others," replied Romig. "She hasn't really been tested yet. Not on her own. Bert Jenkins is probably watching for signs of weakness. I'm not convinced that he would stand by her if he didn't think she was getting good data from you. I think he and Phil are a lot alike; he just doesn't have to deal with the wife-as-property stuff. I think he sees her as an extension of you. I guess he's like Phil in that regard."

"What about you, John? You probably know more about what's going to happen weather-wise, and the life we're headed for than anyone, including me."

"Now that's scary! You have the distinction of being the crazy egghead and I have the honor of being the irrelevant egghead who's married to the nurse. Not bad to be me! Sucks to be you!" They both laughed. The sound of voices came up the hill. The boats were passing through the spruce. The two went down to the water's edge to greet the mourners.

69

To Shrader's surprise, Cathy sat in the bow of the lead boat. His glance asked the question without words.

"Everyone is coming," she answered. "I told them what we were doing, and they all wanted to stand with the Koenigs."

"Do we need someone to take the boats back for more passengers then?" asked Marks.

"No," she responded. "When I started talking about logistics, we found out that every boat has at least one inflatable stashed below decks. When they get them launched, we'll have the whole landing party here. Well, not Phil. He thinks it's not smart to leave the boats unattended."

"So he's staying there alone?"

"Not alone. I told him that I thought it was a good idea and assigned Jenkins to help." She gave him a knowing look. "I remembered that he had pulled out your transducer, and didn't want any more mischief," she added.

With Cathy in the first dinghy were Carol, Marty, and Jeff Koenig. Tiffany Jenkins was also there. The towed inflatable was overloaded with Laura Romig and her two boys, Ben and Cameron, and the Koenig girls, Allison and Sandi. Laura joined her husband, giving him a quick kiss.

"Jeff is really pleased with what you three have done," Cathy offered. "He told his mother that the place is holy, and I now understand what he meant. This is beautiful and quiet."

"Cathy," Marks interrupted, "I'm going to wander off for a bit. I have to think. I'll keep an eye out for when you've finished. John can answer any questions." He spoke the last words loudly enough for the Romigs to hear. "Take them all up to the site," he said. The words were unnecessary. Already Jeff and his family were following the newly worn path to the grave.

"But, Shrader," Cathy began.

"We'll speak soon," he said striking a path under the trees along the shore. No sooner had Cathy and the Romigs joined the procession, than Gus arrived with the second wave of inflatables. In the end, four more boats made the journey. Even Jim Barker, whose fever had broken during the night, was able to make the trek. He was taking it slow and leaning on Tish quite a bit, but his step was determined.

Clustered on the hillside, the group stood in near silence; only the voice of the wind spoke to them. Marty held a canvas bag. At one point she reached into it and pulled out the brass bell from the cabin. "Jeff, your father should have this," she said. He took the bell and set it in the crook of Roland's arm. Its inscription, *Rol's Royce*, caught the light filtering through the trees. Marty turned to her granddaughters with a nod. Allison reached into the same canvas bag and withdrew the Roland's worn codebook that was used to decipher the code flags. From the sack, Sandi retrieved a colored drawing of two signal flags, C-K. On the back were the names of the twelve children of the fleet. After the girls set these in the crypt, there was a silent prayer.

No one had thought about a eulogy or any formal speeches, but Cathy spoke:

"None of us have had much time to think in the last few days, and maybe that's a blessing. I suspect that if we knew what is happening elsewhere, we might lose all hope. But that belongs to another world now, and we can't deal with that. We have to learn how to live in this world by a new way. In the old world, we came to believe that our greatest fear was evil deeds by evil people. Now we understand that we should have had less fear about what others could do, and more respect for our need for each other. In the last few days, we have seen death in the water. People died through no fault of their own, and no one will ever know their fate. We did not leave Roland in the water. He is here in this sacred place because we care, not just about saving our own lives, but about honoring all life.

"We have been learning how to pull life out of the water. We pulled Jim out," she said turning toward Barker. "And we pulled Gus out, and he has proved a very good friend.

"Roland was a lifesaver, too. His phone call gave us Carol and Jeff, Allison, and Sandi. He drew people to life by drawing them to be a part of this group.

"This time and place are now his. Here he is honored, and remembered. He will always be one of us. We are the people who pull life out of the water. We are the people who will watch over each other even if we fall."

As if on signal, Gus and John stepped toward the flat stones that had been placed at the foot of the grave. They lifted one between them and set it across the bottom edge of the crypt. Jeff and Carol followed them. The rock was heavier than they could handle, but Tiffany Jenkins gave them the needed assistance. Soon everyone was helping and the last stone was in place, sealing the body in a stone chamber. The families began the descent to the boats; only Marty and Cathy remained.

Down at the water's edge, some of the children began to run and chase each other among the trees. At the sound, the two women turned. Marty smiled. "They are still so alive," she said.

"It's good for them to be here. Not just to see, but to get out some energy," Cathy added. "Maybe we shouldn't be in too much of a hurry to get back to the boats."

"Cathy, where's Shrader? He was here a bit ago."

"He told me that he had to think. He's wandered off, but I'm sure he's nearby."

"Jeff told me that all this was his doing. I wanted to thank him."

"He knows," answered Cathy. "Shrader doesn't see everything the way we do, and sometimes he just has to sort things out. He's really smart, and clever about how to make things work, but being around other people seems to cloud his thinking."

"Everybody needs to be alone sometimes, I guess. But I'm glad that I'm not alone right now," Marty said, reaching out to hug Cathy. With an arm around each other, they made their way down to the waiting crowd.

When they looked back, Shrader was coming down through the trees toward the crypt. Everyone turned and watched as he piled up some of the dried needles and lit them with a disposable lighter.

"What in the hell is he doing?" questioned Vince Ragni.

"He's going to make a layer of ash," said Romig quietly. "Then he'll mound up some dirt and boulders over the spot. The rocks and the smell of the ash will keep animals from digging around. It's the way ancient peoples protected the tombs of their loved ones."

"Thank God for Shrader," said Marty Koenig.

One by one the dinghies were filled with passengers who pulled their boats through the trees by the jackline. They untethered Shrader's inflatable from the Koenig's dinghy. At last John Romig, Cathy Pearson, and Shrader Marks were left standing alone.

"We have some work to do up there," said Cathy, pointing toward the grave. The three spent the next hour mounding soil and ash and weighty stones on the grave of Roland Koenig.

Tired and winded, they sat among the trees looking at the cairn that was now before them.

"I need a promise from you, Cathy," said Shrader.

"What's that?"

"That you won't waste any time looking for me."

A puzzled expression washed over her. "Are you going somewhere?"

"I already told this to John, but I have to leave tonight." John nodded as Marks continued. "When they realize that I've gone, don't act surprised. Act like it's the most natural thing in the world that I'm away. It is."

"You're going weird on me, Shrader. Where are you going?"

"I'm just going ahead to scout the waters. I might be a day or so."

"And in the meantime, back at the ranch," broke in Cathy with growing apprehension in her voice, "what am I to do?"

"I'm sorry, but I don't really know," he answered.

"What?"

"I mean, you have to get this group north up along the coast. It's going to be slow. We won't have the St. Lawrence River pushing us, and it's the North Atlantic. If storms approach, you might be able to find a coastal inlet, but you might just have to ride it out."

"That's reassuring," Cathy said, mockingly.

"Oh, did I tell you that your compasses will probably not work very well the further north you go?"

"You're just full of good news," she replied.

"Oh, it gets worse," he offered. "John, help me out here. Time to stop being the irrelevant egghead! Tell her what we expect with the weather." Cathy turned to face Romig.

"Well, we don't exactly know," he began.

"This isn't an academic presentation," interrupted Marks, "no disclaimers needed."

"Okay, I get you," said Romig. "It's probably going to get very cold, very fast. During the cold war, it was called 'nuclear winter'. Scientists came up with this idea. They said that the dust from a nuclear war could plunge the world into an ice age. It was seen as political propaganda, but we all knew it was real. It's happened before."

"A nuclear war?" protested Cathy.

"No, not the *war*, the *winter*. In ancient times, volcanoes threw out the dust. For a brief time, there is a blanket effect; the cloud holds in the heat, but eventually it blocks the sun's energy and it gets cold, fast."

"How fast?"

"It would be more like hours or days, rather than months or years. And it will stay cool until the atmosphere is cleansed. It's anybody's guess as to how long, five or ten years, maybe longer."

"So it's going get very cold, but we knew that. That's why we have so many parkas."

"Cathy, most people on the planet are going to die," Shrader added bluntly.

"He's right," John began again. "Everything is connected. There will be no crops because the ground is frozen. That means no food for livestock or wildlife. The people killed along the coasts might have been the lucky ones. Everyone else gets to wait through the cold until their food runs out. And, it will run out."

Shrader jumped into the discussion. "I am going to try to find a cove where we can hunker down, where the animals thrive in the cold. If the caribou make it, then we will, too!"

"And if there is no such place?" questioned Cathy.

"Then the sea will have to feed us. The ocean will stay open beyond the ice edge."

"Which is why we can't stay here, right?" she asked.

"Exactly," said Marks. "The water here, at the mouth of the St. Lawrence, will probably freeze. We need to get out to sea and away from population centers. We can't be much help there. We can only die with them."

"So you're going to look for a safe harbor, and I'm supposed to make everyone think we're on a great adventure."

Both John and Shrader nodded in agreement. "That's about right," said Shrader. "And John will help you."

"But if you go ahead, how will we know how to follow?"

"Stay within sight of the coast. That way we'll be following a narrow corridor. I'll go on the radio at noon tomorrow and every hour after that. If we're within thirty miles of each other, you should be able to hear me."

"And if we pass by each other or something happens to you?" she reflected.

"Then John can help you pick a site." Turning to John, Shrader said, "You know how the 'Red Paints' situated their fishing stations." Romig nodded. "Look for that sort of place."

Shrader stood, brushed himself off, and headed down the hillside. "I guess this conversation is over," said Cathy to John.

"I'll help you as much as I can," said Romig.

"I know, John. Thanks, I'll need it."

As they readied the small inflatable, Shrader leaned over to Cathy. "Be careful," he said. "Remember the first dream? Someone was attacking you. Do you remember how everyone was dressed?"

"They were wearing parkas; I was cold."

"Exactly," said Shrader. "Be careful."

70

Cathy had little difficulty persuading the crews that they should spend a second night at the anchorage. "It will give us a chance to inventory our stores and shift things around to the various boats," she said. Some indicated that they would like to spend a little more time on shore. The thought of trying to track down a disoriented crew member gave Cathy some pause, but in the end she surrendered to the will of those who proposed a buddy system that required periodic check-ins. In time, it proved a useful compromise. A freshwater pond was discovered early on, and the water supplies of the whole fleet were topped to capacity. Vince and Anthony Ragni also proved to be competent at fishing and supplied enough bass to feed the fleet and maintain bragging rights for any foreseeable future.

At the heart of the day's activity was the secret shared only by Cathy, Shrader, and John. Sometime after dark, Shrader was going to put out to sea. The reality was that *Strider* was loaded with many of the supplies needed for the journey. Cathy insisted that if Shrader was going to risk himself and his boat in a night sail, he shouldn't put the community's stores in jeopardy as well. Marks agreed completely.

If the practical reasons for shifting supplies to other boats weren't enough, there was a more ominous concern. After arriving back aboard the rafted boats, Bert Jenkins made his report. In military fashion, he recounted that there had been no incidents. He and Phil had spent most of the time inspecting the riggings and fittings of the various boats and securing the raft itself.

"So you mostly did deck work?" Cathy inquired.

"Pretty much," said Jenkins. "Except when Phil went below on *Strider* to get the things you had left over there. For what it's worth, he didn't find them. Said that they were probably buried under all the junk and he didn't want to disturb anything."

Cathy thanked him, and warned Shrader. "While you are unloading, you might want to check the bilges. Phil was aboard *Strider* while we were on the island."

In general, everyone was surprised by the boxes that Marks brought up out of *Strider*. It began with fourteen cases of canned food, two dozen blankets, freeze-dried fruits, sterno stoves, Sierra cups, and all sorts of backpacking supplies. Very quickly, the decks of the rafted boats were scattered with piles of stores. Cathy moved among them assigning them to particular boats and keeping a master list. The youngest crew members bore the weight of shifting everything to its rightful place. The strongest of the adults had gone ashore by this time and were bringing the water down from the pond. It proved a long, hard trek.

Cathy set Gundersen and Jenkins the task of figuring out how to make each of the boats as seaworthy as possible. The two made an effective team. Gus seemed an inexhaustible source of ideas for jury-rigging, and Bert knew all the weak points. Especially vulnerable, he said, were the larger portlights on some of the cabins. These cabin windows were fine for lake sailing, but would likely collapse inward if struck by the full force of a breaking wave. The traditional "fix" for this problem was to bolt plywood storm shields over the glass. This presented both logistical and psychological problems. The first was the lack of plywood. The second was the fact that the owners of these yachts were not willing to see their beautiful boats scarred by drills and bolts and roughly sawn wood.

The first problem was solved when Shrader offered them the floor boards of the inflatable and had them rip out the settees from the main cabin of *Strider*. No one seemed more surprised or pleased with this than Phil Pearson, who relished the dismantling of Shrader's beloved boat.

The second problem was lessened by John Romig who appeared reluctant, but eventually gave in to the idea of letting the storm shields be applied to *Mewtiny*. Brittany, who had sailed with John and Laura, started to speak, but went silent with a glance from her mother. In that instant, she became a co-conspirator with the small group who knew that the Romigs didn't even own a boat. *Mewtiny* had been acquired for the fleet through an act of piracy. Cathy and Shrader later offered to nominate John for an Oscar for his performance.

Dusk found them all on the island. The fire that had cooked the Ragnis' fish now became the focal point for a clan meeting. Shrader seemed to be drifting into one of his moods, and was wandering about the far perimeter of the firelight.

After a time, he called to Cathy, "I'm going to go back to the boat and turn on the porch light before it gets too dark."

"Shrader," she said, "be careful. Come back." The words seemed straightforward in the fading light, but they carried a double meaning. John Romig nodded to his friend.

"This is the warmest I've been in two days," said Tiffany Jenkins as she edged closer to the fire. Three of the boys, Anthony Ragni, Chris Pearson, and Cameron Romig, had been quietly adding wood to the fire. They did this because they had talked about having a great bonfire. It would have stayed mostly talk, had not the girls protested that they would set the forest ablaze.

Cathy identified the game and headed off Chris as he approached with a handful of dry twigs. "That's enough," she said to her son. "We don't want to set the trees on fire." Without actually sticking out her tongue at the three, Ashley Barker gave them a great facial expression for "I told you so."

"Is this fire a good idea, considering we've been keeping a low profile?" asked Vince Ragni.

"I suppose it would be riskier if I thought that there was somebody out there to see it," said Cathy. "But maybe if we gathered around, we could block the light and have a chance to talk about a few things." After a day away from the terror, most were ready to start trying to put the ordeal into perspective. Words started to flow like a great flood as people recounted the rush of the water, the fire, and their sense of sliding through the wrecks of the lower elevations of Montréal and Québec City. No one mentioned the bodies that appeared over and over like litter thrown at the side of the road. Two sights were clearly remembered. One was the reappearance of *Strider* with Cathy holding a black garbage bag. The other was Marty placing a brass bell aside the body of Roland.

As the stories went on, Cathy sensed that they were beginning to heal. Her optimism, however, was crushed when Phil let loose the volley that he had been holding back.

"What in the hell are you people talking about!" he railed. "You talk as though you've been saved from something! You've been saved from nothing! In fact, you've been thrown into the damn fire. If you weren't here right now, where would you be?"

He waited for a response. When none came, he answered his own question. "If you weren't here, you'd be sitting in your family rooms watching all this on television! You can bet that none of this, I tell you, NONE of this found its way to Sodus Bay. I'll bet that tomorrow in Rochester, people will be getting up to go to work, just like any other morning. And they'll be talking about the poor bastards that got caught in the tsunami. When we get back home, we'll be the idiots who wanted a front row seat in hell."

Cathy didn't interrupt. When his anger died down, she spoke calmly, but she didn't look at him or address him directly. "It's probably true that the wave we passed through didn't make it all the way inland to the level of Ontario. It's also true that we aren't going to be able to turn our boats around to go home. First, the current is running too strong against us, and second, who's to say what happened *after* we passed down the river. It's got to be completely choked by the destruction. In other words, we can't get back now, but we also couldn't get out now if we were on the other side of the devastation. But I want to ask a few questions. How many planes have flown over today? How many rescue helicopters have you heard? How many news media choppers have gone over to get pictures of the destruction?"

Philip just grew red in the face. Laura Koenig voiced the answer that everyone else was thinking, "None. It was totally quiet today; I don't remember a single thing flying over or motoring through the channel."

"Neither do I, Laura," Cathy continued. "Bert, you have an SSB radio on your boat; have you been able to pick up anything?"

"Distress calls, but nothing from the Coast Guard."

"What do you figure is going on?" asked Cathy.

"There are a lot of people worse off than us, but there's something even more distressing. I can't get a single satellite fix on my GPS. I've got three units, and none seem to be working."

"Don't be stupid!" Phil began. "A disaster along the coast doesn't knock out satellites."

"I know that, Pearson," Jenkins snapped back. "If I wanted to name an idiot, it would be you!" Cathy jumped on the comment.

"Settle down, we're all working with limited information. We're only guessing, but let's get everything out so that we can make the best guess. Why do you think we're not able to get a GPS signal?"

"The system has been shut down," said Bert, who did not break eye contact with Philip.

"Why? What's your take on that?" asked Cathy.

"It's a security measure. Everybody who uses GPS uses our satellites for guidance. If they shut them down, it would mean that they don't want anybody in the air. They must figure that this would be a moment of weakness that would be an opportunity for an enemy attack or a terrorist strike."

"It's just like you said this morning," interjected Jeff Koenig. "They are more afraid of evil people than of natural events."

"Still," said Phil who had regained his composure, "if the system is shut down, it'll only be temporary. We could sit here on this island, and turn on the GPS everyday. When we get a signal, we'll know that the national security crisis is over, and we can make plans to go back. By then, relief teams will be going up the river to Montréal, and we'll be right on the supply line."

"There aren't going to be any relief teams," said John Romig softly. He was not one who liked to be front and center in a dispute, but at this moment he couldn't avoid it. "The problems aren't over; they're just beginning," he continued. As carefully as possible, he recounted the conversation that Cathy, Shrader, and he had had early that morning. He had everyone's attention as he described volcanic winter and the likely consequences of crop failure on those who lived in the industrial world.

"It's just an ivy-tower theory," quipped Pearson.

"I agree," said Jenkins. "The same argument was thrown at us by the anti-nuke people, but it's just not provable."

"We'll know in a few days." Romig was not going to back down. "If we stay here, and we plunge into winter, we will have to run to stay ahead of the ice when the fresh water coming out of the St. Lawrence freezes up. The best bet is to get into deep salt water sooner, rather than later."

"I say that we will be safer here." Phil Pearson wasn't about to back off. "The island has already given us dinner, and with all of the supplies we have we should be able to do quite well here. Time will bring rescue teams, and then we will be able to get back to our homes. We won't even have to leave Roland here; we can have his body moved to a real cemetery." This last comment proved an error in his effort to change minds. Marty Koenig sat up straight and spoke clearly and distinctly.

"Someday, you can bring me here to be buried, but you will never move Roland."

"The way I see it," began Cathy, "there are no TV helicopters and no rescue planes because we are not the worst hit area. If that is the case, and John is right, we will get caught sitting here waiting for help that will never come. Tomorrow morning, I will be setting off to the northeast. In the meantime, each of you will have to decide what you want to do. If you want to stay on this island, we will leave a seventh of the supplies for each boat that stays. You can all choose."

The parley was over. Within twenty minutes smaller fires were burning in neatly tended circles, and families were huddled together in private conversation. Phil had wandered off, pouting. Brittany sat beside her mother, and the original fire was nearly all embers.

"Why did God do this?" asked Brittany.

"What do you mean, Honey?"

"It's just that if we weren't attacked and all this stuff is just natural, doesn't it mean that God is making it all happen?"

"Some people think that way, I suppose," answered Cathy. "Everybody feels easier if they have somebody to blame. I think some things just happen, and nobody's to blame."

"But all those dead people?"

"Everybody dies, eventually; we don't get a choice in that. Right now we are the ones who are alive, and that's what we have to think about." Brittany leaned into her mother's hug. Instinctively Cathy began to rock her daughter in her arms, and hum an old lullaby.

By nine o'clock the darkness and the chill made the trip back to the boat uneasy and unpleasant. Cathy, Phil, and Brittany were in the last dinghy to leave the island. Phil was curt and clipped in his speech. About halfway back, words came down the line of boats, "*Strider* isn't there!"

"I guess the rats do leave the ship," said Philip.

71

After leaving the others in the forest, Shrader had paddled quietly to the stern of *Strider*. Climbing up the transom ladder to the boat, he pulled the inflatable aboard and unscrewed the release valves on the air chambers. The hiss of the escaping air sang to him as he walked across to the neighboring boat, *Wave Chaser*. The Morgans had left the companionway open, so Marks ducked below. In the dark he fumbled to find the electric panel. He threw a switch and the cabin lights came on. The sudden brightness blinded him for a moment. When his vision returned, he focused on the panel and threw the switch labeled "Anchor Light". Turning off the cabin lights, he waited until the night blindness had passed. Returning to the bow, he released the spring lines that held *Strider* to its rafted neighbor. He left the lines behind with a toss that sent them whipping over *Wave Chaser's* deck.

The wind was blowing steadily out of the west and the rafted boats turned and faced the air currents, swinging around on *Affinity's* heavy anchor. The sound of his engine would have alerted the others, but he knew that he wouldn't need it. He pushed the bow off with his foot against *Wave Chaser's* gunwale. *Strider* began to turn outward, peeling off from the other boats. Moving quickly back to the cockpit, Shrader waited until the hull was perpendicular with the wind. At that moment, he pulled on the line that opened the roller furling jib. The large sail rolled out like a huge Venetian blind. The wind caught it in its breath and it ballooned out. Shrader wrapped the sheets around the winch and tamed the sail until it became a perfect airfoil. *Strider* began to slip forward; the mast creaked with the sudden pressure of the breeze. In a moment there was already fifty feet between *Strider* and the nearest boat, and she was still gaining speed. He eased up on the sheets, and the forward jib stretched out to take the wind. The boat was now running with the wind and all sensation of air movement died away. The sounds, however, did not die, and Marks knew that he was moving at full speed.

On the right, the dark island blocked out the sky. Shrader could maintain his distance by watching the broad avenue of dimly shrouded sky that still remained above the thick cloud cover. For half an hour, the sky and the shadow gave him confidence in his direction, but then he cleared the island. The forward motion of the craft and the sky pushed the island back to the horizon, but the night was growing darker. No star could penetrate the curtain that was drawn over the sea, and Shrader began to fear the darkness.

His first temptation was to go below and turn on the running lights, but he knew that it would serve no purpose. The red, green, and white lights required for navigation are meant to warn others; they do nothing to light the way. He knew that the masthead light would illuminate his jib like a Chinese lantern, but the closeness of the light would only deepen the blackness of the rest of the sea. He sailed on.

Now it was totally dark. Shrader could not see his hand in front of his face. The air was still, but he knew that to be an illusion. Actually, he knew he was moving with the wind and at the speed of the wind. The sounds of the straining rigging told him he was moving fast. Whatever was out there ahead of him, he could not see. He imagined logs and boats and submerged rocks or waves breaking on a shore. He fought off the despair that has taken many solo navigators, the despair that disguised itself as sleep. Boats and sailors have been lost in the midst of storms by crews that abandon the watch to curl up and sleep. Shrader struggled to stay alert. It was then that the familiar voice began in his head.

"You've come! We are here, too."

"Who are you?" cried Shrader whose own voice sounded hollow.

"We are not what you fear!" came the cryptic reply.

"How do you know what I fear?" he called back. At this point he could not tell if the voices he heard were sounds traveling through air or thoughts from within his anxious mind.

"You fear nothing, Shrader Marks."

Shrader laughed out loud. "I fear everything!" he said.

"No," the voice corrected, "you fear nothing. You fear that we are 'nothing' and you have led yourself into emptiness." To this, Shrader had no reply. "If you want to know us," the voice continued, "you must do as we say. Turn your boat to the left."

"Why? What's ahead?" he wanted to know.

"Only a different darkness. Turn, unless you want to hold onto the present path."

Shrader turned the wheel slowly counterclockwise. He could feel the wind over the port quarter. *Is this how it ends*, he wondered to himself. "Am I one of those sailors who gets disoriented in a fog and ends up going in circles?"

The jib called him back to reality. The turn had made it backfill with air, and he had to release the port sheets and pull in the starboard lines. The boat now rolled to an angle that told him he was on a beam reach, the fastest point of sail. Shrader could feel the wind cut right through him. Still in total darkness, *Strider* leaped and chomped at the oncoming waves. The voices knew that he had turned, and they called out again.

"Come forward to meet us."

Marks did not exactly understand the command, but he knew that *Strider* could hold her course for a while. He fumbled in the darkness for the turning knob on the steering pedestal. He turned it clockwise to engage the set-screw that locked the wheel. He stepped back from the helm and waited. The sounds of the wind did not change, and he knew that *Strider* was holding a steady course. He felt his way to the high side of the heeling boat and slowly crawled forward in the total darkness. He carefully set each new handhold before releasing the last. He took his stand against the mast. With one arm looped about the spar he called out, "I'm here."

"Further!" came the reply.

He sat down hard as a wave slammed the boat up against his backside. Bruised, he inched forward like a crab. At last, he was against the sail that formed a solid wall on his right. With his left hand, he took hold of the forestay, and pulled himself to his feet. At the very edge of the boat, he braced his thighs against the bow pulpit. The salty spray bathed him.

"I am here," he stated unequivocally. "I am here!"

"So are we," came the answer, "and we are not 'nothing'!" Shrader strained to see through stinging eyes, but the darkness confounded him. He held himself on the brink of the bow for countless heartbeats. He closed his eyes. He shut out the wind and the spray and the aching cold of his soaked skin, and then he felt it. The unknown "they" were there and he was not alone.

"I see you," he said. While not literally true, it was truthful. He felt their presence.

The rest of the long night was spent in the cockpit. The blanket he had retrieved from the cabin was drenched, but it was wool and it still protected him from some of the cold. Seated now, he steadied the helm with his foot as he held the blanket tight around his neck. In later times, he could not recall the moment when his eyes caught sight of them, but at some point he became aware of flashes of light and dark to the right and left of the moving boat. In that instant, he could name what he saw. They were orcas swimming alongside, even nudging the underside of the hull to correct the course when Shrader had dozed off.

72

The temperature was in the mid-twenties when the rafted boats began to come to life. Aboard *Affinity*, Chris and Justin were complaining about crawling out of their sleeping bags. Cathy got out of bed and went to the electric panel to check the status of the batteries. The house batteries were at about 75% and the starting battery was still fully charged. She turned on the heating units.

"We're down on power, but we'll be running the engines today," she announced.

Phil stuck his head out of his sleeping bag. He had elected to sleep in Brittany's bunk rather than share a cabin with Cathy. Brittany had slept with her mother in the aft cabin.

"Bet you didn't think about heat," he chided.

"Bet we did," came Cathy's answer. She went back to her bed. "Brittany, you need to roll out, Honey," she said to her daughter.

With a groan, the teenager slid from the berth taking the gathered bed clothes with her. Cathy slid the foam mattress to one side exposing the storage area beneath. Like a magician pulling a string of scarves from an empty hat, she produced three portable twelve-volt heaters. Having slept with most of her clothes on, she put on her jeans and slipped into her boat shoes. Taking a heater in each hand, she walked back through the main saloon. She set them down to lift out the lapboards that closed off the companionway. A blast of even colder air flooded the cabin.

"What the hell!" cried Philip.

"Sorry," she said, as she set the heaters outside in the cockpit. She followed, carrying the lapboards which she dropped back in place once she was outside.

She made her way from boat to boat, asking if everyone had some source of heat. As she expected, *Major Blunder* had both DC electric and diesel heaters. *Mewtiny* and *Rol's Royce* had only AC heaters for use with shore power.

"Anyone interested in electric heat," she bellowed like a town crier. A chorus rose in stereo from the two boats, and hatch covers slid open.

In both cases, they were using their stoves to take the chill off the air and now that little bit of heat was flowing out of the cabins. "I have some small electric heaters that'll run off a cigarette lighter socket. If you don't have one, just cut off the plug and wire it into the battery bank. Be sure to check your batteries. This'll drain them pretty fast if you're already low on juice. If you have to start your engine, we'll need to break up the raft. We don't need to have all the boats filling with carbon monoxide."

The heaters disappeared below as hatches slammed shut. No engines were started, so Cathy felt it safe to return to her boat.

Below, the family was coming to life. "Dress warmly," she said as she handed out granola bars all around.

"What do we have to drink?" asked Justin.

"There may be a few sodas left in the storage under the settees," she answered.

"Chris and Cameron drank them all!" he protested.

"Well, I guess that all we have is water then." Justin stuck his lip out in defiance. Cathy just kept sorting through jackets and warm clothes, making a pile for each of them. "It's going to be cold on deck. Bundle up, we're leaving soon!" she said, taking a bite of granola.

Out on deck, she shouted down the raft: "This is Captain Bly of the HMS Bounty! We will be breaking up the raft in fifteen minutes. If you are staying here, you'll have to set an anchor."

Bill Morgan had come out onto the deck of *Wave Chaser*. "What about Shrader?" he asked.

"He's gone on ahead," said Cathy. "He's got more than ten hours on us, so the sooner we leave, the sooner we'll meet him."

"You two do seem to have a plan," remarked Morgan. "I'm not complaining, but are we ever going to be let in on it?"

"After last night, you know as much as I do. Some of this we have to sort of make up along the way."

"But you must've known about Shrader leaving," he replied.

"Oh, that! He told me that he was leaving, but I've given up trying to figure Shrader out. When he insisted that he had to leave before us, I insisted that all the supplies had to come off *Strider*. But you're right; it really isn't much of a democracy."

"Democracy killed Socrates," he said. "Isn't that what the philosophers used to say?"

"I don't know about philosophers, Bill, but you keep surprising me."

Morgan laughed. "So far, Lady, you are the Queen of Surprises, and we're lucky you're watching out for us!"

"Thanks, Bill. Does that mean that *Wave Chaser* will be sailing with us?"

"Wouldn't miss it for the world!"

In the end, no one stayed behind. When *Affinity* hoisted anchor, six boats were motoring slowly out to sea. Phil was at the helm when Cathy looked back toward the island. She thought she could see the trailing edge of the line that led back into the trees. Jeff Koenig suggested that they go back to retrieve it, but the tide was running out of the estuary. With the water level near its lowest point, the rope was higher in the trees. Rather than waste more time than necessary, Cathy declared the rope a lost cause, and they set out. She hoped the decision would not prove costly.

In spite of the cold air, everyone was outside on deck. Brittany and the boys huddled down beneath the cockpit coaming to stay out of the wind. Though it would have been warmer in the cabin, being below during a sail is an invitation to seasickness. Everyone knew that.

Cathy was not concerned with the cold. She was glad to be following the track that Shrader had set the night before. She looked at her watch. It was nearly nine o'clock, the prearranged time for her to talk with the other crews. She went below and turned on the VHF radio. Out of curiosity, she used the touchpad to scan through the U.S. and Canadian weather channels. There was no signal. She went to channel 16 which is the universal hailing setting. There was no traffic or squawks to indicate boats on the fringe of their range. At last she turned to channel 68. Everyone in the fleet had agreed to meet on that frequency.

At the stroke of nine, she depressed the send button. "There's not much sense of worrying about protocol, we're the only ones here," she said. "Is everyone okay?"

She let up on the switch. One by one, different voices ran through the litany of names: *Mewtiny*, *Wave Chaser*, *Rol's Royce*, *Major Blunder*, *Dream Dancer*.

"Good," she said when all had reported. "Just to review: we're heading north along the coast. We need to keep some distance offshore, but in sight of land. If anyone has a problem, set off a flare or run up a distress flag. Shrader is going to attempt his first broadcast in three hours. All of us should listen for him just in case his signal is weak."

"Is there a prize for whoever hears first?" The voice was Bert Jenkins whose boat was equipped with several high-gain antennas.

"Sure," said Cathy. "The winner gets to choose one piece of electronic gear off *Major Blunder!*"

"No one would want that!" came the reply.

"Bert?" responded Cathy. "If your power supply is adequate, why don't you run a radar sweep every now and again. You might be able to see him."

"He's a small target, but I'll watch," said Jenkins.

"Thanks, Bert. I'm signing off on this frequency." Then she added, "Whenever your batteries are up to full charge, feel free to turn off the stink pot and hoist sail." After waiting a moment for any replies, Cathy shut down the radio.

She returned to the cockpit to Phil who was smirking.

"So you're expecting your boyfriend to call at noon?" he said mockingly. Cathy didn't respond for fear it would merely encourage his belligerence. Brittany, however, perked up her ears and glared at her father.

73

Shrader was invigorated by the sight of the great orcas that paced along with *Strider* between them. He had left the other boats behind nearly thirteen hours earlier, and the time was drawing near for him to break radio-silence. He knew that this broadcast would be relatively meaningless. VHF radio signals could carry ten to twenty miles, maybe thirty if the signals hit just right. By rough calculation, the rest of the fleet was forty miles behind him. Even if he were to stop dead in the water, it would be another two hours before they would be in contact range.

He was tempted to let the noon hour pass and wait another hour for the first transmission. Who would ever know? The temptation was heightened by the steady wind out of the southwest that had driven his boat all night. *Strider* was sailing hard over on a port tack and the idea of slowing down had little appeal. Still, he had promised a first attempt at noon, and he would be true to his word.

He shortened the roller furling jib by drawing in some of the sail. Next, he turned the wheel until the bow pointed toward the wind. As the boat came close to the wind, the jib began to flap around like a fluttering flag. The sail began to backfill and swing the boat back to its original course, but he turned the helm over hard and clamped down the set-screw that locked the wheel in place. The technique, known as heaving-to, keeps the boat in about the same place and requires no one to steer. By having the wheel turned in the opposite direction from the way the sails are set, the boat automatically turns back toward the wind before it can pick up any speed. This combination of starts and stops is like treading water. Shrader was now free to go below deck to operate the radio transmitter.

"What are you doing?" asked the whale which Shrader had identified as Keeper.

Shrader was not sure what to say, if anything at all. He couldn't tell whether he was using words or merely thinking in a wordless language. These great animals seemed to know his thoughts as he thought them, and he, theirs.

"He is calling to others in his pod," said Greyback, speaking from the other side of the boat.

Shrader knew that some primitive societies had killer whale cults. He wore the ancient fetish around his neck, but never considered how the shaman priests could communicate with these behemoths. He assumed that language always needed sound, but these voices lived in his brain, next to his own thoughts.

"You're right, Greyback," he said, "I must call to my pod." He went below and rotated the battery selection switch from "off" to "1". He turned on the radio, but the LED indicator did not light. He pressed the keypad a second time. The radio did not activate.

He turned the battery selector to the second battery, still nothing happened. He set the selector to "All", but there was no response. Both batteries failing at one time would be unusual, but a loose ground wire would mimic a power loss.

Marks grabbed the tool box and leaned into the battery compartment which would normally have been under the port settee. When the cabin was cannibalized for plywood, the batteries had been exposed and were now in easy reach. He loosened and rotated and retightened all the black cables that ran from the engine block to the batteries. He turned on a cabin light and jiggled each wire hoping that the slightest flicker would betray a bad connection. Finally, to remove all doubt, he cut the wires that fed the radio connection and held then directly against the battery terminals. They were completely dead.

"Is there a shark among the pod?" came a thought or a voice that he knew was not his own.

"Yes," he said. "There is a shark." The idea sharpened his vision as he scanned the cabin. In the corner, under the galley table, he saw a small wad of paper with flecks of shiny silver. He crawled across the saloon and picked it up. Slowly, he opened the tightly twisted scrap. It was the discarded wrapper from mint-flavored antacids. He had solved the mystery. The shark had put an antacid in the cells of the batteries.

But why did he leave the wrapper? thought Shrader.

"Because he wanted you to know," echoed Greyback. "When sharks bite, they always leave a scar."

Options, thought Shrader, *what are my options?* He had a small handheld radio with a range of maybe six miles, assuming the batteries held up. Suddenly it struck him, "What if the shark has been there, too?" He slid open the drawer where he kept the walkie-talkie style device. It was still there. He clicked it on and turned the squelch knob until it squawked. It worked!

The danger now rested in the potential of the flotilla's passing beyond the range of his radio signal. If darkness or fog moved in, all bets would be off.

Keeper called out, "It's not much further."

"But I can't go on, not now," Shrader protested.

"Do you find the new path by turning back?" Keeper queried. The orca spoke in riddles, but Shrader took his meaning.

"How far?"

"Very close now, watch the sky."

Shrader turned toward the western horizon. The ground rose sharply to a high plateau. The front of the slope was covered with balsam fir and spruce. Like the island in the Gulf of St. Lawrence, the first line of trees was partially submerged. At the very heights, the terrain was nearly bare on the windswept plain. Here and there, a stunted evergreen clung to its precarious niche. The land jutted out to a point, a spit of land that projected into the sea. Shrader released the wheel and turned the boat back to a beam reach. As *Strider* plowed ahead through the water, the land seemed to come out toward the boat. His new heading would take him around the point. What lay beyond it, he could not tell.

"Do you see it?" asked Keeper.

Shrader did his best to focus, but did not know what he should expect to see. "See what?"

"See what is there!" came the reply. Shrader looked for some sign or feature. The crest was unremarkable. The only feature was a jagged rock that capped the outer ledge. Then it dawned on him.

"*Inuksuk*," he said to the inner voice. In the profile of his vantage point, it looked like a single rock. As he skirted the edge of the shore, however, he saw it that it was not a natural feature.

A second standing stone stood propped against the first, forming a triangle whose apex pointed toward the sky.

"It points the way," stated Keeper.

"To where?" asked Shrader.

"To home," sang a chorus of voices. The sound led Shrader to a question he had not considered.

"How many are you?" he asked.

"Many," came a united reply. Then a litany of names bombarded him. He only heard a few: Fastfin, Sharkbane, Windcrasher, and a small voice of one named Plankton. In all, the pod had thirty members.

"Why do you talk to me?" The question had long haunted Shrader.

"We speak to many," said Keeper, who appeared to be the leader. "But you are the first to hear."

Strider, flanked by her whale companions, turned toward the land. As they got nearer, Shrader could see that the shoreline was broken by a channel that led into a small bay of protected waters.

"This is the place of safety," voiced Keeper. To achieve the entrance passage, Marks tightened in the headsail and beat into the wind. This heading brought him against the full force of the wind. The channel itself was relatively short with cliffs on the right and a low barrier island on the left. Inside the bay, the waves grew calm and the wind lessened in the shelter of the land.

The moderating conditions worried Shrader, who remembered that he had no engine available. If he drifted into a region of dead air, he would not be able to regain the channel to make for the open sea. Here, behind the ridge that marked the southern boundary, his puny radio would be of little use. The hesitation in his thoughts provoked an answer. "We will watch for them."

The wind, though lessened, did not abandon him as he moved toward the shore line. The bay itself was little more than a mile across and a half mile wide. Questions flooded his mind. Was he at high tide or low? Was the water under the keel deep enough, and would it remain deep enough when the tide went out? He remembered the shores around Île d'Anticosti. Was he sailing over the tree tops of a submerged forest? Would the boats be able to drop anchor, and, if they did, would the anchor lines be lost in an underwater tangle?

"You do fear many things," offered his companions, "but we have seen that which you question. The waters are deep enough and little rests below you, other than a rocky beach."

Shrader heaved-to so that the boat maintained its position in the center of the bay. He went below and retrieved his binoculars. With them, he studied the bay, the rocks, and the forest that grew out of the water itself. Everything he saw gave him hope, and a great weight fell off him. In its wake came hunger and exhaustion. He went below, lit the alcohol stove, and put on the kettle. With peanut butter and the last of his white bread, he made two sandwiches. He wolfed them down wondering if he would ever taste anything like it again. By the time his coffee was brewed, his hunger had vanished. He looked at the ship's clock. It would be another four hours before the others would be in range of the handheld radio. Then he would have to sail out into the sea and try to make contact. His newest fear was staying awake during the wait.

"Take your rest," said Greyback. "We will stay on watch for you and your pod." The news was a lullaby, and Shrader collapsed into his bunk. The voices that he long suspected of deceit had become trusted companions.

74

It was four in the afternoon when Cathy went below to listen to the VHF radio for a transmission from *Strider*. When five minutes had passed in silence, she put the microphone to her mouth and spoke to Bert Jenkins.

"Have you picked up anything, Major?" she asked.

"No," came an immediate answer. "It is all very quiet."

"Could he still be beyond our range?" she said.

"I keep playing with the numbers, but I can't see how that would be possible. Even if he is still running at hull speed, we should have gained on him. Every one of our boats is faster," answered Jenkins.

"Well, keep your eyes peeled for any sign of him," added Cathy. "And keep a lookout for somewhere we could put in for the night. Is your radar sensitive enough to show us some shelter along the shore?"

"Well, we can't anchor out here," said Bert. "We have to keep moving until we find something."

"But when it gets dark, we run the risk of collisions. If we put a lot more space between us, we run the risk of losing someone or even passing Shrader in the dark."

"I'll watch the shoreline."

"I'd feel a whole lot better if we had a radio signal from Marks," observed Cathy. "I'm going to keep the radio on for a while. Keep your ears on too, okay?"

"Will do," answered Jenkins.

Cathy replaced the microphone transmitter.

"What if he's not out there any more?" The voice startled her. It was Phil who had slipped into the cabin behind her. "I think he was losing it. I mean, taking off in the dark, he's probably broken up on some rocks somewhere."

"Phil, do you know something? Have you done something to Shrader?"

"I haven't touched him! I'm just a little amazed that you haven't figured him out yet. He's a crazy and you're fronting for him! At some point this idiocy has to stop. You'll only manage to kill a whole lot of people, and I don't intend to be one of them!"

Cathy moved to try and step around him, but he stepped into her, pushing her to the settee. It was then that she noticed that he had closed the companionway so that they could not be seen from the cockpit.

"Phil, I need to go on deck to help Brittany."

"Brittany is fine," he responded. "I just think that it's time that we get a few things out in the open. First, you are going to stop talking, and listen. I'm tired of being treated like a piece of shit. When Shrader doesn't check in during the next hour, you are going to turn the boats around and head back to the island. We'll wait a few days until things get straightened out on shore, and then we head for the coast of New Brunswick. You're not the only one who can read a chart." He was standing over her now.

"What have you done to Shrader?"

Philip caught her throat in his right hand and forced her to look at him. "Let's just say that I cleared up my heartburn! He didn't get anything he didn't deserve. Now, why don't you clean up a little bit; you look like hell." He squeezed his fist until she choked. He let her go as she gasped for air, the red deepening on her neck.

"I'm glad we had this little chat," he said as he moved toward the companionway. "Isn't it much better when we are working together as a team?" Cathy glared, but did not speak as she massaged her throat.

"Look, sharks!" came a call from overhead. It was Justin whose voice pulsed with alarm.

"See what you've gotten us into," touted Phil as he quickly opened the hatch. Cathy was not far behind. The water around them teamed with dorsal fins, some very tall and straight.

"They're not sharks," said Brittany in her best parental voice. "They're whales." She looked at her mother who was still rubbing her neck. Their eyes met in a knowing glance.

"She's right, Honey," croaked Cathy whose voice wouldn't behave.

"Still, they're big enough that they could sink us if they rammed one of us," said Phil in a knowing tone. He disappeared below, only to reappear with his rifle, a 7 mm Remington.

"Phil, don't do anything you'll regret," warned Cathy.

"Weren't you listening?" he said through clenched teeth. "I've given up being stupid. Get out of my way." He clambered up on the deck, and braced himself against the shrouds that supported the mast. The other crews were on their decks and here and there hands pointed in the direction of swimming mammals.

"Just stay where you are," Phil muttered. An orca breached nearby, and Pearson fired off a round. A pool of brightly colored blood clouded the water as the whale rolled over lifeless. The sound of screeching echoed through the fleet, and the whales dove deep for cover. The surface of the water was broken only by the rolling seas as the boats left the great corpse behind.

"And that's how you handle that," said Phil triumphantly.

Cathy gathered her brood around her. Brittany was in tears. "How could you?" she blurted out.

"How could I what?" said her father. "I just saved us from being rammed by a monster. Someday, when your brain kicks in, you'll realize that I'm right!"

75

"The shark has attacked," came the cry that awakened Shrader abruptly.

"What?" he said as he tried to pull his mind in focus.

"The shark has killed. Your pod is very close."

Shrader rushed to the cockpit and surveyed the bay. He freed the wheel and waited until *Strider* picked up some forward speed. As the boat increased in momentum, he steered a broad circle, letting out the jib as the wind came around behind him. The breeze was now at his back. As he ran with the wind, all sensation of moving air disappeared. He felt like he was standing still, but the billowing sails told him otherwise. He pointed the bow toward the channel that lead out to the open sea.

Ahead, he could see the ocean, but the spit of land to starboard blocked his view of anything approaching from the south. He felt the agitation of the whales and his own frustration at his speed. It seemed like the slow motion of running in a nightmare. As he made some distance from the shore, the stern waves grew stronger and he began to surf down the face of the water. Each pulse of the water pushed *Strider* ahead, and Marks fought with the wheel to hold the straight course. At last he was at the end of the jutting peninsula, and his line of sight opened. Six sets of sails lay before him. Six boats were heeled over and reaching with the wind. Keeper and Greyback paced on his left and right.

Over the water, he could see figures mounting the foredecks of the oncoming crafts. Arms began to flail in greeting. Shrader could have used the radio if he had not left it below deck.

Instead, he raised an arm in recognition. He focused on each boat until he identified *Affinity*. Brittany and the boys were in the cockpit. On the deck Cathy looked toward a second figure. It was Philip who sat on the cabin trunk with his hunting rifle resting across his lap.

Cathy looked at Shrader. The distance between them seemed to shrink. She was speaking to him, but no sound reached his ears. Phil looked at him as well. He raised the muzzle of his rifle and pointed it toward *Strider*, as he had in the voyage down the St. Lawrence.

"There is the killer," said Keeper, "the shark that bites with death." Marks held his silence as *Strider* rushed to join the other boats.

On board *Affinity*, Phil sat frozen on the deck. Suddenly Shrader saw the flash of the muzzle and felt a dull thump against the boat. The delayed sound of the rifle's report told him that he was under fire.

What the… thought Marks. *What is he doing?* Quickly he turned the boat around. Abandoning the helm, he rushed below to see if the hull had been hit beneath the waterline. He heard the water before he saw it. Opening the door of the head compartment released a strong surge as if he were being hit by a high pressure hose. He grabbed a towel off the hook and ran back to the cockpit. There, Shrader opened the lazarette and pulled out his aluminum gaff. He climbed out of the cockpit and rushed onto the foredeck where he hooked the towel over the end of the gaff, and shoved it down in the water adjacent to the head compartment. The water rushing through the opening sucked the towel into the small breech caused by the rifle blast.

The leak was reduced to a trickle, but Shrader had no idea how long it would hold. His best bet for saving the contents of his boat was to run it aground. He took charge of the helm and pointed *Strider*'s bow back down the channel into the safe harbor. In his rush, he never thought about the fact that he could still be under fire. His back was now exposed to the sights of the Pearson's rifle. He turned to see the muzzle pointed at him, but this time Cathy was moving behind Phil. Brittany had handed her a gaff, and Cathy was moving with stealth toward Philip who was intent on his target. She brought the gaff down hard on the barrel just as it flashed fire. The gaff hooked the sight and the rifle leaped free, flipping into the deep.

Philip stood up as Brittany called for him to stop. No sounds reached Shrader, however, until he heard Cathy's voice clearly and distinctly.

"Shrader!" she shrieked. It was the dream, awakened.

"Go to her!" yelled Keeper.

"How?" Shrader asked, but he already knew. He noted the heading and locked *Strider's* wheel. The boat would make it to shore on its own or not at all. He leapt into the sea. Down he went in his drenched clothes until he felt himself flying upward under the immense power of Keeper. He hung onto the great dorsal fin and it plowed the water.

"Greyback will guide your boat," assured the great orca.

Suddenly the water around him was teeming with whales. Cathy's cries came clearly now as the distance vanished under the speed of the pursuit. Philip was going toward her with a rigging knife he had pulled from his pocket. He was just two steps from her when two of the whales dived beneath *Affinity*. They obviously threw themselves against the boat's keel because it swung over at a ninety degree angle. In the cockpit, the children were thrown against the coaming. Cathy and Phil were thrown into the sea.

Save her, was all Shrader could think. And then she was on the surface again, supported by one of the whales. There was no sign of Phil. "What about the man?" called Marks.

"Sharks hunt and kill; it is their way," said Keeper, "but they do not swim among the pod." And that was that.

With a gentleness that belied their bulk, the orcas brought the man and the woman around to the stern of *Affinity* where they easily stepped onto the transom ladder. The three children, bruised and frightened, rushed to their mother. With no one at the wheel, the boat had turned into the wind. It was dead in the water. The other boats began to circle and their crews called out. All of them looked for Philip, but there was no trace.

Shrader stood up on the cockpit seat. Braced against the backstay, he looked in the direction of *Strider*. It was still sailing.

He watched until he saw the white headsails disappear into a sea of green branches on the far shore.

76

Throughout the ordeal, the boats had continued to sail forward. On board *Affinity*, the children were in shock. They wanted to search for their father, and expected his head to rise above the waves at any moment. Cathy looked to Shrader, but his certainty offered no comfort.

He took the helm of the vessel and steered toward the entrance to the bay. Keeper and Greyback were alongside. Theirs was an ominous presence. When Brittany asked why they followed, Shrader remarked that "the sea was theirs and they were the ones who knew the ways of the deep." Later he added, "Your father was wrong to take a life." Nothing more was said or needed to be.

In the bay the waves subsided. Cathy coaxed the children below decks where they sank quickly into the escape of sleep.

As at the island, *Affinity* set its large anchor and the other boats rafted alongside. One by one the crews gravitated to the center of the raft, and Cathy spoke in low tones. There were many questions, but few answers. Cathy explained the dreams that had so plagued the two of them. The others looked back and forth at one another, not so much in disbelief, as in the fact that all the answers exploded into unanswerable questions. Shrader sat alone on the bow of *Mewtiny* and did not speak. In truth, he was listening to the grief and questions of another throng of voices which pressed for understanding. His eyes turned to the trees.

As he stared through the darkness, a strange taste seemed to coat his tongue. It was sulfur. The taste of the air took him back to his youth, growing up in mill towns where coke ovens created the fuel to feed insatiable blast furnaces. This was from no human hands, but from the earth itself. The fires had melted, and now the ash would seal the world in ice.

"Shrader?" said Cathy gently. "Are you all right?" He had not noticed that everyone had returned to their boats. How long he had been there, he didn't know. He was not even aware of the cold air or the senses of his body.

"I need to find *Strider*," he said.

"Tonight?" she asked.

"There are still things that we can use aboard her. For all I know," he replied, "she's full of water or broken up."

Laura Romig agreed to stay aboard *Affinity* in case Brittany, Chris, or Justin roused. Shrader borrowed a dinghy from *Rol's Royce* and made his way to the dark shore. In the eerie light of the lantern, the ride felt like *déjà vu* except that it was Cathy who held the light as the small boat came to the edge of the spruce.

Marks rowed parallel to the shoreline. There was no mistaking the point where *Strider* had ripped through the first line of trees. He turned to steer along the path that had been plowed by the five-ton hull. At the extreme end of the swath, they came to the familiar transom that bore the name, *Strider*. Small waves lapped gently against the fiberglass. Shrader shipped the oars as Cathy held on to the transom ladder. The dinghy rocked as Shrader shifted toward the ladder. He stood and released the hook that held the folding stairway in place. Once deployed, it was only a matter of four steps until Marks was in the cockpit and leaning back to take the lantern from Cathy.

She was not far behind. Tying off the painter to the dinghy, she mounted the ladder and entered the cockpit. Shrader steadied her with his free hand.

The foredeck was completely obscured by boughs, and there was little hope of walking over the foredeck in the night. The mast was still standing, but the shreds of the jib were woven through the trees as an indication that the wire rigging was probably ripped away, and the trees, more than anything else, were supporting the mast.

Shrader took a step toward the companionway and noticed a slight downhill sloping. Piecing events together, he figured that

Strider must have been still moving with considerable momentum when the keel hit the earth beneath the water. The boat dug itself into the ground and the bow pitched forward as it hit the hillside.

The cabin was still open. He handed Cathy the lantern and made his way down the steps.

"You'll need the light more than me," she protested, but Shrader knew every inch of his boat. He had not, however, counted on ankle-deep water over the cockpit sole.

"Damn," he cried. He fumbled for the propane lighter that he kept in the galley drawer. Snapping it to life, the cabin glowed faintly as he moved toward the gimbaled oil lamp that hung from the bulkhead. Once lit, the lamplight made the cabin look the same as ever with the exception of the three inches of water that covered the floor boards.

By now Cathy had climbed into the cabin, but took a stand on the last step rather than plunge into the flood.

"I can use that lantern now," remarked Marks, taking it from her hand. He sloshed forward to the head compartment. After a few minutes, he returned. "That towel is wedged through that hole like nobody's business. My guess is that this is the water that came in before I could plug the leak." He moved toward the companionway. "Excuse me," he said making an athletic move to step around Cathy so that she didn't have to move from her perch. He was back out in the cockpit. He pushed aside some springy boughs to get into the lazarette. There he retrieved the stainless steel handle for the manual bilge pump. He inserted the handle and began to rock the lever back and forth. Gushing sounds came from below decks and soon a stream of water was pouring out into the bay.

"That's going to take a while," said Cathy. "Let me help!" He didn't argue. They took turns in five-minute rotations until the water sounds gave way to a gurgle and slosh of air in the lines. Hot and exhausted, they just sat where they were.

"Did you think we'd get this far?" Cathy broke the silence.

"Not in the way it happened," confessed Shrader. "All the plans we made and the lists of stuff that we pulled together, it was all for this place."

"What do you mean?" asked Cathy.

286

"The coats and fatty-food and arrows, all that stuff was meant to give us a toehold on life here. I didn't really think that much about the journey itself. It was more like we *felt* our way through the mess. Remember Gary at the marina said my boat wasn't going to be launched?" They both laughed. "There was *Strider* sitting up on land, and here we are now and *Strider* is sitting up on the land. I know what we've passed through to get from there to here, but I don't have a clue about anything else in the whole world."

"I think it will hit us all later," said Cathy. "Today, my husband died; and I can't even make myself believe it. Maybe it's because if I started thinking about any of this, it would drive me crazy. It's just too much."

They sat quietly for a moment, and then Marks spoke: "At first I thought that I might have killed Phil."

"What?"

"When you went into the water, I told Keeper and Greyback to save you, and they did! But I didn't tell them to save Phil."

"Keeper and Greyback?"

When Shrader realized what he had said, he knew how bizarre it must have sounded. "Maybe that's something I shouldn't talk about. The orcas, well, we sort of think together sometimes."

"But you didn't kill Philip."

"No. It was their sense of justice," remarked Shrader.

"I think that he tried to kill you, and not just with the bullet."

"I know. He put antacids in the batteries. That's why I couldn't radio you. I had no power." A long pause passed between them.

"How do you do it?" she asked.

"Do what?"

"Talk to the whales." Marks stood up and turned toward the darkness that led out toward the sea.

"I don't know if we talk at all. When it started, I thought I was hearing voices. Now I think I just learned to listen. I asked them if they talked to others and they said they did, but I was the first to listen."

"Do you hear them now?" she asked.

Shrader seemed to go into himself. "The boats are quiet. Somebody is snoring on your boat."

"That's Justin," laughed Cathy, "he needs his adenoids out. But I don't think that's going to happen."

"All of a sudden, I'm getting cold," said Marks. He stood up and started down the companionway steps. Cathy stayed outside and could hear him down below straightening things.

"We'd better get back to the others," she said.

"No," he called back. "I'll spend the night here. I'd just stir up everyone looking for a bunk, and I don't think I should stay on *Affinity* given everything that has happened."

Cathy joined him in the cabin. "Nobody blames you for what happened to Phil. I certainly don't," she said.

"That's not what I was talking about," said Shrader cryptically. "I'm talking about the way I feel about you."

Cathy rushed toward him in an embrace. As if every emotion surged in one instant, she began to cry. He hugged her tight against himself. When the shuddering of her body slowed, their lips met. They kissed deeply until Cathy stepped away. Shrader expected her retreat, but she wiped the wetness off her cheeks with her palm. "I must be a sight," she said.

Shrader smiled and gestured her to come closer, but she stood back. She measured her thoughts and then began to slip off her bulky outerwear. Her fingers were shaking at the familiar task of undressing. "You're going to have to keep me warm, Shrader Marks," she said.

Their lovemaking was tender and deliberate. Afterward, beneath the comforter in the v-berth, they cradled each other in the ebbing heat of their passion.

"I do love you," said Shrader. "And I have longer than I am willing to admit to myself."

"I know," offered Cathy. "I don't know when it started, but I know it's real." She gave Marks a quick peck that turned into a lingering kiss. "I have to go," she chided.

"Please, stay," he begged, but he already knew the answer.

"In the morning, the crews are going to hit this island, so you had better be ready for company!" she said with a grin that was broader than her face.

"I just love powerful women," he said with a wink.

In a moment she was dressed, and making her way up the gangway with the lantern in her hand. He jumped out of the bunk, pulled on his jeans and outer jacket. He helped her with the lantern as she boarded the dinghy. They kissed over the transom.

"In the morning, Love," she said.

"I'll see you in the morning," he answered. He watched her light disappear through the trees until it became a hazy glow and then nothing. *Watch over her, Greyback*, he thought.

"She will be safe tonight," came the reply.

Epilogue

Shrader's fears that *Strider* had broken up proved to be unfounded. When daylight came and the boat was inspected, they found very little structural damage. As Marks had guessed, the wire shrouds that supported the mast had been broken away, and the mast was being supported by the canopy of the surrounding trees. All the equipment for making repairs had been packed away by Cathy and Shrader during their days of preparation.

It didn't take Gus Gundersen long to propose a plan for refloating *Strider*. To everyone's surprise, the most vocal objection to the plan was from Shrader himself.

"We don't need any more boats in the water," he protested. "Besides, they're not what we'll be needing. We have to build some kind of foundation under the hull to make sure it doesn't slip off the side of the hill."

The members of the group shared silent glances that said, "Now what?" As in the past, it was John Romig who gave an explanation for Marks' unexpected comment.

"What Shrader is saying," John began, "is that we aren't going to be able to keep the boats in the water, at least not so that we can get them in and out of the bay. Eventually, sooner or later, the water will freeze. We'll need small boats for fishing. Ones that we can move across the ice to open water."

Cathy immediately proposed teams to deal with day-to-day realities and technical problems. Bert Jenkins was to lead a party of hunters to scout out game and make plans for harvesting animals for food. The Ragnis, who had provided fish on the island, were put in charge of fishing. For now they would use the boats of the fleet until other options were explored. Laura Romig and Bill Morgan were charged with health and sanitation. They had to figure out how to insure good drinking water and safe waste disposal. Gus and Jeff Koenig were to come up with a plan to house everyone on land. Finally, John Romig and Shrader were designated as advisors. They were to teach as much as they knew about ancient ways.

The high level of activity over the next weeks drove out any potential depression about the world they had left behind. At night, the company retreated to the boats. In an effort to break the people of the habit of retreating to their cozy settees and stainless steel sinks, John Romig volunteered to have *Mewtiny* grounded in the trees, about forty feet from *Strider*. He, Jeff, and Gus had come up with a design for a longhouse where everyone could gather.

The other crews were appalled that John would so casually destroy his yacht. He kept trying to explain that the side of the hill was the safest place. "When the heavy global snows kick in," he said, "the ocean level will drop. A lot of water will be piled up on the land in the form of ice and snow. When the bay gets shallower, it will freeze and, eventually, the boats will be inside a glacier." The concept wasn't so difficult to imagine; it was the scale that had to be taken on faith.

Once *Mewtiny* was in position, the masts of the two boats were used as ridge poles that ran between the two hulls. Supported by stone columns, the structure was roofed with tarps and insulated with branches and spruce needles. A hole was cut into *Strider's* hull so that it could be accessed from the longhouse. This became the place for meetings, and for couples who needed time alone. *Mewtiny* was only accessible from the outside. Morgan had suggested that it could be used to isolate those with contagious illness. Everyone agreed.

Romig was right. As the water began to recede in the bay, other boats were grounded to become storehouses for dried meats and supplies. Sleeping together in the longhouse provided more security than anyone would have guessed. Romig added, however, that "the textbooks never got the smells quite right."

The group convened each evening in the longhouse as each person reflected on the day's activity. Those with special responsibilities would put forward their ideas. No one said that Cathy was the chief, but all accepted her in that role. For her part, she spent the days trying to perfect ways of stretching hides and preserving food.

One afternoon, after a successful hunt, she was helping to clean a carcass. Nausea overtook her so badly that she became physically sick. When Laura followed after her to see if she was okay, Cathy confided that she had not been feeling well for some time. After examining her, Laura asked, "Could you be pregnant?"

Cathy was visibly shocked at the suggestion. She then paused and said, "Maybe."

Acknowledgments

I acknowledge my gratitude for the many hours of work done by others during the writing of this book. In the early stages, Denise Shoenberger Lo Cicéro was my first reader, and encouraged me to keep writing. Most of all, I thank Nancy Brady Smith, my partner and friend who not only helped me read for errors and continuity, but taught me everything I know about pharmacology.

RBS

BOOK II

Keelhouse

To Nancy

Introduction

If they had accurate coastal charts, the people at Keelhouse would have been able to locate their settlement along what had been the eastern Canadian coast. The charts they did have were no longer reliable. The Atlantic had risen and fallen. First, claiming, then relinquishing the rocky crags of tsunami swept shores.

When they left Sodus Bay on Lake Ontario, their destination was Labrador, a land that had fed and sheltered people through long ice ages. They did not, however, journey as far north as the tundra-taiga interface, that zone between the forested south and a treeless horizon just above the Arctic Circle. When they landed in a protected cove, they were among the spruce and firs of the northernmost continuation of the Appalachian chain. Had they traveled due east, they would have found themselves in Newfoundland, north of what had been the great city, Corner Brook. As it was, they knew nothing of the lands beyond a small region where they hunted and fished for five years.

This was not their land, but it had become their home. A comet strike years earlier had erased all the plans and assumptions of their usual lives. Determination had led them to a very different life. While they did not know the particulars of world events, John Romig and others could surmise closely enough. Chain reactions to the massive impact forced the release of pressure beneath the tectonic plates of the earth. The super volcanoes that were known only in the geological record became active again. A dimming world sheltered beneath the deadly ash. In its shadow the world grew cold, and snow fell. Foot by foot, it deepened in some areas wringing water from sky and oceans so that, over time, sea levels fell as the air was scrubbed of volcanic ash.

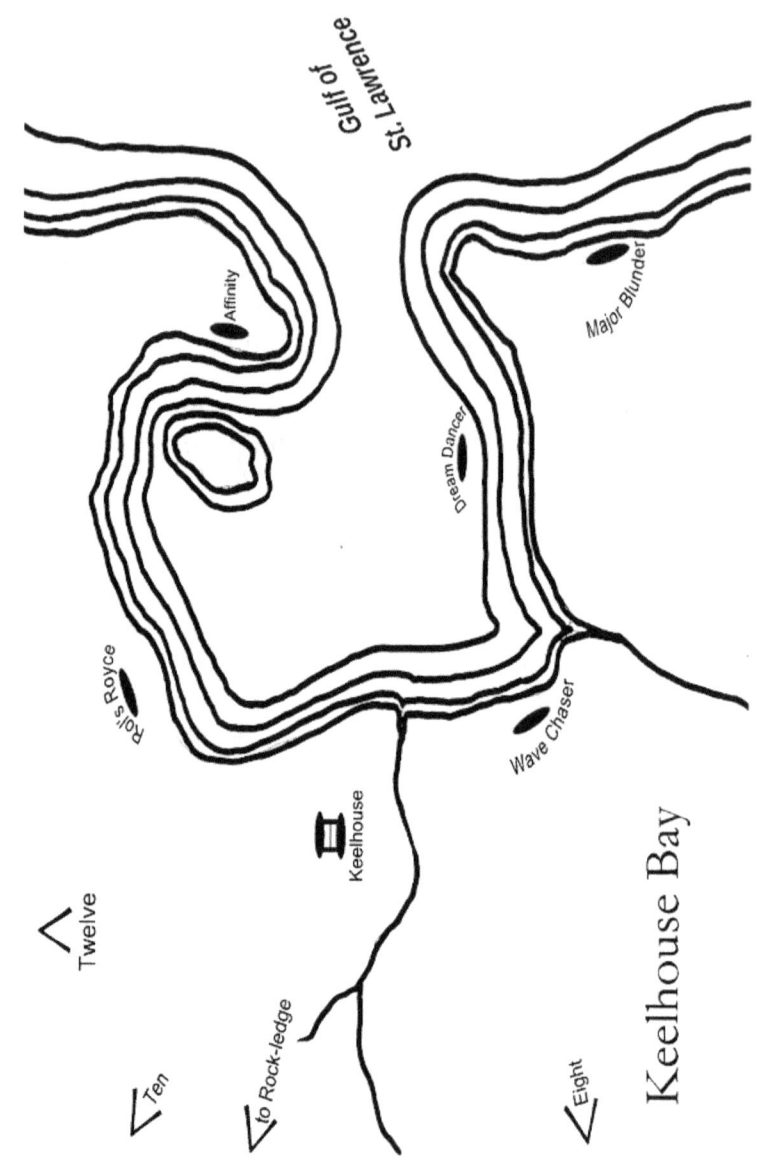

Gulf of
St. Lawrence

Affinity

Major Blunder

Dream Dancer

Roll's Royce

Wave Chaser

Keelhouse

Twelve

Ten

to Rock-ledge

Eight

Keelhouse Bay

"I had a dream, and in the dream a cake of barley bread rolled into the camp of Midian and came to the tent, striking it on top so that the tent fell."

Shofetim 7:13

KEELHOUSE

1

"What are they doing now?" said Bert Jenkins in a hoarse whisper. For the better part of twenty minutes, he, Cathy Pearson, and Shrader had been watching three strangers from a low bluff that overlooked a great herd of caribou. The newcomers were moving slowly around the perimeter of the herd. The largest of the three held a club of sorts, the other two brandished long sticks.

"Surely they're not going to try clubbing one of the cows?" Jenkins was incredulous. Cathy looked down the ridge behind her to make eye contact with Anthony Ragni and Cameron Romig, who stood ready with their compound bows. With a hand motion, she indicated that they should lay low.

"They're not hunting," observed Cathy. "They're scavenging." She nodded to the right, and Jenkins shifted his gaze.

"Oh," he said, "I didn't see that." He was referring to a gathering of wolves downwind of the herd. They were fighting over what remained of an old kill.

"They are not afraid of you!" Shrader stood up from his hiding spot and shouted toward the strangers. He quickly crossed over the ridge and was moving toward the trio. By the time Cathy tried to pull him back, he was beyond her reach. "They aren't afraid of you," he called again.

The largest of the three figures turned toward the sound of Shrader's voice. He raised his club defensively, and the two smaller figures fell in behind him. His stance didn't slow Marks' advance. He repeated: "The wolves aren't afraid of you. They say that *you* don't bite, that you're not like the ones who are following you." These last words brought more response than the mention of wolves. The second figure collapsed, and the man dropped his club and turned his attention to his comrade.

By now, Cathy was down the slope at Shrader's side. "Are you hungry?" she asked. The sound of her voice rallied the fallen figure who managed to speak some painful words.

"You're a woman," said a soft, but distinctly female voice.

"Yes, I am," was Cathy's response. "If you are hungry, we can offer you food."

"That's better than the wolves will offer," said Shrader. "They have already decided that they are not going to share their dinner."

"Who is he? How does he know?" asked the larger figure.

"It doesn't matter," said Cathy. She raised an arm to signal Jenkins who, in turn, sent Anthony and Cameron around the ridge to the edge of the herd. They would quickly dispatch their arrows to bring down an animal. The two were exceptional hunters. Working in tandem they learned to kill quickly so as to avoid the long chase of a wounded animal.

"The wolves say that there is someone following you, someone who bites," remarked Shrader.

"They aren't after us," said the stranger, who had relaxed his posture. Jenkins was now halfway down the hill, and Cathy was kneeling in the snow to see the woman who had fallen. The man spoke again. "They might want to kill us, but they won't waste a bullet if we can stay ahead of them."

"I don't think they've eaten for a while," said Jenkins, who had joined Cathy.

"Please," begged the fallen woman, "we have another child back in the trees."

"How far?" asked Cathy.

"Just there," said the man pointing to a line of spruce on a nearby ridge. "He couldn't walk in the snow anymore, so we left him until we got some food." Shrader was already moving before Cathy could give him the order.

"He'll find him," she assured the woman. "Here, eat this." She had pulled a packet of dried jerky from beneath her parka. "Just a little," she added. "If you haven't eaten for a while, it'll be good to take it slow. We'll have to have the doctor check you out."

"You have a doctor?" said the woman with disbelief. Cathy thought about the fact that Bill Morgan was actually a dentist and Laura Romig was a nurse.

"We have two of them," she answered with pride, "but we need to get you back to our hunting camp."

"But we can't leave without Alain," she protested.

"Shrader will find him and bring him along. Bert," she said turning to Jenkins, "we have to get them back to the camp. Once we get them out of the weather, you and Shrader can come back to help with the kill."

"If they need it," he answered. Looking across the valley, they could see the hunters dragging a cow to a sheltered spot where it could be gutted. The wolves were still busy with their own feast, and, according to Shrader, were not the least bit curious about humans who could not bite.

2

It was only a short hike to the outpost where Cathy could get the three strangers under shelter. She confidently made her way through the fresh snow while Bert Jenkins encouraged the newcomers who were having difficulty maintaining the pace. Once the five were tucked into the rock shelter, Cathy turned to the three.

The woman spoke first. "We should have gone back to get Alain," she said.

"Shrader will be along soon," assured Cathy. Turning to Jenkins, she said, "Bert, would you stir up the coals?" He turned his attention to a glowing charcoal fire in the far corner while the new arrivals were trying to understand their surroundings. When a small flame leaped to life, they began to see that they were in an undercut of rock that had been walled in on the open side. There must have been some sort of ventilation system, for the air was not particularly smoky.

"This is a good place," said the man.

Cathy was wary and merely said, "Thank you." She didn't hint that this rough shelter was an outpost from the main camp. It was a long day's journey to Keelhouse, and another shelter lay between their present location and the bay where their boats had landed more than five years earlier.

"I think some introductions are in order," she said. "I am Cathy Pearson, and this is Bert Jenkins." Jenkins by now had some peat smoldering on the bed of charcoal.

"I am Stephen Durand."

"Étienne," corrected the woman.

"Étienne is my French name," continued Durand. "This is Lainie."

"Ghislaine," added his wife, "And this is Émilie." Cathy noticed that the smallest of the three was a girl.

Without warning, Shrader appeared in the low entrance. In front of him was a boy of five or six, "And this is Alain," said Shrader in a light voice. "And he very much would like to see his mother."

"Alain!" cried Ghislaine.

"Mama," came the reply, as the boy leapt from his wooden stance.

As the commotion died, Cathy spoke. "Shrader, these are the Durands. Étienne, Ghislaine, and Émilie."

"You can call me Steve, if you prefer," offered the man. His wife gave him a sudden glare that didn't go unnoticed. "Lainie swore that she would always go by her Québécoise name," offered Durand by way of explanation.

"Well, you're free to use whatever name you'd like," assured Cathy. Étienne and Ghislaine looked at each other with knowing glances so that Cathy wondered. "What's going on?" she asked.

Étienne spoke hesitantly. "It's just that the people we have been with were not very accepting of people with French names." His eyes were firmly fixed on his wife's as if reading something in them. When he broke his stare, he turned to Cathy and continued. "There were a number of us, Québécoise, in our camp," he offered, "mostly English speakers. One by one, we'd lose a friend, accidents, mostly. Someone would fall through the ice or be shot by friendly fire. After a while, Ghislaine and I noticed that the ones who spoke only French were the first. *The Five* said that it was because they couldn't follow directions."

"*The Five?*" asked Cathy, "Who or what are *the Five?*"

"They're the bosses," explained Étienne. "They hand out the ammo." Cathy, Bert, and Shrader exchanged glances.

"Go on," she urged.

"Anyway," continued Durand, "as time went on, we noticed that there were no French speakers among the hunters. They always had an explanation why no one was promoted. Ghislaine and I had lived for years in Toronto, so we were known by our English names, Steve and Lainie. I don't think that they knew we were bilingual. A couple of weeks ago, one of them, Zimisky, heard Ghislaine say something to me about the kids. It was none of their business, so she spoke French. He just said, 'I thought you were from Toronto?' And I said that we were, but we were both raised in Quebec City. And that was that. The next time we went hunting, I was bullets short and dropped from the team."

"*Bullets short?*" queried Jenkins.

"It's the system that *the Five* worked out. When we'd go on a hunt, each of us would be issued ten bullets. When we returned, we'd have to claim our kills and account for missing bullets. I brought down an elk, but no one would back me up on that. According to them, I had spent every round with no hits. When I complained that I was being set up, they told me that I had twenty-four hours to cool down, and then I would be sent to work the edge of the ice pack, looking for seals. Ghislaine and I guessed that meant that I had been scheduled to have an *accident*, and we decided to follow the caribou south."

"With sticks and clubs?" interjected Jenkins.

"That's what we were left with," answered Étienne. "We knew we couldn't bring anything down, but we did find some wolf kills. We figured that even if we were seen, they wouldn't waste a bullet to shoot at us."

The shelter fell silent for a while. "Well, that's not the way that things work with us," said Cathy, breaking the silence. "We do have rules, but they're for everyone's good."

"Why did they hate the French-speakers?" asked Jenkins.

"I think they were afraid that we could make plans behind their backs or that maybe we spoke French when we wanted to talk about them; that's all I can figure," said Ghislaine.

As they continued to talk, the air took on the hearty scent of broth. Shrader was boiling some fatty meat in a tin by the small fire. The smell had an effect on the strangers. "Sorry that I can't give you better than this," said Shrader as he poured out the watery stew into some plastic mugs. "Still, it's probably better to take it slow and not eat too heartily if it's been a while since you've had a full meal."

"It's been a long while," said Ghislaine as she took the cup from Marks and carefully handed it to her daughter. Shrader passed her a second and then offered one to Étienne before turning to help Alain.

"The boy seems to be the weakest," observed Marks.

"Yes," said Étienne, "his legs are short and he has been really unable to keep up the pace."

"We'll get him back to Keelhouse," said Cathy, "he can rest there. We'll have Royce keep him company." The Durands were not following her meaning, so Pearson elaborated. "Royce is our son," she said nodding toward Shrader. "He's not quite five, but he's got a way of making people well." She could tell that her explanation wasn't helping, so she cut it short. "You'll see what I mean when you meet him."

Whether the cause was exhaustion or the sudden appearance of warm food, a long silence descended on the group as they sat huddled in their rocky niche. Ghislaine sipped slowly from the mug that she held in her cupped hands.

"I'm hungry," she said, "but I don't want to drink it so fast because the warm cup is delicious also." The smile in her eyes was met with understanding from Cathy.

"You all need some rest," she offered. "You'll be safe here to-night. Anthony and Cameron have already gone on ahead and will let others know of your arrival. Tomorrow, one of our doctors will examine you."

"We're fine," broke in Étienne. "We don't need any examinations."

"Thank you," said his wife to Cathy. She gave her husband a sideways glance.

"I'm afraid it's the price that you'll have to pay for our help," said Pearson. "We have our rules, too. They're quite a bit different from where you've come from. We want to know that you are all well, and we also want to know that you're not carrying any illness that can hurt the others."

"If you think that we're too sick, will you turn us out?" asked Étienne with a stiffness in his voice.

"Oh no," said Cathy with a nonchalance that curbed fright and distrust. "Laura and Bill would put you under quarantine for a while, but we don't intend to leave people behind. That's not our way."

"She's telling the truth," said Bert Jenkins who had been un-characteristically silent the whole time. "It'll probably be our un-doing, but we have this 'live and let live' rule that I can't persuade her to drop."

"Bert, I'm going to turn you over to Grandma Marty for reme-diation if you keep talking like that!"

A smile came to Jenkins' mouth. "No, no! Anything but that!"

Again, the Durands looked confused by the sudden change of tone and the introduction of another new name.

"We're confusing you," said Cathy. "There's an older woman in our group, and we all call her *Grandma*. She's sort of a mother-teacher to the younger folk and it's her job to make sure everyone knows the rules. Basically, I just told Bert that I was going to send him back to kindergarten." With that the group understood and laughed at the image.

"How many of you are there?" asked Étienne. Cathy ex-changed glances with Jenkins. It was a question that she was not quite ready to answer.

"A few families," she answered quickly enough to indicate that it was all she would say. "You'll see in a day or so," she added. "The thing to do now is to eat a little and rest a lot. Tomorrow is your appointment with the doctor and then we'll be able to figure out when you can manage the trek to Keelhouse."

"You keep using that word," remarked Ghislaine. "What is Keelhouse?"

"It's what we call our camp," said Pearson. She avoided the use of the word *village*, but it would have been more accurate. "Tonight we'll all stay here. Tomorrow, Bert and I will leave, and Shrader will stay with you. He'll take you to a place where you can meet with one of our doctors. After that, we'll be able to make a decision about whether or not you are ready to make the trek to Keelhouse."

"Is it far?" asked Étienne.

"No," answered Cathy, "it's not far for someone who is fit to travel. But we have the children to consider, too." She nodded toward Émilie and Alain who had already finished their broth and now slept exhausted where they sat.

"Pauvres enfants," whispered Ghislaine.

"They're just done-in," agreed Pearson.

"Bring them over here," said Shrader in low tones. He had pulled some hides together as a crude bed in the corner. Cathy and Ghislaine lifted the two children to their feet and led them to where Marks indicated. Cathy suspected that their staggering steps never disrupted their sleep. "Étienne and Ghislaine, you need to climb under the blankets with them," he added.

"He's right," said Cathy. "We all need to settle in for the night." There was no argument from the Durands. Whether they trusted their new companions, or they were finally overtaken with exhaustion, it did not take the couple long to fall into deep sleep.

Pearson, Jenkins, and Marks were not far behind. Each wrapped themselves with a hide and drifted off. Shrader listened for a while in the darkness, and was the last to descend into sleep.

3

The sound of a buzzing fly was drowned out by a long roll of thunder. Cathy was on the edge of consciousness when she realized that the fly was a dream, but the thundering sound was the call to reality. She sat up quickly trying to exchange the image of a fly for the identity of the real noise. Jenkins was awake, too. The Durands had not stirred.

"Snowmobiles?" questioned Cathy.

"I'd say so," agreed Jenkins, "at least something with a small engine." The ground was shaking with the rhythm of the thunder. They realized that the caribou were running.

"Shrader!" called Cathy, but he was no longer in the shelter. The next sound punctuated the cacophony with a piercing blast. It was a high-powered rifle shot, followed by four others. The adults all sat bolt upright and the children shrieked in terror. Ghislaine pulled them close.

"It's okay," Cathy assured them. "The sounds are far away." Turning to Bert she asked, "Did you see Shrader leave?"

"No," answered Jenkins who was lighting a second oil lamp. "He probably went out before we heard the snowmobile."

"It's Zimisky!" Étienne was speaking, "Or one of *the Five*. They sometimes join the hunt. They're the only ones who use motors."

"But at night?" queried Jenkins.

"It's one of their tricks. They claim it's more efficient. They send in an advance team that sets the web, and then they come on snowmobiles to spring the trap."

Cathy and Bert exchanged glances. "We aren't following what you're saying," she said.

Before an answer could be given, a draft set the two small lights flickering and Marks appeared with a blast of cold air.

"Shrader!" said Cathy with surprise and relief. His look was all business.

"They really have a system," he said. "It seems a bit strange to me, but apparently it works."

"Étienne was just beginning to explain," offered Cathy. "Tell Shrader about this *web*."

All eyes turned toward Stephen. "Well," he started again, "they mak a net of rope. They call it *the web*. An advance team moves on ahead of the herd and sets it among the trees. When the mass of the caribou gets close enough, they use the snowmobiles to stampede them into the wooded areas where they've strung the net. The animals that get trapped and trampled are speared or clubbed by the teams that have hidden in the trees."

"Sounds damn stupid if you ask me," interrupted Jenkins. "Just too much danger involved."

"It's the big kill; *it is* dangerous. They say it saves bullets and feeds the families for the better part of the year." Étienne sounded defensive.

"From what you've said, your village is north on the tundra. Why would they make the main hunt so far south?" Cathy's voice was low and calm. The tension of the moment before was gone.

"They say it's because of the trees down here. It allows us to string the nets to lay the ambush."

"They say it?" asked Cathy, "you mean *the Five*?"

"Yes," said Durand, "but I don't think that's the only reason."

"Why else?" asked Jenkins in less anxious tones.

"Because it gets the men away from the settlement, keeps them busy, and allows for any necessary *accidents*." Shrader was speaking in a quiet matter-of-fact tone. When all eyes turned to him, he directed a simple question to Étienne: "Am I right?"

"Yes. Sometimes the caribou are stampeded too soon, before the men are finished with the nets, and sometimes the men returning home would find that their wives had been used by the other guards while they were away on the hunt." Ghislaine turned her face away to hide her expression and they all knew that Étienne had spoken the truth. Intuitively, Cathy went and sat next to her on the pile of hides.

"The children seem less frightened," she said softly. Ghislaine, glad for a distraction, gave an uneasy smile as she stroked Émilie's hair.

"Yes," she agreed, "it has been a long while since they were able to be this warm and sleep."

The men continued to talk quietly and the sounds from beyond the rock shelter grew more distant. "It snowed all evening; there are no tracks to follow, and the snowmobiles could never manage this terrain," said Shrader to an unasked question that flickered in Ghislaine's eyes, but never came to her lips.

Jenkins turned to Étienne. "You just used the words *home guard*; what does that mean?"

"*The Five* always split up in two and three at hunt time. One group directs the hunt and the other stays at the village with the women and children."

"In other words, the whole village is held hostage to assure the cooperation of the hunters?" said Bert.

"It began to feel like that after a while, but it's not how it started," continued Durand. "They had it all figured out. They could keep the camp safe and guard the stores."

"And rape women in the comfort of their own homes," said Jenkins with disgust.

"No, not that at all! It was part of the survival plan. They said it was a way to produce genetically diverse children." Even in the gloom of the rock cleft, Étienne picked up the knowing glance that passed between Marks and Jenkins. "What?" he asked.

"It's just that we've all talked about this, too," answered Shrader. "When we started we were mostly in family groups. We knew that the more differences we had genetically, the stronger future generations would be. But it's too a big violation of what we all grew up with."

"They said it was absolutely necessary, and to resist was an act of violence against the future."

"But then they killed off the French speaking males!" protested Jenkins. "That doesn't exactly square with their high-minded talk, now does it?"

"When you don't have a choice, you have to hang on to lies," muttered Durand.

"I think there'll be plenty of time to talk about this later," said Shrader, "but we're running out of time to sleep. We can't move on to the rendezvous point until we're sure that they've cleared the region. When the time is right, Cathy will have us move fast, until then, we lay low and rest." With a tweak of a wick, Marks extinguished the oil lamp nearest to him and the weak light of the second lamp became a flickering nightlight in the shadowy enclosure.

4

The sun had risen by nine that morning, but Cathy insisted that no one leave the rock chamber until nearly eleven. With just over seven hours of daylight, the hunters would have to set out early to make any progress on their northern trek following the kill. Just to be safe, they waited long past the sunrise.

Shrader went out first, quickly returning with the news that the way was clear. He, Jenkins, and Étienne made a foray to the hunting grounds, but not before Shrader had given Durand some slotted leather eye patches that were bound with narrow leather straps.

"They aren't for the fashion conscious," he said with a smile, "but they do protect from snow blindness. It's bright out there today, and the new snow will make it worse."

With Jenkins' help, the unfamiliar eyewear was donned and the three looked like fugitives from an amateur production of *Three Blind Mice*. This image set Cathy and Ghislaine to singing. The tune wasn't memorable, but the accompanying laughter of the children stole the show.

The only marks in the snow were from Shrader's mukluks. At the ridge where they had first seen the Durands, the scene was much different. The range was trampled by hooves and scored by the tracks of the snowmobiles.

"The weather is perfect for traveling," remarked Shrader as he pulled back the hood of his parka. "They should be well away by now. I don't get any sense of their being in the vicinity."

Jenkins nodded as though the statement were perfectly reasonable, but Étienne was not satisfied.

"How can you be sure?" he protested. "If they saw the four of us yesterday, they might have left a few behind."

"No," said Shrader calmly, "they didn't."

"You're just going to have to get used to that," said Bert. "Actually, he usually says weirder things. You'll come to trust him."

They followed the trail of the stampeding herd to where it skirted a small copse. Back in the trees they found the evidence of the rope netting. The running caribou had struck it so hard that several of the pines were uprooted. It was also clear where the slaughter had occurred, and the animals butchered. Wolf tracks showed that more than one type of predator had gone away satisfied, and the loud cry of *ke-eer* came from a Rough-legged hawk overhead.

"We are not interested in your lunch," called Marks. The bird swooped to the ground not twenty feet away and began tearing at the entrails of the hunt.

"I have to say that they are efficient," observed Jenkins. "They didn't leave much behind."

The travel plans had been determined by Cathy. She and Jenkins were going to push hard to get back to Keelhouse. Shrader and the Durands would keep a pace that would be more comfortable for the children. Their destination was one of the camps that formed a protective ring around the main settlement. Hunters knew the paths to these outposts that had been set up as way-stations. When the weather closed in, these lightly provisioned shelters proved lifesaving havens. The Durands did not know that their first night with the others was in a placed called Rockledge. It was a camp that gave easy access to the migrating caribou. Being the farthest outpost, Cathy had insisted that it be well provisioned. More than once, expeditions had been hunkered down there for days at a time. The shelters nearer to Keelhouse were less keenly maintained. Shrader was glad to see that this was not the case at Rockledge. Bundled in a corner he found snowshoes to outfit Étienne, Ghislaine, and a smaller size for Émilie. None were small enough for Alain, but Jenkins, Marks, and Pearson had already decided that he was too weak for a five mile trek and would have to be carried. A pack frame was rigged as a carrier. Cathy explained the strategy to the Durands.

"Bert and I are going to go on ahead. Shrader will take you to *Eight* where you will spend the night. One of our doctors will probably be there when you arrive to make sure you're all okay. If one isn't there, you'll just stay there until we get back to you. Don't worry, you'll be safe there." Her words were not completely understood, but the strength of her assurance served.

Once they all had bundled up and donned their goggles, they climbed to the top of the ridge and out of the rocky cleft that concealed the shelter. On top they were hit with the full strength of the sunlight on the snow. Bert and Cathy were already moving across the landscape with the skilled step of those accustomed to snowshoes. Once the three Durands laced their shoes, they began to follow. Shrader carried Alain on his back.

They were making fair time, but it was clear that Jenkins and Pearson were way ahead and outdistancing them. Ghislaine kept looking back at Shrader as if she needed reassurance that they had not been abandoned.

"Don't worry about keeping up with them," he said at last. "In fact, we need to set off a little more to the right. They're following a different path."

As if cued, the group came to a stop. "I did not completely understand what Cathy told us," confessed Ghislaine. "What is the *Eight*?"

Shrader hesitated before he spoke. "It's another shelter."

"But why is it called *Eight*? Do you have eight camps?"

The question was innocent enough, and they did have eight refuge shelters, but that was not why this one was called *Eight*. The emergency shelters were designated by a number that served to point the way back to Keelhouse. Keelhouse was at the center and the numbers of the camps indicated their relative position on an analog clock face. *Eight* was at the eight o'clock position. By following the hour hand of an imaginary clock, a traveler would find Keelhouse. He suspected that the Durands were as they seemed, a family desperately fleeing a hostile situation, but Shrader would exercise caution. "I can't remember why it was called that," he lied. "It might have been from the way two trees had grown together. You know how it is... somebody comes up with a name and it sticks." Of course that wasn't the way it was, but it was best to be economical with the truth. "Maybe I should take the point now that the other two are following a different path." The three ahead stopped as Shrader took the lead. The shift in position also changed the direction of the conversation, or rather, ended the conversation. With Alain still strapped to his back, Ghislaine stepped up and began talking to her son.

"I wish I had someone to carry me," she goaded in a light-hearted way. Alain did not respond other than to pull at the eye pieces of the snow goggles. "Those will protect your eyes."

Shrader could not see Alain's reaction, but he heard a small voice, "*Est-ce que c'est loin?*"

"He asks if it is far," she said.

"Actually, not," answered Shrader, "we are quite close."

"*Non, ce ne pas loin, mon petit chou.*"

This time the voice from his back was firm, "I am not a cabbage."

Ghislaine laughed with delight, "No you are not," she retorted. "I can see you smiling, and cabbages never do!"

"What did he say?" asked Shrader.

"I told him that it would not be far and then added, 'my sweetie,' but in French it literally means 'my little cabbage.' He told me that he wasn't a cabbage. It's a word game that we haven't played for a long time. It makes me think he will be okay."

"Then he gave you a gift," added Marks.

They went on for another forty minutes when Shrader announced, "Here we are, home sweet home." The Durands did not see anything that looked like home or shelter, but it *was there* behind a line of spruce. Having come out of the north, trees of this size and density were not familiar to them. Five years earlier, Cathy and Shrader had intended to lead a flotilla of sailboats to Labrador. When they arrived at the small bay that became their home, they immediately recognized that they were south of their original destination. Here, the trees here grew thickly, especially away from the rugged coast. In a much earlier time, John Romig and Shrader

Keelhouse "Clock" Outposts

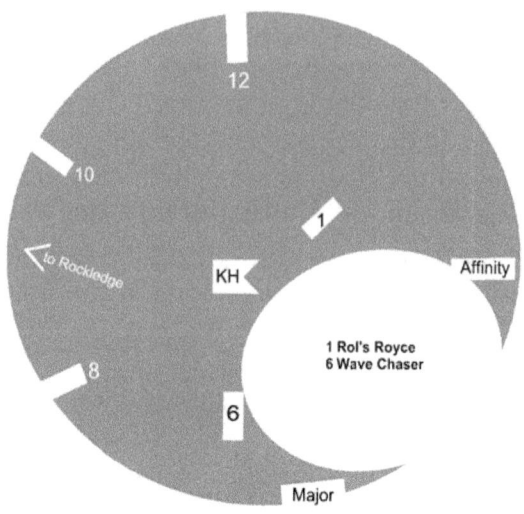

Marks spent time to the north at archaeological digs in Red Bay and Nuliak. Though they never said it aloud, they feared the harsh conditions of the tundra. Now, however, they were in the sub-arctic taiga which provided a richer environment than the life they first imagined.

On the edge of the trees a mist hovered above the balsam pines. Shrader knew that it was not fog, but smoke from a peat fire and a clue that they would soon be met by someone from Keelhouse. The prevailing breeze kept the acrid smell from the travelers, but there was no doubt when they crossed over among the trees.

"That's smoke," observed Étienne.

"Yes," agreed Marks, "they've arrived ahead of us." At this point he raised his voice and shouted, "Permission to come aboard," a reference to their watery passage more than five years earlier.

"It's about time you got here," said a voice from nowhere. "I thought I'd have to go out looking for you."

"Bill!" responded Shrader. Then turning to the Durands, "he's one of our doctors." As he spoke, a head emerged from behind a snow bank. Shrader had already released his snowshoes and was moving toward *Eight* which proved to be a low lying shelter mounded with a drift of snow. He did not see that the Durands stopped in their tracks. Morgan's appearance had been a surprise. He was a large black man, and their faces gave away their astonishment. They covered their shock by fumbling with the unfamiliar ties of their snowshoes. When they had disentangled them, they moved toward the shelter.

"This is Bill Morgan," offered Shrader, "and behind him is Tiffany Jenkins. You met her husband Bert." Ghislaine and Étienne exchanged glances when they saw the smiling Vietnamese face peering around Morgan.

"You have to forgive us," offered Étienne. "We came from a settlement where there was a distrust of people who were different, but you're the doctor."

"And Tiffany is our... what are you, Tiff, I don't think we ever gave you a title?" said Marks. "I guess you've become our resident herbalist."

"More like our resident lifesaver," interjected Morgan. "I don't mean to be indelicate," he continued, "but before we go inside, I'd like to look in your mouths. The light is better out here."

"Still acting like a dentist?" bantered Marks. The Durands did not hesitate, but stepped up one by one. While Morgan examined them, Tiffany whispered to Shrader.

"Royce is here. He insisted on coming."

Alain had drawn the line at opening his mouth. "It's all right," said Bill, "can't blame him. I think I know what I'd find anyway. They're all showing vitamin C deficiency." Tiffany reacted immediately and walked off to a nearby pine tree.

"Do any of you have food allergies?" asked Morgan. The question was so normal for a doctor's office, but so out of place on the edge of the forest. "Are you allergic to pine nuts? It's a common allergy." Morgan waited for an answer.

"No," said Ghislaine at last.

"Good," he said, "That makes everything easier, but let's get inside before the cold catches up with you." At these words, the travelers became aware of the cold for the first time in hours. Snowshoeing over the plateau had raised their core temperatures until their heads were literally steaming. Now, after standing in place, their reserve heat was all but exhausted. Shrader slipped off his pack, and Alain quickly went to his mother. In an instant, Marks dropped to his hands and knees and crawled through a low opening into the shelter. With some encouragement, the others soon followed.

The main chamber was much smaller than Rockledge. That place had been defined by a natural rock feature. This was obviously constructed with rocks and logs from the surrounding area. The low door tunneled up through the floor trapping the warm air in a sort of bubble. Small air vents fueled the flickering oil lamps that dimly lit the room. In one corner, a child was asleep. The commotion of the new gathering roused him.

"Shrader," he said, "I have missed you."

"I missed you, too, Son," said Marks bending over to receive a small bear hug. "This is my son, Royce," he announced to the group. Royce seemed absorbed in his father's affection until he saw Alain and Émilie. He had never seen anyone his own age before, and Alain was almost exactly his size.

"I'm Royce," he said looking straight at the boy.

"Royce, this is Alain and Émilie," said Ghislaine.

"Do you know any stories?" asked Royce. Alain looked at his mother, not sure of the question.

"Go ahead," she urged, "you three can play. The adults have to talk about some things." Émilie gave her a look as if to say that she belonged with the grownups. "*On vous laisse carte blanche*," she added, not wishing to argue. Émilie thought for a moment, teetering between the adult world and joining the two younger ones. Royce stepped toward her and took her hand.

"I know some stories," he said, and her choice was sealed. Ghislaine stood watching for a moment.

"Are you all right?" asked Étienne who had stepped beside her.

"It's just that for an instant, everything seemed normal."

"This is going to be a preliminary examination," said Bill whose heavy voice called them back to reality. "I want to see your arms, legs, and feet. We can set up a blanket as a screen if you want privacy. It's not something that any of us has much of these days."

Étienne pulled off his boots and layers of clothes and the examination began. Morgan kept the conversation going so as to avoid too much self-consciousness. Both Ghislaine and Étienne had lost toes to frostbite, and even now had some black patches forming on their skin.

"I'll have to cut some of that dead skin away," said Morgan. "When we get home, we'll set you up in our isolation cabin and keep those feet elevated until they heal. How long were you out in the weather?"

"Three days, I think," said Étienne.

"Then I think you were very lucky. When I looked at your gums outside, I saw the signs of vitamin deficiency. What has your diet been like?"

"Almost all meat."

"Tiffany is brewing you some pine needle tea. You might not like it, but everyone has to drink it. That includes the children."

"Now, you sound like a doctor," said Ghislaine. "I'm not complaining, it's nice to hear."

"Where you came from," began Shrader, "what did they do about vitamin C?"

"Nothing," said Étienne. "They always said that since the locals didn't have a problem with it, we wouldn't either." Morgan and Marks exchanged glances.

"Were you eating raw meat then?" Bill asked. The blank look on Étienne's face said that they weren't. In the ensuing silence, Royce's voice could be heard whispering in the corner.

"And so Vuhar changed himself into a seal. The bear came close thinking that he would catch the seal, but then, at the last second, he changed himself back into a hunter and killed the bear."

"Did that really happen?" exclaimed Alain.

"Kids, come over here for a moment, the doctor wants to look at your feet," said Ghislaine.

Shrader had moved over next to his son. "Where did you hear that story, Royce?" he asked.

"I dunno, I think I dreamed it."

"Do you have dreams like this a lot?"

Royce thought for a moment and then seemed to change the subject. "Did you know that Keeper was called Greyback before she became the Keeper?" Shrader stared into his son's eyes as if trying to read a meaning deeper than words. For his part, Royce did not avert his gaze, but endured the searching look.

"Yes," he said, "Greyback was not the Keeper of the pod when I first met her. Royce, in your dreams, do you see Keeper?"

"No, I only hear her, and the stories she tells me. Mostly when no one is around."

"Who's Vuhar?" asked Marks.

"He's the hunter. He is like a wolf, but Keeper said that he once hunted a bear who kept the fishermen from the sea. He had to trick the bear, so he learned how to turn himself into a seal. I think it must have been magic."

"When did Keeper tell you this story?"

"The night I was alone. When you and Mom went with the hunters to find the caribou. Sometimes Keeper talks to me when I am quiet."

"You really liked the story."

"Yes, and Anthony liked it, too. He's our hunter. When he came back I told it to him, and he said that Vuhar was very clever. Could a hunter really turn into a seal?"

"A wise one could," said Shrader. He wondered whether Anthony and Cameron were, even now, going out on the ice wearing the skins of seals. They wanted to get a bear, but Cathy and Bert had warned against their trying. Now, Cameron and Anthony had made the trek back to Keelhouse while Cathy and Bert were delayed by the discovery of the Durands. Armed with a tale told by a five-year-old, would they venture out? The answer was a very easy "yes." Shrader closed his eyes shutting out the conversations in the small enclosure. He could not sense danger or trepidation, but the voices within him were silent.

"Can I see Keeper?" asked Royce in a small whisper.

"If she is talking to you, I don't have a lot of choice," answered Shrader. "Keeper doesn't talk to everyone. For now, let's make it our secret, okay?"

"What about Mom?"

"Let me talk to her first, Royce. She will understand, but it might scare her."

"Keeper isn't scary."

"No, not to us. Just promise me that it will be *our* secret for now."

"I promise."

"And, Royce," he added, "tell me, or your Mom, your stories before you tell them to Anthony and Cameron. I think they might try to change themselves into seals."

"I hope so," said Royce with delight in his voice.

"Tea time," announced Tiffany Jenkins. At the sound of her voice, everyone became aware of the pine scent that had pervaded the room. It had taken nearly two hours to brew the herbal drink. As she ladled small cups for each person, she explained the process aloud. "Only the new growth of the needles can be used. The water must be hot, but not brought to a boil. If you do it correctly, it will not be bitter."

"Don't ever ask Shrader to make you some," chimed in Morgan.

"One time!" croaked Shrader. "I messed up one batch, and they never let me forget it!" The laugh that followed told the Durands that the teasing was nothing more than a ritual gesture reserved for this sub-arctic tea ceremony. "Anyway, just don't ask me to brew any ever again!" Leaning toward Étienne he added, "Pretty smart, huh?"

Étienne and Ghislaine exchanged glances. They had landed on a foreign shore inhabited by people who could still laugh.

5

Cathy's arrival at Keelhouse was met with the yelping of the dogs and then by the news that Bill Morgan, Tiffany Jenkins, and Royce had left for *Eight* on schedule. Her daughter Brittany had relayed the news, and then added that Anthony and Cameron had also gone out on the ice. The look on Cathy's face told Brittany that her mother's fears had resurfaced. She remembered the first encounter with a great white bear. The attack had come quickly and suddenly. The hunters had gone out to bring in a seal, and the event ended with Jim Barker lying dead, face down in a frozen pool of blood.

"I know what you're thinking," offered Brittany, "but they had a plan. They're sure it will work. The last time they weren't ready. The bear took them by surprise."

"And how many arrows did they shoot into the animal back then?"

"I don't know. Anthony said four, maybe five."

"And they didn't drop it, did they? Never found the bear." Cathy looked at her daughter, reaching out to push back her brown hair. "Sometimes I get scared for the people who don't get scared for themselves. I know that Anthony and Cameron have wanted to do this, but I'm scared for them... and for you and the baby."

Brittany looked down at her own distended belly. Cathy gently placed a hand so that she could feel the baby's kick. It did not disappoint her.

"My grandchild is a kicker," she said. "And your husband is a scoundrel for taking this adventure when no one was around to talk some sense into him."

"Anthony is a hunter," replied Brittany.

"He certainly is that," answered Cathy. "He and Cameron have been our lifeline, but I wish they'd waited until this could be discussed."

"They knew you'd be against it. But they said they'd met other hunters, and that we'd need to be able to go out on the ice or we'd be opening a Pandora's Box."

"Now they're using my own words against me. We met other people, but they weren't much in the way of hunters and nothing is out of the box. You said they had a plan."

"They had two plans. They were playing safe, just like you always tell us. Vince went with them and took a rifle just in case. Anthony's father and the gun are their insurance. They want to prove that they can take down a bear."

"I know what they want to prove," complained Cathy. "We just don't need to be risking our best hunters."

"That's the mother in you talking. We aren't children anymore."

"No, you're not," agreed Cathy softly. "In the old world you would be still, but as Shrader would say, we already crossed over that threshold." For an instant she thought about her old world with running water and forced-air heat. In that world Brittany would probably be asking for a car to take to college next semester. Now Brittany was Anthony's wife, almost a mother, and in every other way, a peer.

"Walk with me to the memory place," she said. Most of the dogs had gone back to their business of scouring the camp for scraps and rodents, but Sodus, a black lab stayed close by. "Do you remember when the dogs appeared?" she asked.

"Of course, it was just *five years ago*," answered Brittany.

"Seems longer than that," responded Cathy who was drifting into nostalgia. "They came out of the woods to our fires. Somehow they survived the onslaught of the water, but were starving in the wilderness."

"Wolves kill them," interjected Brittany.

"Yes, they knew that they had to throw their lot in with us, and they've made us a bridge with the past."

"John Romig says that the last litter of pups has the makings of a real team and he's going to make mushers out of us all."

"I don't doubt that for a minute. Gus and John will put together a sled, and Anthony and Cameron will be racing to the tundra on the hooves of the caribou."

"They say it's easy to follow them; you just follow the casta-
nets." They both laughed.

"Before all this happened, Brittany, would you have guessed
that you would know about how the bones of caribou click when
they walk?"

By now, the two had entered a small circle cut out of a close
growth of spruce. The center of the clearing was snow-free to the
bare earth. At its center was a heap of nine stones surrounded by
a concentric ring of rocks. It was a place of ritual remembrance.
Shrader and Romig had talked of Scottish clan customs. When
young men went off to war, they placed a stone in a heap. When
they returned to the village, they would withdraw a stone. In
time, a permanent pile would be built up to represent those who
had not returned. In a less somber way, it also counted all those
present in the compound.

"I see that Bert has already been here," said Cathy as she
stepped into the circle, grasping one off the heap and moving it
to the outer ring. "There," she said, "I've checked in."

Only moments before Bert Jenkins had visited this same
place and removed a single stone from its place on the mound.
With eight stones left, Cathy and Brittany were aware that six
adults of the company were away from the camp. Three were at-
tending the Durands and three hunters were on the ice. The two
center stones were never removed. They represented Roland
Koenig and Jim Barker, two of their fallen companions who
would never return to Keelhouse.

"We may have to enlarge the circle," Cathy said at last. She
was intentionally shifting her thoughts from the stones at the
center. "If the Durands choose to join us, there will be a few
more."

"That would be good, wouldn't it?" asked Brittany.

"I think so, but things are different. We now know that
there are others close by."

"So, do you think Pandora's Box has been opened?"

"At this point, Honey, I don't know what to think. The people they were with don't sound very capable, but they are certainly violent. For the time being, I think we will try to keep the
lid on the box, but the whole group will have to decide." Cathy
turned back toward the camp, but Brittany hesitated.

"Cameron and Anthony will come back," she said, looking at the pile of stones.

"I'm sure they will," said Cathy. She reached out her hand to Brittany who followed her out of the circle of stones.

6

The next day brought the Durands to Keelhouse under the guidance of Tiffany Jenkins; Bill Morgan followed behind carrying Alain. Shrader and Royce were not in the party, which made Cathy wonder.

On Shrader's word, they had approached the camp by a straight path. There was no sense of malice in the Durands so no subterfuge was employed. To everyone's surprise, Émilie and Alain willingly stayed with Tiffany as their mother and father toured the settlement with Cathy and Bert.

"Bill says that you are all in good health, aside from diet concerns and some lost toes," said Cathy. Étienne nodded. "We're still going to house you in isolation for a couple of days. That means you'll be in *Mewtiny*."

"No," protested Ghislaine. "We won't cause any trouble."

Cathy realized that in the short time that Keelhouse had existed, they had already created their own language patterns. "I need to explain what I said," corrected Cathy. "*Mewtiny* is one of our shelters. We use it to isolate the sick, but in your case, we thought that it will give you and your family some private space until room can be made in Keelhouse." She gestured to a long rock wall that seemed to jut out of the hillside. "This is Keelhouse, and over here, on the right is *Mewtiny*."

The confusion of the Durands was apparent by their expression, but Cathy abandoned any more explanations knowing that they would understand after they saw the interior of the structure.

A break in the stones proved to be the entrance. After ducking under the low lintel, the passage became vertical and they had to enter single file, carefully setting each foot on a narrow rock step. The result was that they entered a chamber as if climbing through the floor, but to the Durands' surprise, the dimly lit interior was not of rough stone, but polished teak.

"This is a boat!" exclaimed Étienne.

"Yes," agreed Cathy, "and if you pulled away the stone veneer you'd see that the name on the transom was *Mewtiny*, spelled like the sound a cat makes."

"But how did it get here?" asked Ghislaine.

"The water was this high when we arrived. We came by water." Ghislaine nodded as if she understood, but the images were unclear in her mind. Still, the brass thermometer on the bulkhead read forty-five degrees and the chamber felt cozy and inviting.

"The four of you will stay here for a couple of days, at least until you become acclimated," continued Cathy. "The rest of us sleep in the longhouse, and when we can make more room, you'll be expected to join the company." Puzzled looks crossed the faces of Étienne and Ghislaine. "I suppose that our customs here will take some explaining. Right now, I'll just say that all of us sleep in one open area. There's not a lot of privacy, except when couples share their rotation. On the other hand, no one is left out of important discussions or adult companionship." Cathy's words were a blur that passed over their heads. Their eyes were on the neat interior of a cruising sailboat mysteriously dropped onto a mountainside in a spruce forest.

When they emerged from *Mewtiny*, they met a gathering crowd of onlookers. The sun was at its highest and brightest point and the air was still. The youngest males in the crowd were bare-headed in the snow-reflected light. The others kept their heads covered and only their shaggy faces, not their fur-lined parkas, differentiated their gender. An elderly woman wove her way through the assembled throng saying "Ears!" to each of the exposed heads.

"This is Marty Koenig," said Cathy drawing the woman from her task.

"Grandma Marty?" blurted out Étienne. His words stopped Marty short.

"Your reputation precedes you," said Cathy with laughing eyes.

The woman's expression lightened. "I guess so," she said stepping forward. She pulled back the hood of her fur-lined parka exposing her short gray hair to the sunlight. The group behind her let out a collective "ooh" to which she turned with a good-hearted jeer. "I'm always on their case about keeping head and ears covered. You can see what good it does. Look at them. Their ears are always dried out, crusty, and bleeding." As she spoke these last words she raised her voice as if she were a young mother scolding a toddler.

"Marty is in charge of the rules," said Cathy, "obviously, you don't want to cross her."

The introductions were overwhelming to the Durands. Even with five absent from Keelhouse there were twenty-three present, including Cathy, the Jenkins, and Bill Morgan who had already become familiar. They ranged in age from Kelly Barker who was eleven to Gus Gundersen who might have been seventy. They seemed to assemble in natural clusters that Étienne took to be family groups. Their names came too fast to remember, but over time they would learn, not only the names of the original families, but also the pairings that had taken place since the founding of the settlement.

Keelhouse was clearly more than a house. It was a functioning village, and the inhabitants took great pride in showing what they had accomplished in the few years that they had been together. It was obvious to the Durands, however, that this little universe of habitation was bound by a few strict codes. One set of rules centered on cleanliness and sanitation, another on boundaries of behavior.

At night, everyone in the community slept in the longhouse. The result was that there weren't many secrets in this small town, and hardly any privacy. One exception was that couples took turns sleeping apart from the rest of the group. Keelhouse was of curious construction. It was dug or built into the hillside and the two ends were sealed by two boat hulls. The Durands had already been in the right-side boat, *Mewtiny*. Its interior was not accessible from inside the longhouse. In time, they would discover that the left-side hull was a boat called *Strider*. A hole had been cut to allow access from inside the larger dormitory. It formed a sort of upper chamber where a half dozen or so people could gather, and couples could spend their nights when their names came up on the rotating schedule.

At first, it sounded like some sort of regulation imposed on sexual activity, but in time, Ghislaine and Étienne realized that it was also a part of the community recognition of family. There was no privacy in Keelhouse except the courtesy of looking away that members afforded each other. When a couple took part in the nightly rotation, however, they had declared themselves to the entire community. The pattern was set when Marty Koenig and Gus Gundersen asked for time on the rotation. They were close in age, and both had lost their partners after long marriages. It seemed a natural fit that was welcomed by all.

When Brittany Pearson and Anthony Ragni made the same request, people were divided. They, too, were the same age, seventeen. In the world they all had left behind, they would have still been in school. In this new world, Anthony was, by far, the superior hunter and a man in every way except by the acknowledgment of his elders. To their credit, the two held their ground against the parent-tapes of "you are just too young to know what you're doing." They sat next to each other with hands locked.

The break came when Royce climbed between the young couple and asked, "Why are they mad at you?"

"We're not mad," said Cathy sounding like the mother she was, "we just think they are too young to be married."

"They already are, aren't they?" he said.

"Yes, we are," said Anthony as he squeezed Brittany's hand. The simplicity of the statements ended the tension. It was an obvious truth. What followed was an outpouring of emotion, but when everything settled down, Brittany took Royce aside for a big hug.

In some ways, Brittany and Anthony had been a second set of parents for Royce. His real parents, Cathy and Shrader, were often pulled from any nurturing roles by the exigencies of the clan. Cathy's opinion was the stamp of approval on any proposed course of action, and Shrader still seemed to have an accurately uncanny sense of where fish were running or herds of harbor seals were lounging near the ice edge. From what the Durands could tell, Shrader and Cathy were perceived differently than the other couples, but still shared in the rotation in *Strider's* upper chamber.

The settlement that surrounded Keelhouse was elaborately planned. While some duties seemed to be shared universally, there were also strict divisions of labor. For example, cut blocks of peat were carefully stacked in various locations. Some were under an open-sided shelter referred to as the turf house; some were in conical heaps that rose like pyramids between the work areas, and still others were piled against the outer walls of Keelhouse like a thick layer of insulation.

No one was excused from the harvesting of peat. Étienne and Ghislaine got the impression that it was cut some distance from camp, but even the children would be expected to participate. The season for cutting was short. Heavy wet blocks were spread out on the open ground to provide initial drying and lose the weight of water before they were carted back to camp to be stacked. The color and hardness of each block defined its use. The heavy, hard, black turf would be reserved for the long burning fires. Everyone tended the fires, including the strategically placed smolders that were set around the peat bog. These were a somewhat vain attempt to ward off the black flies and mosquitoes that celebrated the cutting with a feast of human flesh.

The complexities of this *simple* existence were beginning to overwhelm the Durands. They understood that everyone was expected to master a handful of tasks, most related to survival. Building a fire from cut turf was one, as was tending it, and cleaning away the distinctive bright red ash. Building a snow shelter was another universal skill. Over and over again, Marty Koenig's name came to the fore as the one who would drill these principles into the newest family as their rite of initiation into Keelhouse.

Before being shunted off into *Mewtiny*, the Durands joined the company in Keelhouse. Émilie and Alain went into *Strider's* upper room with two of the younger girls, Sandi Koenig and Kelly Barker. The gathering was friendly and welcoming, but beneath the surface, there was serious business.

Cathy wanted to know why Shrader and Royce had not re-turned with the others. Bill Morgan could offer little insight oth-er than to say, "We're talking about Shrader."

The second topic of some urgency was the absence of Vince and Anthony Ragni and Cameron Romig. It was clear that the topic made Cathy anxious, but, in the end, nothing could be done, so the conversation was set aside. "I would think that we shall know within two days," announced Pearson. "Shrader says the ice is beginning to break up, so the hunters won't have to travel far to the hunting grounds."

"Isn't it early in the season for the ice to break?" asked Gus.

"We're talking about Shrader Marks," interjected Jenkins, and the Durands found themselves on the outside of an inside joke.

If Étienne and Ghislaine had questions of their own, they were not given the opportunity to ask. They had to repeat the painful recitation of events of the last five years and of *the Five* as the leaders were called. They spoke of their growing dread when they realized that the French-speakers had fallen prey to acci-dents that didn't make much sense. They brought the group right up to the moment when they encountered Cathy, Bert, and Shrader at the edge of the plain.

Throughout the presentation, Cathy and Bert exchanged glances and nods, but didn't interrupt. When the telling wound down into silence, Gus and Marty offered to escort the new arri-vals to their private quarters. To Ghislaine's surprise, Émilie and Alain protested the move. A smile washed over her face. Turning to the company she said, "You people are so amazing; you have saved our children and given us our life back. I will try to be wor-thy of you." Her tears were met, first with applause, and then by hugs all around. When they left, Keelhouse became very quiet.

It was only a matter of minutes before Gus and Marty re-turned.

"They are a very nice family," said Marty.

"And grateful," added Gundersen.

Cathy and Bert made eye contact. An almost imperceptible nod was given by Cathy, and Jenkins whispered. "Down here!"

He gestured the group away from *Mewtiny's* hull that formed the north wall of Keelhouse. The assembly pushed close together toward the south wall, where the fin keel of *Strider* stood out from the rock structure.

"Cathy and I share your opinion completely," he began. "Shrader does, too. I don't know about Tiff and Bill?" he said glancing at his wife and Morgan. They nodded agreement.

"But," he continued, "we haven't heard everything. They are Québécoise, but they lived in Toronto. That seems reasonable, but how did they come to be thousands of miles north in an Inuit village? It had to be around the time that Alain was born. Most people stick pretty close to home or the hospital when that's the case. At least in the old days," he added.

"We aren't ready to push for an answer. If they are intentionally hiding something, we'll just put them on guard. So listen to them. See if you can pick up fragments from their conversation. If they're on the up-and-up, it will come out naturally."

"What if they are not as they seem?" asked Laura Romig. "Not that I think they're faking it."

"I think it would be hard to put on a show with the children around," observed Cathy. "They wouldn't know how to keep a charade going."

"Agreed," continued Romig, "but what if they've been followed or try to contact someone else who's out there?"

"That could be," said Cathy, "if so, we'll have to be watchful. It's like Bert said, it's what they haven't told us that raises the questions. Eventually, we will have to find answers. I suspect that when they trust us, they will open up. We have not heard the whole story. It's not just where they were that haunts me; it's also the story about *the Five*. Why did they come up with such a crazy and dangerous way of hunting? Where were the people who lived in that region? Surely they should have been able to offer some other help and do things that made more sense. You don't survive out here by being clueless, and they're up there trying to slaughter the caribou like the old-time buffalo hunters while their teeth are ready to fall out from vitamin deficiency."

The hushed tones of the conversation melted into a pool of reflection. "Everything they say feels true." The silence had been one of those rare occasions when Tiffany Jenkins' voice took mastery over the clan. Nothing more needed to be said, and everyone settled into the nightly sleeping routine.

Brittany and Cathy spent the night together aboard *Strider*. The space was reserved for the younger couple, but Anthony was out on the ice with Cameron and his father. If Anthony was beyond the limits of sight, Royce and Shrader were beyond the boundary of imagination. The two women did not speak their fears directly, but Cathy tried to listen to the darkness and spoke their names before drifting into sleep.

7

It was midday when the dogs came alive with Sodus leading the chorus. His excitement told Cathy that Shrader and Royce were at the circle removing a stone from the heap. She neglected to pull the hood of her parka over her head as she rushed out to greet them. A choir of young voices called after her, "Bare head, black ears!" The speakers were Kelly Barker, Sandi Koenig, and Ben Romig. The words, however, were one of the maxims from Grandma Marty, who always touted the dangers of frostbite.

Cathy gave them a glance and covered her ears. She did not fear the consternation of Marty, but agreed with the principle. The younger children were attuned to the cold, but their comfort often produced crusty, bloody ears. Better to set a consistent example.

Cathy raced the last few yards between Shrader and herself. They embraced and kissed. Royce was soon crawling between them to get his share of affection, and maybe a little more.

"How could you go off without telling me?" accused Cathy.

"Well, it's really good to see you, Shrader," added Marks.

"I'm sorry," said Cathy, "I didn't mean to put you on trial; I was just worried and scared. Anthony and Cameron have gone out on the ice."

"I know," replied Shrader, "Royce sent them."

"What?" By now others were entering the glade to hear what Shrader had to offer. Whenever he returned from one of his private forays, he always had some curious remarks to share.

"The ice is breaking up early this season," he offered, more to divert the discussion than to supply new information. They had already heard that piece of his premonition. His look toward Cathy told her that the rest of their conversation would have to wait for a less public forum.

"You're losing it, Shrader," said John Romig, "you gave us that news a couple of days ago."

Shrader grinned at his old friend. "I thought you were one of the people who thought that I had lost it years ago!" The banter changed the topic and told Romig that this was not a time for a powwow. With no explanations forthcoming, the excitement evaporated.

"If we are going to get an early thaw, we should make sure that we're clear on turf cutting assignments," said Cathy. The groans which followed left her alone with Shrader. Even Royce tagged along with the retreating swarm. When the circle cleared, Cathy asked the burning question: "Enough subterfuge, where have you been?"

"Anthony is out on the ice, isn't he?"

Cathy was taken back by the question. "Yes, but..."

"He figured out how he could trick a bear from a story that Royce told him, a story that Royce learned from Keeper."

"Oh," said Cathy as the whole thing took shape in her brain. "So he hears the voices, too."

"Yes, and his little head was full of questions and random thoughts. He told me that Keeper's name was Greyback before she became the Keeper."

"So you took him out on the ice."

"I figured that it would be the easiest way to explain what was happening." Shrader was starting to drift into himself and Cathy quickly reached in to draw him back out.

"Did you find the whales? Was Royce shocked or scared by them?" she asked.

"Not at all. Maybe it's his age, but he would have just walked off the ice shelf to see them. I told Keeper not to call to him, but

Keeper couldn't understand how a five-year-old could still be considered a calf. In her world, a two-year-old male can keep up with the pod even if they won't be fully mature until twelve."

"But we don't live in her world." Shrader gave her a look that told her that she was wrong.

"We came to an understanding," Shrader continued. "When she saw that I was carrying Royce, she understood some of the difference. Royce was ecstatic. When I put him down on the ice sheet, he made straight off toward a hummock. Fortunately, it was solid enough for me to follow. Keeper saw what was going on and came under the deformed stuff to a pothole. Close up, her size made Royce cautious. The truth is that it's not very far from here. There's a lot of brash ice and the sheet is breaking."

"Seems early," commented Cathy as she took the meaning of Shrader's remarks.

"Yes, very early. I want to hear what John thinks about it. Maybe enough ash has been scrubbed out of the atmosphere to give us a longer growing season."

"Back to Royce. You said you and Keeper came to an understanding?"

"When she saw how small Royce was, she agreed not to call to him. Royce wasn't happy about that; he evidently liked the stories..."

"Of course," chimed Cathy.

"But the three of us decided to keep all of this our secret. Royce made a very solemn promise to Keeper that he would not tell anyone else the stories."

"He can't keep that promise, can he?"

"Not the Royce I know, but maybe he'll slow up a bit. I told him that he had to tell you and me first, before he shared with Anthony or anyone else."

"Did Keeper have any word about Anthony?" asked Cathy.

Shrader smiled. "Evidently Royce can tell a good story because we're going to have bear for supper. I imagine Cameron and Anthony will be impossible to live with after this."

"I can take that," responded Cathy, "I'm just glad we'll be living with them."

"Must have been some major conflagration, though. Keeper acted like there was a big hunting party involved in the ambush. I told him that there were only three. He just said they were like *Inuksuk*. I couldn't figure that part out."

"That just means standing stones, doesn't it?" questioned Pearson.

"I'm not sure what he meant," confessed Shrader, "but I wouldn't expect Anthony home for a while. There's a Southwester on its way and with the floe-edge breaking, they'll have to get off the ice to take the long way around. I expect that they'll hole up at *Six* until the weather breaks." Shrader was referring to one of the outposts that encircled Keelhouse.

8

The next day fog set in, a sure sign that the southerly winds were sweeping in more temperate air. Cathy sought out Romig.

"What do you make of this, John?"

Romig thought for a moment before answering. "I really can't say. It's unusually warm for this time of year, at least as long as we've been here. But I'd need more data before I could suggest anything."

Cathy smiled, "After all we've been through, you have not changed at all, John Romig. Still the cautious academician. Okay, what would be your working hypothesis?"

"Sorry," said Romig, "it's a personality disorder, at least according to Laura. My working hypothesis? I do have one. From the beginning I thought that eventually the dust and ash would wash out of the atmosphere. It's been five years which is actually mid-range in my theory."

"Which is?"

"That weather patterns will go back to what they were. We've had a lot of snow, but nothing great enough to undo global warming or rebuild the glaciers. Then again, maybe this is just a temporary weather pattern," Romig added.

"Yes, Professor, but I'm going to suggest that it is not. We need to hold a council meeting. I'll tell Shrader. He might have a different sense of the matter."

"He usually does," said Romig.

It was not difficult for the word to spread through the community. That night, the oil lamps would stay lit inside Keelhouse. Cathy's concern was whether the Durands should be included. They were the only ones who would not be gathered in the long-house that night. Actually, Anthony, Cameron, and Vince would not be there either, but that couldn't be helped. Besides, their families would still have a voice. In the end, she decided to include the newcomers. Not doing so would only create needless paranoia.

Shrader seemed to disappear for the remaining daylight hours, but his comings and goings no longer troubled Cathy. A certain part of her was relieved at his absence. Over the years, he seemed to have lost his ability to compromise. Everyone would be thinking one way, but Shrader would lay down an ultimatum. Granted, his dogmatic insistence usually proved right, but it left people with a sour taste in their mouths. Cathy would then try to smooth everything over.

Still, she and Marks spent evenings together as a married couple. Lying quietly together in *Strider's* forward cabin, she would plead her case for more tolerance toward other opinions. It was an argument that was increasingly foreign to Shrader. She knew he would be back in time for the gathering, and he was. But he had said nothing to anyone as far as she knew.

Keelhouse was crowded. Alain and Royce had retreated to *Strider's* upper room with Émilie teetering on the edge of joining them, but wanting to show her maturity by listening in on what the grownups had to say. Cathy opened the discussion.

"We've been here for five years now, and things are appearing to change." Her words sounded ominous in the enclosed setting. "This is the earliest we've had a thaw. It's something that I've been anticipating and I asked John to say something about it."

He began with his characteristic cautiousness. "I don't really need to tell you that before the asteroid hit, everyone was conscious of climate change. This cold spell was the result of all the volcanic ash that was thrown up into the atmosphere. We knew that eventually the jet stream would wash clean. It was just a matter of time before weather patterns would go back to they way they were."

"Isn't it a little early to jump to that conclusion?" interrupted Grandma Marty. "We've had a few days of fog and rain; that's not so unusual."

"I would agree," said Romig, "but..." He hesitated knowing that invoking the authority of Shrader Marks might become the kiss of death for his argument.

"Shrader tells me that open channels are developing. They have nearly reached us and they go all the way south to the Gulf of St. Lawrence." Cathy was using place-names that had not been heard in years.

"Shrader says," said Jeff Koenig with a clear note of sarcasm. Cathy's glance went to Étienne and Ghislaine. They looked like spectators at a tennis match following each word.

"The Atlantic currents are moving," interjected Cathy as if to trump any dissent. Romig took the hint.

"Yes, the temperature differential between the polar regions and the tropics are becoming more normal, at least in the sense that I learned in school."

"Cut to the bottom line," said Gus Gundersen. Marty elbowed him to soften his tone. "I mean, is this just temporary or a sign of things to come?"

"If I'm right," concluded John, "then the change will be more permanent. We'll have longer growing seasons and more open water."

Silence took hold of the space. The focus for years was a system for living in a frozen world.

"So," said Gus, "we get more fish and Tiffany will grow more broccoli and vegetables! What's the big deal?" The comment brought a wave of laugher.

Bert Jenkins' serious bearing ended that. "The big deal is that the waterways will be open longer. We've known for years that we were not the lone survivors, but we also knew that it was safer to stay clear of the kind of thing that was going on out there."

As he spoke, everyone but Cathy turned to see Shrader entering the portal. Cathy's eyes went to the Durands. She wanted to see their reaction to Jenkins' remarks. They looked surprised. Her next comments were directed to them.

"When you showed up from the north," she began, "we were surprised. We had never heard radio conversation from that direction. When we first landed here, however, we used our radio equipment to eavesdrop on the signals from the south. What we heard worried us. It was a cruel game that was being played."

Laura Romig entered the conversation. "We heard two kinds of radio communications, pleas for help and offers of aid."

"Wouldn't that be expected?" asked Étienne.

"That's just it," said Morgan, "there were so many calls for help, but not many who could give aid. We were not in any position to do anything. Our boats were slow, small, and by that time, mostly grounded. But we could use our direction finders to give us an idea where these groups were stranded. We'd chart the signal direction on a nautical chart and figure out where it crossed a land mass. Not very accurate, but we had a general idea."

"Bert and I did most of the surveillance," said Laura. "After a while you could recognize certain voices and signals. And then there were the offers of aid. Sometimes we could hear both sides of a conversation, sometimes only one. The people offering help were always calm and deliberate. They'd ask carefully worded questions: 'What is your location? How many are there? What supplies do you have and what are your critical needs?'

"It sounded like an official assessment by a rescue party," she continued. "But we knew that something was wrong."

"What?" asked Durand.

"The rescuers weren't where they said they were," offered Jenkins. "When the people seeking aid gave their location, it fell on the line that we had drawn on our chart. When those offering help told their location, it was off by a hundred miles. Their actual broadcasts were from several different locations."

"They were triangulating," said Étienne with sudden awareness.

Immediately, Cathy exchanged glances with Bert. In the same instant they had both realized that Durand knew something about radiolocation. Cathy wondered if bringing the Durands into the discussion had been rash on her part, but the deed had been done.

"Exactly," said Laura who had not seen the red flag go up. "After a short time, the voices would shift and the familiar voices of the rescuers were coming from the coordinates of those asking for aid, but they weren't confirming their arrival or describing what they found. They were back to their broadcast offering humanitarian aid."

"Predators! That's all they were," said Morgan. "Cannibals feeding off their victims is what I figure."

"After that," said Jenkins, "we agreed never to send out a message. A broadcast would be traced back here. We'd be opening Pandora's Box if we went on the air for very long."

"We wondered what you meant by that. We heard some of you talking about Pandora's Box, but didn't know what you meant."

"Well, we may have to decide if we need to open it at some point," said Cathy.

"Why?" came an undertone of voices.

"Because the weather patterns are moderating." Suddenly the conversation was back to John Romig. "Overland and over-water travel routes are going to open up."

"Only if the weather is actually changing," said Jeff Koenig, who had been holding his tongue.

"It is changing!" Shrader's voice resonated through Keelhouse. "The cold water currents are flowing in the Atlantic. The water will be ice-free earlier and for longer. We will be able to move, and so will others."

"Give me the word, and *Major Blunder* will be in the water," said Gus as a matter of pride. "When we put her ashore, I told you that I'd be ready to launch when Cathy gave the word."

"You have a boat you can get into the water?" Étienne Durand was sitting up straighter now.

"Maybe two," boasted Gundersen. Cathy would have liked to stuff a sock in his mouth, but the last one had worn out years before. Her steely look, however, accomplished the same thing, but too late.

"Well, maybe not," stuttered Gus. "In theory, we might be able to put a sailboat in the water, but it would be too small to carry many of us." His attempt at minimization sounded feeble.

"That's beyond anything we need to decide tonight." Cathy cut off any follow-up questions. "We know that as the weather moderates, we might find that we are closer to neighbors than we realized. The Durands are proof of that. As travel over distances becomes easier, we may have more explorers."

"Or fewer." Tish Barker added. She had never been outspoken, so every head turned at her surprise comment. Tish blushed as she recovered from the comment that just seemed to pop out of her. "I mean, the Durands got here over snow. The others traveled by snowmobile. We're trying to breed a team of dogs with Sodus to pull that sled that John and Gus have wired together. So far, it seems like travel takes snow on the ground. We don't even know if there are any roads that lead into this place. Maybe you can only get here over snow or by boats."

"You're right," said Cathy. "This place wasn't highly traveled in the past. It could be that we can lay low for many years as long as we don't give away our location."

"Do we want to?" asked Tish. "I mean... and I'm not complaining, but I get lonely sometimes. I don't visit in *Strider* since Jim... Well, we left a lot behind when we sailed out of Lake Ontario."

The room went quiet for a while, and Cathy let the silence swirl softly before speaking. Her voice was hushed but definite. "Tomorrow Laura, Bert, and Jeff will set up the battery system at *Major Blunder*. At this point, we only listen. No transmissions. Understood?"

"Jeff, I want you and Laura to determine whether Gus' invention will work."

"It will," interjected Gus.

"No offense, Gus, but I want another set of eyes on the project before we pull the rip cord on your parachute."

Everyone nodded in agreement, and the confab was over. It was clear that the Durands would have liked to ask some questions, but equally clear that *Major Blunder* would remain undefined for them. It sounded much more like a destination than a mistake. In any case, they knew better than to ask.

9

Though the days were getting longer, there were still only about nine hours of light at the latitude of Keelhouse. By midsummer, the daylight would last more than sixteen. To make the most of the time, the trio set out at daybreak. Even before first light they had loaded a light sled with three bulky deep-cycle batteries.

Though the camp was awake and active, only Cathy and Shrader attended the departing company. Everyone else was about their daily responsibilities. Romig had given his farewell to Laura as he headed out with the dogs to give yet another try with a sled that he and Gundersen had designed. This was the fourth prototype, but the dogs could not pull it farther than a few hundred yards before the drag on the glides was too great. It was the same problem as he had had with other prototypes. The only known solution was to wax the runners, but the supplies that came over with them were too precious to waste on an idea for a dog-powered sled. They were used on the remaining pairs of Nordic skis that Shrader had crammed into *Strider's* quarter berths five years earlier.

Justin Pearson and Ashley Barker approached Cathy with the suggestion that they could handle Bert Jerkins' normal task of walking the north perimeter of the bay to check for animal activity. They had accompanied Bert before, but Cathy wondered if these two were going to follow Anthony and Brittany's example and announce themselves a couple. "Take Aaron with you," she said referring to Ashley's brother, "he needs the experience."

The look that passed between Ashley and Justin told her that her suspicions were probably correct. On the other hand, there was not much else to do. The perimeter patrols were an important part of the routine. The northern edge of the bay would take them out as far as the point where her own boat, *Affinity*, had been beached. It was the easternmost shelter in the

Keelhouse network. From there, they could survey the bay from another angle.

"See if you can catch sight of Anthony and the others," Cathy called after them.

Cathy did not envy the task ahead of Laura, Jeff, and Bert. The three batteries weighed more than a hundred and sixty pounds. The runners of their sled would have to be cleaned many times before they covered the twelve miles between Keelhouse and the ocean-facing beach where *Major Blunder* was at rest above the shoreline. Cathy remembered the long debate about the status of Bert Jenkins' boat and the decision to bring most of the batteries to Keelhouse for safekeeping. Of course, "safekeeping" meant using one of the small wind generators to keep a charge on the batteries. A bank of three batteries was still aboard *Major Blunder*, but they were nearly at the end of their useful life. The wind generator and solar panels aboard that boat had worked fine, but the system was often unattended and the batteries were subject to freezing temperatures. Still, they might be coaxed to hold a charge.

"Should I have sent Gundersen with them?" Cathy asked of Marks who stood beside her in the twilight.

"Maybe" was his response. "Those three will find a way, though, and Gus is laying out plans for harvesting peat."

"Seems early in the season to me," offered Cathy, "but they've all picked up on your idea that spring will be early. Tiff Jenkins is even trying to figure out if she can plant broccoli earlier than normal to assure a large crop. Your word seems to be gospel these days, Shrader Marks."

"She just doesn't like my pine needle tea and wants an alternative, that's all." They both laughed. It was not often that the two were alone as a man and a woman. Yes, they shared time as husband and wife on their occasions aboard *Strider*, but those conversations were hardly private within the small confines of Keelhouse.

"Have you ever thought what our life would have been like if we had been together in the old world?" asked Cathy.

"Probably very boring," replied Shrader. "I would be teaching at a junior college and you'd be worried about the mortgage payment."

"No," said Cathy, "I'd be the CEO of a Fortune 500 company and you'd be holding your own at dinner parties."

"You're right, it would never have worked!"

"Shrader, I've come to believe that almost anything is possible. Well, maybe not you at a cocktail party!" After another laugh, they both fell silent.

"They trust you, Cathy. Even Jenkins! 'Course you earned every bit of it." Though it was still below freezing, the morning was relatively warm so they chanced a brief kiss, but their bulky embrace through leather parkas was more reassuring.

"Enough of this mushiness," ordered Cathy as she cleared her throat. "It's time you got back to work. Better round up Royce before he decides to ask Keeper for another story."

"I trust Keeper's word to not do any more of that, at least not until the pup has grown some. On the other hand, Royce can be persuasive."

"As for me, I just worry about our bear hunters who took their marching orders from a little kid."

"They're okay," added Marks. "I suspect they'll be back in camp today."

Shrader's suspicions turned out to be true. Three hours into the daylight, Sodus began baying. The black lab was joined by the puppies that he had sired. They were a mixed breed, a cross between Sodus and another stray, a mostly-husky bitch they called Nuliak. She was less social than Sodus, and most of her puppies shared a preference for the pack rather than the people. Sodus, however, preferred human company and was always first to greet returning travelers. His barking told the camp that Anthony, Cameron, and Vince had returned from their adventures on the ice.

Brittany was first to greet the hunters. Even her distended belly did not impede her rush to Anthony. After a long kiss, the young man turned to the heavily loaded sled that was harnessed to two tethers that led to shoulder straps worn by himself and Cameron. Vince walked behind to steady the sled.

"You and the baby will snuggle warmly in this," he said lifting a matted pelt of white fur. "It's even warmer than caribou," he added.

By now, everyone had gathered around the sledge. Its cargo was an impressive store of fatty meat. The dogs were also impressed and would not be dissuaded until Cameron threw a generous slab of meat, and they became a barking scrum in a feeding frenzy. Vince, Anthony's father, began recounting the adventure with a clearly undisguised pride in the skill of the two younger hunters.

"I was just the safety valve," he began. "I had a rifle and took position on the high ice toward the shore. Cameron and Anthony found a breathing hole that the seals were using and these two threw seal skins over themselves and settled in about thirty feet apart. I could see the bear working along the ice. I think he sensed the breathing hole or heard the real seals under the ice.

"I had him in my sights the whole time, but I also knew that Anthony saw him, too. When the bear caught the scent, he started to tear across the ice. These two sprung up, like a pair of breeching whales. Well, the bear stopped. It confused him for a split second, and then the arrows flew. Two was all it took."

Like the others, Cathy had been listening intently and trying to restrain the temptation of becoming a shouting mother. Vince's explanation helped her hold her tongue. He was the one who suddenly seemed youthful and reckless. In spite of his six-foot-four frame, his body language recalled an excited terrier reacting to the front doorbell. In contrast, Cameron and Anthony were serious and silent, as though the fuss was an overstatement for what they considered everyday behavior.

"The shooting was impressive. Either arrow would have taken down the animal." These last words sounded an unfamiliar pitch and cadence. Instinctively, every head turned toward the comment. Two men had stepped out of the trees behind the gathered crowd. As if on cue, everyone stepped back except Cathy who held her ground.

"Who are you?" she asked while her mind reeled around the fact that they had slipped into camp so easily. She wondered why the dogs hadn't given any warning, and then she could see the pack still scrambling after the bear meat.

"Excuse us," said one of the men. He held out his arms in a gesture that Cathy thought a strange greeting until she realized that he was simply showing that he was not armed. "My name is Simonie and this is Noah," he said, pointing to his companion. The two had pulled back their leather parka hoods. Their ears were crusty like the Keelhouse children's; their jet black hair and broad features told her that these were two of the people of the land.

As she studied the men, their eyes jumped to something or someone behind her. Cathy sensed movement; the strangers did, too. They looked at the crowd with a sudden moment of recognition.

"Durand, you bastard!"

The sudden outburst startled Cathy. "I don't know you," she said, "but the Durands came to us recently and we offered them shelter. We will do the same for you, but, for now, you are total strangers to us."

"They came as strangers to us, also," answered the man called Simonie. "Like you, we welcomed them all, and then the killings began."

"Étienne has told us about *the Five* already, and about the killings that began to happen like accidents," defended Cathy.

"If he has told you about *the Five*," said Noah who had been quiet, "then he has not told you everything. There were six, and one of them was Stephen Durand.

"*Merde! Qu'est-ce qu'on va leur dire?*" Ghislaine's voice was a frantic whisper. She continued quickly to her husband, "*Comment allons-nous faire pour qu'ils nous croient?*"

"*Dites la vérité!*" Gus Gundersen's words echoed through the crowd and filled the open space of the compound. "We don't need any story," he continued. "We only need truth here!"

In his earlier life, Gus had worked on the St. Lawrence Seaway and had, on occasion, worked alongside his Quebeçois counterparts. This simple insistence on truth came quickly to his lips and surprised everyone when it exploded into words.

It was clear to all, including the Durands, that now only an unembellished account would provide them any hope. Cathy quickly weighed her options. She thought of separating Étienne and Ghislaine to hear their stories separately, then considered that the two strangers, Noah and Simonie, would challenge any misstatements. Though the weather was warm, warmth was relative and the whole company needed to get out of the weather and into Keelhouse.

Anthony protested that his Brother Bear still needed to be stored away. "Take Cameron and make it safe," she ordered. "Then I want you back as quickly as you can."

Keelhouse would not have held such a group had Bert, Laura, and Jeff not been away. Today, however, that would not be the case. Getting the company to make the move indoors was a separate issue. Inuit may have suspected a trap, and Pearson could tell by their body language that they weren't ready to follow anyone into an enclosed space. She backed off her insistence on going inside. The Durands would have to revisit their story out in the open. "The truth now," was all she had to say.

Étienne acknowledged that he had arrived with the other five at the settlement north of Keelhouse. "It happened so very quickly," he began. "We lived in Toronto like I told you earlier. Ghislaine was pregnant with Alain and the baby was due. We wanted him to be born in Quebec and among family. I am, or at least I was a pilot. I reserved a small plane from our flying club, a little four-seater." The blank looks from the group shook his confidence. "A Piper Seminole," he added to clarify, but it did not.

"A small plane," answered Cathy. "Take a deep breath, Étienne, we just want the simple story." Her soft tone calmed Durand. His eyes caught hers and his own demeanor moderated.

"While we were in the air, all hell broke loose. We radioed for instructions, but it was like a switch had been thrown. Our hails were not answered and even the radio beacons stopped transmitting." Étienne's words took everyone back in time. They had not been aware of the plight he faced, but they could taste again the smoke of the inferno that had threatened to engulf their boats.

"Anyway, I had a sort of idea where I was. I flew north somewhere between Ottawa and Montréal. I could see Route 317. Ghislaine and I used to vacation in a wildlife area there. Most planes landed on the lake, but I remembered that there was a little airstrip. I thought that if I could land, we'd we able to drive out easily. It was a mild spring, there was no snow."

His final comment made the others recall the beginning of their own adventure, sailing out of Sodus Bay in shirtsleeve weather.

"We found the strip, just as I remembered. But there were others there, too."

"*The Five?*" Shrader asked.

The tone of the group was changing. "Look," interrupted Cathy, "we can't stay out here; the weather is changing. Simonie and Noah, will you come into our lodge? We need to sit and hear this out."

She was right. A fog was beginning to rise off the snow. The warm air was transforming the icy terrain into a bone-penetrating chill. She knew her question was also a test. These two were wary from the beginning and with the recognition of an old enemy; she feared that they were on the edge of flight.

"We mean no harm," she pleaded. "This place is no trap; it is our home."

Noah looked at his companion and back to Cathy. "We are not armed, but we are also not alone."

"I suspected that," Pearson added. "You came into our camp unarmed, but I know that you were out on the ice when you saw Anthony and Cameron bring down our Brother Bear. Your weapons are somewhere close at hand, and I would suspect that they are not lying abandoned but in the care of others."

"Yes," said the one called Simonie. "There are three others within shouting range." Shrader started to speak, but Pearson's unspoken glance caught the words before they left his mouth.

The dogs had long since finished the meat that had been thrown their way and were settling down. Sodus, however, left the pack to join the humans. His bulky black body wedged between the two men who found themselves being whipped by a perpetually slashing tail.

"Sodus is a pretty good judge of character. He doesn't seem too worried about you." Tish Barker's voice sounded thin in the thickening air, but it was an even smaller voice that broke the stalemate.

"I can show you something really special," said Royce. His extended left arm grazed Sodus as he passed by, but his left hand found the dangling fist of Simonie. The hunter looked down at the diminutive stranger. "It's in Keelhouse. I'll show you."

The man found himself in the tow of a five-year-old, and before he could think to protest, he was getting down on his knees to pass through the low entry into a longhouse curiously built between two sailboats on the side of a hill.

"Your friend has fallen into a trap," said Gundersen. "Royce doesn't look dangerous, but your friend could be in danger of being talked to death."

"What I'm wondering is what he thinks is so all-powerful special! It's probably the pocket knife that I've warned him not to touch unless there's an adult with him," spoke a concerned Shrader.

"Yep, that's our Royce," added Gus.

"Look," said Cathy to Noah, "we offer protection to anyone who comes to us. We gave it to the Durands and we offer it to you. We're not stupid though. The price that we will exact today, from all of you," she said looking at Étienne, "is truth. After that, you can stay or go. And if your companions in the woods need shelter, we can find them someplace out of the weather for a few days until this clears. I expect that it's going to settle in for a while."

Noah looked doubtful at this last comment, but was not about to argue.

10

The ceilings in Keelhouse were high enough for the tallest man to stand at full height. The reality was, however, that no one could endure the peat smoke at the upper altitudes. Life in Keelhouse was lived at floor level. Once everyone was inside they scooted into a large circle around the perimeter of the space.

Royce and Simonie were not in the main room, but in the upper chamber formed by the cutaway hull of *Strider*. It was as

Shrader suspected; Royce had gotten into a box of mementoes that were kept in one of the lockers of what had been Marks' sailboat. When the two were called down to join the group, Simonie looked relieved to be welcomed back into the company of adults.

Cathy called Eteinne and Noah into the center of the circle. "We're going to hear the truth now. Plain truth," she added, "not some technical truth that hides a deception." Étienne nodded his consent.

"You met *the Five* when you landed your small plane."

"Yes. Like I said, we couldn't land in Montréal and we found this small strip. When I put the Piper down, there was already another plane there, an Otter." The last words had drawn confused looks. "A De Havilland Otter. It's an old plane, single engine, but it will carry ten or eleven people."

"Okay, we understand."

"Anyway, they had just flown out of the bush. They had been up north on a hunting trip and got caught just like we did; only they were heading back to the States. Everything was grounded. Lainie, Ghislaine, was almost full-term and we wanted to get to Montréal. It didn't take a genius to figure out that that wasn't going to happen. They asked if I could fly the Otter. It wasn't a problem. Like I said, I belonged to a flying club and we all took every chance to fly any great old plane. I had been in one before and always flew single engine planes."

"Why did they need a pilot?" asked Pearson. "Someone had to have flown them there."

"Whoever their pilot was, he had gotten sick. In fact, they had landed an hour or so before we had. He had gotten really sick during the flight and just managed to get it down. They said that some local people had taken him somewhere soon after they landed. It was then that everything went crazy and they were stuck without a pilot."

"Fred Bristol wouldn't have left that plane!" Noah had interrupted.

"What?" asked Cathy.

"The guy who owned that plane, he was a friend. He had a little transport company. He'd fly people into Jordan, and we'd provide local guides. *The Five* had been hunting with us, and Fred was flying them back to Toronto."

"Well, he must have gotten sick during the flight."

"No, they killed him." Everyone turned to look at Simonie who had spoken from the outer ring.

"They said he had taken ill."

"They lied!"

"They told me..."

"And they told my wife they had killed him. They told her that after they raped her. They told her that so that she wouldn't tell me what they had done. The way they said it was: 'We already killed your pilot friend, and we can kill Simonie.'" The man stopped speaking and there was a long empty silence.

"I didn't know, Simonie. I'm so sorry."

"It's too late for 'sorry'. She bore their abuse for too long. Every time I was sent to hunt they would come take her again, and she finally told me. That night she walked out into the snow and did not come back. Just before Noah and the others were to go out on the big hunt, I went out on the ice knowing that I had a debt to pay. The missionaries, who came to Jordan in the days of our Fathers, gave everyone names from the Bible. But they also gave us words, "Life for life, eye for eye, tooth for tooth.' For me, it will be SIX lives for that one."

"Durand was always on the hunt with us." Noah came to Étienne's defense. "You know that, Simonie."

"But he was one of them!" Again, the room fell empty of words, but not of sound. A woman was crying; it was Ghislaine.

"Yvonne told me what she later told you, Simonie. She didn't talk to the others because they were all holding the same secret. I couldn't believe it, at first, but then she told me that it was only because of Étienne that I was not raped."

"Because he was one of the *six*," interrupted Simonie.

"No, Yvonne trusted me because she knew he was not one of them. None of them had a wife or child with them. She was my midwife when Alain was born; she was first to hold my son. This is true, Simonie. Your wife knew that my husband was not one of them. I was spared only because Étienne was their pilot. As long as they thought they might need him, I was safe."

"She did speak of you as a friend."

"We were friends. She helped me with the baby. We could talk privately by speaking *en français*. They didn't like that. Sometimes Zimisky or Doncaster would yell at us to 'speak English.' Yvonne once laughed at this because they didn't let the women speak Inukitut either. She would say that they were treated like lowlifes, yet they spoke three languages and *the Five* only knew English."

"Did she tell you what they did to her?" Simonie's intensity was rising.

"No, but I knew it was horrible. After a while she seemed to get smaller and would no longer make conversation or even eye-contact. It wasn't just me, but with the other women as well. She didn't talk at all."

"She spoke to me when I came back from the hunting slaughter. She said that they had taken her sexually and they warned her against saying anything to me. They told her that they had already killed Fred Bristol when he would not fly the plane back to Jordan. Freddie knew what they were planning and refused to take them anywhere. When another plane landed, they didn't need him any more. They just killed him!"

"How can you know that? You weren't even there!" barked Étienne.

"Because they told Yvonne many things when they used her. They said that they wanted her to tell me. They said, 'Simonie is a hothead. He'll come after us and then we'll kill him, too.' They thought that they could control her better if they made her afraid. Then Inuit started to have 'accidents' and she blamed herself. After that, she told me. Then," his voice trailed off, "then, she walked out into the cold while I nursed my anger."

The chamber took on an uneasy stillness. Shrader broke the quiet with a soft slap of his hand against his thigh. Eyes turned to the sound in the dim flicker of the oil lamps. He slapped his thigh again, harder now, and then again. A cadence had begun. It became a heartbeat. The others joined in with a slow clap of hand against hand or some nearby hollow object.

Without any apparent signal, the drumming stopped. Cathy's voice seemed to emerge from the last echoes of the pulse: "Does anyone have anything to say to Simonie?"

"She bore pain to protect you," answered a voice, maybe Gundersen's.

"I know how alone you must feel," said Tish Barker in an almost inaudible tone.

"I know that you are telling the truth, Simonie. Yvonne told me these things, too." Ghislaine was talking. "She told me that she was afraid that she would lose you. We spoke *en français*. That's when I was told to speak only English, and I knew that my friendship with Yvonne would lead to Étienne's death. Then, he came up *bullets short* and I told him we had to plan an escape. It was not long after that that Yvonne left the settlement, and Noah and Simonie went too. I had hoped that they had gone together. I am weary of hearing of my sister's death."

"Étienne?" said Cathy.

Durand cleared his throat. "I'm sorry about your wife, Simonie. And, I'm sorry that you thought that I was one of them. Now, I can see how, but I did not know about the killing of the other pilot. Ghislaine was about to have our second child, and we couldn't go to Montréal, all ways seemed closed. *The Five*, as I call them, told us that they had just flown in from Jordan. They said it was a small settlement, but they had a first aid station and would be safe temporarily. They needed a pilot, and I needed a safe place for my family. I know now that my decision has led to your suffering."

The last comment drained the room of words, until Cathy spoke, "We will talk about this again, but not tonight. We have guests and fresh meat. But we have had no accounting of the hunt. I think it best to hear from our hunters before I take the privilege of a mother-in-law and ring their necks."

The heaviness of the atmosphere lifted when Anthony and Cameron returned and began to recall the hunt, and how they had taken seal skins as a cover near a breathing hole in the ice. "It was Royce who gave us the idea in the first place," said Cameron.

"And two grown men blame a five-year-old pup?" added Pearson.

"That little kid's older than Shrader," put in Anthony, "and your grandchild will be born into a warm bearskin bed."

Several versions of the encounter with the white bear were given, but the most graphic was told by Noah who stood to illustrate that moment when Cameron had risen to meet the animal, shedding the seal skin to stand with outstretched arms. He presented a large shape to the bear who had been so near to attack with a gigantic paw ready to swipe sideways across a prostrate form. Uncertainty stayed the blow, and in that moment of hesitation, Anthony had emerged from his own camouflage to get off the first shot. In the course of the telling, Simonie turned to see Tish turn away from the group and bury her face in a blanket.

Cathy saw the shift in his attention and was also aware of inaudible tears. "Her husband was killed by a bear on the ice," she whispered by way of explanation.

"Then that is why the hunt went well," commented the stranger. "The bear's sacrifice was the price of justice." The words spoken so matter-of-factly shivered Cathy's spine.

"It is why we came to your camp," finished Noah. "These men were hunting without guns. Truly men."

"To me, they still seem boys," said Cathy, "but you are right. They are our best hunters, and feed us most of the year."

"Which is exactly why they should not take such risks!" This time the words came from Grandma Marty.

"Wear your hoods."

"Cover your ears." A litany of Grandma Marty rules echoed through the room along with a chorus of laughter that stymied the two strangers.

"Men take risks," said Noah unequivocally.

"Like the risk you and Simonie took when you walked unarmed into our camp?" asked Shrader.

"We were being guarded by others. It was not such a great risk. They are still there, watching."

"Really?" said Shrader. "There were only two of you on the ice, and there were none when you left. No one else followed, nor is anyone hiding nearby. The bear was the only other hunter out there, and he is here now. The ice is breaking up fast, and the seals are drifting on the floes. They are resting, and you are here."

Noah and Simonie quickly exchanged glances. They did not know what to say, if anything at all. Should they acknowledge the truth of Shrader's words or run from the entanglement of their own subterfuge?

"This is not a trap," said Cathy in the face of their confusion. "You have found a safe place. The fog is going to be a problem for now, but you are welcome to stay here."

"At risk of being Grandma-Martied," began Bill Morgan.

"Of course," said Cathy. "You will have to stay in a separate lodging. Bill is one of our doctors and we have strict rules, one of which has already been broken when we let you enter Keelhouse."

"As a precaution against contagious illness, we quarantine the sick... and newcomers," Morgan added. "The Durands are still in *Mewtiny*, but I suppose they could be brought down here and you two could stay there. We'll have some empty berths in the longhouse tonight and could squeeze them in."

A string of thoughts ran through Cathy's mind. The first was Morgan's unintentional declaration that the Durands were in isolation and sleeping away from the group. On the other hand, that could be remedied by the fact that there were empty places in Keelhouse. Laura Romig, Bert Jenkins, and Jeff Koenig were slogging their way through what had to be very wet snow and trying to haul three marine batteries to Bert's old boat, *Major Blunder*. Ashley and Aaron Barker were with her son, Justin, and headed around the northern perimeter of the bay to check the status of *Rol's Royce*, another beached sailboat that formed the shelter now called *One*. At fourteen, Aaron was serving as the chaperone for the two seventeen-year-olds who were building up the courage to ask for community recognition and have scheduled nights in *Strider*. In all, there would be six empty spaces in Keelhouse tonight.

Even if we move them down to the longhouse, thought Pearson, *it would be better if these two thought that the Durands were sleeping apart from the community*. "There's really no need to disrupt Ghislaine and Étienne tonight," she said for public consumption. "There is room in Shrader's hovel. That will give Noah and Simonie privacy and security." To Inuit she said, "It's a small stone-lined shed that

Shrader uses when he needs to be alone. It's warm and safe. But we do have rules, and Dr. Morgan is right. You have not been checked for contagion. So, when you are settled, he will have to examine you."

Simonie's facial color deepened, but he held his tongue. It was Noah who spoke the protest. "I don't understand."

"It's one of our rules," said the gray-haired woman who had been referred to as Grandma Marty. "To keep the people healthy, Dr. Morgan and Dr. Romig examine everyone at the first sign of illness, or in your case, newcomers. We live so close together that disease would spread easily. Anyone new or ill goes into quarantine for a time. Like the Durands who sleep aboard *Mewtiny*. There are other rules, too. If you stay here, you'll have to learn them."

"And so begins your lessons with Grandma Marty," said Cathy cutting off the conversation. She had caught the flicker of the eyes at the mention of *Mewtiny*. She knew that the word would mean little to the two strangers, but they had marked the association with the name "Durand." "We do not mean to offend with our rules," she went on, "but it is our way, and it looks as though you will be our guests for a few days. Shrader says this warm-up will continue, and the fog is not likely to lift for some time."

"Pee soup!" All eyes turned toward Royce who had taken center stage.

"You've never seen a pea much less had any in a soup," remanded his mother. It was true. Royce had learned so many words from the group that had no correlation with any experienced reality. Food names outnumbered the items of their annual diet, but so did the terms of a technological world. The only laptop at Keelhouse had ceased to function long before Royce had learned to crawl. The only exception to the loss of technology was encased in *Major Blunder*, the bilge-keeled sloop that had belonged to Bert Jenkins.

Jenkins spent his career in the Air Force and was stationed in England for several years. During that time, he'd acquired a twin-keeled sailboat that he christened *Major Blunder*. It was his rank at the time, and, according to his sailing buddies, a blunder. They had warned against investing in a yacht that, at the end of his tour, would be on the wrong side of an ocean.

But Bert had different ideas. On a tour of duty in Southeast Asia he had met Tiffany. This young woman lived on the water in a family with too many mouths to feed. After climbing a mountain of red tape, the two negotiated a deal with her father and the government of the United States. The boat they bought in the U.K. was a bridge back to the water. The Irish Sea, however, was a chilly substitute for the Malay Peninsula. With its two keels, it sat easily on the muddy bottom of the estuary when the tide was out. Sometimes Tiffany and Bert would lay out planks to walk across the mud flats to scrape the marine growth off *Major Blunder's* keels. The comments of his friends did not deter his ambition. Jenkins knew his date of retirement, and he and Tiffany had long-known that they would take the southern route along the Canary Current to West Africa and then west toward the Caribbean chain of islands. In preparation for the trip, Bert packed in every manner of electronics from communications to osmotic water filters. In the end, he had an idiosyncratic boat with two keels and the technology of a NASA control center.

"Pee-soup, pee-soup! It's peeing soup," sang Royce as he began to dance around the entrance.

"No, Royce," said his mother, but he had an audience and Alain had come to join him. "He doesn't really understand the words, but he's right about the fog. We get it a lot, but we have lines running between the lodge and the outbuildings. We'll show you where you can stay the night. There's a place where you can even have a peat fire and cook if you'd like."

"Some bear meat would be fine," Noah suggested. "It would need no cooking."

Heads turned toward the two. "White men called us 'Eskimo' for many years. It means 'eaters of raw meat.'"

"Which is why you don't have scurvy," added Morgan.

"I think you are different than the others," confessed Noah. "We were beginning to think that the old stories were true, that, since you were not one of the People, you were the dog-children." The last comment left Cathy's group perplexed, but they as-

sumed it was not a compliment. Judging from Simonie's explanation of his wife's death, perhaps it was a title not undeserved.

"We are not all that sort of *white men*," said Bill Morgan. His
ethnic black features were softened by a broad smile and a chorus of chuckles. Only Royce did not seem to understand, but
clearly he had lost the group's focus.

"And, evidently, my husband was the sacrifice that will fill
your stomach tonight." Tish Barker's soft voice bore a sharp edge
that cut through the dim light. Simonie stared at her a long time
before her eyes caught his, and he broke off his gaze.

11

It was not difficult to get Inuit settled into temporary quarters. For all Jeff Koenig's annoyance at the opinions of Shrader
Marks, the two of them had earlier strung lines from the entrance
of Keelhouse to the hovel where the strangers would bed for the
night. Three hundred feet of braided yacht line easily stretched
past the grounded hull of *Mewtiny* where the Durands were billet-
ed and down the hill to what amounted to an earth-sheltered
dugout that was sometimes used to keep stores safe from wild
animals and sometimes a retreat for Shrader in his more antiso-
cial moments.

If Cathy had the feeling that she was a mother hen tucking in
her brood for the night, those ideas vanished when she reconsid-
ered the proximity of the Durands and Inuit. As an afterthought
she relocated the family of four. Now, as she sat quietly in the
darkness of *Mewtiny*, her mind struggled to fight off sleep. The
Durands were not there. They were sequestered safely in *Strider's*
berths which were accessible only through the crowded longhouse. At that moment, she was the solitary occupant of *Mewtiny*,
maintaining a solo watch for a confrontation that might not happen.

Just when she thought sleep a harmless retreat, she heard a
misstep at the entrance to the boat's cabin. She waited for a mo-

ment. There was a draft of cold air. She silently counted to ten and then spoke with a voice as steady as her nerve could bear.

"Hello, Simonie."

There was silence. Pearson wondered if her imagination was the only sound she had heard. Her heart was thudding so loudly in her ears that she could not hope to sense another. She spoke again.

"The Durands are not here. This is not a trap. We are quite alone. Is that you, Simonie?"

"Yes."

"I will not ask if there is a weapon in your hand. I could understand if there were. But hear me out. I have granted protection for the Durands, and I do the same for you. I think you are wrong about them, but right or wrong, I offer this: tomorrow Shrader and I will come to you and Noah. We will hold council with you. Since we cannot promise justice, we will promise you aid to regain your village. The sea lanes north will open soon and we can set a trap."

"How do you know this?"

"Shrader sees and hears things that the rest of us don't," she answered. "I can't explain it so that it makes much sense."

"Inuit understand such things already," said a voice lowered to a near whisper. "*Mishtapeu.*"

"What?" said Cathy, but the compartment went silent. This time, she knew she was alone. Simonie had slipped silently out of her hearing.

12

While the people at Keelhouse were socked in by the hovering fog, the path toward *Major Blunder* was swept clean by the same warm winds that had already opened the Gulf of St. Lawrence to the south. Laura Romig, Bert Jenkins, and Jeff Koenig stood together atop the ridge that formed the southern rim of the basin that sheltered the community of Keelhouse. To the south and east, the dark Atlantic water was alive with the irregular dancers of the broken ice sheet while the bay on their left was held captive beneath the fog cover. They knew of the acres of ice that lay beneath that blanket, and locked in the ice, another sailboat. When the company had landed at Keelhouse, the boats had been strategically beached as the waters in the bay receded. *Dream Dancer* was the last boat in the water when the deep freeze of winter gripped the coast. It had served its purpose as a sort of emergency exit and coastal explorer. There came a day, however, when the bay made her its unwitting prisoner. That day began as so many others with a hard crust of ice bridging the distance from the shore to the shallow anchorage where *Dream Dancer* lived up to her name, dancing at the end of its chain anchor rode.

The bay had frozen before, and Vince Ragni and his fishing team were used to setting out with their stone axes and poles to break up the ice sheet as they had for weeks. They would work their way out to the anchorage, first on foot where the ice was thickest, then by dinghy when they could break through to the water. Always, they had won their fight against the cold. The relative warmth of the open sea and the power of the sun had been their ally, but ice was forming beyond the narrow neck that marked the entrance to the protective harbor.

It had been Shrader who called off the use of *Dream Dancer*, and Ragni did not take well to being told. But this was one of many bullheaded moments when Shrader would not listen to any argument. "The boat is done," was all he said.

Vince was twice Marks' size, and his strength made him think cold water and ice a feeble challenge, and Shrader Marks even more so. A red-faced Marks stood in his way, and in his face, until Cathy stepped between them with her seventh-month belly creating the most significant distance.

Worst of all, from Ragni's point of view, was that the weather proved Shrader right. The outer edge of the frozen surf became a mountain and *Dream Dancer* ceased all motion. When the white snow deepened it took away all the features of the yacht. For a while, the place was marked by a black pole rising out of the snowpack like a straight proud tree that had dropped leaf and limb. In time, even the tree surrendered its view of the sky. By then, however, *Dream Dancer* had been stripped and sealed, an empty shell that was sealed against the outside possibility that the ice would not crush her completely and that snowmelt would not flood its cabin. For the people of Keelhouse, it had become a rite of spring when the hunting parties returned to camp with the news that the spring melt had exposed a black sapling on the frozen plain.

Today, on the ridge above the fog, the three would not see any of that. Their goal was another boat, *Major Blunder*. They were at the meeting in Keelhouse when the Durands first heard of *Major Blunder*, but Cathy had not elaborated, and for good reason. When the boats first took shelter in the protected bay, the ocean levels were artificially elevated. As the atmosphere cooled and snow began to pile up on the land, water levels receded. It was then that the decision was made to ground most of the sailboats that had carried them out through the Gulf of Saint Lawrence. With the onset of volcanic winter, Cathy and the others knew that it was better to convert their sailing vessels to land shelters rather than risk losing them in a deep freeze. There were two exceptions. *Dream Dancer*, the boat that had carried the Ragni family, was kept afloat as a fishing platform and a potential sacrifice to the crushing ice. *Major Blunder*, with its unique underwater shape, opened other possibilities. With its two keels, it could sit on a beach when the tide was out and re-float when the tide returned. Gus Gundersen first raised the idea that such a boat could be lifted out of the water and launched again at a later time. The lifting was easy. It meant bringing the boat close to the land during a spring tide (near the time of the vernal equinox). As long as the surf would not pound the hull to pieces, *Major Blunder* would sit grounded through the entire cycle of the moon. By the end of that first cycle, Gus had designed a set of rollers mounted on log rails to sit beneath the twin keels. A deck winch and chain were salvaged from *Rol's Royce* and anchored on the hillside. This time, as the tide went out, *Major Blunder* was chained to the rocks like Prometheus to endure the wind and elements. Eight tons of boat seemed a dangerous prisoner, but Gundersen was confident that the captive hull would hold safe in its wedged position. The launch would be "easy", he argued. Log rails would be extended to the water's edge, and teams would catch the rollers as the boat passed over and move them further along the track as the boat moved downhill. All this would take place in controlled slow motion thanks to the winch and chain, a foot at a time, very slow, very deliberate, very easy.

Gus was the only one who believed it would happen. Cathy signed off on the project only when Gundersen explained that the winch would be attached to the shore and not the boat. No one would have to actually be onboard when the thing was fed down the line to the water. If the boat took a tumble, it would not take anyone with her.

"Well, she's still hugging the shore," said Laura when she saw the gold mast of *Major Blunder* pointing through what was left of the snowdrift that disguised the familiar hull shape.

Getting down to the boat and clearing away the ice and snow from the deck was the first task, but before the daylight had begun to slip away in the late afternoon of the arctic, the three were aboard with their cargo of batteries. Bert had rigged the small wind generator and the power was on in *Major Blunder*.

He set about re-familiarizing himself with all the instrumentation aboard his old boat. It had been more than four years since he had used any of the digital devices, and recalling the settings took more effort that he had first imagined.

Laura was the mechanic in the group, and she removed the companionway steps to pull away the cover off the engine compartment. She was somewhat surprised when she saw a hand crank strapped to the bulkhead.

"Can this engine be started manually?" she asked. Bert looked up and realized what she meant.

"In theory," he answered. "The owner's manual says so, but I never knew anyone who could get one to turn over."

"I'll have to put Gus on that one," she said turning her attention back to the diesel monster that sat in front of her. She found the threaded plug that would cover the drain hole in the engine block. "There's ice in the bilge," she said. "Is there anything in your bag of gizmos that could put some heat in here?" She laughed at how odd the words sounded. After years of living with the cold, the cabin temperature seemed fine. She wanted heat, not for creature comfort, but for removing a potential water bath in the engine compartment.

"If the inverter still works," replied Jenkins, "I could have this place toasty in a few hours."

"Let's not get carried away," she bantered, "I'd have to tell Cathy that I'm now experiencing hot flashes. Where's Jeff?"

"I think he's outside clearing everything around the boat and inspecting the rigging."

As if on cue, Koenig reappeared in the companionway. "Is this a boat or a tank?" he asked. "She's as solid as the day she came out of the mould."

"Certified by Lloyd's," said Jenkins, remembering a measure of quality that probably had no meaning anymore.

"Remind me, Bert," said Laura, "didn't they certify the Titanic? Before we launch, this boat will have to meet my standards." Her threat was real, but completely unnecessary. Long after darkness fell on the outside world, the three were seated in a warm, lighted chamber and the only concern was for the fuel supply, and that was back at Keelhouse where it had been pampered like a vintage wine by Gus who kept it dry, strained, and treated.

"We got the batteries here," Bert offered, "we ought to be able to bring twenty gallons of fuel oil."

"It better be soon," warned Jeff. "The weather is changing out there."

"I'm surprised that Gus hasn't proposed a plan for our rendering animal fat into something that will power an old diesel. Maybe I could suggest it," said Jenkins.

"What do you mean about the weather changing?" asked Laura, picking up on Jeff's comment.

"Just that the snow is getting wetter. If we get into a thaw or even freezing rain, we're not going to be using a sledge."

"We should be able to turn the radio on," said Burt. "There, we are now monitoring channel 16 if such numbers mean anything." He twisted the sensitivity knob on the faceplate until it squawked, then backed it off slightly. Nothing.

"Even in the old days there wouldn't be much chatter this time of year. With the ice, there wouldn't even be commercial shipping," said Jenkins. "Land-based stations wouldn't be using this frequency."

"Who's to say that the radio is even working?" asked Jeff.

"Simple," said Bert. He lifted the radio mike from its hook on the nav station, depressed it and spoke into the transmitter. "This is the sailing vessel, *Major Blunder*, calling for a radio check."

"Jenkins, what are you doing?" screamed Laura. "We're not supposed to transmit."

"It's just a joke," he said blowing it off. "What are the odds? There are no boats at sea. Who would have functioning radios or would even be monitoring them for five years? For now we are all alone, at least until the shipping lanes open."

"Still," she chided, "it's a stupid risk."

"No risk involved," agreed Koenig.

"Come again, sailing vessel, we did not understand your message."

"Shit," said Bert, hitting the off switch. "That should not be possible."

"We all heard it," said Romig. "What's the damage?"

Bert thought for a quick moment. "Not much," he said. "They asked us to rebroadcast because they didn't get a fix on us, that's all. They can't know where we are. They didn't even get our boat name."

"But they know we are," said Laura. "And we know that they are relatively close."

13

"I promised Simonie that we would give what aid that we could to help him get his village back," began Cathy. "It is not my intention to enter a war. We have seen enough death on the way here, but these people are despicable. I think we all heard enough yesterday, even the Durands do not argue that point." Étienne nodded and Ghislaine hung her head.

"Still," she continued, "they have been driven by fear and if that is taken away, maybe they can be redeemed."

"They deserve death," said Simonie, "and I am not afraid to give it."

Cathy let the sound of the words drain into silence. *I wish Shrader was here,* she thought wondering where he had slipped off to. The breaking weather stirred a restlessness in him that she could not penetrate. During her encounter in *Mewtiny,* she had promised this council, and it could not be avoided. She was glad that Bert was not here. It was in *his* nature to design a war strategy, and that was something she wanted to avoid. She did hold information and resources that her Inuit visitors could not guess.

"Can you get all your people out?" she asked.

The question sounded like surrender. "Why would we leave our homes?"

"Because the men who are terrorizing your people are weaker than you already, they just don't know it. In time they will destroy themselves, but you have to get everyone else out." she said.

"So we go out to face the weather and let them have the supplies? They would track us down on the tundra."

"Only if you stay there," she offered. "If you knew that food and shelter were waiting here, couldn't you move fast and light? From what you have said about them, they need their motors and guns. They know that you have the skills to survive in the bush, but they would also think that they could outrun you and catch up with you when you had to create temporary shelter. What they would not suspect is you having allies along the way and safe shelter after just a few days."

Noah, who was more levelheaded than his friend, understood what she was saying. Pearson was offering an alliance. "You're right," he said. "They live off the blood of others. If we leave, they will die. They have guns, but not skill. They would not hunt bears with arrows."

"If they try to follow, they will not expect that you would get very far. By the time they chase you down, they may find themselves extended too far."

"And caught in a trap," said Simonie.

Cathy pretended not to hear his comment. "They only have the power of a threat that they can't really use. If they use their only force, they will use it up. That's why they keep the wives and children so close. If we get them out, *the Five* will be nothing."

"You have truly spoken," said Noah. "What they don't know is that our families are strong, too. This bullying did not happen all at once. At first, we welcomed these men back into our homes. We knew that terrible things were happening, and it was not long before we lost all communication with the outside world.

"The strangers shared our lot, and we counseled just as we are doing here. We pulled our resources together, closed down some of the houses so fewer would have to be heated, and pooled all our ammunition. Like you, we knew that the old ways would be better, and we still had the harpoons of our grandfathers. What boy has not used such a tool?" He smiled at these last words and looked toward Simonie who smiled back. "We have not forgotten ourselves," he added with pride.

"And we have had to learn about ourselves," agreed Cathy. "You have seen our hunters."

"Yes," said Simonie, "but what do you know of spear fishing and dog sleds?"

John Romig's ears pricked up at this last comment. He had several prototypes for sleds; none had worked even though he built them from models he remembered from his anthropology books.

It was Cathy's turn to laugh. "I think that there is much you can teach us. We grabbed what we could when we left our world, but we're not yet fully suited for this one. We are still in-between. But we've carved out a place here, and we can be your haven until *the Five* have surrendered."

"Or are dead," said Simonie.

"Yes," she reluctantly agreed, "or dead. But our weapon will be a seige. The first task is to evacuate everyone. How many people are we talking about?"

Now Noah became guarded. In this place, the truth seemed to hold the best advantage, but he had been fooled before. "Between two-hundred-fifty and three hundred," he said.

"Does that include those who were within shouting distance when you came into our camp?" It was Shrader who had just entered the lodge. He knew that, in spite of their initial claims, the two had come alone

"We...," began Noah.

Simonie leaned toward him and whispered "*Mishtapeu.*" Noah nodded as if he understood and went silent.

"You came alone yesterday," said Shrader, "and it is why I trusted you then and why I trust you now."

"There are seventy or eighty of our number," said Simonie. "Ten or twelve are probably hunting now, unless there has been *another* accident."

"And they are not far from where we heard them three days ago," said Marks. "They have been busy dressing their kill. They had not counted on the wolves being so curious." Shrader laughed. "They set up a butcher shop on the taiga and they wonder why they are drawing new customers. The caribou have not been bothered by the packs; they graze unmolested, and the wolves are scavenging the entrails that get left."

"You know where they are?" asked Noah.

"The herd comes to us every year," said Anthony. "We've been hunting them. They are not far away, right now. That's how we found the Durands."

"Are there people you can trust among your hunters?" asked Cathy. "How secure are their encampments? Could you get word to them?" Her questions came quickly and did not disguise her train of thought.

"It might be better to join them when they are setting the net," offered Noah. "It's heavy manual work that's left for the ones they think expendable. If we knew where they were planning to direct the stampede, we could find my friends."

"Cameron, Anthony," said Cathy.

"We're on our way," came a unison reply.

"No," said Pearson, "Anthony, you are not going anywhere near the herd. You will stay here with your wife, but first I want you follow the north ridge and bring back Justin, Aaron, and Ashley. They've gone to check the perimeter since Bert's not here."

"You sent Ashley and Justin out together?" protested Anthony.

Cathy laughed. "Do you think they're too young, old man? They have *little brother* along as a chaperone, but no one thinks it will be long before they strike up the courage to sit together in the hot seat of the council. I wouldn't expect you to protest too much over your wife's little brother."

The smiling eyes of everyone present told Anthony that his best bet was to swallow hard and shut up.

"We'll bring them back right away," said Cameron, rescuing his hunting partner from public humiliation.

"Good," said Cathy. "That is the first step. I have a vague idea of how we can smoke out *the Five*, but I need to hear from others. Shrader, Noah, Simonie, Gus, and," she hesitated, "Ghislaine. I would like to meet in private council."

"But," began Simonie, "she was..."

"A friend of your wife's," Cathy interrupted anticipating the complaint. "She knows better than anyone how things are when a hunting party is away. I could have asked Étienne. He knows *the Five* the best."

"But maybe you have been fooled," said Noah, "and *the Five* is *Six*."

"I don't believe that," said Cathy. "Neither does Shrader. I will trust until trust is betrayed. But I think we need one other so that Ghislaine is not hounded."

"I will sit with her," said a small voice. It was Tish Barker.

Cathy smiled. "I would not have forced you into the council," she said, "but you are my choice."

With that, the rest of the camp fell into the familiar routines of their hunter-gatherer life. There were fires to tend and meals to cook. Their quiet redirection of activity spoke well of the *sailing DNA* that was the foundation of the Keelhouse community. The crew knew its business, and each took to the work at hand without orders or complaint.

As the others went about their work, the council spoke in low tones with Cathy outlining a strategy. "I propose," she began, "that we get them looking in one direction while we are moving in another. What would happen at the base camp if they thought there was trouble with the hunting party?"

After a long pause, Noah asked: "What sort of trouble? An accident with one of *the Five*? An uprising? A desertion?"

"I don't know," said Pearson. "It's our job to try to guess the reaction to each and choose the one to our advantage."

Simonie was first to speak. "If they thought they were under attack, they might harm the women and children. They may draw them closer as hostages."

"Same if one of them was hurt or killed," agreed Noah. "I think they'd think it an opportunity for some sort of uprising. The people in the village were always their insurance against rebellion."

"What if some of the village men were killed?" asked Ghislaine.

"You are of *the Six*," challenged Simonie. Ghislaine cowered away.

"Enough," barked Shrader with an intensity of a man on the edge of rage.

"You are safe here," said Cathy to Durand. "What did you mean?"

"I didn't mean that anyone should be killed, only that if they thought that some of the hunters—not their own—were killed, then they might behave differently."

"They wouldn't blink," said Simonie.

"My anger can out-burn yours," said Shrader. "Stop blinding yourself with rage. She is giving you a gift and you can't see it. The loss of lives may not bring *them* any grief, but the loss of muscle might. They'd wonder if they had enough men left to keep their hunt going."

The truth of the matter was so plain that it stunned Simonie. After a long pause, he turned to Ghislaine and spoke in a low tone. "I am sorry. You were a friend to my wife, a friend of Yvonne."

It was a moment of epiphany, both in the awareness of a common goal and in the direction of an idea. "They would have to figure out how to get all the meat back to the village," said Cathy, "how would they do that?"

"They'd have us pulling sleds," said Noah. "If we weren't there, they might try towing a line of sleds with their snowmobiles. It would be a slow job; they'd have to balance the loads just right, and still the sleds would roll over pretty easily unless..."

"Unless what?" asked Pearson.

"When a dog is pulling a *komatik*, the driver stands on the last board in the back. It tips the runners up in the front. Keeps everything moving forward instead of digging in."

"Do they have dog teams that can pull?" asked Gus, who had been quiet until one of his more frustrating projects was invoked. "How do you get the runners to glide without wax?"

Cathy and Shrader seemed perturbed at this new line of inquiry, but Noah and Simonie put on long grins.

"Wax?" said Noah. "We must teach you how to spit!" The remark must have meant something, because they both broke out in a laugh while the others looked on blankly as the outsiders of an inside joke.

"Later, Gus," said Pearson. "Do you think that they would bring in some of the women or children to ride as counterweights?"

"They would if it was the only way," said Noah.

"What do you mean by *the only way*?" asked Tish.

Noah looked quickly at Simonie and spoke. "We do not have a problem living here. This is our home and the home of our ancestors. You have learned much by being here these years. *The Five*"–he looked at Ghislaine–"have learned nothing from us about this land. We tolerated their ignorance and started to go back to the ways of our people. That's when the killings began, and everyone of us were held hostage, not by their cleverness or strength, but by the lives of our families being held as prisoners.

"Since they have learned *nothing* from us, they will not know why sleds no longer work or what would fix them. If the hunters tell them that going for the others is *the only way*, they have no choice but to believe."

"But they're not stupid..." began Gus.

"No," said Noah, "they are ignorant and proud. It is a bad combination. I've heard that you've built many sleds, but have not been able to get your dogs to pull them."

"That's right," said Gundersen, "we haven't found the right design, that's all."

"But I have seen one of your designs, and it would run well if I were the driver. You have failed because you do not know the trick of taking water in your mouth and spitting it out on the runners until the edges are coated with ice."

"Of course," said Gus, "that's brilliant!"

"No, it's not," argued Simonie. "It is what every child in our world knows and takes for granted."

"And that's what we will count on with *the Five*," said Cathy. "They have survived, so far, on what they thought was their greatest strength. But they were ignorant. Their greatest strength really was the knowledge and skill of the people they tried to control. As long as they still have confidence in their strength, they will not be dangerous, so we are going to leave them with two things, their guns and their delusions. Is there a way to infiltrate their hunting camp?"

Noah thought for a moment. "At night," he said. "The people who have guns do not want us near them when they sleep. And the wolves, they fear the wolves and the dogs."

Pearson was a bit confused by Noah's train of thought. "Dogs and wolves?"

"We run our dogs," said Simonie, "and *the Five* stay with the snowmobiles. They don't trust the dogs because we work with them and they do what we ask. I think they're afraid we might use them to attack. The wolves are attracted to the blood of the animals we kill, so they have us stay near the carcasses until everything is processed."

"How long would that take?"

"On a big hunt where we take fifteen or twenty large caribou, it takes a couple of days. We can only dress them during daylight, and we're not in any hurry."

"What about the wolves?" asked Gus.

"They really aren't a problem," said Noah, "they are hunters, too, so we pick a spot to dump the entrails. They eat well and respect us in return. But they make a lot of noise at night. Makes us happy to think how much it scares *the Five*."

"Why do they kill so many at one time?" asked Cathy.

"That's what we argued," said Ghislaine. "The women would talk, and I was told that it was not good to take such risks on long hunts when the sea and the ice were nearby and would give us food."

Simonie studied her for a moment before speaking. "They fear what they do not understand," he said at last. "They understand guns, but not the way of the animals. They understand having stockpiles and inventories, but not trust in the land. The big hunts gave them security of a full larder, and a way to keep the rest of us in camp. They hold families captive and threaten to track us down if we set out on our own."

"We thought they were after us," said Ghislaine. "When we heard their engines, we abandoned what little supplies and equipment we had left, but I think they weren't after us, they were just following the herd."

"You and Noah left," said Pearson to Simonie. "They didn't follow you."

"But they did," said Noah. "That's why I am here."

"What?" said Gus.

"I'm a spy," said Noah with laughter in his dark eyes. "When Simonie walked off, they were going to run him down."

"And I would have fed them to the sea," said Simonie.

"Or gotten killed," offered his companion. "I told them that his leaving was Inuit custom. He had to make peace with the land or terrible things would happen to the clan. Of course, they said it was all mumbo-jumbo Eskimo superstition. Then I agreed, but said that if Simonie did not come back, it would set everyone else on edge and bring trouble at the big hunt."

Shrader laughed, "Is your totem a fox?"

From first contact, Noah and Simonie had been curious about Shrader. It was Simonie who voiced the traditional question.

"Are you human or are you a spirit?"

Cathy turned to Marks with sudden empathy for a man who might have been suddenly stripped naked before a group of strangers. The others from Keelhouse went silent.

In the old days, when he was an instructor of anthropology, he could have quickly come to a clever answer. But cleverness was a form of pretense, and Marks had little left.

"I can no longer say."

* * * *

After Shrader's remark, the mood of the council changed. The plan was simple, straightforward, and risky. What was not uncertain was the resolve of those gathered in the circle. Simonie and Noah kept looking to Marks for assurance of success; Ghislaine to Pearson for kindness, and the others to the sounds of reasonable expectation.

As Cathy explained, they would have to move quickly as the big hunt was nearing its end. Noah would make a sudden reappearance in the camp. "Tell them that you felt the movement of the herd and knew they must be close," she said. "Tell them that Simonie was killed by a bear out on the ice." Tish cringed at this, but held her tears. "Explain that it is not a good omen."

"We'll have some of our own people nearby," she continued. "You will have to convince your friends to bring the dogs out to where we will be stationed. We'll bring them back here, except for one team. They will go north with Simonie, back to your settlement. You should be able to make good time. That's assuming you can get one of John's sleds to work for you."

Simonie smiled at the prospect. "The dogs will pull anything for me."

"Good," said Pearson. "Will they pull for the others as well?"

"We are Inuit," answered Noah as if that should settle any doubt.

"Then we will let them choose as many of John's sleds as they can make usable and take supplies north to set up camps along the way," she continued. "When Simonie brings out the people, they will be moving fast and light. They will outrun any pursuers, and those giving chase will not suspect the support of so many allies. If we play it right, there will be no one to come after you."

"I agree," said Noah. "We will say that the wolves came for the dogs so we let them off their tethers and they scattered. Then we'll tell them that the men had to go after them, or how else could we pull the sleds back to the village?"

"But the men won't return," said Simonie. "They will be running north to meet up with us."

"Exactly," said Pearson, "but you mustn't get there before Noah fuels their fear of losing the entire kill."

"They won't have too many choices," said Noah. "They can sit and wait for the men to return with the dogs..."

"Which they won't," interrupted Gundersen.

"Or they can go after the men using the snowmobiles," continued Noah.

"Would they do that and use up all that fuel?" asked Tish.

Cathy smiled at Barker's contribution. "You're right, they'll not risk their precious resources," she said. "It's at this point that I can't see how they'll react. Will they run north on their snowmobiles and arrive in time to use their motors and bullets to go after the escapees, or will they wait to see if the dogs are rounded up?"

"They are not patient," said Simonie.

"Doesn't sound like it," agreed Cathy, "I leave it to Noah to convince them to save the kill by using the snowmobiles in place of the dogs and tethering the sleds. When the rig flips, tell them that they need to send someone back to the village to get people to steer."

"But there'd already be enough people there! You're forgetting the other hunters?"

"Well," said Cathy, "we'll have to make them disappear, too. Some will have taken off after the dogs. We could stage it so that it will look like the others were scattered, even dragged off, by wolves."

Noah and Simonie burst into laughter. "We just keep playing into their fears."

"That's the way I see it," said Pearson. "The *deserters* could actually come here and help set up the pathway along the coast. As for *the Five*, we'd have them spread out. There'd be two in the village, two at the hunting site, and one enroute. Or would they send you, Noah?"

Noah considered this. "You're asking if they would trust me with their lives. I can't say. It would depend on what they feared the most, and whether any of them were willing to risk the idea of traveling alone. They wouldn't like me taking one of their precious snowmobiles, but I'd have to in order to make speed without having dogs... they might."

"It's something you should push for," offered Gus. "When you got back to your village you could create some chaos with the fact that people need to move quickly south. Getting everyone ready and supplied quickly would cover preparations for a total migration in the another direction. You could take one group and instruct the others as to where to meet Simonie."

"That's if they believe any part of it," said Shrader, breaking his silence.

Gundersen looked confused.

"Noah comes back out of nowhere with a snowmobile and a story. They won't have heard the wolves or seen the men scattering after runaway dogs. They might think it an ambush."

Everyone went silent at Shrader's words. They knew what he said was true. The men at the camp would be subject to a different set of fears and would be skeptical.

"You must have fixed rendezvous places in mind," said Marks. "Don't go back to the settlement. Meet with Simonie at the place where you could gather the people for a trek south. Then walk into Jordan together, the two of you. Do they really believe that you went out to find him?"

"Yes," said Noah. "I think they feared his temper and thought that his leaving might be for the sake of setting an ambush."

"And you said that it was his grief that drove him. By coming back, you would prove your word." Again, Shrader's comment brought a burst of thoughtfulness that had to settle out.

"They would want to interrogate me, maybe both of us," said Simonie.

"Then your stories have to be the same," said Cathy. "If they want to isolate you both, well there's only two of them, right? They will not be able to pay attention to anyone else while they are questioning you. That's when the others can begin to move away from the village."

"But we wouldn't be able to tell them the plan," protested Noah.

"Which is why we need a third person to slip in after they sequester you two," said Pearson. "It has to be someone the people would trust. Ghislaine?"

Durand's head jerked up at the mention of her name. "Some would trust me," she confessed, "others..."

"Then it can't be you or Étienne," agreed Cathy. "We don't want to start an argument that will just get loud and slow everyone down."

"I'm getting a little old for this," said Gus, "but the truth is that I am the most expendable. Nobody lives forever, you know."

"Thanks, Gus," said Cathy, "but this trip is going to be rugged. You aren't anywhere close to your expiration date, but there's no point in pushing it."

"I guess that leaves me," said Tish Barker softly. "I would hardly seem a threat, even if I am an unknown."

"And you are proof of another settlement," said Simonie. "If I was to tell them of an escape plan, well, they might think that I'm risking all their lives on a mad attempt to get even."

"I wouldn't ask you to do this, Tish, but I thought you were the right person all along," said Pearson.

"This is all fine," said Noah, "but two things are still bothering me. First, where are you going to put all these people? They can't all bed down in your longhouse."

An hour earlier, Gundersen would have protested revealing to strangers that a ring of shelters existed around Keelhouse. The Durands already knew about the hunting shelter they called Rockledge and the outpost referred to as *Eight*. Ghislaine spoke up when Noah asked if they could be supplied sufficiently for as many as a hundred people.

"Étienne and I have seen two of their smaller camps," she said, "between them they might house a couple dozen."

"We have other places, too," interjected Pearson, "we would not offer you this plan if it was not possible."

"More?" said Noah quickly. "How many?"

"This would only be temporary," said Cathy, "people can be squeezed in for as much time as we'll need. We just need to make sure there are adequate provisions. You won't be able to bring much with you."

"We do have a bear." Brittany spoke from the upper room of Keelhouse that had once been Shrader's sloop. She spoke with a measure of pride for her husband, Anthony. "And the caribou herd is still nearby," she added.

"You've been eavesdropping!" said Cathy.

"I didn't mean to. The baby is just acting reckless, and I came up here to lie down."

"Are you having contractions?" her mother asked.

"You said there were two things, Noah." Shrader pulled everyone back to the topic.

"It may seem small to you," he began, "but while...," he forgot Barker's name, "the woman is helping with the escape, Simonie and I will be held at gunpoint."

Shrader's laughter was disconcerting, but it heightened everyone's attention. "Your chance will come when they're distracted. Do you think that they will actually hold you at gunpoint?"

"No, they'll just want to talk–like it's regular guy stuff–*except* they'll be wearing sidearms and staying on opposite sides of the room. What do *you* mean by *when they are distracted*?"

"Wouldn't they turn when one of their companions comes back on a snowmobile? They'll hear him coming a mile away."

"Who?" asked Noah.

"I don't know," said Shrader, "who would I look like riding in with my parka pulled over my head and a rifle slung over my shoulder? Would they think it was some kind of surprise attack, or would they come out to see why I was back?"

"Maybe you are the fox," said Simonie.

"Where would you get a rifle?" asked Noah, who was still trying to imagine Shrader riding in like one of *the Five*.

"You saw Vince with one out on the ice. He was the back-up in case the boys missed the bear," said Gundersen.

"We did not see a rifle. Of course, we were distracted by the real hunt." Noah searched his memory and did not find Vince Ragni poised to shoot from behind a great hummocking block of ice.

"We have a range of weapons and ammunition." Cathy noted. "We saw them as a transition to weapons we could make on our own. The boys took to the bow quickly, and we stockpiled the rest for special situations."

"*Special situations!*" Simonie's voice boomed. "You mean we have enough firepower to knock them out? Why did you keep this from us?"

"We have kept nothing from you that is important. What you should have seen is our way of being open to strangers and defending those under our protection." It was Shrader Marks who spoke, but there was anger steaming in his voice. Simonie stepped back. He had already called Marks a *Mishtapeu*, a shaman seer, and asked straight-out if he was human or a spirit. Something in the tone of the man in front of him no longer sounded human.

Cathy intervened. "We have taken no hurt from these men, though we do not doubt that you have. Floating bodies were the markers along our path to this place, but we pulled people out of the water; that is our way."

Her speech felt like a liturgy and not normal language. Gundersen spoke next.

"They pulled me from the water, and I found a life here that I had not expected." Cathy smiled at the words and touched his arm softly.

"And Gus has touched everything in this camp to make it better. He can make things work," said Tish.

"Well, I don't know about that," said Gus, "it's Marty that keeps us well."

"Grandma Marty?" said Ghislaine, "I thought your doctors did that."

"They do," said Cathy. "They brought knowledge of medicine and treatment, but much of their world was left behind with the tools of technology. Grandma Marty brought *Torah.*"

"What matters in this case is that we will extend hospitality if it means saving a life," Shrader continued, "we will bring your people back here. *The Five* you leave behind will have fewer choices once you are gone. In time, we will go to them. What they do after that will determine their fate. I will hold the gun. When I come into camp, they will be distracted. One or both will come out to me. If they both leave the building, I want you to bar the door against their return and be ready to come when I call. If only one comes out, I will fire the rifle once this first man out is under my control. At the sound of the discharge, you must overpower the one with you. Do not get his blood on your hands. Do you understand?"

Noah answered more quickly, but both agreed.

"Unless one of our lives is threatened," added Simonie.

"Yes," answered Marks, "unless another life is in danger."

14

Before the afternoon sun had set, a small party of men was bedding down at Rockledge. The next day they would send scouts to locate the hunting party, and Shrader would come to join them from Keelhouse.

Simonie and Noah did not speak openly as they quietly assessed the small fortification. It was fully supplied with peat and hides, everything necessary for survival with the exception of meat. Surprisingly, the caribou were still close by and Cameron Romig and Aaron Barker were anxious to move to the perimeter of the great herd, looking for a chance to isolate an animal, but they held back out of fear that they might be seen. As it was, the group was carrying an ample supply of bear meat, and did not need a kill. Still, they had to be restrained. They wanted to prove themselves. Anthony Ragni was the usual captain of the hunting party, but he was confined to camp by his mother-in-law until Brittany delivered. Cameron, a veteran in his own right, wanted this chance to lead the party, and Ashley's younger brother much preferred the role of second hunter to that of tagalong chaperone. Still, the two were uneasy with Cathy's insistence that Noah, and not Cameron, was to have the final word in all matters regarding this particular expedition.

"It doesn't seem right," said Aaron in a low voice. "What do these two know how we do things?"

"Shut up," said Cameron. "I'm the one who should be insulted, not you. I was out on the ice with Anthony and my arrow was as straight as his."

"Can we even trust them?" said Aaron.

"It doesn't matter whether we trust or not," answered his partner. "Cathy made the assignment and she's the one we have to trust. If something goes wrong, stick with me."

That evening the four were bedding down in Rockledge. The conversation was nearly non-existent. Noah and Simonie sometimes spoke in what Cameron and Aaron could only describe as guttural sounds, but they dared not say anything knowing full well that *their* words would be understood.

The low flame from the peat fire cast long shadows over the rock walls.

"You were one of the hunters of the bear," said Noah in the semidarkness.

"Yes, I was," said Cameron, who had forgotten that the kill on the ice had been observed.

"You did well," said the stranger. "It is no wonder that your clan leader trusts you to lead us."

Several things in Noah's comment surprised young Romig. First was the reference to Cathy as a *clan leader*; he supposed that the designation was right, he had just never thought of it that way. The second epiphany was that Noah thought him the leader of this party.

"I'm not the leader," he protested.

Noah smiled. "When you are older, you will see differently," he said. "You have led us to this place, and tomorrow you'll find the people we're looking for. You will watch us walk unarmed into their camp. If we are not killed, we'll come back to you so that you can lead us again by showing us the way to another place–a place that we don't yet know. Your chief calls it *Twelve*."

"Yes, *Twelve* is one of our outposts," said Cameron. "It's not hard to get there from here."

"If you know the way," said Simonie breaking his silence. "That's why we look to you two to lead us. Some of the people that we may meet tomorrow could have rifles."

"Then we will need stealth," said Cameron, quoting his geologist father. "That's how people live in the bush."

Noah laughed outright. "We have heard that expression before and it always comes from strangers. They say we live in the *bush*, but that's one thing that is very rare on the tundra and the ice."

It was an obvious truth, and all four laughed.

"How do you come by your stealth?" asked Noah. "Does Shrader teach you?"

"Shrader?" said Aaron, "he's an odd bird. Gus and Cameron's father and mother are the clever ones when it comes to figuring out problems. Grandma Marty looks out for us, too."

"How did you figure out the seal skins as a way to trap the bear?" asked Simonie.

"Royce told us," said Cameron.

"The little boy?"

"Yes, he told Anthony and me the story of Vuhar, the hunter. A bear kept terrorizing the hunters when they went out on the ice to get seals. The people were starving, but Vuhar learned a trick for turning himself into a seal. When the bear saw him, he thought that he could easily catch a basking seal that was sleeping near a breathing hole in the ice. The bear came closer and closer singing a lullaby so that the animal would not awaken until it was too late."

"But it was not a seal, was it?" said Simonie.

"No, it was the hunter. And as the bear crept close, Vuhar changed back into his human skin and rose up and harpooned the bear."

"He was a great hunter, then," said Noah, "and from that story you knew to wrap yourself in pelts."

"Yes," said Cameron. "I guess we did learn stealth from Royce's story."

"Where did he hear it?"

"I don't know. He makes things up all the time."

Noah and Simonie wondered.

"I will tell you a story about a hunter and a bear," said Simonie. "I've never heard of your Vuhar, or how he became a great hunter. My story begins with a man who was a very bad hunter. Everyday he would go out to hunt and everyday he would return home empty-handed.

"One day he went out to hunt and saw a polar bear out on the ice. As I said, this one was a poor hunter. I don't know if he was ignorant of the power of the animal or whether he was so desperate that he was willing to give up his life to the bear. As he crawled toward the creature, the bear heard him and rose up. Instead of attacking though, the animal said to the man, 'If you do not kill me, I will tell you how to become a powerful hunter, so powerful that whatever animal you think of, you will be able to catch it.'

"The man stopped his approach and thought about what the bear had proposed. He wanted to be a great hunter so that his clan would always have food to eat. He put down his lance and the bear said, 'Come with me.'

"The man climbed on the back of the bear who told him to close his eyes. They went a long way through air and water until they came to an igloo, and the bear led the man inside where there was another bear, but this bear was wounded badly. It had a spear lodged deep in the flesh of his haunch.

"'If you can make this one well,' the bear said, 'you will be a great hunter.'

"The man broke off the long shaft of the spear, and then eased its sharp head from out of the bear's heavy muscle. When it came free and he had cleaned the wound, he told the bear that it would heal. Then the first bear did a curious thing, he took off his skin, and he was a man underneath. The wounded bear did heal, and one day the second man put his bearskin *anorak* on again and told the hunter to climb on his back.

"The bear took him through the water until they were back at the very spot where the adventure had started. When the man went back to his people, he was surprised to find that he had been gone so long. He thought it was for a day or two, but they said that it had been a month. From that day on, the man was an excellent hunter, the very best of his people."

"Wow," said Aaron, "that's a great story."

"It's true," said Simonie.

"Do you have more?" asked the fourteen-year-old.

"We have a good many stories," said Noah. "Many are about monsters and creatures that you are too young to have seen. They are all true."

"You don't mean *really* true," said Cameron, "do you? The bear couldn't take off his skin and be a man."

"What did your bear think when the seal he was hunting became a hunter?"

"Bears don't think," said Aaron.

"Have you seen them hunt?" asked Simonie. "Don't they wait at the hole in the ice for a seal, and don't the wise seals watch for the shadow of the hunter in the ice above before they come up for air?"

"He's right," said Cameron.

"Hunter and hunted are of one skin," said Noah. "Do not despise your own skin."

"It is a true story," whispered Simonie, who was now thinking about Shrader's words against killing *the Five*.

The cave was silent for a time when Noah began a low chant that might have been a song. It was about a man who had paddled his kayak toward land as winter began to melt away. He grew sad as spring approached because the winter had left him so weary he could not see the beauty of the changing season.

"Tell me a story about Shrader," said Simonie.

"What?" asked Cameron.

"Shrader," insisted Simonie. "He is your *Mishtapeu*, your *holy man*."

"He's kinda weird," said Cameron, "but I don't think anyone has ever called him that."

"Maybe he has not yet taken off his skin," said Noah with a seriousness that told the boys that this was not meant as a joke. "What have you seen that you think him weird?"

Cameron thought before framing any words. "When we first arrived," he began, "I was only eight and mostly below decks in the cabin of our boat. It was a scary time. Our parents kept us in the cabin because the water was rough, and they were afraid that we'd get washed overboard. We really weren't good sailors. At the beginning of the trip, Brittany, Anthony's wife–but she was the age that I am now–she was helping us learn to sail, but she had gone back to *Affinity*. That was the Pearson's boat. On the last day, we were at sea and, I remember that there were whales swimming along with us. They were orcas. We all wanted to see them, and came up to look at them. Anyway, Brittany's father had a rifle. I never heard why, but he was firing it. He shot at Shrader's boat–you can still see the bullet hole at Keelhouse–then he turned and shot one of the whales.

"I had never hunted before. It was breeching when he hit it and it screamed. The other whales got upset and started rocking Cathy's boat. They must have pushed and pushed against the keel because it was knocked down, and both of Brittany's parents were thrown into the water. That's when it happened."

"What happened?" asked Simonie.

"Shrader jumped into the ocean and one of the whales came up under him, and he rode it—just like you'd see in those big tanks at zoos and aquariums where trainers ride on the backs of whales. And another whale lifted Cathy."

"What about the other man?" asked Noah.

"He couldn't change his skin," said Cameron. "He was gone."

"He asked me if I was the *fox*," said Noah. "He is *Whaleman*."

15

Five years earlier, when Shrader first led the company to the relatively calm waters of this isolated cove, the decision was made to beach most of their boats among the spruce trees at the high water mark of the rising ocean. When the snow began to fall in the succeeding *nuclear winter* scenario, the water levels dropped, leaving the hulls stranded high on the hillside.

At first, the family groups thought in terms of their nice suburban homes. But Shrader, Cathy, and John set to work constructing the longhouse which incorporated the hulls of *Mewtiny* and *Strider*. Three other boats, *Affinity*, *Wave Chaser*, and *Rol's Royce*, stood at the same elevation on the slopes that ringed the perimeter of the protected bay. One by one, the families who lived in these outposts moved to the central security of Keelhouse. In time, these, and the other early homesteads, would come to be known by either the names on the boats' transoms or by a number corresponding to their position on the face of an imaginary clock. The boats were all clustered around the bay; the numbered shelters were further out and served primarily as refuge for the safety of hunting parties.

Though rarely used, these remote sanctuaries became integral to the plans before them. They were going to be essential in housing any refugees from the north, at least temporarily.

Cathy assigned crews to outfit five of the stations. It was a test of strength, an undertaking that stretched the limits of her clan's human resources. With Bert, Laura, and Jeff already away at *Major Blunder* and Cameron and Aaron at Rockledge with Inuit, the *children* who had come down the St. Lawrence River five years earlier were now leading expeditions. Her son, Christopher, was assigned to ready the boat that he had grown up on. Chris, now fifteen, was heading for *Affinity*. Justin, his seventeen-year-old brother, went to *Rol's Royce*, and Teresa Ragni, sixteen, was given charge of *Wave Chaser*, the Morgan's sloop. Ashley Barker, seventeen was assigned the long trek to *Ten*, while her mother, Tish, led a more experienced crew to *Twelve*, the northernmost outpost and, hopefully, the rendezvous point for the fleeing villagers that would be led out by Noah and Simonie.

Fortunately, the weather turned cold again, and the foggy, bone-chilling drizzle was replaced with light snow that could handle the weight of a toboggan weighted with blocks of cut peat and food supplies. Grandma Marty, along with Bill and Connie Morgan, tried to imagine the strain that this sudden influx would have.

"I think they will have better skills than we do," argued Bill. "I doubt that there will be any frostbite."

"But I'd think that we will want everyone staying close for awhile," said Grandma Marty. "It will take awhile to gauge the reaction of *the Five*. Suppose they come pursuing with rifles? How will we protect everyone with groups so spread out? They will be afraid, maybe angry like Simonie, and probably in tighter quarters than they are used to."

"We can worry about the tight spaces and make sure that the camps can handle these numbers without creating a disease risk, but I'm guessing that something will have to be done about *the Five*," answered Connie.

"If it's up to Simonie," offered Bill, "they'd gut them, and feed them to their dogs."

"Sounds worse that Shrader's pine needle tea," said Marty. "Besides, I think the dogs might deserve something better." The three laughed and the humor cleared every mind.

"Once they have no hostages, they'd be the ones who are vulnerable to ambush," said Bill.

"You're probably right," said Connie, "but I think Cathy would have something to say about that. It would take something major to have her sign off on a killing spree, even if they are despicable."

"They're trapped," said Marty. "They can't continue the way things are, and they must realize that as soon as they lose their one source of power, they will be at the mercy of the people who they've been victimizing."

"It's like hunting," said Bill. "The most dangerous time is when the animal sees no way out. Sometimes they'll hunker down and take the inevitable, but sometimes they come at you with all they got. And size doesn't matter. A squirrel will attack as quickly as a caribou."

"What if the trapped animal sees an opening to escape?" said Connie.

"They'll take it," said Grandma Marty. "Or they might die trying."

"If it comes to that," said Bill, "somebody else will have to make the call."

While these three settled in at Keelhouse to discuss matters of health and hygiene, their counterparts were stocking the outposts. Though the daylight was lengthening, Cathy instructed the teams to stay the night in their assigned locations and return the following day.

That night, even with fifteen people, the longhouse seemed empty. Shrader was anxious and moody. Tomorrow he would rise early and move out to intercept Cameron, Aaron, Noah, and Simonie, who would be moving along the route of the caribou herd.

"Ugh!" said Brittany suddenly. Every head turned toward the sound, and she jumped at the release of her mucus plug.

"Her water has broken," said Cathy who turned toward the Morgans.

Bill had been a dentist in his previous life, but now he was the camp physician. When Royce had been delivered, Laura Romig, a nurse, had been in charge of the delivery. She was also a first class mechanic, and Cathy cursed the fact that she had sent her out to inspect *Major Blunder*.

She kept all doubts to herself. "What do you think, Bill?" she asked.

"I don't think there's much choice," he answered. "The baby is going to come whether I'm up to it or not. I wish Laura was here. She's had a lot more experience at this."

Cathy was not about to weigh-in. There was nothing that could be done in any case. No one could be sent to bring Laura back in the darkness, and she knew that if the delivery did not proceed quickly, it would not bode well for the baby or her daughter.

"I have helped with births before," Ghislaine's voice was soft but firm, and a welcome relief to Morgan whose experience could be counted on one finger.

Regardless of the positioning that was taking place outside Keelhouse, Cathy had become a mother again. Her daughter was more important than the child, and the child more important than the hunters encircling *the Five* in order to offer an escape for the desperate. Leadership, however, demands self-denial, and she understood the obligation. So did Marks.

"Go ahead," he said, "see to your daughter. Everything will be fine."

She wanted to believe him. She had to believe him in order to let go of the world.

Shrader's view of taking charge, however, defied logic. He spoke briefly with Gus and Marty, drew Royce up into his arms, and left the compound. As he walked into the deeper darkness, he turned to see them watching him. They nodded, and turned back to the longhouse.

16

Shrader always liked the morning best when the sun greeted him from across the ocean. He had taken Royce through the darkness to one of his high places. It wasn't very far from Keelhouse, but it was one of his *quiet* places where he could escape the confusion of competing noises that now perplexed him when he was in a close group. Royce's presence was never a distraction at these times. He seemed to know when to settle down, and when his father's moodiness went to that internal space which contained the horizon of the curving earth.

Shrader never considered this aspect of his relationship with his son. The intensification of consciousness (or was it the displacement of all ego?) pulled him away from time and from the immediacy of a little boy standing so close. Today, however, he saw Royce in his peripheral vision. It was an epiphany that jolted him, for the boy stood, not as a solitary form, but as a tall mirror image, shoulder to shoulder with his father, adjoined reflections.

"Royce," he said breaking his internal reverie. "What are you doing?"

The little boy did not respond immediately. His voice returned like a shadow moving across the horizon. "Listening," he said.

"What do you hear?"

"Sometimes I hear the ocean," he offered. "Sometimes you are singing with the others."

Shrader didn't ask any more questions. He couldn't easily abide the idea of loneliness for his son that he accepted for himself. "There is a dangerous place, over there," Marks said pointing toward the path that led south and followed an eroded path that would become a cascading torrent in the spring melt.

Royce looked in the direction of his father's gaze and recalled the familiar route that they had often taken. If he had questions, Shrader's answers came first.

"When the rains come," he said, "ice will wash down through that hollow and make a lake. It will look like snow on the ground, but it will be a deep swamp that would swallow a herd of caribou."

"Not the great herd," answered Royce with a recognition for exaggeration. Shrader smiled.

"No, not the great herd, but the family of Keelhouse could get swallowed by it."

Royce took in the words. "Then I would have to make it spit everyone out."

17

When the ocean breeze shifted slightly, Shrader could catch a hint of peat smoke on the morning air. Those staying at Keelhouse would not have slept much the night before. Brittany was the first of her generation to experience childbirth, and she would do it as her ancestors had for millennia, without the aid of sterile drapes and medical equipment.

He didn't sense any turbulence from the camp, but, in his heightened state, he felt life. It had been an awareness that strengthened with time. He could not say exactly why, but the world seemed more alive than it had been. He could not say if this was a product of his own increased sensitivity over the past five years or a change in the fabric of the creation.

When he was a college instructor sailing his old sloop on Lake Ontario, he tired of being labeled *liberal* by some of his friends when he warned of climate change. "It's a natural cycle," they would argue. "It's just a liberal *opinion*. You're entitled to your *opinion*, even if it's wrong."

Shrader was not much of a political animal, but he was often tempted to join the fray by shouting back, "Yes, everyone is entitled to their *own* opinion, but they are not entitled to their own facts!" As a sailor (screw the scientific argument), he knew that the Atlantic currents were shutting down. There was not enough cold water from the Arctic flowing south to sink beneath the warm water of the tropics in a ritual dance that made the currents swirl in a smooth clockwise dervish of life-giving renewal.

This simple mechanism of nature provides the balance of hot and cold, spawning the plankton and providing food along the paths of the deep. Maybe that is what he sensed that morning as he looked eastward toward the sunrise. He did not wear his snow goggles in the early light. He always met the sun unveiled and with his own voice singing with the dawn. There were other voices, too, but only one song. At these times of reverie, he felt less alone than in the company of Keelhouse.

"I can't understand all the words," said Royce who had come quietly up behind his father.

"You were so still, I thought you were asleep," said Marks.

"It's hard to sleep here."

"Why? Are you worried about something?"

"No, it's so loud."

Shrader stopped to listen to the thin silence of the crisp morning. "You are right," he said. "In this place you can hear and see everything."

"We're at the center," said Royce as he climbed into his father's lap. "Us two," he said, "we can see every direction into the sky, under the sea, under the ground."

"Underground?"

"Keelhouse is like being underground, isn't it?"

"I suppose it is," agreed Marks.

After a long pause, Shrader spoke like a person startled awake after a dream. "I am going to have to take you back there now. Your mother will be very busy with Brittany, but I'll have to go away by myself for awhile."

"I think Brittany is going to be okay," said Royce. Shrader paused and felt the breath of the morning.

"I think so, too."

18

Cameron stepped more lightly that morning in spite of the snowshoes that sent puffs of new white powder out ahead of him as he shuffled forward. Simonie and Noah followed with Aaron in the final position of the line of figures that moved toward the massive herd. Though the sun's light was still dim, they had donned their goggles against a blinding light that would gradually overtake them if they were too intent on their task and not aware of the power of light in an arctic landscape. They *were* intent on their task.

Now they could move quickly and openly. They would hear the buzzing engine sounds of any snowmobile before its rider could focus enough on the tan parkas of the four who would blend with the blur of caribou at the edge of the herd.

Men on foot might come in silence, but Noah was sure that *they* would be friendly. Their first mission, however, was to make contact with the people now being held captive by fears for friends and family held hostage in the north.

For the first time, Cameron Romig felt that he *was* the leader of a hunting party. He had always played second to Anthony Ragni whose nerves were currently unraveled by his wife's labor. Though he was only thirteen, he stood taller than his companions, and the bulkiness of the parka, or *anorak* as Noah called it, hid the lankiness of his youth.

For the most part, Cameron's job was done when he brought the team downwind of the herd which showed no signs of twitchiness. The winds were light, and the increased sunlight was syncopated only by the sounds of the clicking joints of the large animals.

Suddenly Simonie spoke in hushed tones. "There they are."

Noah's eyes followed the direction where Inuk pointed. "Of course," he said recognizing human shapes moving along the edge of the herd in the familiar patterns of stalking. Both he and Simonie knew how such a hunt would proceed and could anticipate the movements of their counterparts. "Wait here," Noah said as he stepped out of formation and headed away from the three.

"Now we wait," said Simonie.

Aaron scanned the perimeter of his field of view. "Shouldn't we find a place to hunker down?" he asked.

Cameron didn't like the open terrain either, but before he could suggest an alternative, Noah turned back and gestured to Simonie. Already, Noah had thrown back his hood and was embracing another bareheaded man in a welcome greeting. "We can go to them now," Simonie said stepping forward so that Aaron and Cameron could only follow.

It was only a matter of minutes before Simonie was locked into a similar hug.

"We thought you were dead," said a stranger who was later introduced as *Matthew*.

For young Cameron, the sounds of *Matthew*, *John*, and *Thomas* spun around three unfamiliar faces. He was not aware that these were missionary names like *Noah* and *Simonie*. They were the public names, but there were probably deeper identities locked beneath the syllables of Inuktitut. After greeting their friends, the strangers turned toward the young men.

"Who are they?" asked the one referred to as Thomas. The words, however, were not English, and Aaron and Cameron felt suddenly like geese being poked with sticks.

"Friends," said Noah using a word the two could understand. "They have offered to help us, but we have to find a place to talk where we won't be seen if someone else approaches."

"They look like pups," said one of the men, this time in English. Cameron felt himself bristle, but Simonie silenced all reaction with a hand to his shoulder and a shake of the head.

"They have a good plan," Simonie offered. "Judge them after you've listened." The calm words sounded more like something Noah would say. The fact that they came out of Simonie's mouth ended any potential protest.

"We'll hear them if they come," observed one of the strangers, "but you're right, they will see too many shapes in the snow if we all stand out here together."

"Cameron and Aaron will stay with me in plain sight," said Simonie. "You can go with Noah back into the trees," he said indicating a stand of spruce not far away. "We'll be the decoys."

"They can't be carrying bows over their shoulders," said Thomas. Aaron and Cameron instinctively clutched the grips of their compound bows.

"They can lay them down in the snow. I've seen them shoot. By the time a sled gets close enough for anyone to see their faces–well, it will be the very last thing they ever see."

The boast sounded as though it was meant to be flattering, but it was troublesome to Cameron who had never considered placing a human in the path of an arrow. Noah told the story of the bear and ended by saying "the hunter and the hunted are one skin." Would killing a human be any different than a bear or caribou?

He and Aaron did not hear what passed between Noah and the strangers. They were standing out in the open and in the company of Simonie who seemed invigorated in this odd situation.

"What do you supposed they're saying?" asked Cameron.

"He's telling them of the plan," was Simonie's shorthanded response. "It's a good one, one that *the Five* won't be expecting. Of course, I'd be less sure if we didn't have a *Mishtapeu*."

It was clear to Aaron and Cameron that Inuit had a quite different view of Shrader than they did. They had often defended the moody man in the face of their peers who had adopted the reservations of a few of the older men. Cameron's family, the Romigs, had been longtime friends even before sailing from Sodus Bay. Aaron had a deeper connection. He had seen Shrader pull his father's mangled body out of the fast rushing waters of the St. Lawrence. The action was heroic, even if his father's saved life did not continue long beyond the establishment of Keelhouse. He was only fourteen now, and sometimes the emptiness he felt was almost overpowering. He didn't know whether he was feeling it for himself or for his mother whose loneliness was impenetrable to her children. The feeling had come over him again during the brief stay at Rockledge. He heard it in the voice of Simonie when he told the story about the hunter and the bear.

He also *felt* it in the sounds of the chanting, not as Noah had led it, but as Simonie had drummed against his thigh and mouthed voiceless words.

Simonie's sadness from the night before had all but disappeared from the animated figure that stood before them in the brightening day.

"You seem happy," said Aaron.

"It's time we start," said Simonie. "Your *Whaleman* makes me feel strong again."

"Why do you call him that?"

"Because that's who he is. He sees things." The boys let the comment go and turned their eyes to the plain of snow.

"If they were to come this way," asked Aaron, "what would they expect to see us doing as they approached?"

"You have the makings of an elder," said Simonie. "We should look like we are trying to scout the direction of the herd. The problem is that you don't want your bows to change your silhouette."

"We could drag them, couldn't we? Or carry them in a bundle?" offered Cameron.

"Yes," agreed Simonie, "but maybe the others will not be so long in their talk. Let's act like we are taking a rest. They would just think us lazy. I'll show you something." He slipped off his snowshoes and began tamping down the snow beneath his feet. "This would be better on a solid surface," he said after packing an open circle to where it held his weight.

"Come into the ring and hold out your hand," he said. Aaron extended his palm. "Higher," said Simonie, "over your head."

To the surprise of the boys, Simonie stripped off his parka and laid it on the ground at the center of the packed snow. He stood just a pace back from Aaron's outstretched hand, took a two-legged hop toward him and kicked his right foot upward until the tip of his mukluk touched Aaron's open hand, then flexed the same leg back beneath him to land on the kicking foot. It happened in such a short moment that Cameron and Aaron were taken by surprise.

"It's one of our sports," offered Simonie, "being good at it will save your life on the ice floes."

Cameron and Aaron made several awkward attempts to match the feat, and Simonie smiled broadly at their attempts. "We will hear their engines if they are coming," he assured. "They will only think that we are just *dumb Eskimos* goofing off, but your bows are right here."

* * * * *

Not far away, Noah was speaking of the plan. Those who listened were excited at the prospect of striking back, but Noah reminded him of his agreement with Cathy that their first weapon would be to isolate *the Six* rather than to kill them. He was hesitant to acknowledge that he had encountered the Durands at Keelhouse, even more wary to subtract Étienne from the number of their enemies.

"Has Simonie agreed to this plan?" asked Matthew. The other two nodded as if this were the crucial question. It was not that they trusted Simonie's insight as much as they knew his desire for revenge.

"Yes, Simonie agrees. That is why he is here." Noah continued, now addressing all the unasked suspicions of Matthew's inquiry. "They have a *holy man* among them."

"They?"

"It is a village of people who were not here before. They have done well and respect our ways. They have food and shelter enough for us all. That, in itself, would not convince Simonie, but the man called Shrader has the gift to see what others cannot. That is why Simonie trusts this plan. Look at him now."

The four looked between the trunks and boughs of the spruce cluster just in time to a one-legged high kick.

"He seems like a boy again," noted John.

"That's because he sees a way that will work," said a voice from behind them.

If Noah needed any other additional argument, it was made by the stunning quiet of Shrader's sudden appearance among the trees. The three jumped defensively at this stranger who had a scoped hunting rifle slung over his right shoulder.

"This is the man who has so impressed our brother," said Noah.

"And he has a rifle that could make easy work of men on snowmobiles," said a voice that came from one of the hunters.

"Which is why I will carry it," answered Shrader. "We did not come here by an easy way, and we don't intend to start killing people who have done us no wrong."

"They have done us wrong," said Thomas, "ask Simonie about his wife."

"I have heard his story, and if the time comes, I'm sure we will do what's necessary. *Sharks don't swim with the pod,*" he added cryptically. "But until then, we have seen enough death. For now, we'll set them free to live with their ignorance so that they can learn the meaning and power of fear."

"*Mishtapeu,*" said the three in near unison.

"You will need only blood, wolves, and quick action," said Marks. "Each will bring the others. Noah will play the dangerous part."

All eyes turned to Noah whose jaw was set as firmly as his resolution. "I have faced danger since I was a boy learning the high kick," he said nodding toward the place where Cameron and the others played. "Simonie and I will bring out our people and take shelter in the camps of our new friends."

There was no sense of negotiation or compromise in his voice, so the discussion was over.

* * * *

Darkness came in the early evening under the northern sky. Cameron, Aaron, Shrader, and Simonie had hunkered down in a temporary shelter in the spruce forest after the others, including Noah, had set out to find the three armed men on snowmobiles.

As suspected, the three were cautious and excited by Noah's return. They detained him for questioning while the others were sent back to their chores. For his part, Noah played the trusted lieutenant reporting his dreadful discovery. In his telling, he had caught up with Simonie, or what was left of him. Every sign indicated that he had been attacked by a wolf pack and brought down more easily than an antlered bull.

At one point Noah had to stop his telling as he recited how he had seen a pair of arctic foxes playing tug-of-war with his friend's entrails. The description seemed to please his questioners to the point where they failed to ask any questions that may have unmasked the charade. In the end, they sent Noah back to his friends to help with the packing of the recent kills and tending to the dogs.

In truth, he had no intention to follow any assigned task, and before the night was given over to the stars, most of the dogs and men were following Cameron and Aaron to an outpost known as *Ten* where Aaron's sister, Ashley, was preparing for their arrival. Before they left, they tore apart their hunting camp to make it tell a story of violence and mayhem. The soft tissue of a caribou was dragged around to create a bloody swath, but they took care to leave no parts large enough to identify. Only Shrader and Noah stayed near the campsite that night.

"We can hope that the blood will call the wolves," said Noah.

"That's no problem," answered Marks, "they will be here tonight and will be grateful for a meal that cost them little effort. Snow would be nice, to cover the tracks of the others, but that's not going to happen."

"The mess that we left will confuse them," Noah continued, "those three are not curious about danger; they all avoid it by sending others. The scattered tracks of the dogs will feed their fear and suit our needs. I will tell them that the wolves attacked us as we slept, and that they killed John outright, dragging his body away before we could help. The dogs scattered, and the others went to find them."

Shrader smiled at the story's simplicity. "*Man-eating wolves* ought to chill their quest for adventure."

"*Inuit-eating wolves* is the way they'll see it," said Noah. "They will hold the loss of a man less than fear, but either way, it will serve our purposes."

"Your hate runs deep," observed Marks.

"I believe that you see many things, but I have seen things that you have not. I have given my word that we will not kill if it can be avoided, but that is not how I feel."

"But it is your word."

"It is my word! If we are provoked, though, not one of us would regret an execution."

At first, the word *execution* surprised Shrader, but it was the unspoken death sentence that had been passed long before. It would have been the fate of the Durands as well, had not Cathy intervened. At the same time, Noah and Simonie seemed to be making a cautious exception for Étienne, perhaps because the presence of a wife and children distinguished him from *the Five*.

"Fair enough," said Marks, "*sharks don't swim with the pod*." The thought had come from Keeper long ago when he had witnessed the death of Cathy's husband, Philip.

"Sharks?" asked Noah, and then he thought better. "Yes, I understand, *Whaleman*."

19

Keelhouse was quiet now. Even the smell of blood and amniotic fluid had mostly dissipated. Ghislaine's presence had rescued the dentist Bill Morgan from an anxious nightmare scenario in which he would have to deliver a child without the help of Laura Romig.

The baby girl's cry and a nod from Morgan when the afterbirth was delivered let Cathy breathe easier. Brittany, her nineteen-year-old daughter, was apparently as tough as her hunter of a husband, Anthony Ragni. At first Cathy thought that Anthony might be disappointed when "It's a girl" undercut the baby's transition to being an air-breather, but, like her, he seemed mostly enamored with Brittany's endurance and her delight. The new family was quickly sequestered into the privacy of the upper chamber that had been *Strider*.

The baby took quietly to the breast and showed every sign of being as strong as mother and grandmother. The truth was that Cathy, the grandmother, was not feeling particularly strong at the moment. Shrader was away from camp with Royce tagging along. She wanted to talk with him alone, but that was not possible, so she settled for being alone and made her way to the hovel that Shrader used when he needed to be alone. This was the same small shelter where she had barracked Noah and Simonie on the night of their arrival. Once inside the small room, she threw herself face down on the pile of hides that were stacked in one corner.

She tried to order the stampede of competing ideas that muddied her thoughts. Brittany had come through the ordeal, her granddaughter was healthy; why did she suddenly have this urge to run and hide? The time of joy was quickly buried beneath heavier burdens. Maybe she could not be a mother anymore. Her fears were running with those setting up the outposts and the sleight-of-hand she had proposed to strangers whose first instinct was to violence. Even beyond that was the survival of her clan. She had heard all the academic discussions between John and Laura Romig and Shrader. They always looked outward, beyond the day-to-day necessities of keeping people alive. Then there were the pragmatists. Bert Jenkins and Gus Gundersen engineered the systems for gardening and sanitation. Tiffany knew what environment was best for growing anything green, and Grandma Marty was raised within *Torah* and understood practices that preserved health. John, Laura, and Shrader worried about esoteric subjects like genetic diversity. How many different individuals would be necessary to make a gene pool that would be viable beyond a few generations? When Brittany and Anthony announced their marriage, the trio's discussion ignited again. Should reproduction be held by tightly bound social contracts like marriage? Multiple partners for each woman would stir the genetic mix; they argued in long discussions about the use of ritual prostitution among primitive peoples as a means of maintaining tribal fidelity in places where too close of interbreeding became a threat to tribal survival. The discussion stirred anger in the others. "We are just speaking theoretically," said John in defense of the topic, but academic ideals made little sense to mothers whose children were listening. When the Durands appeared, followed by Noah and Simonie, the scientific triumvirate smiled as if the initial problem were solved. Cathy was not so sure. What would they unveil next? These *academic discussions* usually distilled into a decision that she would have to enforce to insure some distant future that none of them would live to see.

Here in the darkness, it all came down on her. She wanted to be a real grandmother, one with the future she had always envisioned. She wanted to join with Anthony and Brittany in *oohing* and *aahing* over a first somersault on the living room carpet in the fragrant atmosphere of Thanksgiving turkey baking in a holiday oven. That was not to be the future, and never a fond memory.

She found herself alone in tears. The soft sounds of her own broken breaths sounded even more remote than the movement of someone outside the shelter. Cathy quickly wiped her cheeks and tried to clear her uncooperative voice.

"Yes?" she said aloud.

"I don't mean to barge in on you," came the soft reply of a woman's voice. It was Connie, Bill's usually silent wife.

"Connie, come in. Is anything wrong? Did Bill send you?"

In the darkness, Cathy could not possibly see the smile that crossed Connie's face. What she did see and smell was the glow of orange embers floating on a scorched wooden trowel.

"I thought that you might like a little light and heat," said the intruder, "maybe, some company?"

"I'm fine," lied Cathy.

"Bill wasn't so sure."

"He was busy with the baby, how would he..."

"In our world, he was a dentist, remember? He saw a lot of anxiety on the faces of people and learned to tell the difference between standard panic and the deeper kind." She gently blew on the embers that she had placed in a shallow bed of kindling. "He thought you might need someone to talk to."

A small flame leaped to life throwing shadows against the low walls.

"Your husband sees more than he ever lets on."

"Yes, he does." Connie turned her deep brown eyes toward Cathy who quickly shifted her gaze away. "Of course, you are not particularly hard to read right now," she added reaching toward Cathy's still moist cheek.

Cathy could not will the next droplet not to fall.

"I'm sorry," she said, "I shouldn't be so weak."

The space around them glimmered and Connie's broad smile appeared like a mother consoling an overwrought younger mother.

"You'd have trouble convincing me that you are weak. I'm just relieved to see you so human."

The words stopped a flood of emotion. Cathy looked at her friend.

"You've managed to hold us together for five years, and made everyone strong in the process. Just take care of your daughter, and trust the rest of us to do our part. We're pretty much on our own as it is. Except for the radar that you and Shrader seem to have, there's not much you can tell any of us anyway. Most of us are out of earshot, and so much depends on Noah and Simonie anyway."

"What do you think of them?" Cathy had never heard Connie express an opinion on any of the plans or forays at Keelhouse. She was more inclined to let her husband take the lead.

"Bill doesn't trust Simonie's hotheadedness," she began, "but I think he'll be different now that he has hope for the future."

"Hope?"

"Don't tell me, Sister, that you haven't seen what's going on." Cathy must have stared blankly because she went on. "Tish and Simonie! Surely you've seen the looks pass between them. I figured that's why you stationed Tish at *Twelve* where Simonie is to bring out the refugees."

"I didn't..." began Cathy.

"See, you even do the right thing by accident."

"Why didn't I notice..."

"You can't see everything. Let this grand plan go. Your daughter needs you. Sure as snow Anthony won't be much help with a new baby. He may be able to bring home a bearskin, but he's going to find out that little girl is tougher. What's her name?"

"I don't know," Cathy confessed. "They've kept everything a secret between them. I suppose when Shrader and I gave Royce his unique name, we left the door open for all sorts of innovation."

"All the more reason that you have to get in there and issue some grandmotherly wisdom. Anthony's so into hunting, he might suggest something like *Little Scat*."

"That would be the end of his sorry butt," said Cathy. The two women were laughing openly, and the tears on Cathy's face came from release rather than burden.

"In any case," offered Connie, "it's your time to be 'mother', not 'chief'. Bert and the others can handle all this other stuff, and Shrader won't let them stray too far."

"Thanks," said Cathy. "Do you think it's too soon for me to be the nosy mother-in-law?"

"Not at all."

20

"How far does our signal carry? Will they be able to figure where we are?"

"I don't think so," said Bert responding to the second of Laura's questions. "Damn, why did I do that? It was stupid."

"It was stupid," agreed Jeff Koenig.

"Now," began Laura, "there might not be too much damage if they couldn't focus on our signal."

"I don't think there's much chance of that, as long as we don't broadcast anymore," answered Jenkins. "I never suspected that anyone would still be listening after all these years. Cathy will need to know this as soon as possible." He reached over and turned the radio on to make sure the remote transmissions had stopped.

"They must be relatively near," Jeff added. "How far *can* a VHF signal carry?"

Bert felt relieved to be on the technical side of a question rather than the guilty side. "Maybe twenty miles or so if we were on the water with a mast-mounted antenna. We're up another forty feet, so maybe we're a hundred miles apart–just a guess."

"Come again, sailing vessel, your signal is weak, we couldn't understand your message." The radio crackled between the calm resonate syllables of a baritone voice.

"Could we get a fix on them?" asked Laura.

Bert powered up circuit boards that had not experienced an electron flow for years. "If they keep trying to hail us, yes."

"Come again, sailing vessel, we could not understand your message."

"They're southeast of us; that's about all I can determine," said Jenkins, "I'm really not calibrated for any kind of accuracy."

"That's good enough," said Laura. "I'm sure we could pull out the old charts and find a corresponding land mass. Probably Nova Scotia or Prince Edward Island."

"The bad news is that they now know we're here," said Koenig. "I just hope that they don't have search boats to send our way."

"Monitoring air waves is pretty benign," offered Jenkins. "But sending out an expedition to try and find us? I don't know about that. They'd have to calculate the cost. Firing up diesel-hungry engines would be pretty wasteful. If they have fuel reserves, they'd want to know that whatever they went out to get would be worth the getting."

"Maybe there's nothing sinister in this at all," said Laura. "We survived to this point; why shouldn't a lot of people have made it as well? Maybe people in the provinces and states are coming back."

"I suppose it's possible," said Jenkins, "but I'm not ready to stake my life on it."

"Neither am I, for that matter," said Laura. "I just felt that I needed to raise the possibility."

"If a recovery was widespread and governments were functioning, wouldn't there be more signs? We've never seen any indication of shipping," said Jenkins, "never even the sound of a jet engine or sight of a contrail."

"Could we defend ourselves, if we had to?" asked Jeff. The three went silent.

"Well, I need to get back to face a court martial called 'Cathy'."

"We'll be character witnesses," offered Laura.

"On the other hand, you are both witnesses for the prosecution. In any case, we're nearly done here. It still looks as though Gus's launch contraption still will work."

21

Shrader was glad to be alone as he turned his back on Keelhouse and moved northwest. The thawing that had seemed so remarkable two days ago had declared a respite, and snow was falling thick enough to cover the telltale waffle prints of his snowshoes. Tonight he would sleep in a snow bank, and tomorrow, if all went as planned, he would ride north on a snowmobile delivered by Noah. The thought of a motorized vehicle seemed so unwelcome compared to the healthy cry of the little girl Brittany and Anthony introduced as "Canada". The name was met with general approval, especially by Royce who was already planning a life curriculum for his little niece. Since, however, the baby showed no interest in beginning her lessons, he quickly retreated into the old quarter berth where he fell into a deep sleep. Only Shrader had heard or noted Royce's whispered promise of: "And I'll tell you all the stories I heard from Keeper."

If there were any human eyes on the vast land that lay ahead of him, they would have easily spotted his dark silhouette against a field of pure white. He had left the thinning spruce behind and was heading northward where he now knew a settlement to be, the one called Jordan which was home to Simonie and Noah. As much as he was grateful for the safe delivery of Brittany's daughter, he was glad to be away from the cacophony of voices that had become Keelhouse. He felt stretched by the details of this planned intervention, never mind that many of the details were his own. He had nearly forgotten the old world of his life with meetings and timetables and lines of accountability.

Here, in the snow, the noise could be shut out by the wind and swirling chill and only one voice told him to start piling snow into a mound. The snow beneath his feet was deep enough to accommodate a snow cave, but he wanted to raise it above the plain. When the mound was in place, he waited for it to settle and he could safely dig into it. As he hunkered inside the snow chamber, he ate from the packet of meat he had carried with him.

When the light was gone from the sky, the walls of his cave lost their translucence. Still, Shrader knew that his own breath was condensing into ice on the thickening shell of his shelter. *This is a peaceful place*, he thought as sleep took him.

His dreams were vivid, but not of snow. The sun was warm, high in the sky, and shielded only by green and yellow alternating panels sewn into a Dacron sail that ballooned out over the bow pulpit of a sailboat.

This was no night terror, but a reminder of bright light throwing stars over the ripples of wind on water. He recognized the sail. It was the spinnaker that lived in a light blue sail bag stuffed in the starboard quarter berth of *Strider*. If *Strider* was under sail, the dream was memory, not omen. The water around them would be fresh, and the *them* would be he and Lynn. She would be sunning herself on the foredeck or coming up the companionway steps, but Shrader was afraid to look. That world had vanished in a flash of molten rock, and had forced every one of his companions to renounce all memory of schools and friends, of careers and possessions, of loves and hates. Keelhouse was the world of their existence, and it helped to relegate older memory to a black hole of irretrievable loss and forgetfulness. Here in his dreams, the black hole seemed to defy gravity and spewed a single happy moment. He would look.

The companionway was empty; she wasn't below deck. He then straightened to look over the cabin top toward the bow where he fully expected to see a raised knee above the wide brim of a straw hat. It would be Lynn, reading a paperback in the comforting warmth of the sun. But there was no woman, and the rigging was all wrong. Shrader broke into panic, "Lynn," he called in his now fitful sleep. He was awakened by a cold spray that choked his breath. It was salty.

22

"Canada is perfect." There was no two-mindedness in Cathy's thoughts or words. Five years earlier, she had cradled Royce in her arms, but this was a grandchild. Somehow it seemed the normal progression of life. Royce was born on the divide between two worlds. Canada would be a grandchild, and the herald of a new generation.

She felt suddenly free. A private life was never hers at Keelhouse. She had become a public person; everyone had. There was little that she could point to as her personal property. Even Shrader and Royce were more a part of a public circle than the others. In spite of the close quarters, couples were still couples. Tish Barker was the widowed exception; she seemed to be losing more as her children explored the rather limited possibilities of their own adult relationships. The freedom she now felt was Connie's gift, a simple permission to step out of the role of tribal leader and become something as normal and ordinary as a grandmother.

The Ragnis also came closer. Anthony's parents had always stood estranged from both Shrader and the reasoned caution of those whose leadership prevailed. Now, they were family, sharing the watery-eyed delight of a nearly naked baby nestled snugly in the warm fur of a polar bear. At this moment, the events on the coast at *Major Blunder* were unknown. The supply teams were on their way to the outposts, and the planned drama, more like a sleight-of-hand, that was about to take place near the great herd, were dim ideas that fell into the recesses of repressed memory. The baby, on the other hand, was real and, for the moment, making little sucking movements with her lips.

"I think she wants you," said Cathy handing the tiny package to Brittany, who seemed as confused as a new mother who has yet to learn the subtleties of baby-speak that comes without red faces or cries. "She wants to be nursed... see her mouth moving?"

Brittany understood, and awkwardly adjusted the baby into position. Rhonda, Anthony's mother, helped her sit up to give more access to the breast. Cathy found herself in a small moment that seemed outside time. She was looking at the people in front of her as though they were in a picture on a wall and she was the unphotographed observer looking at some documentary display of a past long-gone. She understood that Canada was the first to graft the politics of Keelhouse into a family tree; everything would be different.

The baby had no trouble drawing milk from her mother's breast, and a creamy globule sat in the corner of the little mouth so tightly clinging.

"She's strong," observed Cathy.

"Of course she is," answered Brittany, "her father is a great hunter."

"And her grandmother is the leader of a people," added Rhonda in what sounded more like a credo than an observation.

"Right now, I'm just a proud grandmother like you," said Cathy smiling. The two women's eyes met, maybe for the first time. And, they felt the truth of the words. Any other claim of authority would have sounded hollow, and none were made or argued.

23

The sound of Noah's approach on the snowmobile was audible long before Shrader heard it. His focus was elsewhere as he lay curled up in his snow cave. His normal morning ritual would be to watch the sun come over the sea. This day, however, the water was beyond the horizon of this treeless open landscape.

He was a creature of the sea with legs that anchored him to an increasingly alien terrain. Unconsciously, he called to Keeper and, behind closed eyelids, saw the emerging high dorsal fin breaking between the crests of the waves.

"Your little pup keeps calling to me, too," said the whale. Shrader knew that she was referring to Royce who seemed to have inherited his sensitivity to voices out of the deep.

"I know," he answered, "but he's still a pup and doesn't always fully understand the things you say."

"But it is that way between us. You tell me that it is cold, but I tell you it is warming and the cold water is now flowing very deep."

Shrader's mind went to charts that had been a part of an older world, charts of the Atlantic currents that created a clockwise rotation that allowed movement east and west between the continents. Sailors referred to it as the "milk run" which ran toward Europe at the northern loop and west from Africa at the southern circle-back.

"Keeper," began Marks, "are there boats on the water?"

The thoughts of the whale went silent for several heart beats, and Shrader could sense uneasiness. "Only near the shores," came the reply, "small men with sticks and guns who try and kill us."

The thoughts were obviously painful, and Shrader let silence linger. Long ago he had stopped apologizing for the excesses of his species. Perhaps the hunting of whales in coastal waters was a symptom of desperation. Orcas had saved his and Cathy's lives, however, and the idea of taking them for food felt like cannibalism. Still, the caribou, bears, and fur seals had become staples of the Keelhouse diet, and he thought nothing unusual about that.

"You are moving north in our direction," he said changing the subject.

"Yes, the waters are opening and we are following the ice shelf."

Shrader understood the ways of Keeper and her pod. They were mammal hunters who, like his own people, ate from the harvest of the seals. He also knew that Keeper was implying that other pods were heading in more of an easterly direction and following schools of herring. "It will be good to see you again, Brother." Of course Keeper, like all pod leaders was female, but the subtleties of politically correct language did not function well between two who understood only a common kinship and not the divisions that seemed to be a vestige of human culture.

He was fairly certain that Keeper was his own age, about fifty, but there were no standard markers for them to compare. Humans relied on pivotal events that marked the calendar. Events like birthdays, graduations, and legal drinking age no longer made any sense as the world had changed. Age now was a product of functionality, and Gus Gundersen was, at times, as young as Anthony. He knew that wouldn't last, but Keelhouse had become strong enough to care for the weak and would not have to resort to a remark Keeper once made. It had sounded like a proverb, a saying of orca wisdom when Shrader first heard it:

When I cannot swim with the pod, I will seek my rest on the shore of the high tide.

Even at the time, it did not feel morbid or menacing, but Marks took the meaning, and thought about the many hypotheticals that could transform it into reality through age, infirmity, or injury.

The buzzing was much louder now, and Shrader knew that his morning ritual was over. He crawled out of the snow cave and was immediately blinded by the snow-reflected light. Fumbling for the leather straps of his eyewear, he climbed the snowy hillock and lifted his arms in the direction of the sound, waving at a figure that he could not fully recognize at that distance. The driver of the snowmobile turned in his direction. Shrader slid back into his snow shelter and retrieved his pack and rifle.

The distinctive noise which announced the approach of the sled was the first indication that the plan was running its course. But how could Shrader know if the snowmobile was being driven by Noah? Shrader adjusted his goggles and saw that there was no rifle barrel protruding over the shoulder of the operator. That was a good sign.

"Did everything go as expected?" shouted Marks over the drone of the motor.

Noah did not respond immediately, and Shrader didn't know whether it was his reticent spirit or misgivings. "They weren't sure I could be trusted," he said finally.

Shrader looked at the man with an intensity which demanded more explanation.

"It wasn't anything that was said," Noah continued, "they told me to take one of the snowmobiles and go back to the village. They said that I should bring whatever dogs and sleds I could and the hunters' wives to drive them."

"The wives?"

"Yes, I don't pretend to understand their plan, but I'd guess they're backing up their pieces by having hostages that the men would respect if they're going to lie in ambush."

"Which means they are wary of us," added Shrader. "That's good."

"Good?"

"They expect an attack rather than a retreat. If they wait until they determine it's safe to move, we'll have more time."

"That's true enough, but what will they do when they find we've flown?"

"I'd leave a bear a way to run," said Marks. "An animal that is forced to stand and fight is more dangerous than one with options. You know that."

"I do," said Inuk. "I also know that they don't think like you. They believe in force."

"But I am thinking like them," offered Shrader.

"How?"

"They are hunters and I am thinking like a hunter. They are being herded into the net on the edge of the forest. They have not yet learned to think as prey."

The immediate task before the two was how to get Noah to a rendezvous with the team from Keelhouse which was moving north. They were placing supplies along the route to become the escape conduit for the women and children on their way south. They now had a snowmobile, but a limited supply of gasoline. Noah was confident the fuel would be adequate to make it to Jordan, but just barely. In the end, the two decided to take a direct path toward the village and part company at a point where Noah could strike eastward to join the others moving along the coast.

Shrader feared more for Noah than for himself. They had brought enough food-stuffs for the two of them, and they distributed everything into two packs, the larger going onto Noah's back. Coordinating movement was crucial, and ultimately, the whole plan rested on Noah's timely linkup with others who were also on the move.

"Are you confident about the rendezvous?" said Marks nervously.

"I am one of *the People*," Noah remarked in a tone that could not be argued with.

"You are," answered Shrader, "but my people are not, and I'm not so sure they could always find their way."

"Simonie and I know the signs. From this direction, I look for three standing stones on a pinnacle that marks the direction to the sea and if you don't watch your footing, you'll tumble over the ridge that will hide the company as they move north."

"*Inuksuk?*" said Shrader.

Noah smiled at his friend. "You understand."

Shrader kept track of Noah's progress along the horizon until his dot became the mere shadow of a snow dune. He spent his time shoring up the snow cave he had hurriedly built the day before. He would have another night here to give time for Noah's reunion and the rescue company to get into their final position for the secret assault. He had given up the idea of focusing on the details of a scenario that might not happen as imagined. Instead, he turned his mind to feeling the place. He sensed the cold, and heard the sound of his own breath merge into the stream of the wind. These hours, or were they moments, were better than sleep to Shrader.

When ego brought thought to consciousness, he was in the snow shelter and hungry. In the darkness he fumbled among the food stores for a bite of meat. He apologized to his Brother Bear, and ate. The pitch black of the tiny space pulsed in his mind, but there was another light calling from outside. He pulled himself out into the night where the green glow of the aurora borealis awakened words almost forgotten:

> You fearful saints, fresh courage take;
> the clouds you so much dread
> are big with mercy, and shall break
> with blessings on your head.

He had sung those words many times before, but the most memorable time was five years earlier in the nightmare of the Saint Lawrence. They had come through a sea of destruction to a place that gave them life. What mercy would come from this night? Would it be the fragile and tentative mercy that he and Cathy hoped for five murderous thugs? Or, would it be the mercy of delayed justice becoming a offering to Simonie's grief? Keeper's sense of ethics was not so highly nuanced. "Sharks hunt and kill, it is their way," he told Shrader, "but they do not swim among the pod."

The old world of philosophy came back in a rush. There were clans in this new age, and they would be governed by the old rules of power. Maybe the egalitarian fairness of their new life was about to end forever. What mercy would come of that?

24

Keelhouse felt empty after Cathy sent Anthony and Vince northward to join the others in establishing the supply gauntlet for a swift exodus from the Inuit village. She was pleased by the protest of the new father. Somehow the passion for adventure had been reduced by the soft desire to hold a child. In time, and with the coaxing of his father, the two set out to intercept weary and unarmed refugees who may be pursued by armed bullies.

Sodus seemed the most disturbed by the turn of events. Even in his napping position, his hyper-vigilance showed itself with a jerk of the head at every sound. It was a nervousness that came of a broken routine. His function in life was to be the perpetual greeter of his humans, but not many were near at hand. Marty and Gus were handling the daily cooking and fire tending chores for Brittany, Rhonda, and Cathy who were focusing on the new baby. Royce was somewhere. Ben Romig and Sandi Koenig grudgingly accepted the task of watching Alain and Émilie while

their older peers were setting up the outpost camps for some undefined adventure.

As lost as she was in grandmothering, Cathy was beginning
to be anxious for the return of Jeff, Bert, and Laura who had gone
to inspect and power up *Major Blunder* which was still in her
launching berth along the coast. Some of her unease came from
Shrader's warning about the frazil ice that had washed down
along the watercourse that ran to the south. The alternating early
melt and freeze had created an ice river which would block the
trio's easy return. If they recognized the danger of the slushy ice,
now disguised as snowpack, they would avoid the path they had
taken out, and stay high on the ridge. By doing so, they would
cross above the ice melt and skirt the cascade which showered
the ravine in crystal shards.

"They know to look for ice there," she consoled herself.

"What?" asked Brittany.

"Just thinking out loud, Baby," she said.

Her daughter laughed. "Are you still allowed to call me 'Baby'?"

"Old habits! My mother used to call me that, too. Canada will
probably be next."

"I suppose so," agreed Brittany. "What were you talking
about—just now, to yourself?"

"Just that Shrader told me that the mountain is throwing off
a lot of ice right now, and the three that went out to the boat are
due back soon."

"They'll know," assured Brittany. With tiny sucking sounds,
the newborn began to wriggle against her.

"I think she's hungry," said Cathy.

"Are you hungry again, Baby?" said Brittany and the automatic words caught them both in laughter.

25

"That is one tough Lady," observed Bert as he lowered his
binoculars.

"What's that?" said Jeff as he turned to follow Jenkins' gaze down from the heights and to the small inlet that sheltered Keelhouse. "Oh, I see."

What he saw was a sailboat at anchor floating amidst the ice floe of the thawing water. The deep blue hull of *Dream Dancer* had survived yet another winter's freeze.

"Ragni is going to be bragging again," said Bert.

"And complaining," said Laura who had joined them to see what had drawn the attention of her companions. "It still looks like a boat," she continued, "but it's all façade."

"Well, he's still bitter that his boat is the one we left in the water after we did so much work to save mine." With this Bert turned toward *Major Blunder* which was sitting high and dry on its two keels.

"It's an argument of passion," offered Romig. "At some level he understands the logic of what we've done; it's just that it looks so perfect sitting there when the ice melts off. Forget that everything has been stripped out of it, the steering cables snapped two years ago, and the rudder dropped into the bay soon after."

"Still, it's local ambience," offered Koenig with a grin sliding sideways across his face. "If we ever start to draw tourists, you can bet it'll be in the background of every postcard that gets sent home."

"Are we expecting tourists soon?" Laura asked glancing at Bert Jenkins.

"They can't have gotten a reading of our location," he protested. "We have a better fix on them than they do on us... Yes, I will report my stupidity when we get back," he added feeling the unvocalized reprimand.

The damp air carried the coldness into their bones as they stood on the ridge and looked out over the rocky coast which stood at the conjunction of water, earth, and sky.

"With all the freezing and thawing, we might have trouble at the lower crossing in the valley." Laura and Jeff understood Bert's concern.

"You're thinking of the ice off the upper falls," said Koenig.

"Exactly," said Jenkins. "If we take the direct route and hit a field flooded with ice shards off the escarpment, we'll have to backtrack, and it'll take longer than just assuming bad ice conditions."

"But if there's not enough ice to clog the gorge, the upper route will be that much longer than the straight path," offered Laura.

"True, but we know cause and effect. I'd guess there's a problem and we should bet on the trail along the ridge."

"What do you think, Jeff?" asked Romig.

"Bert's probably right on this one."

Laura turned toward Jenkins. "You're not just stalling to put off facing Cathy, are you?"

"Mostly *no*, but that, too." The three laughed, but the sound was carried off by a gust of cold air.

26

It would have been easier for Noah and Shrader to take the snowmobile across the tundra to meet with Simonie, Tish, and the others who were just a few miles to the east. The problem was the fuel supply. There was enough gasoline for a direct approach, but the reserves were too meager to squeeze out the extra miles which would have been necessary for circling around and coming in with the others. The big problem for Shrader was coordinating his grand entrance with the apprearance of the others. He was slated to arrive *after* Noah and Simonie had pulled away the two guards who would demand an explanation of both Simonie's departure from the camp and his willing return. Marks would also have to allow time for Tish to get into the compound among the women and children to alert them and gather what they could for an impromptu exodus.

His first difficulty was the sound of the engine. Sound traveled too well for the buzzing signature of this motor to be confused with anything native to the tundra. Before he would be able to see the settlement, his presence would be heralded by the trumpeting exhaust. His second was knowing how close he could come to the camp before he would be too close! He had never been this far north, and any recognition of the guiding landmarks, such as they were, was known only through the sparse words of Noah. In the end, he decided to err on the side of caution and left the snowmobile sooner rather than later when he went in to scout out the enclave.

By the clock, the hour was not late, but the dimming world distorted time and the distance involved. Marks killed the engine on the snowmachine and took particular notice of where it sat in the barren landscape. He needed to come straight back to the sled. After the others were in place, the droning hum would become a cover for his subterfuge. The sky turned to being his friend by providing starlight enough to walk for nearly an hour before geometric shadows along the horizon told him that he was getting close. The shapes were the roofs of houses, and only one seemed alive with the harsh white glow of a fluorescent light.

That's where they are, thought Shrader. He could only guess what that meant. Did they always burn electric lights? He doubted that such extravagance could be afforded on an ordinary basis. A motorized generator would use too much precious fuel, a wind generator would require storage batteries that would, after five years, be nearing the end of their useful life. If an electric light was on, something was happening. Where were Simonie and Noah?

The lighted window was his best clue. His suspicion was confirmed when a figure appeared at the window. It was Noah, or Noah's back as he paced inside the room. They were already there. The stage was set.

Shrader had to trust that all the others were at their assigned places. Barker was in one of the other houses, talking quietly in the dark to strangers who had no reason to accept her words other than the fact that Noah and Simonie had pushed her toward them as they moved to meet the two guards.

Shrader rued his caution. Had he ridden the sled directly into the village, he could be drawing out the two and cutting short the interrogation that had to be going on. *Maybe not*, he thought. *I might have arrived too early, drawing out one of the guards while the other watched, armed and alone, from a window.* It was true. He needed Inuit in the room when the motor called one or both of the men to the door. It was also true, that he had a second long walk before him. The steps from the snowmachine now had to be retraced, and every delay lengthened the danger for those who were now on the inside. He quickly surveyed the juxtaposition of the buildings and the open space that would become the place for the face-off.

Once away from the lighted window, his eyes adjusted to the return path. On his earlier trip, he was walking with his face into the wind, a fact that helped muffle the sound of his approach. Now, the wind was at his back and lightened his step. It had taken him nearly forty-five minutes to cover the two miles over the untracked snow, but only a half hour to retrace the path.

The snowmachine fired immediately and Shrader moved quickly toward the compound. As defense against recklessness, he now tried to calm himself and looked to the dim horizon as an antidote to the race of wind and motor. He could not see himself in this world of carbon fume, but if he had, he would not have recognized his own silhouette as he stopped the noisy engine and dismounted. He fought every impulse to panic. The fact was that, at any moment, an armed man would appear in a doorway, and the rifle he had inconveniently strapped to his back would be useless unless he could casually shed it in the manner of a man loosening his tie after a long day in a suit.

A shaft of dim fluorescent light made a rectangle on the snow in front of the sled. Shrader turned toward the snowmobile as if tending to some maintenance detail. He tried to sense the other man, but there were too many noises in his head and he felt like he was in a room full of people, all confused, all looking for an exit. He knew from Noah and Simonie that this man would be wearing a sidearm. Was it in a holster or a hand? In either case, Shrader was giving him his back. He reached back to peel his rifle over his head. He wanted it to look like he was relieving an aching back rather than drawing a weapon. He counted his heartbeats, one, two, three...

"Tomstock, is that you?" came a strange voice.

He ducked his head under the elevated strap and brought the raised gun down slowly to where it cradled gently in his right arm. Evidently, he looked like someone called "Tomstock." How would Tomstock gesture a greeting? How would he turn? That's what Marks had to do now. He had to turn as though it was as natural as pulling back his hood to meet the face of a friend. He counted his heartbeats, one, two, three...

27

At Keelhouse, Canada was fussing in Cathy's arms. She had held her own children and was always able to calm them by holding them tight and swaying side to side.

"Shoo-shoo-shoo," she breathed quietly into the baby's face. The infant was not impressed, and Cathy felt her own frustration mounting as she realized the problem.

"Babies can sense a person's mood," she said handing the small bundle to Rhonda, who welcomed another turn at being an overprotective grandmother. The baby settled down immediately. "I didn't think she was hungry," Cathy added. "She must feel my tension."

"What do you have to be tense about, Mom?" asked Brittany.

"Oh, nothing," said Rhonda in a low voice that wouldn't disturb a tiny, wrinkle-faced bundle. "Her daughter just delivered an angel, she has almost everybody else out on some mission to trap men with guns, and who knows where Royce is?"

"Besides that, I mean," said Brittany. The three laughed in very low decibels.

"I wish it sounded like a more normal day, when you put it that way," answered Cathy. "Canada is the only one who seems to think that I have a problem. She's your daughter, Britt, and you're going to be spending a lifetime trying to figure out her moods."

"Is that what you did with me?"

"Not always that well, Baby. But I think I'd better listen to her." With that Cathy, leaned over and kissed her daughter then gently stroked the baby's smooth fontanel. "She is so beautiful," she said catching a glimpse of Rhonda's watery brown eyes. "Maybe tomorrow we can go to the mall and pick up some onesies," she said to her counterpart, referring to a life and a world long gone. A second laugh followed, and Cathy announced, "I think I'd better check on Royce."

Though such things are a parent's universal excuse, but she was not really worrying about Royce when she stepped down into the longhouse. In fact, she spotted him immediately. At times it was hard to think of him as a little boy who was not all that far out of the toddler stage, but this was not one of those times. He had crashed early and was asleep on a pile of soft hides. At that moment, he was her angel and she crawled in next to his small sleeping form.

She looked at him for a moment as dread returned. Something was bothering her, but she couldn't name it. *Is this the way Shrader feels all the time?* she wondered, and *where is he now?*

"He's okay, Mommy," said a small voice at her side. Cathy turned. Royce was sleeping quietly.

28

Shrader's slow count to three ended as he pivoted slowly in a clockwise direction, the barrel of the rifle moving like the sweeping second hand that would suddenly stop on the darkened shadow that spoke to him from the half-open door of the house. In the old world of his life, he had never really handled a gun other than a pea-shooter at the county fair when he was a boy. At Keelhouse he had become more proficient with a flint point than a bullet, but here he was, a stand-in for the sake of mercy. Simonie would have fired by now, but Marks stood with ambivalence with all the words of the warnings ringing in his brain. *If you point a gun at an armed intruder, you'd better be the one who fires first* was the admonition that came to mind.

His paralysis, however, would not cost him. The entrance of the sled had created the right illusion, and the shadow had not yet drawn a weapon.

"Who are you?" said the shape, and Marks knew that the *Tomstock* assumption no longer held. Before he could answer, an explosion of activity came from inside the house and the stranger's head turned just in time to see his own partner flying through the doorway like a two hundred pound sack of potatoes. The collision was spectacular, if not graceful, and two bodies flew off the stoop and landed near Shrader's mukluked feet. Simonie and Noah were swiftly behind the two prostrate shapes who, by now, were staring into a muzzle and were beginning to understand their plight.

The internal argument in his head was pushed away in favor of a pithy aside. "Who am I? I am the man who just saved your life. Simonie and Noah would have preferred to see you dead."

The strangers knew the statement to be true, and that death would likely be a sentence handed down by other courts, even those higher than vigilante. They did not contest a ready surrender. In an instant their sidearms were in Inuit hands, and the two were sitting out of diving reach on the frozen ground. Marks looked at Simonie as if reminding him of a difficult promise. Simonie nodded. He kept his word, and stepped down from his thoughts of revenge.

Shrader raised his rifle in the air and casually fired a round into the ladle of the Big Dipper. The report was sharp and vibrant. "Just so you know that we are not alone," he said cryptically. Within the minute, a deeper, twelve-gauge blast came from beyond the line of houses. A skyward trail of sparks became a red glow shining like a dwarf star. It was, of course, an expired emergency flare from the flotilla that had become Keelhouse. Shrader felt a cynical wave of pleasure at the sight. It confirmed both the long held suspicion of expiration dates and the decision to keep the old pyrotechnics in storage.

"There are more than three of us," he continued. "The people you have been holding are now armed. I could ask them to come out to show you, but I suggest that you stay close to me."

"There are more of us, too," said one of the men. Second gave him a *shut-up* look.

One snake still thinks it still has venom, thought Shrader. "And I rode in on one of their sleds," he said aloud. For emphasis, he turned the muzzle of his gun toward the dark shape of the snowmobile and squeezed. As soon as he had done so, he regretted it. *Suppose the damn thing explodes*, he thought, or *Tish shoots another flare, or everyone comes out of the houses?* Fortunately, none of those things happened, but the usability of that snowmobile as an escape hatch was suddenly and seriously in doubt.

"I would not expect help from the other three; they have problems of their own right now," he said with all the false bravado he could muster. Relief came only when Anthony and Vince stepped into the scene. "Go to your friends," said Marks to Noah and Simonie. They understood, but as they left they held on to the weapons that they had taken in the scuffle.

If the two on the ground thought Shrader's position weakened, their thinking changed with a better view of six-foot-four Vince Ragni and his Winchester M70. If they had known, they would have feared more the new father with his compound bow and quicker reflexes.

"Inside," said Shrader. "You have no friends in this village. We're your best... no, we're your only bet, so no games."

29

Until Canada was born, Royce had been the youngest person at Keelhouse. Though he knew Cathy and Shrader to be his mother and father, all ordinary boundaries were twisted by an extended family of more than thirty who lived and breathed the same air of the longhouse. Instead of being the only child of doting parents, he was more like the thirteenth born into a household of aunts, uncles, and siblings who felt no hesitation in alternately reprimanding or ignoring his comings and goings. Of late, *ignoring* was more in fashion as it became clear that Royce shared the peculiarities of his father, and, though he said he was five, he was really four-and-a-half, going on fifty.

When Shrader left him, he was standing on one of the high places on the edge of the escarpment that was the demarcation between that plateau of the wooded lands and the bay that protected Keelhouse. Now that his father was away on some errand, Royce made the same pilgrimage to the place each day. Mimicking his father was, at first, a form of play for a boy who had no contemporaries. With the appearance of the Durands all that had changed, but only on the surface. Alain was his age, but he had his sister as a playmate. By then, Royce had an interior world which would not permit the inclusion of new friends. Now in the confusion of some large adventure to the north and the birth of Canada, he could slip into that world to hear the stories that Keeper told. This was the voice he missed, a voice that had become all too silent in recent days. The morning greeted him on the heights, and he listened through the ranges of silence until a sound turned him westward. It was a strange sound, more of a buzzing than a call, and at a distance he saw a fast moving silhouette like two men riding low to the ground on a dark shape. If it was an animal, its legs were very short and churning up an arc of snow that drifted back over its snaking footprints.

They *were* men, and they saw Royce as he turned and stood watching their approach. The animal slowed with a lower pitch in its voice. It was shiny like a wet fur seal, but Royce realized that it was fiberglass like the sides of Keelhouse, and not alive at all. The man seated in the second place drew a strap over his head and pulled a rifle from his back. Royce saw the morning light flash from the scope. He quickly looked right and left to see if some game animal was standing near him on the heights. The first man pointed his direction and pushed aside the gun's muzzle. His partner tucked the rifle away across the seat in front of him. The sled turned and started to crawl slowly toward Royce's position. He recognized it as a sled because now he could clearly see that the front paws of the beast were runners bouncing over the snow. He started walking downhill toward their approach.

The snowmobile's original course had given Royce a momentary start. Had the two men continued in their first direction, they would have intersected the watercourse that, in a few hundred yards, became the cascade that rained frazil ice into the gorge beyond the escarpment. Today the flow was hidden under a layer of blowing snow and a plate of thin ice born of the nighttime cold. Beneath that skim coat of glass, however, was a

SHRADER MARKS & KEELHOUSE

moving flow which would accelerate into a flood as the thaw deepened.

Royce waved his arms in greeting. These men were hunters, but he wondered if they had ever heard of anyone as clever as Vuhar who had been able to turn himself into a seal. Anthony had managed the trick, but would these new people figure out the riddle?

30

The morning brought a flood of confusion that vacillated between outrage and release, and Shrader found that the only way to keep any semblance of order was to sequester the two prisoners, well away from the villagers, who crowded into a room that had become a communal dining hall. Keeping any internal psychic order was out of the question. The least aggressive of Noah's people simply wanted to spit on Mallory and Doncaster, the two men he had *met* the evening before.

He found *them* difficult to read, and he could not focus on anyone. This is where, in the normal pattern of Keelhouse, Cathy would step in and Shrader would step out to some place of solitude where he could listen to more distant voices. The voices in this camp were only loud, accusing, and angry. In a sort of momentary flashback, he saw Royce beside him in the sunrise, and then the image was gone, and he was back to separating the sheep from the goats.

Mallory and Doncaster were the easiest to cut out of the flock. They willingly went to a small room to sit with Vince and Anthony or, when their shift ended, Tish and Cameron. In all, they were tightlipped about their years in the village, but seemed disinterested in any scheme to escape their captors and rush into the larger adjoining room where the victims of their leadership sat with Shrader, Simonie, and Noah.

When the grand plan was discussed at Keelhouse, the obvious strategy was to evacuate people to the outposts that formed the perimeter of the settlement. Food and shelter had already been supplied, but food and shelter were also at hand in the village.

The easy capture of the two by Noah and Simonie (who had appeared to have come back from the dead) made the potential return of the other three more seem benign. Maybe, even safer than leaving Jordan for an expedition over the tundra to a new place controlled by strangers.

"These are all good people," said Noah, but everyone looked to Simonie for corroboration.

"They are," he agreed. "They follow a *Mishtapeu*," he added whispering and nodding toward Shrader. At the moment, Shrader's fidgety confusion brought no merit to the argument. Vince radiated a more imposing aura, but he didn't say much and was relegated to guarding prisoners.

In the end, three groups were established with only a few wavering between options. The first group would stay in their homes and defend against the three when and if they attempted a return. Noah was to stay behind and Cameron, who had shared stories with Inuit at Rockledge, agreed to stay as well.

A second group was composed of those whose trauma could only be healed by some respite from the village. It was clear that the sudden events of the night before initiated a cascade of pent-up emotion. Some, who had borne their captivity well, were abruptly overpowered with anger, grief, and a powerful feeling of violation. Their lives and their space seemed poisoned by memories too recent to ignore. These were the ones who elected to take to the unknown adventure south, and they were emboldened when it was clear that Simonie would lead them. Tish, a soft-spoken woman, would go with him. She was seen as a strong person. Though none knew her personal story, she was the brave woman who ventured into the camp with Noah and Simonie. She sat with the others in the darkness, raising the hope of release, and, at the correct time, fired the signal flare that sealed the capture.

The third group was also the most problematic. It was the prisoner escort detail which consisted of the Ragnis, Marks, and the two who, at the moment seemed docile enough, but had tried to turn venomous the night before. They could not be trusted on the open tundra. This was particularly true if they took the path that Shrader had taken which would lead them to the place of the hunt and potentially into rifle range of their allies. No, it seemed clear to Marks that the only reasonable path lay to the east along the way that had been fortified by teams from Keelhouse and followed by Barker and the others.

The only problem was related to timing. Traveling with the captives among those already traumatized was out of the question. Shrader would either have to set out first and put enough real estate between them and the others to keep everyone separated, or delay leaving and return last to Keelhouse. No one was willing to step up to vouch for the character of Mallory and Doncaster. Clearly, they were not seen as men of honor who would be above making their own plans to escape, including overpowering escorts and waiting in ambush for a fresh group of hostages following close behind.

The best plan was the second, the one Shrader hated the most. It was to sit and wait. He would wait with the others while a disorganized group got ready to move. Wait while a slow-moving semi-hysterical throng set a crawling pace toward uncertainty. Long hours would have to pass before the trailing group could begin without fear of overtaking the others.

Marks settled his anxiety with the memory of Noah's words at the snow shelter. In his directions, he told Shrader that *Inuksuk* would guide the way. For Marks, that meant they would come near the coast. The prospect of hearing and smelling and feeling the ocean gave him hope, the hope of being alone with his thoughts and hearing the voices of the earth.

31

"What is that called?" asked Royce, pointing to the black sled with its leggy front runners and rear track that extended on the underside like an insect's abdomen. The question confused the two riders almost as much as the appearance of such a young boy so obviously alone. They looked nervously for some adult to mount up like a bear to defend its cub.

"It's a snowmobile. Are you out here alone?"

"It moves fast," said Royce whose interest in the fiberglass and steel completely drowned out the second question.

"Do you live around here?" asked the man seated in the second position. He dismounted, taking with him the rifle that he had laid across the seat. He threw it back over his shoulder.

"I live at Keelhouse," offered Royce with a nod toward the path that paralleled the more deeply cut ravine which had become a trough of white frazil ice.

"Would you like a ride?" asked the driver.

Royce had learned to respect the size of an animal and was not sure that this one should be approached until better known.

"*Whaleman* worried that there were bad men nearby." The words crossed into Royce's consciousness and broke a long silenced conversation.

"Keeper!"

The two men looked at each other, not understanding Royce's excited response.

"You say you live down that way," spoke the driver, pointing toward what looked to be a clean, flat snowpack. "We'll just take a short ride; just a little loop around down there and come right back here. You can point to that house you talked about."

"I'm not allowed to go that way."

"It'll be fine," said the driver, gunning the engine, and to prove his point, he left his companion standing and pointed the sled toward the open snow. He had not gone more than twenty yards when the snow appeared to swallow him like some gaping maw that closed its white lips over him and sucked him down.

"What the..." began his partner. He started to run toward the vanishing point.

"No!" shouted Royce with an urgency that cut the man short. "It's ice!"

In a moment a head bobbed up from the icy quagmire. The stranger moved toward it, but with caution, carefully testing each foot before placing it down in front of him. He understood when he reached the nearly invisible seam between the snow and the pond of frazil ice.

"I'll get some help," said Royce taking off running in the direction of a higher path.

32

When Cathy laid down next to Royce, she had intended only a short powernap and then a return to grandmother duty in the upper chamber. Several times during the night she was awakened by soft cries from above, but each time the whimpers transitioned into sucking noises. Brittany was doing well, and Cathy had regained the super hearing of a new mother. Royce, on the other hand, seemed oblivious to the voice of his niece. Cathy's sleep was fitful, and she envied the deep quiet that enveloped his small body.

Her sense of restlessness must have left her in the early morning because she was surprised to find Royce gone when she awoke. It was not the sound of the baby that brought her back to life; it was the insistent barking of Sodus. Something was going on outside the longhouse.

"Someone was swept into the floc!" It was Gundersen calling from just outside the entrance well. "Cathy, do you hear me?"

"Who is it?"

"Don't know, Royce didn't know either. I'm headed up the gorge." Cathy could hear the final words drifting away as Gus began to move. She pulled on a parka and retied her foot coverings, and was in sight of Gus before he had reached the scene. It was Cathy's first recognition that Gus was getting old. He was carrying a large coil of line which he was shifting between his right and left shoulders. Royce, even with his shorter legs, was running uphill fifty feet ahead.

"Let me help with that," said Cathy taking the rope. Gus didn't protest. *How old is he*, she wondered. *Seventy-five? Eighty?*

Gundersen didn't respond with his normal bravado. "Thanks," he said. "I'll be right there; I just need to catch my breath." Cathy hugged the bundle against her chest and began to run to catch up with Royce. She caught him just beyond a cluster of spruce. Here the view opened, and she could see the pooled ice with four figures gesturing frantically at something in the water.

Three of the figures were recognizable. They were Bert, Jeff, and Laura pulling the skin-covered sledge they had used to drag the batteries back to *Major Blunder*. The fourth figure had a rifle and seemed to be stepping back from the approaching trio.

"Pearson!" shouted Jenkins as he saw Cathy's approach. "Good, you brought rope! We'll need it! We can float out on the sled, but we'll need to have some way of pulling it back."

"The rope was Gus' idea; he's coming along behind." The stranger looked back along the path beyond Cathy.

"How many of you are there?" he asked with a tone that modulated between curiosity and anxiety.

"Royce came and sounded the alarm," offered Cathy ignoring the question.

"The little boy?" asked the man, but his desire for information was swept aside by the body in the icy pool.

"We'll use the coracle to get out there," explained Bert. "Somebody will have to be in it to steer and grab hold of him. We'll tie on the rope and use it to pull them back once he has a grip. The line will have to be around the person in the boat. That way, if it tips, we'll get him back and not just an empty boat."

"Be sure to thank John," said Cathy to Laura. Everyone but the stranger understood the cryptic remark. John Romig built all the prototype sleds with the insistence that they also double as boats in the event that anyone fell through the ice.

Bert used a bowline to secure a loop at the end of the line. Without asking, Jeff Koenig slipped it over his head and shoulders and clamped it under his armpits. By now, Gus had joined the effort, immediately understanding the plan. "You're going to have to use your hands to paddle and pull yourself through that crap," he said.

"I know," said Jeff. "It would be nice to have something dry to put on when you pull me back."

"Do you have a kit in the sled?" asked Cathy referring to the extra pelts and supplies that Grandma Marty demanded as standard equipment on any foray into the bush.

"Always," said Jenkins, "lie down in the sled, Jeff. Keep your body weight low and wedge yourself in just in case it tries to flip."

"You're not helping my confidence." But Koenig did not hesitate to do exactly that. Bert, Laura, and Gus set themselves to the task of pushing the sled toward the point where it would slip into the ponded ice shards.

The rifle-carrying stranger grabbed Gundersen's shoulder and pulled back. "Better let me do that, Gramps."

Gus stood up. He was not the imposing man he once had been. "Okay," he said. "Let me hold that." He reached for the strap running across the man's chest and started to lift away the rifle.

"No!"

"Your friend will freeze to death before he drowns," Gus protested as the man tried to break Gus' grip. The words dissolved the man's quick resistance, and he peeled the band over his head to hand the weapon to Gundersen.

"Thanks," he said as he dived into a task which took every ounce of his strength. The slushy snow had frozen the runners in place, but the three finally broke the inertia and the coracle dipped and rolled before it stabilized, and Jeff reached over the gunwale and began to paddle.

"Whoa," he cried. The three holding the trailing line were momentarily confused. Was he telling them to stop? No, it was a reaction to the temperature of the water. "I'm all right," he shouted, "let's do this fast."

Koenig's admonition was an understatement. Had the man been conscious he could have gripped the small vessel, but he was unresponsive. Jeff's reaction was to grab a handful of wet clothes, but the weight shifted the small boat's buoyancy and water and ice spilled over the lip of the boat. He let go of his hold and the light craft bounced back. His nearly frozen fingers reached to break open the knot that held the line around him.

"What the hell are you thinking?" cried Jenkins who was watching closely.

"I've got to get the line around him!"

"Leave it alone! Grab on to him. We'll pull to keep you balanced."

"The sled will flood!" protested Koenig.

"Just hold on!" said Gus.

The power of command is sometimes underestimated, especially when it has the power to inaugurate irrational acts of bravery. Jeff did not pause to consider the physics; he reached forward to recover his hold on the lifeless form. Ice immediately swirled over the gunwale, and the men pulled hard. The horizontal motion pulled the boat to a flatter plane, slowing, but not stopping, the rush of cold slush. By the time the runners of the sled were impaled in the more solid snow bank, two men were pulled from the water. Gus and Cathy tended Jeff while Laura and Bert turned to the stranger.

Jeff was wet, shivering uncontrollably, but alert. Quickly they stripped him of his wet clothes and wrapped him in one of the dry hide blankets from the emergency kit, drying his exposed skin as best they could.

The stranger was less fortunate. "Cardiac arrest," whispered Laura to Bert as she began cutting away the man's clothes.

"Who are you?" asked Cathy of the man standing before her. He turned to face her.

"My name is Tomstock; we were hunting caribou and saw the little boy." Cathy's mind filled in a lot of the blanks, but her face didn't offer any recognition. For now, she was satisfied with keeping this man distracted from his partner. Out of the corner of her eye, she saw Bert's eyes widen as he uncovered a Ruger Redhawk beneath the man's cutaway down jacket. He quickly tucked the high power revolver beneath his own parka and turned to see if he had managed the sleight-of-hand. His gaze met Cathy's, and his nod met her best poker face.

Laura put her ear to the man's exposed chest. She sat upright, raised her arm and brought her fist down hard on his chest. She listened again. "Get that sled free and wrap him tight," she ordered. "Jeff, are you all right?"

"Yes," he answered without hesitation.

"What is your name?" she asked to Koenig's chagrin.

"Jeff Koenig," he said defiantly.

"No hesitation, no slur! He's okay for awhile. Sorry, Jeff, you'll have to walk. This guy's in no shape." She looked down at the pallid face of the man beneath her. "Quickly now."

Everyone knew what to do, and the cortege was soon moving hurriedly along the path, making its way toward the shelter of Keelhouse.

"My name is Cathy, Cathy Pearson. You said your name was..."

"*Tomstock.* That's all I've been called for years. *Tomstock* or *Tom.* Where are we? I thought we were alone out here."

"We did, too," said Cathy trying to slow the pace so their arrival at Keelhouse would be delayed. Thoughts were forming in her mind. If she was right, the Durands would need some time to become invisible.

33

Everyone's spirits lightened at the sound of baying sled dogs. Simonie and Noah had to leave them behind when they came into the village a day earlier; otherwise their exuberance would have betrayed the whole enterprise on the night of the capture. The hunters also returned to their families with tales to tell about the charade that they had carried out with wolf howls and scattered dogs.

There was also a good deal of interest about their neighbors to the south, the people of Keelhouse. Only Noah and Simonie had visited the longhouse, but these hunters had rested at one of the outpost camps and swapped stories with new friends. Their dogs ran freely before the curious sleds that had been built by John Romig. He was rightfully proud of their performance once he knew the secret of spitting water on the runners.

The emotional realities within the village did a flip flop. Some who had despaired of staying for fear of the return of the other three now felt fortified and ready to fight. Those who had decided to stay and defend were now anxious to join with Simonie and head south to see this strange new world called Keelhouse.

Overall, hope returned and drumming broke out in the hall. At the center of the celebration were Tish Barker and John Romig. Tish felt useful and needed, a feeling that had abandoned her, and John had hopes of becoming a great musher. Shrader was the only real basket-case. He kept circling the halls trying to keep the group on-task, but his efforts could not ignite any sense of urgency to counteract the great relief that had taken hold. On the third round, Anthony pulled him aside.

"Give them an hour," he said. "Those who are staying will need to post a guard, but the three men we left out in the field are not going to arrive after dark. They are too afraid of the night noises. The few who decide to go south will be traveling light. They'll move fast with the dogs setting the pace. Everything is preset, and they'll get help from our people at each new outpost."

Shrader looked hard at Anthony. He wanted to ask: *Who are you?* But he knew full well that their best hunter was also becoming a strategist. "What do you say is next?" he asked aloud.

"Take care of yourself. Go somewhere quiet. Dad and I will protect the prisoners, and in an hour Simonie and Tish will round up their goslings and fly south. Tomorrow, we'll follow, and my guess is, we'll make better time and get to Keelhouse just after they do."

"Even though they have dogs and sleds?"

Anthony smiled broadly as though he was an amateur ready to announce "checkmate" to a master. "Yes, even with John Romig's magical sleds," he answered. "If you haven't noticed, it's thawing out there. They'll need cold nights to firm up the snow-pack. Near the coast, they may find their feet faster than runners!"

Shrader considered the wisdom of the words and knew them to be true. "I think you're right. If you're okay, it would be good to have a few minutes to myself." As he spoke, he was unconsciously moving toward his parka and heading to the door.

Anthony smiled. "Don't get yourself lost, now!"

Marks' quickened pace began to fall back to normal with each step he took away from the compound. The sound of the people was sealed off when he shut the door behind him. The sound of the wind was the next song in his hearing. By the time he reached the tundra beyond the perimeter, even the wind became silent, and the voice he heard was his own singing.

He stood atop a small hillock and faced the south-sailing sun.

"You miss the sea," said a familiar voice. It was his friend, Keeper.

"Where does the pod swim?"

"Not far from your calf, but perhaps not near you."

Shrader understood Keeper to mean Royce, even though the whale thought a five-year-old past infancy. "Did Royce speak to you?"

"He called from the place where you have stood, but I did not answer at first."

"At first?"

"He was puzzled by men riding a strange animal, and I knew that you had seen bad men. I did not intend to break our promise, but there was danger."

"You were right to warn him, Friend. Do you know what happened?"

"After that there were so many voices, so much noise." Shrader knew what Keeper meant; he had just escaped the same chaos.

"There may be trouble, Keeper. If Royce needs you, speak to him. Where are you now?"

"The seals are feeding us well, and the ice has broken up around the *dark-shape-that-is-not-ice* in your cove."

Marks understood the whale's idiom. In earlier times, Greyback had called his boat the *dark-shape-that-blocks-the-sky*. In winter, ice is the sky. Now, he was saying what Laura, Bert, and Jeff had also noted. *Dream Dancer* was floating free on her mooring chain.

"I will come to you soon," promised Shrader. "If your pod is well-fed, will you listen for my call?"

"Yes, *Whaleman*."

The time of quiet was over. Shrader's feet moved in time with his thumping heart.

34

Everyone at Keelhouse was aware that something momentous had drawn Cathy and Gus away, but it was Sodus who first announced the arrival of the impromptu rescue party. Among those waiting for a call to action was Étienne who blanched and stepped back when he saw the face of Cal Hemmenburg sticking out from its hide wrapping like a death mask on a mummy.

"Take Alain and Émilie and go to *Rol's Royce*. You know how to get there?" barked Jenkins. Before Durand could give an answer, he added: "Better yet, take Ben Romig or Ashley Barker with you. They can come back with supplies if there's not enough there."

Étienne knew what Bert did not. He didn't know that the outposts had already been supplied for the potential arrivals from the north. This, however, was not a time for a briefing; it was a time for haste. He moved quickly, fearing that the man on the sled would open his eyes at any moment.

"There were two of them," Jenkins called after him. Étienne began to run.

It was only a minute or two later when Tiffany Jenkins came out of the longhouse. She greeted her husband, then turned to face the shrouded form of Jeff, who tried a weak smile through his shivering.

"Most everyone is gone," said Tiffany. "We expect Noah and Simonie to return with more refugees soon. Oh, and Brittany had a girl." She had not noticed Cathy's arrival with a stranger.

"Jeff decided on a swim," said Bert gesturing toward his companion, "he needs to warm up. Make some tea. That will help, and bring some to *Mewtiny*. I'm going to have to take this one there since he hasn't been through quarantine."

Tiffany looked at the bundle that Laura and her husband were pulling in the sled. Expecting that it was just a load of supplies, she had not given it a glance. Now she saw its human cargo and wondered. She then saw an unknown man standing near

Cathy, and Gus approaching further back with a rifle over his shoulder. She didn't know the details, but she knew her task. She took Jeff by the arm and turned toward the entrance to Keelhouse. Gus went in after them. Without instruction, he knew what he had to do. He had to make a gun disappear into the bilge of a sailboat that had been sitting high and dry for years.

"I'm sorry, Tomstock," began Cathy, "but I can't take you straight into the shelter. We have strict rules. We have to make sure you're not carrying anything."

"I have a knife," said Tomstock, "the old guy took my rifle."

"No, I mean, we worry about people carrying sickness, but you'll also have to put aside any hardware that you're carrying, at least for the time being. We have two doctors, Laura is one, but she's with your friend. The other is Bill Morgan, but..." She was going to say *after the baby was born, he joined one of the teams that went out to meet Simonie*, but she caught herself short of saying it and added simply, "he's away."

"Jeff is really cold, but I don't think he's in any real danger, thank God." Marty Koenig came out to report about her son. "He never did have much sense about staying out of trouble," she added.

"He was incredibly brave," said Cathy in Koenig's defense. "This is Tomstock. The man Jeff rescued is his friend."

"Whoever that guy was, he didn't hesitate a second."

"He's my son," said Marty, "and I am proud of him even if he scares me to death sometimes."

"Tomstock's friend wasn't so lucky. Laura is with him, and since Bill is away..."

"You want 'Grandma' Marty to make sure there's nothing contagious. I understand."

"Marty has the reputation of being our chief rule enforcer," Cathy said to the outsider who, in turn, took a long, second look at the silver-haired woman. He wondered what sort of rules this little old lady could really enforce. "Take Gus with you down to the drying shed." No sooner had Cathy said this than Gus also emerged from the low entrance that baffled the air and kept Keelhouse warm.

"He's the old man that took my rifle," said Tomstock.

"Hey, that's my 'old man'," said Marty, "and he'll not appreciate the moniker."

"That's Gus," said Cathy. "He's quite a man. He can make anything work or figure out a way to do without it."

"What about my gun?"

"It's safe. You won't need it here at Keelhouse, and, if you decide to leave, you can take it with you."

Tomstock didn't see much room for argument and the better part of discretion was to watch and listen. "That sounds fair," he said trying not to sound concerned. "What do I do now?"

"Now," said Cathy, "you have to lay aside all modesty and let us examine you physically. If Morgan were here, he'd give you the checkup."

"How many people are at this place?" interrupted Tomstock.

"He's our principle doctor," continued Cathy ignoring a probing question. "Grandma Marty takes care of hygiene mostly, but she can recognize any symptoms."

"We need to see that this fellow has a clean bill of health," she said turning to Gus who nodded with understanding.

****

The physical exam did not last too long. Marty had a way of making middle-aged people feel seven and completely obedient when having to down a spoonful of nasty medicine. She didn't like his gums and called for a dose of Tiffany's pine needle tea. Gus did not like the discovery of three knives, including a small one sewn into the lining of his down jacket. On the other hand, hunters would carry knives. It was the concealment that was troubling.

In the end, Gus and Marty left him resting in the warmth of the shelter. "You've been shaken pretty hard," said Koenig. "Rest! We'll bring you food in a bit. Hopefully, your friend will be in better shape by then and we can show you around so that you can get your bearings."

"So, you're saying I'm confined to this shed?."

The tone of the statement caught Marty off guard. "No, you're not confined. I just think a bit of rest will do you good."

The answer seemed to satisfy the newcomer, and they left him wrapped in caribou blankets and sipping on the last bit of warm tea. Exhaustion eventually overpowered his latent distrust, and Tomstock dropped off to sleep.

He awoke with the uneasy feeling that he was being watched. He was. The shed was heavy with the dusky smell of peat, and near the doorway sat a small figure.

"Why do you wear such funny clothes?" asked Royce.

"Funny?" Tomstock looked at the outerwear that lay in a heap on the floor. Beneath the warm hides he had not missed the rather tattered and grimy synthetic fabrics of his old life. The boy's outer parka was tawny brown, an *anorak* in Inuktitut. "These are the clothes that I brought with me when I came here from the States," he explained to a small face that showed no sign of recognition. "You didn't come from here, did you?" he asked.

"I was born here," said Royce. "Everybody else came from another place without snow. Except for Canada, but she's new; I don't know about Alain and Émilie."

Now it was Tomstock's turn to look confused. Part of his problem with deciphering the list of names was the inclusion of *Canada*, and after that the other names were a blur.

"Why do you hate Simonie?" asked Royce.

That name was not a blur, and Tomstock knew only one person who carried it.

"Is he here?"

"Not now, but they're coming back soon."

"Who's *they*?" asked Tomstock, but he guessed the answer. By the time Noah's name came out, Tomstock was remembering Noah's return to the hunting camp and the decision to send him on a snowmachine to Jordan to get help. "That help won't be coming soon," he said aloud to no one but himself. In his mind, he imagined Mallory and Doncaster face-up, bleeding out from slit throats, and lying in a pool of congealing blood.

"I am feeling a lot stronger now," he said in his most optimistic voice. "Do you think you could take me for a walk around, Royce? That is your name, isn't it?"

"Sure," said the boy. "I know all the paths. I'll take you where you can see the boat in the water."

Of course, thought Tomstock. *They must have come in boats.*

The tour did not last long. The watercourse to the south was in full spate and the gorge was sated with frazil ice. He had already seen the longhouse, at least from the outside, and knew it was a long ridged-roof strung between two sailboats. He wondered how they had been lifted so high on the hillside, but didn't ask. He let Royce offer his five-year-old assessment of this place called Keelhouse.

"This is the best view," said Royce proudly pointing toward the bay through an opening in the thick spruce.

"There's a boat there!" said Tomstock.

"That's *Dream Dancer*," announced Royce. "Anthony came in that boat. He's our best hunter."

Tomstock was troubled by yet another male name and by the attribution of being a great hunter. *How many people were in this place, and how strongly are they armed?* His weapons had been taken from him. He reached into his pocket to feel for the stiffness of the metal blade he had sewn into the lining. *Damn!* It was gone. These people were thorough and clever.

"So you still have boats that are ready to go out into the water," observed the stranger.

"Just one," said Royce. "It even has a motor. Shrader says that it will make a very loud noise when it's turned on, but it will move the boat without having to paddle. Your sled made a loud, funny sound. Was that a motor?"

"Yes, it was," said Tomstock. "Of course it was ruined when it went into the ice and water."

"After the snow melts, we'll be able to get it," offered Royce.

"But it won't work anymore. Motors are tricky. They have to stay dry and have the right kind of gas."

"Do they burp?" asked Royce. Tomstock laughed an honest laugh.

"No, not *gas* like a burp. It's a fuel, a liquid that makes the motor go."

"Like diesel?" asked Royce. It was not a word that Tomstock expected.

"Exactly. How do you know about diesel? I thought you didn't know about motors."

"Shrader tells me things that I don't understand yet. Diesel is something that Gus fixes or takes care of because it can turn rotten. They took it to pour into the boat so that it will be ready."

"Is the boat ready?"

"Laura and Bert would know. They're the ones who took the diesel."

"You need to be careful around here," Tomstock turned to see Gus approaching from behind. "Royce can talk your leg off. Is he being a pest?"

"No, he's a perfect gentleman," said the visitor. "I thought that a little exercise might do me good, and he was good enough to give me a tour." Tomstock was in full charm mode, and Gundersen had no reason to doubt it.

"Good! It's time to put some food in you. We'll go into Keelhouse and you can properly meet Jeff Koenig, the man who went in after your friend. By the way, Laura tells me that he's resting comfortably. It's too soon to tell if he's okay, but his pulse is strong and he's warm to the touch. She says that it's not really surprising that he's not regained consciousness. When there's a big trauma like this, the brain shuts down for its own protection. He'll wake up when he's ready."

****

"How is he doing?" Laura looked up to see Bert coming into the main cabin of *Mewtiny*. Beside her on the settee berth was Cal Hemmenburg who appeared to be sleeping quietly with his head and arms resting on the outside of a blanket resting over a grossly bloated body.

"What's with this?" asked Jenkins looking at the shape of the man's distorted torso.

"Sodus," answered Laura. Beneath the blankets came a muffled urgent whimper of a dog who wanted to give a proper greeting. "We're using our canine heater, and it's working just fine."

"Well, I can sit with him awhile. You should check Jeff, but he's doing fine. What you probably need is a little food and rest for yourself."

"I won't argue," said Romig. "Have you heard what all's going on around here? We left for a few days and the place is almost unrecognizable."

"From what I've been able to piece together, it's been Grand Central Station. We knew about the Durands; they turned up before we left, but then two Inuit came, and today–these two who are armed to the teeth. In the meantime, Brittany had her baby that they've named Canada, and most of the others are on some sort of raid on that settlement where the Durands came from."

"And to think all we had to do was power up a boat and make sure she is seaworthy," said Laura.

"I'd like to tell Gus that we're ready to turn the key and fire up some of that diesel that he's been nursing to extend its shelf life, but our *big* news doesn't seem important."

"Bert, you still have to report the radio contact."

"I know, and I will."

"Funny, isn't it," said Laura, "all these years we thought we were alone and we've been surrounded. Villages to the north, hunters from the west, and sail south and you're in the arms of someone who has an operating radio station and who knows what else."

"I guess I worry about the *What else?*" said Bert.

"Or maybe the *What next?*"

35

Anthony was right, and when Shrader returned to the compound, those traveling south were sorted out and ready to move. Actually, there were only seven besides Simonie and Tish who now wanted to make the journey. Most of the others had been calmed by the drumming and felt that they were on the way toward cleansing the place of its recent putrid past.

With such a small group planning to leave, it became clear that the trip back to Keelhouse would be fast. They didn't even take the time to gather stores. After all, feeding stations and emergency shelters were already in place, thanks to the parties from Keelhouse which were now stationed along the route.

"Shrader, you're back," said Anthony with relief in his voice. "We're ready to move, and it's going to be a fast passage. The first group will have dogs, which means that the prisoner escort can leave about the same time since we'll be snowshoeing it."

"I'm not going with you."

"What the..." Anthony didn't finish his sentence. This was, after all, Shrader Marks, a man who had often infuriated his father with his random shifts in mood or direction. "Is something happening?" he asked.

"I have to find the other three. I need to know where they are." answered Shrader.

"So you're going to head toward Rockledge."

"Two days, if I push it, but maybe I'll meet them sooner."

Anthony knew better than to argue or to ask for the details of what Marks was going to do. He suspected that when Shrader took these sorts of moods, he himself could not explain motive or intent. "You have to take a gun with you!" Though Marks was, at the moment, doggedly determined, Anthony stood resolute. "There are three of them and they have high-powered rifles. You are a lot of things, Shrader Marks, but you are not much of a hunter."

"You noticed," came the unexpected reply. "A rifle will weigh me down."

"Then you'll have to carry a handgun. *The Five are* hunters," continued the younger man without a pause. "They brought an arsenal with them and now we have the spoils of war."

Is this a war? Marks drifted into one of his internal debates so quickly that he was oblivious to the fact that Anthony had left the room and was now returning with a blue barreled revolver which he offered to Shrader.

"It's a Blackhawk."

Marks reached out to take it from his hand. "It looks like a toy cowboy pistol that I played with as a kid."

"Maybe," said Anthony, "but it's evolved some. It still uses the same rounds as a Colt .45 and could take down a buffalo. Dad

436

said that with this long barrel it'll have the same muzzle velocity as a rifle, but it won't shoot nearly as straight."

"Which means that if I'm in their sights, I'll be in more danger than they are."

"Yes, but at least you'll have a shot. Six to be exact. After that you won't be able to reload. The only bullets we found were the ones already in the chambers."

"So, after six shots it turns into a hammer," said Marks with uncharacteristic humor. He weighed the pistol in his grip. "Thanks, Anthony. Six will be enough." He paused for a moment to consider whether it wise to say more. "In spite of what some say, I am human and I do get scared," he added. With that he went back to renew the supplies he had carried on his back the day before, or was it in a different lifetime?

The first wave of refugees left with a public show of exuberance that had quietly found its way into the people as if they had crossed over into a new land. The second "wave" was intentionally unheralded. It was a foursome, two Ragnis and two prisoners. Vince was not happy with the reduced number.

"It's classic Shrader," he fumed. "Do you know how much harder this is going to be with only two of us to keep watch at night? We can't both sleep with these two."

"I don't think we have too much to worry about from them. We're their best hope, Dad," Anthony argued. "Where are they going to go on their own?" Of course he was right, but there was a river of bad blood to wade before his father would be satisfied to let Shrader go off on his own.

"Hostages!" said Vince, "they could take us back as hostages."

"Before we lose the light we'll meet up with Bill. Besides, I don't really think you should be helping them brainstorm all the negative options," protested Anthony with a nod toward the two men walking ahead of them. That fact finally quieted his father's words, but not his suspicions.

****

Shrader wore his smallest frame snowshoes in hopes of moving faster across the frozen ground. In his favor, the night had been cold and clear so that the tread path that he left with the snowmobile allowed a fast pace. He cursed his impulse that put a bullet through the lightweight engine block of the sled. That was the first time he had fired a gun in more than four years. Now he was aware of two things: three pounds of steel that he carried beneath his parka, and the knowledge that his journey would have been much easier if he was riding a snowmachine south until the fuel tank was drained.

Still, he made good time and rejoiced when the snowpack lost its telltale tread marks. He was now past the point where Noah had met him. He walked several more miles before he had to find somewhere to shelter. He made a snow cave, ate a hasty meal, and tried to focus on sounds other than the wind and senses beyond the cold, but exhausted sleep robbed him of such luxury.

A sound did awaken him, but it was the sound of thunder. Thunder over the snow is one of those curious signals of changing weather, but these particular claps were sharp and short. What he heard was not thunder, but the report of a rifle. It was a long way off, but with increasing frequency. *One, two, three...* he began counting the blasts. *Was it more than one weapon being fired?* He could not tell for sure. Some shots seemed more muffled or distant than others. *Was it one rifle fired in different directions—a single shooter fending off assailants on all sides? Did people from Keelhouse come out to meet the three? But the hunters are all deployed to meet refugees!*

Fifty-seven was the count when silence finally settled in. Shrader could not guess how many rounds sounded before the thunder invaded his sleep. He was alone.

36

"Looks like you have a friend," noted Bert Jenkins as soon as he crouched through the entrance of the longhouse. He gestured toward Royce.

"Seems that way," said Tomstock. "Actually, he's been pretty good company."

"Your friend is asking about you."

"He's awake?"

"And hungry," said Jenkins. "He's burned a lot of calories bringing up his body temperature. We'll start him easy, though. You can take something to him if you'd like." With this Tiffany Jenkins ladled a bit of stew into a plastic bowl which had become an indestructible heirloom of the past. She also poured out some tea.

"That stuff is nasty," commented Tomstock.

"It's an acquired taste that saves lives," Bert interrupted, "and my wife makes it best." He winked at Tiffany as Tomstock looked quickly trying to catch every reaction. He was somewhat troubled by the lack of questions here. Any stranger coming into his camp would have been cross-examined and debriefed before anything else. Here, his only examination was medical, and he seemed to have the run of the place. *Why wasn't everyone more curious?*

Cathy, who at first seemed to be someone of import, was now preoccupied with the sounds of a baby on the other side of a doorway cut into the hull of a sailboat that had been decommissioned to become the south wall of the building. Still, the cries told him that children were being born here, and some invisible part of the population was of childbearing age.

The most obvious reason for the lack of interest in him and his past was the use of familiar names in Royce's conversation. *Noah, Simonie, Émilie,* and *Alain* had all been mentioned, in which case, his history was known to these people already, and it was told them through the words of enemies. He and Cal were sitting in a comfortable trap, one too nice to escape, one that could close tightly at any moment.

"I'll take that food to Cal right away," he said without hesitation. "Seeing him awake and doing well will be my best medicine, too." They gathered up what they needed, and Bert led the way carrying a sloshing mug of pine needle tea.

"I brought you a familiar face," Bert announced as he stepped up into the main cabin of *Mewtiny*. This boat formed the north side of the longhouse, but was only accessible from the outside and a little draftier. A small peat fire in the vented wood stove, however, kept the teak-lined chamber warm and friendly.

Tomstock tried to take it all in. He had not anticipated the upholstery and joinery of a yacht after the crude interior of the large common room that sat between the two hulls. "You have everything here, even a furnace," he said pointing to the stainless steel rounded box.

Jenkins was slow to realize the point. He said, "most of our boats had heaters that could be used at anchor. The propane and diesel burning ones had to be adapted to burn peat. This one was always a wood-burner.

"Now Tom here has already pronounced this stuff toxic, but you both need to drink it. It's full of Vitamin C," said Jenkins

"You're beginning to sound like a commercial," said Tomstock, who was surprised by the stranger's easy laughter.

"You need to be told what's good for you," retorted Bert, "and that ought to sound like Grandma Marty." Cal Hemmenburg looked puzzled by the remark, but Tomstock took the reference.

"I'll leave you two a chance to catch up," said Bert standing and turning to leave. "Royce seems to be your sidekick anyway. Send him if you need anything." The two looked to see the diminutive figure tucked back in the foot well under the chart table.

"Will do!" said Tomstock. When Jenkins left, there was a long pause to make sure that they would not be interrupted by a sudden return.

"You were out for a long time," began Tomstock. "They said that you just regained consciousness."

"I've been awake for awhile," said Hemmenburg, "I just kept my eyes closed for awhile–resting, I guess, and listening. What about him?" He nodded toward where Royce seemed to be absorbed in some form of shadow game against the smooth white fiberglass hull liner.

"That's my buddy Royce," said Tomstock, "he's been a big help. He's helped me get my strength back by walking me around the camp. He knows a lot about this place; he even knows Simonie and Noah, don't ya?" Hemmenburg's eyes widened.

"They're our friends," answered Royce. "I'm glad you're not mad at them."

"Never!"

"While I was *resting my eyes*," said Cal, "I heard the name Durand."

Tom nodded. "Royce knows Alan and Emily," he said with higher volume. Then, in a low urgent whisper: "If we stay here, we're screwed!"

"What about Zimisky? He's still out there waiting for Noah."

"Noah won't be coming in the way he expects. Besides, we lost our wheels when you took that swim." Tomstock looked to see if Royce was following any of this, but the boy was intrigued with trying to use his fingers to project floppy bunny ears against the bulkhead.

"There is a way out," whispered Hemmenburg. "The man and woman sitting with me were talking. They were on their way back from getting a boat ready when they got involved with the rescue."

"There's a sailboat sitting at anchor just offshore. This whole settlement is built on boats; look at this room. They must have kept one in the water."

"They've had a lot of confusion, and it didn't start with us. I guess there was a baby born, and the men went north on a raid of some sort..." Cal stopped, mid-sentence. "Noah and Simonie!"

"I think the only two people who can be helped at this moment are right here, and I don't think we have a lot of time."

"I think you're right. Have you ever sailed?"

"When I was a kid we had a sailing dinghy. I guess I know something of the physics involved," said Tomstock.

"From what they said, that boat you saw is ready. That's what they were coming back to report when I was in the water."

"I sailed little boats; I wouldn't know how to get something that big rigged or turned around to get out of the bay. At least I couldn't do it fast enough to go without notice."

"But could you do it if you had time?" asked Cal.

"I suppose. I'd have to figure out the hardware and how the sail attaches. We'd be sitting ducks out there on the water. They have at least one rifle with a scope—mine!"

Hemmenburg had saved the best for last. His broad grin gave it away.

"What?"

"Let's say it's a turnkey operation. There's an engine with clean diesel in the tank. I'll bet the key is in the ignition or nearby."

"Hotwiring is not difficult," Tomstock answered. "If we can get it away from here, I could figure out the rest while we're moving."

"We'll head south. They had a radio signal from there."

"They have a radio that works. We could be going home! Just one catch."

"What's that?"

"The boat is a couple hundred yards from the beach. I doubt if you're in any mood to try and swim it."

"Royce?" said Hemmenburg addressing him directly for the first time. "Tom says there's a boat out in the water near here. How would anyone get to it? The water is so cold."

"It's easy; we'd use one of John's boats."

"A jon boat. I wonder if they have an outboard for it." Cal gave Tomstock a sideways glance. At that, he turned back to Royce.

"It doesn't sound easy to me," observed Hemmenburg.

"I could do it," bragged Royce.

"By yourself?" Royce paused in self-doubt. "What if we just helped you with the heavy part?"

"Then I could do it."

"You know," began Tomstock, "that Cal here has not seen anything and he really needs some exercise. How 'bout tomorrow morning we all walk around and you could show him what I saw? You could show us the jon boat and prove that you could really do it. In fact, maybe they'd let you sleep here tonight. It'll be a boat party. We'll stay in this boat and go look at another one early tomorrow. Sound like fun?"

"Nice touch," whispered Hemmenburg.

"I know how to get out to *Dream Dancer*," Royce said proudly in his most parental voice, "but you'll have to do exactly what I say!"

"Yes, Sir!" was the unison response which was followed by a mock salute.

37

As disquieting as the night had been, the morning dawned with fresh, crisp clarity. Shrader faced the sunrise with a renewed sense that he was not alone. He looked into himself and captured a rhythm that became a song. When he finished his sacred reverie he turned expecting to see Royce, but he was alone on a seam of the earth. He was in the tundra-taiga interface. Ahead of him were the outliers, trees struggling to find light on the ground between boreal forests and the treeless north. Behind him was the true tundra where, in deepest winter, the sun never rose above the horizon.

As if an alarm had sounded, Marks began to gather himself for the journey ahead. The gunfire of the previous night made him wary of what he would find, but the wariness held no deep fear. It was not long before he realized that he wasn't alone. A Rough-legged hawk hovered over the path ahead. *What is it seeing?* He wondered as he approached a black shape laying in a deep rut. It was the overturned tread of a snowmobile half buried in a snow bank. *How did it end up here, and where is the driver?*

His attention went back to the hawk. *I'm not in its circle; what is it seeing? Is someone else out there?* If there were, that someone might, even now, be watching Shrader through the scope of a rifle.

Marks dropped to the ground and crawled parallel to the machine. Only then did he dig beneath his parka for the revolver. If he was being observed before, he did not want to be seen drawing a weapon. He calmed himself, shedding the emotional panic of sudden adrenalin in favor of listening to his surroundings. The hawk called from overhead, but it was not interested in him or the foul smell of gasoline next to him. Instinctively, he recoiled from the fumes and rose to his feet. He stepped away twisting his head toward the shoulder that had been nearest the sled. Then he breathed deeply trying to catch an odor. *Did I just get soaked with gas?* He looked back to the spot where he dove for cover. The snowpack that held his body's impression was packed down, but still white with no oily trace.

What happened became clear to Marks. Whoever the driver was, he was driving in the dark and too fast. He was out-speeding the range of his headlamp and hit the rut hard enough to be thrown. *But where was he now? Was he alone on the sled?*

Shrader had names to put with the *he*. He had heard them before from Noah and Simonie, and again from Mallory and Doncaster. The driver could be Zimisky, Hemmenburg, or his silhouette twin, Tomstock. *Was there a passenger?*

Last night he had counted fifty-seven rounds fired. That was a lot of ammo for one shooter, but the reports were uniform in pitch. Perhaps not too many for one panicked man suddenly stranded in a world he feared.

The hawk continued to hover; was it preparing to dive on some unsuspecting rodent or waiting for Marks to get further away? *The driver is nearby*, thought Shrader.

The shallow ridge that had overturned the sled was one of many crests over the surface of the rippled land, and he did not have to go far before he found the man curled in a fetal position between two drifts. His right boot was no longer oriented correctly to its accompanying leg.

"Poor devil," said Shrader looking at the frozen body still holding fast to a scoped rifle and floating in a sea of shell casings. In his mind, Marks synchronized the image at his feet with the soundtrack of the night before. There was no blood, so the bone did not break the skin, but the bleeding within might have been profuse. In pain, the stranger took his defensive position against wolf howls and imaginary shadows of predators. He shot at them all, and hit nothing real. Then either the bullets ran out or pain and cold took him.

He pulled the rifle free, lifted it to take aim at a distant hillock and fired.

Click, and Shrader knew the truth. The man was alert and waiting to die in the jaws of something that was not there.

The hawk would have liked to scavenge, but Marks sent him away empty. "Sorry, fellow," he said. "This one's not yours." The idea of human remains being scavenged by animals was not particularly repulsive to him. As an anthropologist he knew that some cultures honored their dead by setting them on pyres in high places and giving the corpse back to the timeless cycle of life. No, his concern was more pragmatic. Other predators would be drawn to this place. At night the owls would feed; foxes, bears, and wolves would also be attracted. He did not like the idea of the larger animals feeding on this flesh, and learning that humans were just a form of prey slower than caribou.

He looked around at the ground. The only patterns in the snow came from the sled, a crawling man, and his own snowshoes. He dragged the body, and after several attempts, managed to balance it on the flat tread of the snowmobile.

This is really stupid! he thought. Then again, if he was careful, it might actually be better than *doing nothing.* Gasoline is not a fire starter; it is an explosive. Still this machine had been draining all night, and fiberglass burns very hot. He walked well away from the sight of the wreck and lay down on the far side of another snowy ridge. He had put a bullet in a snowmobile before and nothing exploded. Gasoline needs a spark and it would have to be a lucky, or unlucky, shot to make a bullet spark against metal. He only had six bullets.

His Colt ammunition was clearly not the right tool for this job, but he had another option. Properly speaking, it was not different ammo. *Properly speaking,* however, was a wordplay game between the United States and Canada. *Guns* were not permitted to be carried across the international border into Canada, and this included *flare guns.* Over the years, sailors learned to answer the question *Do you have any firearms on board?* by saying, *No, but I do have the pyrotechnic signaling devices required by law.* Shrader's pyrotechnic device was rated *twelve-gauge,* and it was the white practice flare version of what Tish Barker had fired two days earlier. She was red; he, white. Each was the planned signal response to a single gunshot, and intended to announce: *I am here, too!*

From his prone position, he took rough aim at the sled. This was not how the rocket was meant to be fired, but it would come out as burning phosphorus. With gasoline fumes floating around the sled, close would be close enough. It was.

The fireball was more dramatic than the explosion. He had feared creating a flying zombie blasted from an ejection seat, but the fire took control. It burned hot with toxic black smoke that rose like a pillar against the morning sky.

"If anyone else is out there," said Shrader, "I am here, too."

38

"The kid is gone!" said Hemmenburg in a near panic. He was standing in the main cabin of *Mewtiny*, and it was his first attempt at walking since he was bundled into the berth.

"Relax, he's probably close by; he's a kid, after all, he can't go too far. Maybe, he just had to take a leak." said Tomstock. "How're you feeling?"

"I'm on the right side of being dead. Look, they must have brought us some food." He pointed to the galley counter and a collection of what appeared to be some sort of meat stew and strips of jerky. They both fell to the meal without question.

"We haven't thought about food," said Tomstock through his full mouth.

"They said the boat was ready, but that might not mean that there were provisions aboard," said Cal.

"That kid, Royce, seems like he always wants to be helpful; he might know where there's a larder we can raid. We just have to ask him carefully."

"For all we know, he's reporting to the others right now. The longer we're here the more dangerous it is."

They heard a rustle outside the door and the excited foot-work of Sodus' body being shaken by his high-spirited tail. "You stay here," said a small voice. "I'll see if the sleepyheads are awake."

When Royce appeared, Tomstock and Hemmenburg were seated like two old friends getting ready to swap stories.

"Where have you been, Royce?" asked Tomstock. "I was worried about you."

"Oh, I just went to do my morning things," said the boy. Hemmenburg and Tomstock let it go. Their normal morning ritual was to empty their bladders. Royce probably did the same. They would not have guessed that he also hiked up to his morning spot on the escarpment and greeted the dawn. It was a bright morning, and he thought he could hear his father singing.

"There's food here," said Tom. Royce looked over the fare, and took a piece of dried meat and began to chew.

"We were just talking about how good the food is," Cal began. "There must be a big place where they keep enough food to feed all these people." The two men waited to see if Royce could be baited to talk.

"Gus and Bert are the ones who know how to smoke the meat," he said examining the strip of jerky in his hand. "Sometimes it's too hard for me to chew."

"Do you remember you told us that you knew where the jon boat was?"

"I remember. Do you want me to take you there now?"

"Sure," said Hemmenburg. "I feel a lot better this morning, and I think a walk would make me feel even better. If we go before people are up and around, we can surprise them with how well I'm doing when we get back." Royce seemed to ponder the last statement as if it didn't quite make sense.

"Everybody's already awake," he said finally. "They won't care if we take a walk."

"Will we pass the place where they smoke the meat?" said Tomstock.

"No," said Royce, "it's too smoky, but there's a place with stone walls where we keep it after it's done. I can show you that."

If they had hoped for a stealthy escape, it was thwarted by Sodus who was waiting for Royce's exit. He welcomed the boy with a fresh round of barks.

"Has Laura given you your walking orders yet?" It was Gus speaking primarily to Hemmemburg.

"Just giving my legs a little test drive." The fact was that he was already feeling an energy drain, and he hoped Tomstock would not have to rely on him to haul the rowboat to the water.

"Should the dog be coming with us if we're going to go to the place where the meat is stored?" asked Tom, who was beginning to fear complications in the scenario that he was still working out in his mind. Making it to the boat at anchor was a must. Making it with a pint-sized hostage would be insurance, but Sodus kept nosing his way between the boy and himself.

"Sodus, go find Cathy!" The dog sat down and looked hard at his small master. "Go find Cathy!" The dog gave a barked reply and then bounded off.

"How much farther is it?" asked Cal who was getting winded and raised a hand to indicate that he'd like to take a time out before moving on.

"Royce, why don't you take me quick to where they store the food and then Cal can get a little rest before you show us how you'd get out to that big boat." The plan seemed reasonable to Royce, and by the time the two returned, the color had come back into Hemmenburg's face. A large smile ran across Tomstock's.

"I take it you were successful," said Cal.

"Very," said Tomstock who was carrying a bundle of what looked like hides. "We decided that we'd take some meat back to Keelhouse and save someone a trip down later." Royce nodded his agreement.

By now they were nearly down to the level of the bay, and Royce seemed to find new energy as he bounced ahead. The two men stayed together, trailing a little behind. At some point Tomstock spoke to his partner under his breath. "Back in that cold cellar, there was a knife for cutting the meat." He let his words sink in. "It's not there anymore."

Near the water's edge, Royce suddenly turned back and ran into a thicket of stunted spruce that bordered the rocky beach. "It's here in the trees," he called.

"Stay here," said Tomstock. He followed the little boy and lifted the lower branches of a conifer. He turned to look back toward Hemmenburg, then reached under and started to draw out a six or seven-foot long oblong shell. He turned it upside down and shook out the snow that had dropped from the nee-dled boughs. He held the lightweight craft in his right hand and carried it back like a valise.

"I thought you said it was a jon boat," Tomstock chided.

"It is," protested Royce. "John made all these boats. They real-ly, really work."

Tomstock did not look convinced and set down the flimsy sapling-ribbed boat with its hide covering. He looked at Hemmenburg with an expression that asked the big question.

"Do we have a choice?" was Cal's response. The answer was known, but not voiced.

Royce, however, was very excited. This was his moment and his five-year-old confidence seemed infallible. "Now, you have to do just what I tell you!"

The two men had the feeling that they were listening to a re-cording of some parental instructions that had been embedded in Royce's memory. If that were the case, maybe this flimsy pea pod could put to sea with passengers other than an owl and a pussy-cat.

"Take the boat down to the water!"

The task was more difficult than the weight and shape of the coracle suggested. The beach was littered with blocks of ice as large as a beached whale. Tomstock lifted the boat and crossed the craggy floes until he reached the place where free water lapped and splashed against the ice face. The thickness of the ice boulders put him several feet above the surface of the sea. He was not aware of the fact that he was walking out on an ice shelf and was already over deep water.

Royce and Hemmenburg followed his path with more diffi-culty, Royce because of his short legs, and Cal because his energy was ebbing.

"Put the boat down in the water," ordered Royce. It floated high and bounced and rolled like a fishing bobber. "This is im-portant," said Royce with all the authority that his little voice could command. "The heaviest person has to get in first. Hold on to the sides, and stay low."

Tomstock now understood. This tipsy thimble would gain stability with the ballast of passengers. "You first, Cal," he said, thinking that he would be better able to hold on than his companion.

Hemmenburg sat on the edge of the ice with his feet dangling over the bouncing skin boat. Slowly he lowered his weight into the craft, and it gained stability as his weight pushed it deeper in the water. In a moment he was scrambling toward the farthest end of the craft. As he shifted his weight, the end nearest the ice lifted out of the water and Tomstock limited its rise by extending his legs over the ice shelf. Slowly he lowered his bulk into the boat which now, with ballast fore and aft, sat securely in the water. A small paddle was wedged next to a woven thwart. He drew it out and handed it to Cal.

"Now it's your turn, Royce," he said reaching out one hand to the boy while the other clung to the gritty ice ledge. Instead of taking the extended hand, Royce stomped hard on the ice-frozen, gripping fingers.

"What the fuck..." Tomstock cried in pain as he lost his grip and the little coracle rolled back into the retreating waves.

"Here are the bad men," said Royce to nothing except the waters now suddenly swirling with flashes of black and white. A dorsal fin broke the water's surface, and the two men became a beach toy in an aquarium act. Hemmenburg raised the wooden paddle to strike at a diving shape. "Don't make them mad," called Royce. "They won't hurt you. They'll push you out to the boat... I told you that I could do it!"

39

Sodus had a way of being persistent when there was something he wanted to communicate. He pushed his way into the longhouse with unrelenting barking that could not be scolded away. Cathy pulled on her heavier clothes in the knowledge that there would be no peace until someone acknowledged the black dog's protest.

"Okay, okay, I'm coming," she said.

Once outside, Sodus turned and jogged along the downhill path toward the water. After ten feet, he stopped and turned back to see if he had been understood. "Where are you going?" she asked.

The answer came when she reached the point in the path where a vista of the bay opened. In the distance was the proud form of *Dream Dancer* riding on her mooring chain. The foreground, however, revealed a ring of circling shapes, like animated standing stones orbiting around a dark earth-tone object. Recognition came in pieces as each aspect of the scene fell into shape.

"The orcas have returned," she said aloud to no one. Their proud dorsal fins looked like gray granite slabs rising above the flashing turbulence of the dancing water. The point at the center of the circle was less obvious, but coming into focus. It was two men, hunkered low in a skin boat, arms splayed between the gunwales, hands gripping tightly by white clenched fingers. "Royce!" she called, now running down the path with Sodus keeping pace.

Her run slowed to a walk when she came out of the spruce and stumbled into the smooth stones of the bank gravel. The footing here would not afford running feet, but her need for speed lessened when she saw her son standing atop an ice floe. He turned to her, his face beaming.

"It's Keeper!" he yelled in her direction.

"Is Shrader back?" she asked.

"She said she'd come."

"Is your father here?" she asked again looking left and right for some sign of the *Whaleman*. "Royce, what is happening?"

The boy twisted his body to face his mother. His sudden sobriety, however, did not erase his exuberance. He kept turning his gaze back to the water to watch the progress of what looked like an unusual game of water polo.

"The bad men wanted to see *Dream Dancer*. I told them about John's boat, and said that I knew how to get them out there. I didn't tell them about what Keeper promised."

"Keeper promised?" Cathy jumped up to the level where Royce was standing, scooped him up in her arms, and hugged him tightly.

"Look," said her son as he rolled back in her arms. Cathy followed his pointing finger. The whales had floated the coracle to the side of *Dream Dancer* and one of the men risked being spilled out to grab hold of the toe rail that defined the outer rim of the larger boat's hull. Once contact was established, the orcas withdrew and the coracle settled in the water as the now-standing shape walked the little dinghy back toward the stern of the larger boat where they scrambled up the stainless steel boarding ladder mounted on the transom.

If they meant to reach over the side to snag the coracle, the orcas denied them the opportunity. Without the ballast of the humans, the craft was light and buoyant and more like a bale of twigs wrapped in seal skin. It became the perfect toy for the prisoner escorts. Two of the younger whales flipped it back and forth out of the water.

"They're bringing it back," said Royce. While they were successful in this last endeavor, *what* they brought back was no longer a boat. The saplings that formed the frame were now floating toothpicks out on the bay, and what washed back toward Cathy and Royce was seal hide in an undefined shape.

"Good thing John made several," noted Pearson. "Do you think that will ever be a boat again?" she asked Royce who only giggled as he waved his right arm wildly in the direction of the two men. They were looking back at him, but did not return the wave.

"How did you know they were *bad men*?" asked Cathy.

Royce was not fully conscious of how he had reached his conclusion. Keeper had warned him when they first approached on the snowmobile. Was that it? "They didn't like Simonie," was the answer he spoke aloud.

"And you really do, don't you?"

"Yes," said Royce. "Sometimes he seems sad."

"That's right," answered his mother. "Sad things have happened to him, and those two men did some of those bad things."

Royce looked back over the water. Even at such a distance the frustration of the prisoners was evident. They thought of this boat as their escape, but it was their prison. Instead of being fully equipped to sail, it was rudderless and stripped. There was probably a foot of water in the bilge, but they'd find a pump mounted in the cockpit locker and drain it dry.

"Simonie isn't sad when he's with Tish," said Royce.

Cathy started at the observation. "She isn't as sad, either," she added quietly and to her own surprise.

40

The story of the prisoner transfer lost something in translation from Cathy's point of view. On the other hand, she preferred the misattribution that emerged within public opinion. Everyone marveled at Royce's cleverness and the seaworthiness of Romig's little boat. The appearance of the whales, however, was completely understood to be one of *Shrader's* peculiar interventions. This twisted thinking even survived the initial confused looks and persistent denials made by Marks after his return. His Keelhouse homecoming came later the same day, but the rumor of his involvement with the pod was already too firmly fixed.

It had been a day of reunions. Word reached Keelhouse that Simonie and Tish had begun to settle a smaller than expected group of refugees at the outpost known as *Twelve*. Word was also sent around to the other outposts that the teams at the other stations could come back to the base. Group by group, they all returned. Just after midday Vince and Anthony appeared with two new prisoners, Doncaster and Mallory. They had pushed ahead, choosing not to stop at any of the established perimeter shelters out of concern that their charges might not be safe within close proximity to the people that they had abused for so long.

A day earlier, there would have been a long debate over what to do with the captives. With the earlier pair, allowing the freedom of the camp had been Cathy's veiled attempt at house arrest, but Royce's intervention provided a clearly more effective alternative. Being marooned as they were, they were safe from assassins, and being guarded, as they were, by a pod of killer whales, all plans for escape were worse than bleak.

The immediate problems were the practical matters of supply and transport. The *prison barge*, as *Dream Dancer* was now called, was hardly livable. It had long ago been stripped of all usable parts. Below decks the wood cabinets and bunks had been scavenged leaving only the structural bulkheads. The wood-burning cabin heater had also been left behind under the early delusion that, in winter, the ice-bound boat might become yet another outpost accessible to hunting parties trapped on the ice in sea fog. Now there were two men living in that cell, and two more awaiting transfer.

In her mind, Cathy knew that the earlier trick that Royce had managed could be repeated. On the other hand, the supply of Romig's coracles was limited, and it was doubtful that Royce would understand the necessity of convincing Keeper to keep her youngsters from play. "John can fix them," he said with full confidence in the ingenuity and power of adults.

Shrader's return postponed the discussion while the story of Royce, Keeper, and the prisoner transfer was repeated yet again. By the third time Marks heard himself described as the *orca-master*, he understood Cathy's sideways look and dropped his protest.

In his turn, Marks relayed the story of the nighttime rifle firing and the discovery of the nameless corpse under the hovering gaze of the hawk. He also proposed that the last two of John's prototype coracles be strung together in tandem. He and Royce would paddle the lead boat with the second on a tether carrying the captives. Supplies could be distributed between the two boats to balance the load.

"Why Royce?" asked Jeff.

"He can keep an eye on the other boat while I paddle. He won't take up a lot of room or give any added weight that will limit the amount of supplies that we'll need to carry over."

"I doubt that they'd try anything out on the water with Shrader there," observed Jenkins. "After all, the bay is full of giants and the one who called them out would be right there in the lead boat."

"Exactly," said Marks with a wink toward Cathy. Royce had turned away from the boring conversation and made no protest.

"There's something else," offered Bert Jenkins. "When we were outfitting my boat, I did a quick radio check."

Cathy's eyes widened. "What!"

"It was a lark. I knew that no one could be out there after all these years."

"And?" pressed Pearson.

"I was wrong. My hail was answered–but I didn't transmit after that," added Bert defensively.

"They came back asking for clarification," said Laura. "We shut down our signal, but they kept hailing back and Jenkins got a good directional fix on them. They're from the same direction they were five years ago, mostly south and a little east."

Shrader could see Cathy's fear beginning to mutate into anger. "This won't hurt us," he offered in the cryptic tone that everyone had grown to understand as meaning: we won't talk about this. "The real question is whether Jenkins' boat can be launched."

"No doubt about that, Gus engineered it well." said Koenig, and Laura and Bert agreed.

Cathy's mood lightened. "Did you hear that, Gus? Where's Gus?"

"He's here," said Grandma Marty softly. She began to cry. The sleeping figure in the corner was Gus Gundersen, but he was no longer sleeping. "His ankles were swelling again," she said. "He just wanted to lay down for awhile."

41

There came a day when Gundersen's ideas were put to the test, and they stood. *Major Blunder* slid from its high perch on Gus-designed log rails and then muscled its way through surging waves with an engine powered on Gus-filtered diesel fuel. Now that old engine was to be used for one last adventure. Aboard her were her captain, Bert Jenkins, and an experienced crew consisting of Vince Ragni, Bill Morgan, and Tiffany. They also had another passenger who was the most excited. For the others, this maiden voyage of the recomissioned craft was both a serious business and a chance to be at sea after years of puttering along the shoreline. For Royce, however, it was a chance to swim among the pod. Keeper was nearby, and Royce stood forward in the pulpit where the leading edge of the hull surged against its bow wave.

Soon the engine would be straining under an unusual load. It was to tow a prison barge, the derelict shadow of what had been *Dream Dancer*. Aboard the tow was an uneasy group of four. They were uneasy because they weren't in control, nor could they imagine how this day might end. The fifth passenger seemed far less concerned, and sang as he worked the deck of a rudderless, hollowed-out hull. Shrader brought a ditty bag with him when he stepped off the rail of *Major Blunder* and on to *Dream Dancer*. His instructions to the four were simple: "Sit in the cockpit while I ready the boat. I am going to show you how to find life, what you do after that is your business."

If his words sounded cryptic, the silent threats were more ominous. The first threat was seated on the cabin top of the lead boat where Vince Ragni sat with a Remington Bushmaster across his lap. It was not his favorite rifle but, with its scope, full-camo stock, and semi-automatic action, it impressed the four whose eyes were wide open when he showed it to them across the water. It was part of the unused arsenal of Keelhouse, a weapons stash that was no longer necessary for a people who had adapted to bow hunting and stealth. The second threat stood a little over three feet high at the bow. It was an odd man-child who somehow trained whales to follow his commands. The whales were all around, always circling.

From the hillside, Cathy watched the two boats in the bay. The four prisoners had settled into well-behaved slumps, and Shrader would be busy for awhile. He had yet to run a double towline from the base of the mast forward to where it could be passed off over the bow and picked up by the crew of *Major Blunder*. The more time-consuming task was to free *Dream Dancer* from its mooring without losing eighty feet of heavy chain rode. Metal had become precious. Pearson knew that the day might come when they would be limited to the technologies of a Stone Age people; until then, if they could salvage, they would. They meant to keep the steel that had anchored *Dream Dancer* through wave and ice.

She heard movement in the nearby woods and recognized that someone had entered the quiet place, a clearing in a close growth of spruce. She followed the sounds and found Grandma Marty standing quietly before three center stones. Cathy waited until Marty's eyes turned toward the sky and walked to the center to stand with her.

"He would have been proud of the part he played," said Marty looking down at the newest memorial stone.

"Yes, he would," agreed Cathy, "but he'd not be willing to hear anyone talk about it too much. He was a modest and remarkable man."

"Two of those men were my husband," said Marty pointing at the stones, but remembering the lives they represented. "When Roland died, I thought that was it, but I was wrong. I know Gus felt the same when Cassie died." Cathy's face must have indicated confusion. "Cassie was his wife when they lived in Massena Center," Marty added.

Cathy nodded. She suddenly marveled at how little she knew about Gus and Marty. They breathed the same air of Keelhouse, but the intimacies that passed between the two seniors remained secret.

"It's very different," continued Marty. "I know Gus felt that, too. Our first partners were our sweethearts. With Gus and I, well we were the only ones." She hesitated, "that didn't come out well. What I mean is: it's different now."

"Different? You mean falling in love?"

"Maybe not *love*, but *marriage*. Gus and I talked about it a lot in the beginning. We wondered if we were together because we loved each other or because everyone else thought that we should be together. Before all this, in the old days, we wouldn't have run in the same social circles. We probably never would have even met, and if we did, we probably would have concluded that we had nothing in common. Here, what we had in common was the fact that we were both lonely, and we knew all the words to the same songs. Everyone thought we should at least like each other, but is that enough?"

"Was it?"

Marty paused before answering. "Yes. My two marriages were so different, but I was married to two wonderful men."

"Do you think Tish will be happy?"

"I don't know if she and Simonie know it yet, but everyone thinks they belong together. It'll make our neighbors into cousins, won't it?"

"I expect so," offered Cathy. "I think it's time that Keelhouse broke up."

"What?" said Marty.

"We're getting crowded. It would be better if we were spread out a little more. Maybe we could make *Rol's Royce* into a permanent settlement."

Marty teared at the name of her old boat. "That would be the second great tribute to Roland."

"Second?"

"Royce was the first." Both women went silent and Cathy's sight went back to the little boy who was ready to put out to sea with the whales.

"We'll be so much safer with neighbors. If trouble ever came to our door, it's nice to know that there's someone down the road that will help." Marty understood.

"What about you and Shrader?"

"What do you mean?" asked Cathy.

"Is he the man you would have chosen?"

Cathy thought for a moment. "He's not the most romantic." Both laughed. "And, you're right. I probably wouldn't be with him in the other world, but I'm so very glad that I am in this one."

Marty turned her gaze at the three central stones in this place of remembrance. "If we do this right, my stone will be here next," she said.

"No, don't think..."

"There is a natural order to things, child. I am not afraid of dying. *You* have to teach the others, to not be afraid of living."

By the time Cathy returned to the place where she had fuller view of the bay, she saw Shrader standing in the cockpit giving instructions to four seated men. *Major Blunder* was on the far end of a tether steaming out to sea. She thought that she might have caught sight of a whale breaching, but it may have been a trick of the light on a whitecap.

Had she heard Shrader's coaching, she would have heard him explaining a system of ropes that he had jury-rigged on the stern of *Dream Dancer.*

"I'm not going to hide anything from you," he was saying, "this boat is in its death throes." As soon as he said this, he wished he hadn't. These men were creatures of land and already believed that the water was not a friend, and the orcas were the enemy. "I don't mean to scare you," he added quickly. "It's your best lifeline."

"How do you figure that?" asked Tomstock.

"This way," said Marks with an abruptness that said he was not looking for the gentleness of political correctness. "I saw your friend Zimisky dead, not too far from where you left him. You would be dead too if you were placed in the hands of the people you have been abusing. My opinion is that, if you were dead, you would have suffered no injustice at their hands.

"This boat is giving you a choice, and you have two." The men suddenly sat up to listen more intently. "Your first choice is to head southeast. We have heard radio signals from that bearing. We have no idea who these people are, whether they govern as you did or as we do. They have been there for five years, but they have not found us.

"We are going to leave you a small handheld radio. The rechargeable batteries in them have been charged for the last time. In about six hours, the signal from that little radio will be in their range. If you call them, they will be able to track you, and, perhaps, intercept you. That is your first choice."

"And our second?" asked Hemmenburg.

"The second will be more demanding," said Shrader. "It was our choice, but does not need to be yours. You can sail southwest. You will find an island that will give you game and fish, but they will come with hard work and no people to subdue." He let that sink in a bit. "It will be your choice. This derelict of a boat is a gift from us, and it's a gift of life."

SHRADER MARKS & KEELHOUSE

The four were in no position to bargain. There was no advantage to rushing Shrader in hopes of having a hostage. He was not afraid of them, and the sniper aboard *Major Blunder* would be no match for the knife that Tomstock had lifted from the meat locker at Keelhouse.

"What do we need to know?" asked Mallory.

"That's the right question," said Marks. He then spent the next half hour showing the four how to steer the boat by winching a drogue to the left or right. "This boat has no steering," he kept reminding them. "What you have here is an emergency technique to help you set a general direction." Then he raised the cruising spinnaker. It caught the wind and ballooned out with its green and yellow starburst. It was a light sail that would allow them to sail only with the wind behind them. They could not, he told them, "turn back."

This was the solution that had come out of a council at Keelhouse. They would sacrifice *Dream Dancer* to rid themselves of prisoners who were universally hated for acts they had done in desperation.

Vince Ragni, the owner of *Dancer*, gave the loudest protest. It did not help that Shrader made the best argument. "The only thing left to salvage is an aluminum mast and a lead keel. We can't keep it at anchor in the mouth of the bay. It would be like hanging out a shingle for an invasion fleet from the south."

Now Vince was the one cradling the Remington on his lap; he would release the tether to free both his boat and four prisoners to a decision of their own making. The signal came when Shrader hoisted a green and yellow sail that ballooned out from the foredeck of *Dream Dancer*. He threw off the lines, and *Major Blunder*, still under engine power, peeled off to starboard carefully avoiding the free floating tether.

As the wind caught the sail, *Dancer* took on speed. Shrader ordered Mallory forward to pull in the loose line. With the wind at his back, he adjusted the southward course by balancing the trailing drogue.

"In a moment, I will leave you," he said. "I told you before that the batteries on the radio we're giving you will not last long. You will need them in six hours, so keep it turned off. However," and he used an inflection that underlined *however*, "turn it on when I step off the boat. I have one more critical thing to tell you." The remark was meant to feed their paranoia, but not their psychosis. It worked.

Major Blunder came along side of *Dream Dancer* and Shrader, standing amidships, stepped easily between the two boats. Before he could go below decks on *Blunder*, Tomstock had already powered the handheld.

Marks turned on the VHF and turned the radio to its low power setting so as not to broadcast a signal too far south. "*Dream Dancer, Dream Dancer, Dream Dancer.* This is *Major Blunder.*" Somehow the correctness of the transmission seemed to matter.

"Go ahead," came the incorrect response.

"Within the next six hours you need to decide to go east or west," said Shrader. "The sail bag that I carried aboard with the spinnaker has a few other things in it. Go below and see what's there. It'll give you options for whatever you decide."

"Okay!"

By now, *Major Blunder* was close-hauled under full sail and widening the distance between themselves and the prison barge. Bert Jenkins was at the helm, and the breeze flowing off the Dacron sail wiped all the age lines from his face.

"What was in the sail bag?" he asked.

"Some survival gear, fishing nets and lines (that sort of stuff), what else? A nylon tarp, oh yeah, a six-round .45 caliber hammer."

Jenkins looked back over his shoulder. "I don't think it would do them much good at this distance."

"That was the idea," said Marks. "They might need it for hunting. It's not much, but it could buy them some time while they work out their survival skills."

"What if they go east?" asked Jenkins.

"If I was them, I'd push diplomacy rather than a shoot-out."

"They aren't you! What if they ransom their own skins by telling the predators about a *City of Gold* called Keelhouse?"

"And how would they tell that story without sounding delusional or suffering from post-traumatic stress?"

"What do you mean?"

"They'll arrive in a gutted boat with one sail, using a drogue for steering, and telling of how they were imprisoned by a clever five-year-old who talks to whales."

It was true, and they both laughed.

How does a sailboat move?

If you've ever seen a leaf floating on a puddle, you've seen that a floating object is completely at the mercy of the wind, and travels across the water wherever it gets pushed. How then can boats move in a different direction than the breeze?

It's just physics similar to what makes an airplane lift off a runway. The key is the shape of the wings. The wings of planes, called *airfoils*, shape the way the air flows over the wings. The faster the airflow the more the wing-shape creates lift. To maximize lift, the plane faces into the wind and the pilot races the engines to get a fast running start. At the right moment, the wing flaps are positioned to bend the air currents, and the plane rises.

Traditional sailboats fly the same way. The difference is that the observer can only see one of the wings on this *flying* vessel. The second wing is underwater and is called a *keel*.

While winged aircraft need to accelerate to get the wind flowing over the wings, sailboats rely on the density difference between air and water. To understand this, think of air as a very thin, light liquid (like the atmospheric *river* that meteorologists talk about). The liquid under the boat (water) is so much thicker than the liquid that fills the sails (air). The wind wants to push the boat sideways like that leaf floating on the puddle, but the wing under the boat (keel) resists being pushed. (It's like the difference between waving your hand in the air and then waving it under water.) The result is that instead of going sideways, the shape of the keel (like a wing) controls how the water flows around it, and it squeezes the boat forward. The sailor at the helm pays attention to the wind direction and changes the angle of the sails to achieve the best forward speed. The angle of attack is called the *point of sail*.

By changing the angle of the sails in relation to the boat's hull, the boat achieves its greatest speed as illustrated in the following diagram:

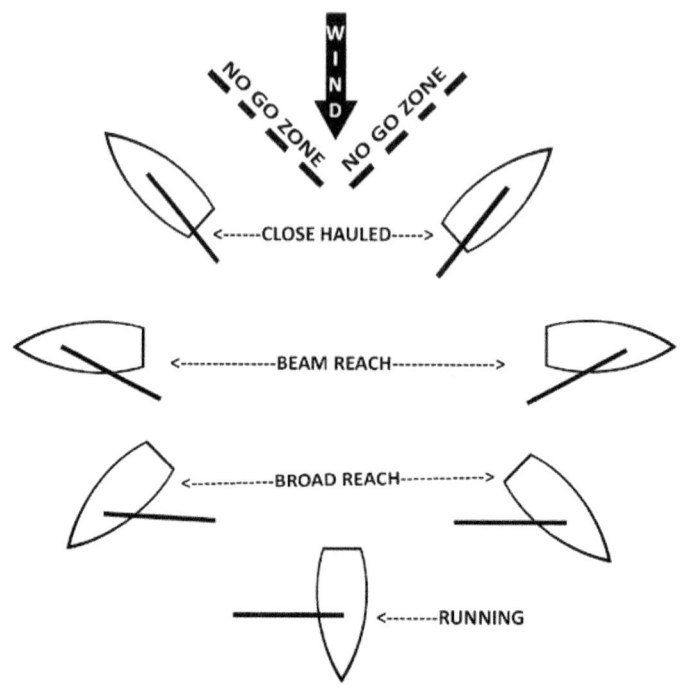

Points of Sail

Note the NO GO area. Sailboats cannot point too close to the wind. Why? Because when the wind is coming head-on the sails flap like a flag so there's no sideways pressure on the keel. The boat will then stall. When it does, it is called *being in irons*. In order to travel in the direction of the wind, the boat has to zigzag, that is it has to sail close hauled on a starboard tack for awhile, then come about and sail for awhile on a port tack. The average between these two legs of the journey will be in the direction of the wind. It's a slow slog.

(Quick question: Did you understand that last paragraph about zigzagging? If so, you might be a sailor!)

If you wonder, each point of sail feels different to those on the boat. Sailors get used to feeling the direction of the wind against their faces, but they can also feel it in the movement of the boat. The next few bullet points describe how each of the points of sail will feel on the same day with the same wind conditions.

- When close hauled, the wind feels strong, the boat heels (leans) over, and passengers brace themselves as the boat plows into the waves. It feels a bit like flying into the wind.
- A beam reach is more comfortable, the wind is coming from the side, the waves are more rolling and this is actually a fast point of sail.
- At a broad reach the breeze feels lighter, the waves roll into the back (stern quarter) of the boat. Strong waves will lift the stern of the boat and push it forward with a sudden rush. (This slide forward is called surfing.)
- When running the wave action is even more noticeable. The people on the boat may no longer feel any breeze at all. This can be the pits on a sunny day. You may, in fact, be moving at the same speed as the wind, but it will feel like a dead calm. Whoever first pronounced the Irish Blessing saying, *and may the wind be always at your back*, was not a sailor.

A final word about a heavy topic: the KEEL. Wind in the sails is a powerful force which should never be underestimated. The underwater wing/keel has to be structured to resist that substantial push of air pressure. As a result the keel is weighty. Many are made of iron, lead, concrete, or, as in days of old, smooth boulders placed deep in the hulls of square-rigged vessels.

In short, traditional sailboats are very bottom-heavy. They can get knocked around, but as long as no water floods into the hull's interior, the boat will stay afloat. They may wobble, but they don't generally fall down.

In conclusion, sailboats are slow, heavy, and subject to the vagaries of weather. On the other hand, without fuel or engines they have been safely circumnavigating the globe for centuries.

Glossary of Selected Terms

Atlatl, *n.* a spear flinging device used in Stone Age cultures to hurl darts on a fast, powerful trajectory. Some anthropologists view it as a precursor to the bow.

Bilge keel, *n.* a keel defines the underwater shape of a sailboat and keeps the boat from drifting sideways thus converting the power of the wind into forward thrust. A fin keel consists of a single "wing" that extends downward. Bilge keels or twin-keels are paired. In latitudes marked by high tides, this design has the added value of allowing the boat to sit upright on the seabed when the tide is out.

 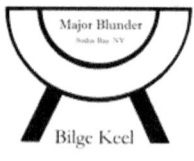

Brash ice, *n.* floating ice made up of an accumulation of relatively small fragments (2 meters across or less).

Drogue, *n.* any object towed behind a vessel in order to slow it down. In an emergency, drogues can be rigged to provide rudimentary downwind steering.

Floc, *n.* a cluster of frazil particles.

Frazil ice, *n.* fine needle-like crystals, plates, or disks of ice suspended in water. It forms in super-cooled, turbulent waters.

Hummock ice, *n.* a ridge of broken ice created by upward pressure.

Ice floe, *n.* a free floating sheet ice larger that a meter across, but smaller than an ice field.

Ice sheet, *n.* a thick sheet of ice covering an extensive area for a long period of time.

Inuit, *n. pl.* literally *"the People,"* the name native peoples from Greenland to W. Canada use to refer to their ethnic identity. Properly speaking, when used as a noun in English, *Inuit* (*"the People"*) is not used with the definite article. When used as an adjective, an indefinite article may be used. (*source:* The Translation Bureau of Canada)

Inuk, n., a person (see *Inuit*).

Inuksuk, n. standing stones erected to guide navigators in arctic regions where there are few natural landmarks.

Inuktitut, n. a name applied to Inuit languages of Eastern Canada. Several different dialects are spoken by native peoples.

Komatik or *qamutik,* n. a dog sled.

Mishtapeu, Mishtapeuat (pl.) according to Innu mythology, these spiritual beings are sent in time of need to communicate with animal masters. They are described as belonging to another world, *Tshishtashkamuk. (source:* Armitage, Peter. "Religious Ideology Among the Innu of Eastern Quebec and Labrador.")

About the Author

PHOTO CREDIT:
AL FREEMAN

Rob Smith is a native of Youngstown, Ohio who spent his teenage years in the Cleveland area. As a boy he rode his bike seven miles to the shores of Lake Erie where he could watch sailboats ghosting on the horizon. He wondered what it would be like to be aboard one of those boats. Decades later, he was regularly sailing on Lake Erie and currently lives and writes from Ohio's north coast.

Besides being the author of eight novels, he is a nationally recognized poet who served two years as his city's (Huron, Ohio) Poet Laureate. In 2006, he received the Robert Frost Poetry Award from the Frost Foundation in Lawrence, Massachusetts. Prior to relocating to northern Ohio, he taught religion and philosophy at Wright State University in Dayton. He holds a bachelor's degree from Westminster College in Pennsylvania, and both master and doctoral degrees from Princeton Theological Seminary.

When not writing, he is continuously refurbishing an 1850's cottage which was built by a ship's carpenter turned lighthouse keeper. He has many hobbies like sailing, carpentry, and photography. While still enjoying bike riding, he prefers the four minute walk to the shore of Lake Erie.

Rob and his wife, Nancy, share a home with a stray cat named Regulus Black.

www.ingramcontent.com/pod-product-compliance
Lightning Source LLC
Chambersburg PA
CBHW051939020726
47501CB00001B/199